Wayward Kin

By Andrew J Landis

Chapter One

The sky split with a flash of amethyst lightning as the ground shattered. Lidria stumbled backward, wooden buildings collapsing and sinking in front of her. Her longsword clattered to the cobblestone, impossible to hear over the thunder above and bellowing earth below.

Lidria scrambled to her feet. A sinkhole spanning fifty feet mere inches from her had swallowed a handful of buildings. She peered into the shifting maw and tried to ignore the distant din of battle. Far below, she spotted organized movement.

Scooping up her sword, Lidria glanced around to get her bearings. The stone wall of the city peeked over the roofs of the still intact buildings on the far side of the sinkhole. Behind her, the wide street cut a path to the eastern barracks. She could run or stay and fight.

Lidria fled toward the garrison. She couldn't survive on her own—not against the coming tide. Her heart pounded. She checked her chainmail armor and found one of the buckles undone. Without slowing her pace, she refastened the clasp.

The earth trembled, and Lidria wavered. The Quela were close now. Allied soldiers appeared down the street, and her spirits buoyed. Lieutenant McCrear barked orders at the head of the gathering masses. His reputation for averting disasters inspired confidence.

"Breaker," McCrear called above the rumbling earth. "Good to see you didn't get swallowed by that sinkhole. I'm going to need you on the front."

Lidria saluted McCrear with her offhand, unable to part with her weapon. "As you wish, Lieutenant. They're close." He nodded and turned his attention back to his men.

Lidria turned her back on her fellow soldiers and glanced at her left arm. A swathe of intricate tattoos covered her bare skin, forming a pattern of chains inscribed with potent scrip. Raised scars broke several chains; however, a dozen more remained intact.

"Ready yourselves," McCrear hollered, drawing his longsword. The mass of soldiers shifted and prepared to march. "Forward!"

Lidria stepped forward, two hundred soldiers moving in unison. The force behind her solidified into a palpable presence, but she feared it wouldn't be enough. Their enemy could kill several soldiers before falling themselves. Without mentioning their shaman's terrible magic.

The sinkhole appeared again, but, instead of a barren expanse, a throng of Quela marshalled at the edge. They stood, on average, time and a half taller than a man, with gnarled horns growing ever upward. Thick, matted fur covered their bodies beneath hardened chitinous armor—shock troops.

Lidria surveyed the enemy weapons and her own. The beastmens' dwarfed hers, but she could—and would—do significant damage. Her grip tightened.

The Quelan shock troops stood tall and crashed their arms against shield and armor. Frightened murmurs arose behind Lidria, but such brutish displays no longer phased her. She continued forward, outpacing her fellow man.

Lidria's eyes wandered to her left. McCrear remained at the head of the column, not content to let his men do all the work. With a man like him at her side, they might survive. She turned her attention back on their enemies, a small grin tugging at the corner of her lips.

A Quelan near the heart of the pack raised its head high and snarled a guttural bellow. Tiny bells affixed to its horns tinkled in the invisible flow of magic. Lidria shot a glance at McCrear, acknowledged his shallow nod, and sprang into action.

The front rank of Quela jerked back. Their weapons came down a second later, forming a patchwork wall of blades. One of the Quela let out what Lidria interpreted as a laugh as she approached. She ignored the mockery, and her right arm fell in a wide arc.

Feet before she hit the ranks, Lidria swept steel across her body. Weapons shattered. Grunts of surprise emanated from the beasts, and they took a collective step back. She continued, ignoring the weaponless troops.

Lidria pulled her weapon back and close to her chest. The shaman in the center of the herd lowered its head, staring her straight in the eye. Her heart skipped a beat, and she thrust forward. To her surprise, nothing stopped her.

Piercing the caster's chitinous armor, Lidria buried her blade to the hilt. The Quelan made no sound. She stared at the creature as its life faded away, baffled by its lack of self-preservation. A quick yank freed her sword, and she danced away before its comrades could collapse upon her.

Amethyst lightning streaked down from the sky, crashing into the fallen shaman. The impact knocked Lidria back. She bounced off an immense figure and tumbled toward the lightning strike. She managed to stop as the mangled corpse rose.

The reanimated Quelan staggered forward, limbs bent and movement wooden. Lidria swung at the creature's neck. An alien appendage burst forth from the Quelan's shoulder, catching her swing in bloated flesh. She tried to retract her blow, fruitless in her effort.

Lidria closed her left eye and focused. A stitch of magic slithered through her arm, sending chills down her spine. One of the chains on her tattoo sleeve snapped with a sharp tingling sensation. Strength coursed through her, and she tugged. Blood flew, sliding free.

Screeching, the shaman recoiled and lowered its horned head. The beast charged Lidria as she backpedaled. Horns came close, but they didn't concern her. A swipe from her long sword knocked them away, yet the abomination kept coming. Three limbs flailed at her.

Lidria hopped away from the shaman's natural appendages, but the new, monstrous one managed to grab her left arm. The immense pressure left no mark on her flesh or nerves. No pain shot into her body, and her bones didn't snap. She remained resolute.

The Quelan took the opportunity to move closer. Lidria struggled against the creature's grip, raising her sword to its throat. Ignoring the threat, her captor pressed on. The tip sank into the Quelan's soft flesh but drew no reaction of any kind. She stared, dumbfounded.

Lidria withdrew her blade and raised it high. She swung down, severing her captor's limb at the wrist. The appendage spasmed and spurted black blood while the giant hand remained latched to her arm. She spun and bolted for the edge of the enemy ranks.

To Lidria's surprise, the beastmen let her pass without incident. Their shattered weapons and shaman behind gave them little incentive. She ran to her allies, and they greeted her with shocked expressions. McCrear glanced her way, but she didn't pay him any attention.

"Archers," McCrear shouted. Knocked arrows and drawn bowstrings sounded from the back row of soldiers. "Loose!"

Lidria pivoted. The creatures raised their shields skyward. Arrows pinged off the bulwark, but several met flesh. Three stuck out from the shaman's body, but the abomination appeared unconcerned. No matter how much punishment it received, nothing seemed to slow it down.

A second volley sailed overhead; however, the tide moved forward. Somehow, fewer arrows found their marks. Soldiers behind Lidria lowered their spears and made ready. A sergeant called for her to fall back, and she followed their suggestion.

Quela crashed into the defensive line. The ranks gave, sagging, and human and Quelan cries mixed into an ear-splitting cacophony. Lidria pushed back. Her comrades needed aid, and she lent her strength with gusto.

Lidria spun around a fellow soldier as he flew back from a Quelan. Using the momentum, she whipped her sword around. She struck at shoulder-height, slamming into its torso. Sparks flew from the strike of metal on metal.

Armor plates squeaked and gave way. Blood gushed from the gash as the blade continued slicing through flesh and bone. The Quelan cried in pain, but a soldier's spear silenced the beast. He lanced its skull before the creature crumpled to the ground, bisected.

Lidria glanced at the man. A self-satisfied grin quirked his face, which she tried to ignore. She had taken care of the issue; he didn't need to intervene. In his defense, few common soldiers ever experienced a breaker in action.

Placing a hand on the man's back, Lidria shoved him forward to plug the gap in the line. He let out a surprised noise. A small grin curled her lips, but she didn't dwell on her amusement. The front row began to crumble.

McCrear cut through a weaponless beast, carving his way across the forward line. A giant spiked club clobbered a soldier beside him. He slid in to fill the opening and hacked at his opponent's wrist. The monster showed no reaction.

Lidria rushed forward as another Quelan lunged at McCrear with a crude spear. He dodged, but the club-wielding beast attacked him from the other side. Lidria kicked her leg up, planted her boot on the Quelan's thigh and shoved. Bones snapped, and the creature collapsed to one knee.

With a swift swipe, Lidria lopped the beast's head off. McCrear caught his assailant's spear under his arm and yanked. To her surprise, the Quelan stumbled forward a step. McCrear extended his sword arm before driving the blade into the creature's exposed armpit.

The body stepped forward but toppled and became motionless. McCrear shot his gaze up to Lidria. They locked eyes, and he nodded. He turned his attention back on the enemy and shouted a command. Despite his best efforts, the exhaustion in his movements shone through.

A streak of lightning cut through the ranks of human soldiers. Twenty men and women fell to pieces. Lidria's head snapped to the right, ignoring the mangled, scorched corpses of her comrades. The reanimated shaman stood at the front of the gap, head lulling to the side.

Lidria focused on her left arm. Pins and needles followed a sharp snap of pain bolting up her arm. She shuddered, overwhelmed by the surge of energy. Her hand slid across the flat of her blade, and azure flames ignited in a glorious blaze.

Lidria held her sword parallel to the ground with both hands. Arm and blade vibrated with energy, and she rushed the shaman. The creature blinked. A guttural growl twisted into something resembling a laugh, sending a shiver down her spine.

Before her strength diminished, Lidria drove her blazing sword into the shaman's chest. The flames melted its black armor, and the abomination caught aflame. She shoved the Quelan back five feet and ripped through burning flesh.

A ripple of magic expanded from the charred remains, and Lidria's heart leaped into her throat. She spun around. An explosion rocked the street, decimating men and Quela alike. Screams of terror and pain rang out and filled her ringing ears.

Lidria crashed into a hard surface. Her shoulder popped, followed by the rest of her body slamming against coarse stone and splintering wood. She bounced off the wall, dropped to the street, and rolled a turn and a half. Her mind as cloudy as her blurred vision.

The ground rumbled and shook. Lidria propped herself up, limbs trembling. Around her lay groaning or motionless bodies. She searched for the shaman, expecting to see her efforts all for naught. To her surprise, and relief, nothing stood.

Several forms amid the wreckage began to rise. McCrear stood. Lidria took a step forward, toward him, and her leg crumpled beneath her weight. She cursed and stumbled a few steps. Her eyes came back up as a Quelan attacked McCrear.

The beast moved slow and awkward but so did McCrear. He grasped the Quelan's horns and held it back. Lidria tried to hurry, but her legs refused to listen. Bodies strewn in her path slowed her further. No matter how fast she closed the gap, she wouldn't make it in time.

The brute let out a terrible cry and tossed McCrear on his back. He scrambled away, his gaze darting sidelong. A sword lay to his left, and he extended his arm. A cloven hoof, however, slammed down on his elbow.

McCrear screamed, and Lidria stopped in her tracks. The stories she heard of the man painted a picture of a stoic leader. Such raw agony struck her as something beneath him, yet he screamed. Her eyes darted to her left arm. Sympathy bloomed in her chest.

Lidria hobbled forward. Desire to save McCrear flooded her—severing another link would suffice. The creature needed to die regardless of whether the lieutenant survived. She preferred he lived, but she couldn't afford to spend more for one man.

Bending down, the Quelan snatched the armament beside McCrear. Lidria's breath caught in her throat. She held her sword out to the right in both hands and aimed. Her arms shook from the weight, but she swung back and hurled her weapon.

Time slowed as Lidria's sword spun. She pressed on, fearing her feeble attempt wouldn't end the threat. Her blade caught the beast in the shoulder, and a screech filled the air. Despite her best efforts, she had acted too slow. Crushing force hacked McCrear's arm off.

Crimson blood spilled on the scorched and broken stone. Lidria ignored McCrear's cries and grunts and closed what little of a gap remained between her and her target. She tripped forward, reaching for the hilt of her sword imbedded in the Quelan. Her fingers wrapped around tight.

Lidria drove deeper, her weight adding more force than her muscles. Her legs gave out, and she collapsed. The blade tore through the Quelan's flesh until striking armor. She gripped tight, her dead weight wrenching leverage.

Ripping through soft tissue, Lidria's blade shot skyward. She crashed to the ground; her arm extended above. The weight of her sword, combined with her exhaustion, proved too much. She let the weapon tumble from her grasp.

The Quelan stumbled backward, wet patches of warmth trickling down Lidria's back. A heavy thud sounded behind her to signify the all-clear. She heaved a long breath. Her heavy eyes closed, but McCrear's labored gasps reminded her of the situation.

Lidria spun around, still seated, and inspected the lamed lieutenant. His severed arm lay inches away, blood pooling at his side. She tried to lock eyes with him, but he stared to his left. She pushed herself up, feet unsteady, with a hand on her knee.

A tattered banner lay seven feet away. Although a mess, Lidria saw nothing else at hand. She limped her way to the standard, bending over and gathering the cloth. A silver phoenix emblazoned on azure stared back at her. She *humphed* and shook her head.

Lidria strode over to McCrear. His eyes met hers this time, and his face shifted from agonized to stoic. He didn't need to act tough for her sake; she understood. Her left arm twitched, a sharp pain spiking from her shoulder. She grit her teeth.

McCrear shifted upright, but Lidria clasped his shoulder. "Take it easy, Lieutenant. I'll have it wrapped up in a minute."

"Thank you, breaker," McCrear said, his voice strained.

Lidria tore away a shredded part of the banner, tossing the useless section aside. She stepped around McCrear until she could get at his wound. With a grunt, she bent down beside him. His blood stained her clothes and armor, but she didn't care.

McCrear whispered, "Such a pathetic display," as Lidria wrapped the cloth around his stump.

Lidria paused her ministrations, deciding if she should say anything. Her empathy won out. "It's all right, sir. Losing a limb isn't easy."

"That's not what I'm talking about." Frustration broke McCrear's façade. "Our forces were torn apart, and there was nothing we could do about it." He lifted his head. "Doesn't sound like the rest of the city is faring any better either."

The ground shook, threatening to ruin Lidria's work. She held off until the tremors ceased. "You're right. I haven't seen anything like that before."

“Nor have I. They must really want to wipe us out if they’re resorting to methods like that.” McCrear winced as Lidria applied pressure to his wound.

“What should we do, sir?” Lidria asked.

McCrear’s eyes focused on Lidria’s. “Are you still able to fight?”

“Yes.” Exhaustion weighed Lidria down, and her remaining links precious, but none of that mattered if she died.

“Are you sure?” The uncharacteristic concern in McCrear’s voice surprised Lidria, and she averted her eyes.

“Yeah, I’m sure,” Lidria brought her eyes back to McCrear’s, “sir.”

McCrear nodded. “Go help at the citadel—they’ll need more people like you if they’re going to hold off the tide.”

Lidria tied off the end of the cloth, having done all she could. “What about you?”

“I’m going to try to round up any survivors and help where I can.” Lidria frowned, and he smiled. “I’ll try not to waste your hard work.”

“That’s not—”

“Go,” McCrear ordered. “I’ll be fine.”

“Be careful.” Lidria rose, her knees aching.

“You, too.”

Lidria picked up her sword, hefted the blade onto her shoulder, and headed north. The brass-tipped peaks of the citadel shone purple-gray as the sky flashed with lightning. Clouds had rolled in since the fight began, and they pressed down with oppressive force.

An ear-splitting shriek caught Lidria off-guard, and she recoiled. A bulky, winged monstrosity swooped down out of the clouds. The creature landed atop the citadel’s spires, wrapping its forked tail around the stone. Another screech pierced the night as lightning spewed from its dual maws.

Chapter Two

The monster splayed tattered wings and swept out of sight. A ripple of hope spread through Lidria but dissipated when the beast shrieked. One of the buildings near the citadel crumbled, and a shiver ran down her spine. How could she fight something so monstrous?

Lidria intended to move forward—she had a duty to uphold—but found herself taking a step back instead. She cursed her cowardice. People needed her. She forced herself toward danger, but she struggled with each step.

The closer Lidria got to the heart of the city, the more life she encountered. Civilians, hunkered down in their homes, peeked out of shuttered windows or cracked doors. Silence hung in the air. She couldn't fault them, but they weren't safe indoors or anywhere.

Lidria staggered as the ground shook. The homes next to her toppled, crumbling before her eyes. Screams from inside rose above the thundering collapse of stone, wood, and earth. She ran, disinclined to add her cry to the haunting din.

Lidria's thoughts wandered as she jogged down the vacant road. Even if they held the citadel, the rest of the city would be little more than inhabitable rubble. The recovery would take decades if anyone survived at all. Her head spun with the scale of the disaster.

A selfish thought played in the back of Lidria's mind: run. She could turn from her comrades, from her duties, and flee. No one would know, and she could live out her days in peace. Her skills and knowledge would make a smooth trip. She need only turn.

An image of McCrear popped into Lidria's head. He wouldn't abandon his people, even when wounded to the brink of death. Her consideration of running—however brief—shamed her. She was grateful no one witnessed her weakness.

Shouts echoed off the buildings in the upcoming courtyard. Lidria spotted several human forms. They rushed to the right, and she picked up her pace to join them. A bone-chilling screech ripped through her being. Two soldiers flew past.

The winged monstrosity clambered forward, smashing into a nearby building. Lidria's blood ran cold. Bulbous muscles rippled under dark fur as the abomination stalked a group of terrified troops. She willed herself into motion, but one of the heads swiveled toward her.

Slit russet eyes stared at Lidria. She struggled to control her breathing, and she trembled. All rational thought fled her. She wished she had given in to her selfishness. The beast blinked, and its eyes bled crimson before lashing out.

Lidria leaped back, avoiding gnashing jaws. She whipped around in an arc. Her blade connected with the beast's snout but bounced off. Rearing one head, the beast's second came to bear. Teeth snapped at her waist, and lightning oozed from the muzzle.

A jolt of electricity ran through Lidria's leg. She recoiled from the unnatural excretion, muscles spasming. Her teeth rattled. The two heads flanked her—each mouth could swallow her whole. If she didn't act quick and careful, she would forfeit her life.

Lidria severed a link. The slight tingle of magic danced up her spine, and the world slowed. The creature lunged and nipped at her. She darted to her left and forward, avoiding certain death. A shrill cry accompanied the heavy beat of wings

Lidria slid across the cobblestone and broke a second link. Strength flowed through her, and she thrust upward. A long gash formed in the wake of her blade, showering her in murky brown blood.

Lidria finished her slide and popped upright, spinning around to face her foe. The aberration batted her away with a ponderous swipe of a giant paw. She flew several feet before crashing to the ground. She sprang back to her feet and dodged a follow-up blow.

The monstrosity flared its wings and beat them down. Lidria braced herself. Wind rushed around her, and her feet slipped an inch. Enraged, the beast shoved both heads within two feet of her, maws agape. A white-blue light bloomed from deep down its throat.

Lidria's eyes widened. Her heartbeat pounded in her head. She dropped into a crouch and tumbled forward. Lightning erupted, crashing into the building behind her. The aberration's heads moved to follow her underneath—its breath unending.

Stone erupted into charred chips, spinning through the air. The terrible sizzle urged Lidria forward. She slipped under the monstrosity's body, weaved around its legs, and emerged on the other side.

With a grunt of exertion, Lidria leaped up. Her boots struck bone, and the creature rolled its back from side-to-side, trying to shake her off. Ooze spewed as the heads swiveled around. She fell and pressed herself against the furry mass.

Lightning arced and crackled. Lidria held tight, her eyes shut, waiting. More of the static-ooze dripped from above. She fought the shocks and endured as best she could. Her muscles ached, and she couldn't stop them from quivering.

The assault stopped. Lidria loosened her grip and opened her eyes. Soldiers surrounded her and the beast, spears at the ready. They proceeded with caution. She needed to aid them; they wouldn't survive by themselves. Her body screamed at her, but she stood.

Lidria raised her sword, flipping it. Left hand on the pommel, she plunged her weapon into the monstrosity's flesh. The beast shrieked and thrashed. She leaned all her weight forward, and the blade sank deeper.

Not content with only thrashing, the aberration bounded skyward. Its forked tail slammed into a line of soldiers, sending them flying. Lidria knelt and gripped the hilt until her knuckles turned white. In her haste, she hadn't thought her plan through.

The creature sailed up in a spiral around the citadel. Any higher and Lidria would be out of options. She stared over the side at the flat gray-silver stone. Several ledges hung out nearby, yet the odds didn't favor her. However, what other choice did she have?

Lidria pulled back and leaped off. She sailed through the air and crashed. Hitting one of the balconies, she slipped. Reluctantly, she dropped her weapon, grabbed a decorative statue with both hands, and prevented herself from spilling over.

Lidria hauled herself up on the balcony proper and stared upward. The beast continued to wheel into the sky. Shame crept in, but she wouldn't have survived if she fought longer. She had wounded her adversary, in which she took some solace.

From atop, the city spread out before Lidria...what remained anyway. Too many spots were devoid of buildings. No doubt those were where the sinkholes originated. Fire and smoke rose from all around, creating an oppressive haze. Sounds of battle came from all directions.

Things were worse than Lidria believed, and she already thought little of their survival. Thoughts entered and left her mind before they registered. Her knees buckled, unable to support her weight. She reached for something, anything, to steady herself.

A steel door squeaked behind Lidria, snapping her out of her despair. She turned around expecting a soldier, but a kid popped his head out through the crack. Lidria frowned. The kid cocked his head. Disheveled, shoulder-length brown hair fell sideways.

"Miss," he said in a high voice. He couldn't have been more than eleven years old. "Are you a soldier?"

"Yes." Lidria took a shaky step toward the door. "Are there any other soldiers nearby? I need to get—" Her left leg gave out, and she collapsed on one knee.

The boy slipped out the door, and a woman yelled from inside. He ignored the voice and rushed over to Lidria's side. "Are you all right?"

Lidria glanced at him and nodded. "I will be, yeah. Go back to whoever called you."

"That's just mom; she's fine. You don't look so good. Is that your blood?" He tilted his head to the side again, getting too close.

"Some of it might be, but, like I said, I'm fine. Go back to your mother." Lidria rose, unsteady.

"Hector, get back in here." A middle-aged woman with the same brown hair as her son emerged. She scowled until she spotted Lidria. Her demeanor softened.

"Mom, this lady's a solider and needs help," Hector shouted beside Lidria.

Hector's mom strode over to Lidria and offered her shoulder to lean on. "Come on; we'll take care of you inside."

Lidria hesitated, but her body ached. She took the woman's aid, letting her guide her inside.

Dozens of families sat together. Benches, cots, and tables scattered about were occupied with either people or their belongings. Every set of eyes in the room focused on Lidria. Pressure and disgrace drained her further. She cursed her weakness.

"My name's Nell," she said as she eased Lidria down on an empty bench. The simple act of taking the weight off her strained legs comforted her.

Lidria grimaced as her back spasmed. "Lidria. Thank you, Nell."

Nell smiled. "You're welcome, Lidria." She turned to Hector. "Hector, go get some cloth and water so that I can help your friend here."

"Okay, mom." Hector beamed and rushed off around the corner.

"He's a handful," Nell shook her head, "but at least he listens sometimes."

Lidria opened her mouth to say something, but nothing came out. Her eyes closed. Nell chuckled. "It's all right. I can see you're exhausted...and a little battered."

"I can't believe I let myself get this far gone," Lidria admitted.

"The work of a breaker is never done, eh?" Curiosity brought Lidria's eyes open.

Lidria stared at the other woman. "I didn't realize our work was common knowledge."

"My brother," Nell wore a somber smile, "was also one."

"Ah." Lidria's gaze wandered to the others in the room, and their prying eyes shied away.

Nell turned her head and sighed. "Don't mind them; you're fine. They're just not used to seeing someone covered in blood. Looks like you got in some good blows."

"Not as many as I would have liked to." Lidria tipped her head down at her blood-soaked armor.

"Things aren't going well out there, are they?" Nell's voice came out soft; the cheer and friendliness there a moment ago gone.

Lidria locked eyes with Nell. "No. A good portion of the city has been turned into sinkholes. Our forces are being overrun. And, on top of that, the Quela are showing new behavior, so we have no idea what to expect."

Nell went rigid, silent. Lidria chewed her lip. A civilian shouldn't know all the details, not at once, not now. She opened her mouth, but Nell beat her to words.

"If things go south here," Nell glanced around, "can you keep an eye on my son?"

Lidria frowned. "I don't think—"

"Out of everyone here, you're the most likely to survive. I'm not asking you to go out of your way or anything, but, if it's within your power, please try. That's all I ask." A grim resolve shone behind Nell's vibrant brown eyes.

"I—okay," Lidria conceded. "I'll see what I can do if it comes to that."

Nell breathed a sigh of relief. "Thank you."

Water sloshed on the floor from a bowl in Hector's hands as he hurried back. Nell turned and shook her head, but a faint smile clung to her face. Memories Lidria would rather forget drifted back to her. An ache blossomed in her chest, and she tried her best to appear composed.

"Sorry I took so long." Hector handed his mother the bowl and some rags. "The mean old lady downstairs thought I was just playing a game."

"It's all right. Your mother's been great company." Lidria cracked a weak smile.

Hector beamed. "Mom can be fun...when she's not trying to make me clean things."

Nell grabbed Hector by the ear and pulled him close. "Go play with some of the other boys while I help Lidria."

"I want to help, too," Hector whined, pouting.

"I can take care of it myself." Lidria sat awkward, wooden. No one had ever doted on her before. "I'm grateful for your help, but you don't need to waste your time on me."

"But—"

"Come on, Hector," Nell said, with a frown. "She's been through a lot tonight; let's give her some space. I'm sure you can talk to her later."

Lidria nodded.

Hector hung his head and kicked at the stone floor. "Okay, but I want to hear about your soldier adventures later."

Lidria found herself smiling. "All right, Hector. You have my word."

Nell dragged Hector away, nodding as she went. The two of them crossed the room to another small family. They peered at Lidria, a mix of judgement and fear in their eyes. She sighed, leaned against the wall, and submerged a rag in the lukewarm water.

Wringing out the excess water, Lidria buried her face in the damp cloth. She wiped down, taking pleasure in the soothing cleanliness. A quick squeeze in the bowl flushed out the dirt, and the water turned a murky reddish-brown. No wonder people stared.

Lidria untied her bun, letting her hair spill free around her shoulders. Blood and dirt matted her blonde locks, and no amount of wiping or squeezing cleaned them. She gave up on the venture and rubbed her bare arm. Her tattoos shone through.

The other rag Lidria used to clean the filth from her clothes and armor. Her chainmail shone in the firelight, but the recesses between the rings remained black. Unrecognizable muck stained her brown leather pants, and her blue gambeson fared little better.

A runner in blue and silver livery stumbled through the door. "The Quela are breaking through. We're evacuating the citadel."

Lidria tossed the bloody rag to the side and crossed the room. The soldier's eyes widened as she approached. "Evacuate to where exactly?"

"There's a secure route to the north. We don't know how long it'll hold, so we have to move now." The man refused to meet Lidria's gaze.

"Give me your sword," Lidria demanded, holding out her hand. "I'm going to help these people evacuate, and I'm going to need a weapon."

The soldier unfastened his scabbard and handed it to Lidria. "I'll lead you to the path, and then you'll be on your own. Several squads are holding the route along the way, so you shouldn't run into any trouble."

"All right." Lidria fastened her new weapon to her belt. "Give them a few moments to get ready, and we'll be on our way." He nodded and informed the room.

Lidria strode over to Nell and Hector. She kept her voice quiet. "Stay near me."

"Okay," Hector said, staring up at Lidria with anxious eyes.

Nell stepped close. "Thank you. I appreciate what you're doing."

"You're welcome. Now, grab anything you have and let's go." Lidria turned from them and headed for the door.

The civilians murmured, afraid, but they went about collecting their possessions. Lidria stepped out into the hallway while she waited. The hall extended fifty feet in both directions. Voices drifted up from the right—more people than the handful behind her required protection.

Hector swept up beside Lidria, rocking back and forth on the balls of his feet. She gazed down at him, and he grinned. She gave him a weak smile in return. The messenger came out next along with several civilians. Nell joined Lidria before they headed off.

The group made their way down, picking up more members as they went. Uneasiness grew within Lidria. The route sounded safe enough, but if one checkpoint fell, things would get messy. She lacked the strength to fight.

Outside, battle echoed down the streets. The runner clasped Lidria's shoulder. "Head down the Promenade. It's mostly a straight shot, but soldiers further down will direct you through. Good luck."

Lidria took two steps forward, and the sky ripped open. Amethyst lightning crashed, raking the side of the citadel. The structure shrieked and groaned as huge chunks of stone broke away. Civilians panicked and ran despite her attempts to maintain order.

The upper half of the citadel toppled. Lidria glanced up—the debris would crush them. She pivoted and grabbed Hector. He yelped as she scooped him up and carried him forward. Splintered and broken stone rained down around them.

Massive sections of rubble crushed buildings and people alike and fractured the ground. Lidria toppled, losing her grip. Hector flew several feet in front. Something substantial struck the back of her head, and the world went dark.

Chapter Three

Lidria groaned and forced her eyes open. Her vision swam. She rolled onto her back, every muscle aching in protest. Wracking coughs strained her dry throat as she cursed. Each of her senses rebelled against her, and she wished to return to unconsciousness.

"You're awake," a familiar voice exclaimed.

Lidria's blurry eyes focused. Hector stood beside her, bouncing on the balls of his feet. Seeing him alive gave her a flicker of joy, but she suppressed the emotion. What little energy remained in her body would be better spent on anything else. She stared up at the white canvas of a tent.

"How—" Lidria grimaced as her voice came out garbled. Her throat burned, and she hacked out a series of coughs.

Hector moved from Lidria's side before returning with a cup. "Here, you must be thirsty."

Pain shot down Lidria's spine from the base of her skull, but she grasped the cup Hector offered. The lukewarm water stung at first as the sensation went all the way down. Soon, the unpleasantness turned soothing. She drained the rest and breathed relief.

Hector grabbed the empty cup and went for a refill.

"How long have I been out?" Lidria asked, folding her aching legs. Baggy, cream-colored clothes draped her huddled frame.

"Three days, I think." Hector returned and handed Lidria the filled cup. "Ren wasn't sure you were going to wake up, but I told him you would." He beamed at her.

Lidria frowned. "Ren?"

"He said he was a le, lew," Hector shook his head, "some important soldier guy. He said he knew you."

"McCrear." Lidria couldn't believe he had lived.

"Yeah, that's him. I heard some other soldiers call him that." Silence filled the tent as Lidria finished her second drink. "Do you know him?"

"Only a little." Lidria spun the empty vessel between the tips of her fingers. "I fought beside him for a while in the attack before I met you and—where's your mother?"

Hector shied away from Lidria's gaze. "I don't know. She was near you when I left to find help. But when I got back, she was gone. Ren told me not to worry, but…"

Hesitation crippled Lidria. Part of her wanted to comfort Hector, but she didn't know how. What did she think she could do? Nothing she did turned out right. She banished her dark thoughts, set the cup aside, and lifted her arms in a halfhearted gesture.

Hector's wet eyes met Lidria's. She nodded, and he hopped up into her embrace. A sense of reassurance filled her. She hugged him tight. His little body trembled, but the tears she expected to follow didn't come.

"We'll find your mom," Lidria whispered.

Hector stirred, and Lidria loosened her hold. "You're so nice, Lidi."

"Lidi, huh?" Hector nodded, a broad smile brightening his face. No one had ever given her a nickname before.

A giggle echoed in Lidria's ears, and Hector plopped down on the edge of the cot. She followed suit and swung her legs over the side. Her feet touched the ground, drawing a grunt. A couple of crates filled the tent—her equipment gone.

Lidria stood, Hector following. "Can you show me where McCrear is?"

"He's in the big tent outside," Hector said, making his way toward the exit. Before he got to the tent flap, he turned to Lidria. "Do you like him, Lidi?"

Lidria stopped mid-stride. She forgot how…imaginative kids were. "He's a great officer, but I don't even know him."

Hector frowned. "He's going to be disappointed; he seemed to like you a whole lot."

"What do you mean?" Lidria cursed herself for humoring Hector.

"He went right over to you when I got him and some other soldiers. He carried you all the way back here. And he's checked on you every day. He's going to be so happy to see you awake, but…" Hector trailed off and hid his eyes.

Lidria's eyes drifted to her left arm. The tunic sleeve stood in her way, so she rolled back the cloth. A heavy breath escaped her as she took in the sight of her tattoos. "He was just paying back a favor. He needs people like me to help him. It wasn't personal."

"Okay." Hector stared at the ground.

Fixing the sleeve over her shoulder, Lidria opened the tent flap. "Come on."

The campsite outside extended far beyond Lidria's imagination. Rows of tents stretched out hundreds of feet in all directions but south. The Vel drifted behind her, disturbed by a handful of fishermen and the occasional small group of people doing laundry.

Lidria swallowed before she turned her gaze on the city two miles away. Sporadic buildings stood tall, but many no longer existed. The citadel, which dwarfed everything, peeked over the roofs. Smoke rose, and she wondered how the hell she had survived.

"Ren said being along the river would be the safest place," Hector said, breaking Lidria from her brooding. "Said they hate water."

"Yeah." Seeing her home destroyed should've crushed Lidria, yet only emptiness filled her. "The Quela stay away because they don't want their tunnels flooded."

Hector snatched up a stick and swirled it around as if he held a sword. “You must be really strong to fight those things. I want to be strong, too.”

“In time.” Lidria folded her right arm across her stomach and held her left wrist.

Hector’s curious eyes fell on Lidria’s tattoos. “Why’d you get those?”

Lidria clenched her teeth. “It’s not something I like talking about. Long story short, I got hurt and needed magic to save me.”

“Do you know magic?” Curiosity turned to excitement, and Hector bounced in front of Lidria.

“I can’t use magic myself,” raised, scarred flesh passed under Lidria’s thumb, “but I can tap into the spells the mages gave me and use that.”

Hector’s eyes grew wide, and a smile slid onto his face. “That’s amazing! You’re so cool, Lidi.”

Lidria’s cheeks flushed. “Thanks.” She pivoted, looking back at camp. “Let’s go see McCrear.”

Lidria attempted to discern what provisions were left, but people’s bewildered stares distracted her. Between her being a breaker and a kid leading her around, she didn’t blame them. She sighed. Cotton fabric unfurled as she covered her tattoos back up.

Hector stopped at a larger-than-normal tent and waited for Lidria. The guards posted outside spoke to him; they acted used to him being around.

Lidria approached, and one of the soldiers smiled at her. “Finally awake, I see.”

“Is the lieutenant here?”

"Yeah, you came at the perfect time. He just finished with some officers, so he's all free. Head on in, breaker." The man saluted her, stepping aside.

"Hector," Lidria spun halfway around, "stay out here."

"Okay." Hector kicked a loose stone.

Lidria pulled the flap back and stepped inside. Papers, various supplies, and equipment lay strewn about either on crates or the floor. A clear path cut through the mess. McCrear sat at the table, his head snapping up as she entered.

"Lidria," McCrear exclaimed. He reeled his surprise back. "Breaker, how are you faring?"

"I'm doing fine, lieutenant. Still feel like hell, but I'm in one piece." Lidria's eyes snapped to McCrear's wrapped up stump. "I—"

"You of all people don't have to apologize. But," a flicker of agony danced across McCrear's face, "now that we're on the topic, I wanted to thank you again."

Anxiety rose, and Lidria pushed away. "I didn't really do much, sir."

McCrear caught Lidria's attention, his gaze unwavering. "You saved my life. If that's not doing much, I don't know what is."

"I was just in the right place at the right time." Lidria didn't think her actions warranted gratitude. "I'm sure anyone else in my position would have done the same."

"That may be true," McCrear admitted as he strode over to Lidria. "But it was, in fact, you." He placed a hand on her left shoulder.

Lidria glanced at McCrear's hand and up into his eyes. They shone green, like hers, but a deeper shade. She shied away, not worthy of standing in his presence. He stood for courage, strength, and she cowardice and weakness.

McCrear backed off. His eyes drifted down, staring at Lidria's arm. A twitch on his left side ruffled his loose, pinned sleeve. She stared at the ground, and her shoulder ached. Human contact had become a rarity she didn't realize she missed.

Silence permeated the air. Lidria's eyes wandered until they fell on McCrear. The pain on his face retreated. A weight rested on her chest, crushing her ability to breathe. She wanted to say something to break the awkwardness.

Lidria swallowed hard. "I understand how you feel. It took me a long time to adjust, even after I got," she held up her left arm, "this.

"It's not the same as a natural one, and I still have problems. I—if you ever need to talk or anything, you can count on me." Lidria attempted to smile but failed.

"Lidria," McCrear said. "I appreciate that. You…you're far too kind."

Lidria opened her mouth—

"Lidi's nice to everyone," Hector chimed in, bursting inside. Quick feet hurried over to Lidria's side, and he beamed up at both her and McCrear.

The tent flap flipped open again, and one of the guards popped his head inside. "Sorry, sir. He got away from us."

"It's all right, Deeter." McCrear chuckled. "Thanks for the effort." The guard nodded and slipped back outside.

"Hector," Lidria said, crouching down. "I'm not done with McCrear yet. It's important, so you'll have to be quiet."

Hector considered Lidria's words for a moment. In a soft voice, he said, "Okay."

Lidria shook her head and went to stand. Her legs refused to listen, and she grimaced in pain. McCrear put his hand under her arm and lifted.

With their combined efforts, she managed. Embarrassment exacerbated her pathetic display.

"Thanks."

"No problem." McCrear took a step back and relaxed his posture. "I assume you want to know how things are going?"

Lidria nodded. "How did you manage to round up so many survivors and keep them safe?"

"We lost a lot along the way," McCrear admitted. "I was surprised myself at how many we found, but the Quela seemed more interested deeper in the city.

"After we got out, we met up with stragglers. At first, we barely had any supplies, but we have been scavenging since. All things considered, we're in a decent position."

"Yeah, things seem pretty nice here." Lidria stared at the floor, not wanting to meet McCrear's gaze. "I wish I could've helped."

"Don't worry." Lidria didn't raise her head. "Besides, you did help. Without you, I…"

"You don't need to say it." Lidria fought down her anxiousness and stared up into McCrear's eyes.

A curious expression formed on McCrear's face. "You've already helped. And you'll be able to from now on." He grinned. "I'm sure I could find a use for you."

Hector popped up next to Lidria, startling her. "See, Lidi, I told—"

Lidria clamped her hand down over Hector's mouth. "Hector, what did I ask you to do?"

"It's all right…Lidi," McCrear said. Lidria stared at him, wide-eyed, and he tried his best not to laugh. "Hector's a good kid, let him speak."

Lidria removed her hand. She expected Hector to move away from her, but he instead inched closer. "Are you sure you don't like him?"

Lidria tilted her head down and glared at Hector. “This is not the time,” she warned.

“That’s not a no.” Hector ran out of the tent before Lidria reacted.

McCrear raised an eyebrow. Lidria shook her head, sighing. “He hasn’t known us for more than a couple days, and he’s trying to play matchmaker. For all he knows, you have—”

“I don’t.”

“Oh.” Lidria didn’t expect McCrear to entertain Hector’s nonsense. “Neither do I.”

McCrear shifted in place. “Good.” He cleared his throat and met Lidria’s gaze. “I mean, I’m sorry to hear that.”

“It’s fine, lieutenant.”

“Please,” McCrear smiled, “call me Ren.”

“All right…Ren.” A yawn escaped Lidria—a perfect excuse. “I’m still exhausted, so I’m going to head back and get some sleep.”

“I can imagine so. Have a good evening and rest well, Lidria.” Ren threw her a salute, which she returned without hesitation.

Lidria turned to leave, but she stopped and peeked over her shoulder. “You get some rest, too, Ren. You look tired yourself.”

“I’ll try.” Ren yawned and grinned. “If they let me.”

“Good luck and goodnight.” Lidria took her leave.

Outside, Hector didn’t show. She expected him to be waiting, either to say something smart about her and Mc—Ren or because she had promised him she would do what he wanted. However, with Hector out of the picture, she could sleep, which sounded terrific.

Chapter Four

Lidria straightened her chainmail and tugged at her left sleeve. Voices leaked out of the command tent, but she didn't eavesdrop. The officers—promoted in desperation—kept the peace. However, she noted a distinct lack of direction. She couldn't blame anyone.

With a growl, Lidria tore off the constricting sleeve. The guards eyed her, but she didn't care. People could think what they wished; she wouldn't let them dictate her existence. She owed her life to the magic binding her arm, and that fact endured. Errant assumptions didn't matter.

Wind gusted and blew a loose strand of hair across Lidria's face. She hooked a finger under and tucked the lock back into her bun. Her sword slipped down her back, so she tightened the scabbard's strap across her chest. Confidence filled her; she belonged in uniform.

"You look a lot better today," one guard said with a grin.

Lidria snapped out of her thoughts, her posture rigid. "I had some time to recoup."

"That's good. I have a feeling the lieutenant is going to need you in top form."

"She doesn't need any more pressure put on her," the female guard chided. She shot Lidria a reassuring smile. "Don't mind him."

Lidria shook her head. "It's all right. I'm used to it."

"I'm sure, but—"

The tent flap flipped open. Several soldiers adorned in officer pins filed out. Ren brought up the rear. He shook hands with the two men and women before they saluted him and left. His gaze met Lidria's, and he flashed her a smile. She smiled back in spite of herself.

"It's good to see you all sorted," Ren said, his eyes flicking over Lidria's shoulder. "I hope I'm not pushing you too hard."

"No." Lidria straightened her back and shoulders. "I'm ready."

"Come on in." Ren gestured behind him with his head.

Inside, the heat of the day remained trapped. Lidria breathed deep, but she coughed halfway through. The stillness didn't suit her. A clean spot cut through the mess to harbour a rolled-up sleeping bag. Ren took her advice; he needed the rest more than her.

"So," Lidria said, ignoring the curious expression on Ren's face. "What do you need me for?"

A flash of recognition came over Ren. "Ah, right." He strode over to the desk and poured over a map spread out over the surface. "We had a group of scouts go missing," his finger tapped a section of the map, "here."

Lidria stepped up next to Ren and leaned over the table. A small farm village lay a mile to the east. She hadn't been there before, but the nearby landscape filled her mind. Forests lined the land between the camp and the farms.

"Were they trying to scout those farms for food supplies?" Lidria asked, turning her head toward Ren.

"Not exactly. Some civilians spoke of men carrying tomes and scrolls heading into the forest." Ren swallowed but didn't turn to face Lidria. "I sent a detachment to follow after them, but they never returned."

"The Enclave," Lidria breathed. Ren nodded, and she frowned. "But why would they run from your men, or kill them? We're on the same side."

"Honestly, I don't know." Ren turned face-to-face with Lidria. "I would go to find out myself, but I'm needed here and…" his eyes flicked down to his missing limb.

Lidria stared up at Ren. "You can count on me. I'll figure out what's going on and bring the mages back."

"I know." Solemn countenance played in Ren's eyes. "And if they're not willing to come back, I want you to end them. We can't be dealing with renegades of their caliber at a time like this."

"I understand." Lidria glanced at her left arm. "You know, if I can get those mages to come back, you could—"

"Become a breaker?" Ren interrupted, bitterness in his voice.

Lidria's heart stopped. She took a step back and shied her eyes away from Ren. "I-I'm sorry. I'm going."

Ren grabbed Lidria's arm before she got to the exit. "Lidria, I didn't mean it like that. I have no secret disgust for you or people like you.

"You…you're a strong person, and I'm glad you survived. I'm just not sure it would be the right thing for me. If that makes any sense."

"I guess it does." Lidria reined her emotions back in, relaxed, and eased back into the tent.

Ren's hand fell. "Good. I didn't want you to think I look down on you. I understand the sacrifices you've made, and I didn't want you to think I was belittling them."

"Ren, I understand." Lidria turned toward him, tried to smile but found she couldn't. "Don't worry. I promise I won't hold it against you."

"Okay." Ren nodded. "I trust you."

Lidria forced a weak smile. "Thank you."

"You're more trustworthy than most of the people here." Ren placed his hand on Lidria's shoulder.

"That means a lot to me," Lidria managed, putting her hand on Ren's outstretched arm.

"Be safe out there," Ren whispered.

Lidria squeezed Ren's arm before hers fell to her side. "I will." She turned, exiting the tent before either could speak further.

Lidria hiked down a narrow path, cutting her way through the forest. Trees rose tall and spread out enough to let the high afternoon sunlight drift in. She glanced to the left at the babbling creek. Several frogs ribbited to each other in the distance.

A twig snapped, and Lidria dropped into a crouch. Her head whipped to the right. Through the sparse treeline, a small, cloaked figure hurried forward. Twenty yards separated them. She hung low and hoped the person had not spotted her.

The individual glanced around before they knelt. With quick and practiced motion, their index finger drew in the soil. Lidria craned her neck. She couldn't make anything out and decided to remain inconspicuous. Giving away her position now would be foolish.

Pale blue light flashed. The figure shot upright as the illumination faded, and their cowl fell back. Silver hair, framing a feminine face, glinted in the streaming sunlight. She pulled her hood back in place and rushed toward the forest's edge.

Lidria stood and followed the woman. She expected a difficult time finding either of the missing parties, but luck appeared to be on her side. If she didn't cause her target to panic, her mission would succeed.

The edge of the forest halted Lidria's advance. She watched the woman cross a crop-filled field, heading toward a cluster of squat, drab homes and barns. No signs of life, besides the mage, made themselves apparent. At least if things went south, no one would get caught in the crossfire.

As soon as her mark slipped inside one of the buildings, Lidria moved. She kept to the ground and used the young crop of corn to mask her approach. Sneaking up on supposed allies churned her stomach, but she knew what needed to be done. This method proved far safer.

Lidria picked her way through the small village. She treated all windows as potential threats, avoiding walking in front of them. Nothing suggested immediate danger, but she didn't want to take any chances. Ambushes were a complication she didn't have energy for.

Anticipation held Lidria's breath as she crept up. She took up position on the right of the door in case the woman proved hostile. The wooden wall wouldn't put up much resistance against magic, yet the slight advantage soothed her nerves.

Lidria reached out, steeled herself, and knocked on the door. Boots scuffed against wood and footsteps came closer. She reached over her shoulder, gripping the hilt of her sword.

Wood groaned around the hinges as the door creaked open. Through the narrow crack, sunlight glinted off silver hair, and a golden eye stared back at Lidria. She attempted to appear non-threatening, but her preparedness gave her away. The woman flinched, slamming the door shut.

Lidria lowered her arm; there would be no altercation with this woman. The tricky part would be getting her to open up or at least explain the situation. She knocked again.

"Hello," Lidria called. "Lieutenant McCrear sent me to find out what's going on here. I assume you're a mage of the Enclave, so we're on the same side. I just want to talk."

Silence.

Lidria frowned and took a step away from the wall. She didn't want to force her way in, but she would if pressed. Rot and age would make kicking the door in easy, without resorting to using a link. She took a deep breath, readied herself, and—

The door squeaked open if only a foot. Lidria relaxed. A young woman's face appeared in the opening, golden eyes glinting in the sunlight. Her eyes flicked down at Lidria's left arm, and Lidria sighed. The woman met her gaze with a blank expression.

"Greetings. My name is Selis." Her lips twitched in a failed attempt at a smile. "What is yours?"

"Lidria." Selis' eyebrows twitched, and she set her jaw. "Are you the only one here?"

Selis pulled her long hair over her shoulder and fussed with the braid. "Currently, yes, but I am not alone. My master will be back presently."

"Thank you, Selis, for speaking with me." Lidria smiled despite herself. "For a moment, I thought you were going to run."

"You are not a threat." Selis' eyes widened, and her hands gripped her braid tight. "I am sorry. That did not come out the way I intended. I meant to say; I know you are not here to do me harm." She opened the door the rest of the way and stepped outside.

"No offense taken." Lidria shifted her weight onto the heel of her right foot, easing away from Selis. "What are you and your master doing out here exactly? I thought you would want to join with McCrear and his men."

"The common citizens often treat us with distrust or even fear. We did not want to cause any unnecessary problems or tension. As a breaker, I am sure you understand." Selis locked eyes with Lidria as she spoke, but Lidria could tell the mage forced the gesture.

"That's not—" Lidria snapped her mouth shut and sighed. "I suppose you have a point. Still, we need to band together in times like these."

Selis' expression turned sorrowful. "I agree with you, Lidria. I feel we should help. My master, however, does not see it that way. He has been quite obsessed with keeping our distance."

"Forget your master," Lidria offered. "If you want to help people, come back with me."

"I cannot."

"You said he would be back soon, right? Well," Lidria leaned against the house and folded her arms across her chest, "I'm going to wait and have a little chat with him."

"I advise against that," Selis warned, fear clouding her eyes. "He has not been stable lately. He is likely to see you as hostile and attack."

"I have to try." Lidria's confidence wavered. "We…could really use someone like you."

Selis glanced at Lidria but shied away from her gaze. "I—"

"Selis," a masculine voice barked, causing the woman to jump. A robed man marched down the dirt path, another by his side. "What are you doing?"

Lidria turned to face Selis' master. He sat two inches shorter than her, ten years older, and his head bald. She frowned; he seemed familiar. However, no matter how hard she wracked her brain, she couldn't remember his name.

The man ignored Lidria and stopped inches away from Selis, staring her down. "Selis, I told you to keep yourself hidden. What happened to the wards?"

"I-I am sorry, Master Flinn. I intended to stay hidden as you said, but Lidria was sent by Lieutenant McCrear to see if we required aid." Selis never met his gaze.

Flinn turned his attention on Lidria, a peculiar, thoughtful expression on his face. "Breaker, I assure you we are quite fine on our own. You can tell your lieutenant we do not require aid. Good day."

"I'm afraid I can't leave it at that," Lidria said, drawing Selis' wide-eyed stare. "Several of our scouts went missing in this region, and I intend to find out why. If you would be so kind as to cooperate."

"We have not seen these scouts you speak of," the man beside Flinn impressed.

"Cent, quiet yourself." Flinn regarded Lidria with a sceptical eye. "My servant has the right of it, breaker. We have seen no scouts at all. With everything that's happened, perhaps they simply went AWOL."

Lidria glared at Flinn. His dark brown eyes never wavered. "I highly doubt they would. We're all on the same side—why the secrecy here?"

"You wouldn't understand," Flinn spat, turning from Lidria. "You're just a lowly soldier."

Lidria's memory clicked, and she remembered where she knew Flinn. "I've been trying to figure out why you looked so familiar." He glanced over his shoulder. "You're the mage that led the ritual to make me into a breaker."

Flinn raised an eyebrow. "Oh? What of it? You should be thankful to have your limb back, so show me your thanks by leaving."

"I can't yet," Lidria pressed. "Even if you're not interested in helping the survivors, Selis wants to. I want to take her back with me."

"Out of the question." Flinn waved his baggy sleeve at Lidria. "She is my pupil, and she is going to stay right here."

"Selis, is that what you want?" Lidria hooked her thumb through the belt loop at her waist.

"N-no." Selis turned toward Flinn, avoiding eye contact. "I want to help people. I am not helping anyone here."

Flinn *humphed*. "Help people? Bah! They don't want your help; you're nothing but a freak to them. Why would you want to help them?"

“They may look down upon me or call me a freak, but they need help.” Selis raised her head and met Flinn’s gaze head-on. “And I am capable of helping.”

“You? Capable?” Flinn shook his head. “Don’t make me laugh, child.”

Emerald flames ignited in Selis’ hands. She thrust her right hand, palm-out, at Flinn. A quick flick brought his up, and the magic spiralled. The flames dwindled into sputtering wisps, vanishing into the palm of his hand. He snared and chanted.

Lidria drew her sword and leaped between the two mages.

Chapter Five

"Step aside, breaker," Flinn growled. "This no longer concerns you."

"Yes, it does. I came here to bring you back into the fold. If only one of you is willing," Lidria extended her sword, "I won't let you get in the way."

Flinn held his hand out at Lidria. "Fool. You could have lived, but I cannot allow that anymore."

A shriek pierced Lidria's ears as steel crumpled and folded. She tossed her weapon, and Flinn caught it in midair. In the blink of an eye, the rest curled into a tiny ball. He flicked his hand to the side, the bit of metal disappearing.

Magic tingled up Lidria's arm as she severed a link. She pushed forward and rocketed toward Flinn. The mage brought his hands down in a sweeping gesture. An invisible force pressed down on her. Her legs pumped hard, but she got nowhere.

Flinn flourished his right hand at the end of an arc while he moved his left. Emerald fire erupted to life once again, and Selis stepped forward. Cent, who had remained motionless, interposed himself. His eyes glowed pale yellow.

Selis' flames collided with nothing, flashing pink as they dissolved. Cent raised a hand. "Do not do this, Selis. There is only one way this will end."

"I cannot turn my back on those people, Cent," Selis shouted above the roiling.

"Then, you have left me no choice. I must protect the master." Cent thrust his arm at Selis, and the vanishing flames turned and shot back at her.

Selis dove to the ground. Cent pointed down, and the fire froze above her. She rolled onto her back and pushed upward. Flames cascaded down, yet none of them touched her, rolling off on either side.

Lidria moved if only a foot. She reached out and grabbed Flinn's wrist. The spell upon her broke, and her full speed returned. She yanked him forward, bringing her knee up into his gut. He crumpled with a grunt of surprise and pain.

Tossing Flinn, Lidria stood over him. His eyes shot open, and, with them, a gust of violent wind carried her upward. She flipped twenty feet into the air. Her mind raced. Memories of the winged monstrosity and her helplessness paralyzed her.

Lidria plummeted, but something tugged at her waist. A gentle breeze flitted around her. She glanced down at Selis, still on her back, with her hand outstretched. Lidria took a cautious step forward, the space beneath her foot tangible. She rushed down to Flinn as he righted himself.

Flinn snarled. He shouted a word Lidria couldn't identify, and the footholds vanished. She dropped, collapsing on one knee. She cursed, ignored the pain, and shot back to her feet.

A dazzling blade of rosy light formed in Flinn's left hand, and he thrust at Lidria. She twisted to the side, avoiding the stab. Heat flushed her face and sizzling popped in her ear. The blade connected with her chainmail, melting metal before deflecting away.

Lidria hopped backward as Flinn pressed his advantage. He cursed at her and flailed his blade around. The inexperience in his movements, his strokes, amused her. She dodged this way and that, staying out of reach. In a minute, he would wind himself, and she would strike back.

Lightning crackled and Lidria tumbled. The bolt of electricity sailed over her, striking a nearby building. The old wood went up in flames. She snapped her head in the direction the lightning came from. Cent stood over a motionless Selis.

Lidria's heart leaped up into her throat. If Selis died, her mission failed. She needed to finish this before anything happened to her. Her eyes flicked to Flinn. He stood, panting, holding his conjured weapon. There would be no diplomacy here. She launched herself at him.

Flinn attempted to dodge out of Lidria's reach, but she snatched his left wrist with her right hand and squeezed. He yelped, and the light-blade dropped from his hand. She leaned forward, scooped the conjuration out of the air, and put the blade to his neck.

Pain bit into Lidria's hand, and she grit her teeth. "Cent," she hollered. "Leave Selis alone, or I slit his throat."

"As you wish." Cent lowered his arms and took two steps away from Selis.

"How does it feel, breaker?" Flinn asked, venom dripping from his voice. "It must hurt an awful lot. Oh, right. You are probably happy you can feel anything in that limb of yours."

Lidria snapped. Shouting, she jammed the point into Flinn's neck. She expected blood, gurgling, decapitation, anything, but nothing came. The weapon froze a fraction of an inch from his delicate throat. Her hand burned, and she tossed the magic away.

Flinn broke into a fit of laughter. "Good work, Cent. I knew she could not hold for long."

Lidria glared at Flinn and then Cent. Cent shrugged. "I obeyed your wish: Selis is unharmed. You never said anything about not stopping you, though."

"You bastards," Lidria breathed, her speed returning to normal.

"Now do you see how foolish it was to meddle in our business, breaker?" Flinn stepped toward Lidria and grinned.

Lidria's breath came sharp and shallow. "What is so damned important you would turn on your own?"

"I already told you." Flinn paced in front of Lidria. "You would never understand."

"You never know."

Flinn shook his head. "Some things are better kept as secrets. You might have learned that one day, but…" He raised his hands and then lowed them, and the same invisible force from before bore down upon Lidria.

Light flashed above Flinn's left shoulder. His head spun around, and a curse slipped from his mouth. He released Lidria, floundering back and to the left. The illumination winked out of existence before a flare of energy rushed out.

A clean-cut hole the size of Lidria's fist appeared in Flinn's shoulder. He howled in pain, covering the wound with his hand. She glanced around. Selis leaned against the building to her right. Her chest rose and fell in an erratic rhythm, but she appeared relieved.

"How dare you," Cent roared, stepping over to Selis and backhanding her. She collapsed. "He is your master."

"I cannot," Selis struggled against gasping breaths, "I cannot allow him to do as he pleases if it is going to harm decent people."

Cent grabbed Selis by the collar and hauled her off the ground. "You…I do not know what he saw in you, but he was clearly mistaken. I will take responsibility for your disobedient actions and deal with you accordingly."

"Let her go," Lidria demanded, taking several shaky steps toward Cent and Selis.

Cent laughed. "Do not be so impatient, breaker. You are—" His head snapped backward.

Selis swayed in Cent's grip, her jaw set and a grimace on her face. He released her, and she dropped to her feet, managing to stay upright. Her hand shot to her forehead. Lidria stood still, mouth agape.

"Cent." Selis lowered her hand and stared him down. "I never wished any ill upon you despite your mistreatment of me. However, I will not hold back any longer."

Cent regained his composure and stared daggers at Selis. "You? Hold back? You do not have enough power in your little body."

Selis closed her eyes. A wordless chant played upon her lips, and Cent wrinkled his brow. Her eyes opened a moment later, and they glowed a brilliant yellow-gold. Cent reeled. His mouth hung open and eyes wide in shock. She lifted a hand.

"Stop this instant," Flinn bellowed as he held his wounded shoulder. Selis turned her head, but her eyes remained fixated forward. "You do not know what you are messing with, Selis. Do not go down this path."

"It is too late, master," Selis said, indifferent. "You showed me the way. I am merely following your tutelage; you should be happy."

Flinn closed his eyes and turned from Selis. "You are lost to me."

"That is acceptable." Selis focused on Cent. "Goodbye, Cent."

"I always did hate you, Selis," Cent whispered.

"I know."

Emerald fire and amethyst lightning mingled in a vortex between Selis and Cent. Flinn inched forward, but Lidria held him back. He stared at her with nothing but sorrow in his eyes. She didn't understand, but she trusted Selis more than her master.

Cent's eyes glowed yellow, and he put a hand between him and Selis' vortex. Pink light sparked as the flames and lightning swirled. He staggered backward and threw his other hand up. She remained static, motionless, as he disappeared.

Lidria stared as the maelstrom consumed Cent. He made not a sound above the roaring magic. She blinked and retook stock of Selis. The mage stood a fraction of Lidria's size, but she held incredible power. A thrill of terror ran down her spine.

"Lidria," Selis said, turning toward her. "Please subdue Master Flinn. I am afraid I—" she crumpled to the ground in a heap of robes and hair.

Lidria stepped in front of Flinn and stared him down. "Well, are you willing to come peacefully, or am I going to have to force you?"

Flinn shook his head and blinked. He stared past Lidria. "Do you really think I would come with you after what has happened?"

"I have no delusions that you'll cooperate," Lidria admitted. "But, one way or another, you'll be coming with me."

"No," Flinn hissed. "No, no, no. You cannot know. I will not go. They must not be found." He lurched toward the building Lidria had found Selis in.

Lidria let Flinn pass, but she struck him in the back of the head. He staggered and flopped forward, motionless. She nudged him with her foot; he made no sounds, nor did he move. Content with her handiwork, she walked over to Selis.

Lidria knelt and brushed Selis' hair aside. She still breathed. A flutter of relief danced inside her, but she suppressed such a ridiculous emotion. She lifted Selis—the effort more than she expected—and carried her to the nearby house.

The dim interior hid any furnishings. Lidria navigated through the room without dumping Selis. Her muscles strained as she set the mage down, propping her up against the wall before heading outside.

Flinn, despite his small stature, proved far more cumbersome than Selis. Lidria grabbed him under the arms and dragged him into the house.

She tossed him on the floor near the outer wall. She would wait until Selis regained consciousness to leave.

Lidria plopped down near Flinn and waited. Her eyes adjusted to the lack of light. In the far corner of the room, several travel packs lay. She regarded them with curiosity, noticing blocky protrusions. Flinn wanted to protect something.

Selis stirred, and Lidria jumped to her feet. She padded over to the young woman. "Selis, are you all right?"

"I," Selis blinked and gazed up at Lidria. "I do believe so. I apologize for the inconvenience."

"Don't worry about it." Lidria forced a smile. "You saved me out there."

Selis frowned. "I did save you, but it cost Cent his life." She lowered her head. "He did not deserve that."

Lidria sat next to Selis, causing her to flinch. "What's the story between you two? Flinn called him his servant but you his pupil."

"Cent was born into serving the Enclave. Mas"—Selis shook her head—"Flinn was in charge of his family and, while he couldn't cast magic himself, he had been given artificial power he could tap into."

Lidria's gaze fell to her left arm. "That—"

"Yes," Selis affirmed. "It is similar to the process of creating a breaker. You are your own person, however. He was given power to be Flinn's tool."

"Sometimes I've felt that," Lidria swallowed hard and shied away from Selis' blazing eyes, "the only reason I was saved and turned was so I could simply be someone's tool."

Selis took Lidria's left hand into both of hers. The warmth didn't reach her. "I will not lie: breakers are not usually made for any other reason but to serve some purpose not their own. However, Lidria, if you ever were just a tool, you are no longer."

"I-I don't know what to say," Lidria stammered, her eyes fixated on Selis' hands around hers.

Selis released Lidria's hand and brought her own back into her lap. "That is okay. I do not require validation of my words."

Lidria tilted her head back up to meet a warm smile. "Thank you, Selis."

"You are quite welcome, Lidria."

"I'm sorry." Lidria frowned. "I asked you about your relationship with Cent, and then I went and made it all about me."

Selis wrapped her arms around her legs, pulling her knees to her chest. "You are fine. I would rather speak about you than Cent's jealousy or what I did to him. I am surprised by my actions."

"I was surprised, too." Lidria cursed her bluntness. "By how powerful you are, I mean. How long have you been studying magic?"

Selis cocked her head to the side, thoughtful. "Fifteen years, I believe."

Lidria stared at Selis, her brow furrowed. "No offense, but that doesn't seem like long enough for you to be where you are."

"I have undergone several invocations to enhance my magical capabilities since I was little." Selis spun the tip of her braid between her fingers. "One of them went awry and gave me my silver hair and golden eyes."

"Oh." Lidria took a moment to take in Selis' eyes and hair. "Well, I think they're beautiful, Selis. You're one-of-a-kind, and you should be proud."

Selis offered Lidria a halfhearted smile. "I appreciate the gesture. I believe I still need some time until I can believe that or follow your advice."

"I understand, but I want you to think positively." Lidria held Selis' gaze as she spoke.

"I will try," Selis said, determined. "I can assure you."

"Good." Lidria nodded, got up on her feet, and extended a hand down to Selis. "Can you walk?"

Selis released her legs, stretching them. "I feel weak, but I think I can." She took Lidria's hand and stood.

"What do you want to do about those?" Lidria asked, pointing to the full travel bags in the corner.

Selis padded over to the bags, knelt beside one, and yanked open the drawstring. "I would like to bring all the tomes with me, but I cannot carry much." She pulled out random tomes and placed them on the ground beside her.

"I could use a link to carry Flinn and the extras if they're that important to you," Lidria offered, discounting how wasteful the effort would be.

"No." Selis shook her head. "I do not wish to make you waste your finite power." She continued to make several stacks of books. "While I desire to take them all, only a few will suffice."

"We can always come back and grab the rest later." Lidria strode close to Selis and the books.

Selis placed several volumes back in the bag. "I will make do."

Lidria stood, frowning, and tried to understand Selis' logic. "It's not a big—" Selis shoved something at Lidria.

"Take this." As soon as Lidria opened her hand, Selis dropped a bit of rolled-up cloth inside. "This is a compress made of thistle, dawndew, and lyme. It is used to disrupt the flow of magic. Place it on Flinn's skin in case he wakes up."

Lidria nodded and strode across the room. She unwrapped the cloth. A pungent odor wafted off the pastel green paste, causing her to wrinkle her nose in disgust. She applied the compress to Flinn's neck and pulled away.

Emerald flames ignited the stack of books. "Selis, what are you doing?"

"If I cannot take them with me," Selis turned and gazed up at Lidria, "I must destroy them. Flinn was right about one thing: some secrets are better kept secret."

"I don't…" Lidria stopped herself. If this was what Selis wanted, she couldn't stop her. "I'll trust you on this."

"I will prove your trust is not misplaced." Selis hoisted the travel bag and slung it over her shoulder. The weight sagged her body. "Shall we?"

Lidria shook her head. "All right." Selis' smile broadened, and she took the lead. Lidria, as she made for the door, paused to scoop up Flinn. She wrestled with his weight and stepped outside to greet the setting sun.

Chapter Six

Selis strolled into camp, the sun set, with Lidria at her side. She had seen the campsite from afar two days prior, but she had not realized how few survivors remained. Guilt weighed heavy. If she had helped during the attack, perhaps more people would be alive. Her gaze shifted to the man responsible for her inaction.

Flinn looked pathetic—defeated and slung over Lidria's shoulder. Selis sighed. She could not believe she let him rule her life for so long, but he had been her master. Everything she knew about the Flow, he had taught her. She owed him her way of life.

Selis shook her head. No, Flinn had gone too far. Without Lidria's intervention, she would have continued to kowtow to his manic demands. Weakness suited her, something everyone she met reinforced except Lidria.

Selis glanced at Lidria, and her chest tightened. Lidria's hair hung loose from her bun, her face and clothes dirty and torn, and her chain mail melted by magic. She carried herself like nothing happened, save for a faint limp in her stride.

Lidria turned her head. "Is something wrong, Selis?"

"No." Selis locked eyes with Lidria. "Thank you for helping me stand up for myself."

"I couldn't leave you with them, not after you said you wished to help." Lidria smiled.

Selis' heart fluttered. She shied her eyes away from Lidria's, but she did not stop a smile from curling her lips. "If you had not shown up, things would have remained the same."

"I'm not sure what to say," Lidria confessed. She shifted Flinn on her shoulder with a grimace. "But I'm glad you're with us now."

“I am glad as well.” Selis stared up into Lidria’s vibrant green eyes. “I have not been accepted by anyone in a long time.”

Lidria frowned and stopped in front of a tent. Her eyes flicked back to Selis. “You’re welcome to stay with me. There’s plenty of room.”

“That would be wonderful,” Selis said, smiling. “I know I can trust you.”

Lidria’s face twisted, and she chewed on her lip before she composed herself. “It’s nice to hear that.”

“We outcasts have to stick together.”

Lidria shifted her weight, awkward. “Yeah, I guess we do.” She half-turned and gestured toward the entrance. “I’m going to dump Flinn here for now. Get some rest; I need to report to Ren.”

Selis grew anxious at the thought of being alone with Flinn, even unconscious and surrounded by strangers. “All right.”

“Don’t worry.” Lidria held the flap back for Selis. “It won’t take me long.”

Selis nodded and entered the tent. The sparse furnishings made for a lot of open space. She took the corner opposite the cot, swung her pack off her shoulder, and plopped the bundle down. Her body swayed forward with the motion, and she feared she would follow.

The canvas rustled as Lidria staggered inside. She dumped Flinn on the ground, letting out a sharp breath. Her back didn’t straighten for a moment. Selis frowned and stepped close before placing her hand on the small of Lidria’s back. Lidria went rigid until she exhaled a shaky breath.

Selis focused the Flow through her hand and into Lidria’s body. Points of pain flared, causing Selis to flinch. She continued and guided her magic to the sore spots, and they faded. She did not eliminate them, but given how much time passed, her work proved satisfactory.

Lifting her hand from Lidria, Selis staggered backward. Lidria grabbed her and prevented her from toppling. Selis smiled up at the taller woman. The support Lidria offered vanished, and she stood on her own.

"Selis—"

"I am all right," Selis asserted. Dizziness washed over her, and she stumbled to the cot. "You were hurting because of me. It is only right that I help you."

Lidria's expression softened, but the concern did not disappear. "You're exhausted, and you have every right to be. I wasn't hurt any more than a night or two of rest couldn't fix."

"You may be right," Selis' arm shook with the effort of holding herself upright, "but it did not feel right when I could do something."

Lidria shook her head before gazing down into Selis' eyes. "Thank you." A shy smile slid onto Lidria's face. "I do feel a lot better now."

Selis beamed up at Lidria. "You are most welcome."

"I'm going to go report to Ren now." Lidria stood straighter. "If you want to sleep, go for it. Don't wait for me to get back."

"I do not think I am comfortable enough here, despite my exhaustion, to rest alone." Selis pulled her legs up onto the cot, managing to fit her small frame, and hugged her knees to her chest.

"I understand; you've had a rough day. I promise I won't take long." Lidria exited the tent, abandoning Selis.

Selis sat and stared at her former master. Guilt flashed through her before she reminded herself why events had turned out this way. He needed to be stopped; the day couldn't end any other way.

The Flow-inhibiting compress on Flinn's neck stood out. Selis knew how he would feel if he woke up: empty, isolated, desolate. Every mage experienced the effects at some point in their training to learn how to cope. She hoped she never did again.

Selis tore her eyes off Flinn, cupping her hand like so many times before. A tiny spark of emerald flame danced to life in the palm of her hand. She stared and sighed. Fire—her fire—soothed her. Cent's face appeared, contorted in intense hatred.

Selis swung her arm out to the side and dismissed the flame. A shiver ran down her spine. She should not have killed Cent; he had been a companion of sorts, but he meant to kill her. Her meek nature, however, did not permit her own murder. Not when her power prevented it.

Power. Interactions always came down to power. Selis never considered herself powerful—more a result of the fact everyone belittled her than self-depreciation. Flinn had spent years molding her, feeding her magical strength. Despite several blunders, he had succeeded.

A thought came to her: why did Flinn, being the egotistical man he is, want to make her strong? He held her leash; she did not dispute that. He need only point, and she would jump. She had been a tool to him, not a person. People did not fear, nor were they jealous of, tools.

Movement outside startled Selis, stopping her breath in her throat. She calmed herself when the tent flap flipped open as Lidria stepped in. Lidria gave her a warm smile when their eyes met, and her anxieties vanished. Something about Lidria put her at ease.

A man swept up beside Lidria. He stood half a head taller than her, which meant he dwarfed Selis. His disheveled brown hair had no doubt seen better days. His green eyes drifted from Flinn to Selis. Shock played on his face. She had become accustomed to the stares people gave her.

Selis unfolded her legs and rose, stepping over to Lidria and McCrear. "Greetings. I am Selis. It is good to make your acquaintance, Lieutenant McCrear."

"It's nice to meet you, too, Selis," McCrear said, offering his hand. She stared for a moment before she complied. "Lidria tells me you're a pupil of Master Flinn."

"He is no master of mine any longer," Selis spat. "Nor is he worthy of being anyone's ever again."

McCrear's eyes widened. She had to admit; she shocked herself. "What has he done to warrant such hatred from a former pupil?"

"My reasons are my own, but I know what you are interested in. He killed your scouts and refused to help the people of Odwyn." Selis held McCrear's gaze, resolute.

"Fair enough," McCrear scratched the back of his head, "but why did he kill those men? They weren't hunting him."

Selis glanced to Lidria, and she nodded. "He is quite obsessed with keeping certain knowledge safe. I do not see things the same as him, so here I am."

"It's good to have you, but I'm concerned about Master Flinn's condition. We don't have the means to keep a mage restrained." McCrear's attention drifted from Selis to Flinn's motionless form.

"Do not worry," Selis said. She walked across the tent, opened the sack, and pulled out a satchel containing more Dauein. "There is enough of this to render him magic-less for quite some time."

"And what exactly is that?" McCrear asked, craning his neck.

Selis unfurled the small satchel to reveal a row of several compound compresses. "Dauein. It is a compound that inhibits the flow of magic in a person's body, thus rendering them unable to use magic."

"That's good," McCrear acknowledged, but Selis noted he did not comprehend the concept in its entirety. "We'll have to make sure the guards know what to do when we take him to be detained."

“I would like to change the subject to something other than him.” Exhaustion crept up on Selis, legs trembling under her weight. “I came here to help.”

McCrear cocked his head to the side before a flash of recognition sparked in his eyes. “I’m sure Doctor Silvon would appreciate someone with your skills, Selis. There are quite a few injured we can’t care for with mundane treatments.”

“That sounds perfect.” The world swam, and Selis tipped over. Lidria lurched forward and caught Selis in her arms. Selis, face against Lidria’s chest, stared up into her concerned eyes. “I apologize.”

“Don’t worry about it,” Lidria said as she righted Selis. She expected Lidria to remove her arm, but she did not. “I’ll take you to meet Silvon tomorrow after you get some rest.”

“Speaking of tomorrow,” McCrear interjected. “I decided to break camp in several days and march to Reilk where we can get some relief. But first, I wanted to let the people go back into Odwyn to collect anything they can find and to say goodbye to their home.

“I would like you to accompany us in case there are any lingering Quela or more renegade mages.”

Lidria’s grip on Selis’ arm tightened. “Of course.”

The tent flap rustled, and a small form bolted in. “Lidi!” a young boy called before throwing himself at her. “You’re back.”

“Hi, Hector.” Lidria stood rigid against his enthusiastic hug.

“Where did you go?” Hector asked, releasing Lidria. “What were you doing? Did you have to fight any bad guys?”

McCrear chuckled, receiving a quick glare from Lidria. “I was on a mission for Ren. I would like you to meet—”

“Whoa,” Hector exclaimed. “Your hair is so pretty!”

Selis smiled, her cheeks flush. “Thank you, Hector. My name is Selis.”

Hector rushed over to Selis. “Can I—can I touch it?”

“Y-you may.” Selis knelt to Hector’s level and pulled the rest of her long braid free from her hooded robe. Her silver hair cascaded over her chest.

Hector’s hand shot out and grabbed Selis’ hair. She yelped as she was jerked forward by the kid’s excitable, absent-minded strength. Pain radiated from the top of her head, and she grimaced. Her hair would be torn from her scalp if this continued, yet Hector did not appear concerned.

“Hector,” Lidria scolded, grabbing his arm and pulling him away. “Be gentle. Selis is nice, and you should be more careful.” She released him.

Hector let go and lowered his head. Selis let out a breath of relief. “Sorry.”

“It is all right, Hector.” Selis eased back from him and stood. “I am not used to being around someone as enthusiastic as yourself.”

“How did your hair get like that?” Hector asked, his curiosity coming back to the forefront.

Selis played her braid between her fingers. “It is complicated, but to put it simply: magic changed my eyes and hair.”

Hector stared. “Can you do magic?”

“I can.”

“That’s so cool! You and Lidi are awesome.” Wonder shone bright in Hector’s eyes.

Selis smiled, unsure how to respond to such excitement directed at her. “Thank you, Hector.”

“Can you show me some magic?”

Selis sat down, folding her legs. She flipped her hair back and held out her hands, cupped. Small pinpoints of multi-colored light danced to life. Hector leaned in close. A small smile curled her lips, and she poured more magic into her little show.

The lights grew brighter and rose from Selis' hands. Hector's head snapped upward, his mouth agape. Lidria smiled behind him and nodded her appreciation. Selis poured the last bit of energy into the beams, and they flared into fleeting flames of corresponding colors.

"Awesome," Hector breathed.

Pride ran through Selis, and Hector's childish wonder reinvigorated her. His excitement proved magic could be more than destructive—it could captivate, excite. The alternative uses could, and should, outweigh the violent ones.

Hector grinned. "That was amazing. Do more, do more!"

A wave of dizziness washed over Selis. Even such a small display took a toll on her; she had nothing left. "I—"

"Hector," Lidria said. "Selis has had a rough day. I'm sure she'd be happy to show you more magic some other time, but she needs to rest now."

"Okay." Hector frowned for a moment before a smile broke through. "Thanks, Selis."

"You are welcome, Hector," Selis said, returning his smile. "I will be glad to when I am feeling better."

"I'll get a tent set aside for you," McCrear offered. "It shouldn't be more than a few minutes."

Selis shook her head. "No need. I am staying here with Lidria."

"Oh." Surprise played across McCrear's face. "All right. That works, then."

Lidria turned to McCrear before she gestured at Flinn. "Let's take care of Flinn so Selis can get some rest." Lidria glanced at Selis. "You can use the cot tonight." She stepped over to Flinn and, with a grunt of effort, hoisted him off the ground.

"Goodnight," Selis managed. The thought of being alone put her on edge.

"Goodnight, Selis." Lidria gave her a mesmerizing smile, and she wanted to ask Lidria to stay. "C'mon, Hector. Say goodnight to Selis."

"Goodnight, Selis," Hector sang, waving his little hand at her. She offered her own, albeit less enthusiastic, wave farewell.

McCrear locked eyes with Selis. "I'll make sure Master Flinn is properly detained. So put your mind at ease. If you need anything, let me know." He gave her a shallow nod before he slipped out of the tent, following Lidria and Hector.

Once everyone exited, Selis moved. Her legs trembled at the exertion, but she managed to stand. Her eyelids weighed heavy, and further dizziness threatened to topple her. She padded over to the cot. Strength vanished.

The simple act of laying on something other than the cold, hard ground elated Selis. She heaved a contented sigh. Any reservations she held about taking Lidria's bed drifted away. She closed her weary eyes, curling up. Oblivion swept her away.

Chapter Seven

Lidria kicked a loose stone, and it tumbled and skipped down the rubble-strewn street. She told Ren she would stay, but, after the initial shock from the devastation, the venture grew boring. She didn't have much in the city—nothing she cared for.

Lidria gazed down the street. A sinkhole thirty yards out cut it off, forming a ring of debris. A building, half-collapsed, sat at the edge of the sinkhole. Ren led a group of six people up to the building as a soldier slipped out. He nodded, and the group headed inside.

Outside, Lidria turned her attention to the remaining civilians. They milled about, some disappearing into buildings. One of the soldiers glanced around before they, too, entered a battered building alone. Lidria frowned at the odd behavior. Why would they break away from their post to—

Lidria froze midstride. She had become so entrenched in her views that she hadn't realized how the destruction of Odwyn had affected others. To her, the city represented little more than a collection of buildings. To the other survivors, their whole lives.

With a shake of her head, Lidria shied away from the civilians. She ducked around a corner to a side street to be alone. The stone brick pressed chainmail into her back as she leaned against a wall and tilted her head up. The sky above shone bright blue.

Lidria swallowed. The world turned blurry, and loneliness enveloped her. Everything she once held dear had been ripped away from her. Only a void remained, and she had done nothing to repair or fill it for years. She had neglected so many things.

Steeling herself, Lidria lowered her gaze. She wiped away what remained of her few shed tears and blinked several times. The narrow street around her became claustrophobic, stifling. She wanted to move, to leave, but her body didn't listen.

"Breaker?" a feminine voice called out. Lidria turned her head as a dark-skinned soldier strode down the street toward her. The same woman from outside Ren's tent. "Is everything all right?"

Lidria shook her head. "Y-yeah. I just needed a moment."

"I can sympathize." The soldier leaned against the wall beside Lidria. She took off her helmet, and jet-black hair spilled out in a tangled mess. Her almond-colored eyes met Lidria's.

"What's your name?" Lidria asked.

She stared at Lidria before smiling. "Joan. Joan Heln."

"It's nice to meet you, Joan. I suppose you already know mine." Lidria frowned. "Well, part of it. Not many people know my last name; it hasn't been a priority. But," she swallowed, "it's Avar."

"What's wrong, Lidria?" Joan asked, concern masking her face.

"I've been thinking," Lidria confessed, turning away. "I haven't told anyone in years. I think I'm ashamed of it, or it's too painful to remember. I'm not the same person I was when I went by that name."

"I've never personally experienced that, but I think I understand where you're coming from." Joan paused, staring at Lidria's arm. "It must have been tough, becoming a breaker. I've only heard stories."

Lidria ignored Joan's gaze and pressed forward. "It wasn't a horrible experience in and of itself.

"I didn't take it well, though. I was depressed after nearly dying and my inability to cope with this," she lifted her left arm, "and I turned self-destructive and pulled away from everyone I knew. I was such a wreck my family left me."

“I’m sorry to hear that,” Joan said, placing a tender hand on Lidria’s shoulder. “I’ve known some people who acted similarly after being gravely wounded or crippled in service. It’s never an easy thing.”

“Looking back, I don’t know what I was thinking. I had been given a second chance, unlike most in my situation, and I didn’t realize how lucky I actually was.” Lidria shook her head and let out a nervous chuckle. “No wonder they left.”

“What was your family like?” Joan asked. “If you don’t mind me asking.”

“It’s all right; I’m the one who brought all this up.” Lidria tilted her head back until the top touched the stone wall. “I was married and had a daughter. My husband, Ian, was a baker. We met back when I was fresh in the military.

“My daughter, Evelyn, was only three when Ian took her. I wasn’t a perfect parent, even before everything happened. He mostly took care of her after infancy. I was too busy trying to climb the ranks to devote much time to her.”

Joan shifted around, cradling her helmet in the crook of her arm. “I have to say; I’m surprised. I mean, that Hector kid hangs around you; you can’t be as bad as you’re selling yourself.”

“Thanks,” Lidria managed. “But I don’t know why he’s like that. I just hope his mother turns up. For his sake.”

“If she hasn’t by now,” Joan started, “chances are pretty low she will. Not to be a downer or anything.”

“No, you’re probably right.” Lidria lowered her head. “I don’t understand where she went. She was right beside me the night of the attack, and she survived the citadel collapse.”

“Things were pretty chaotic.” A distant expression took hold of Joan’s face. “Any number of things could’ve happened.”

Sighing, Lidria stared off into nothingness. “Yeah.”

“You’re not his mother, but at least he has a friendly face to turn to.” Joan smiled when Lidria glanced her way.

Lidria frowned. “I don’t—”

“Lidria, Joan.” Ren jogged over to them. “There you are. We’re moving on in a few minutes. Is everything all right?”

“Yep,” Joan affirmed, chipper. “We were checking things out when we got a bit distracted. Nothing to worry about, sir.”

“I’m glad you two are getting along.” Ren smiled.

Lidria forced a halfhearted smile. “I have something I want to take care of. You go on ahead, and I’ll meet back up with you at Willard Square.”

“Okay.” Ren frowned. “Be careful.”

“I’ll be fine. I just need to get something.”

Ren locked eyes with Lidria. “Go. I won’t stop you.”

Lidria strode down the battered and debris-filled streets. She passed two sinkholes, and she hoped it hadn’t been devoured like so many other buildings. While her world wouldn’t end, her coming to terms with who she was would face a setback.

Forgotten red stone appeared. A sigh of relief escaped Lidria. She strode up, yanked the door open, and took the steps two at a time. Doors lined the hallway at the top of the stairs; she ignored all but one.

As expected, the door remained locked. Lidria lifted her right leg and aimed below the latch, kicking forward. The old door snapped and splintered inward but stayed on the hinges. A puff of dust kicked up in her face.

Holding back a sneeze, Lidria pressed inside. Sunlight streamed in from a window in the back, illuminating the room. Dust lay everywhere except where her boots left a distinct footprint. The table, a chair in the corner, and the worn armoire sported full dust finishes.

Lidria opened a small closet. She pushed all the old, dusty clothes to the side and groped around in the dim light. In the back-right corner, she found the object of her search. She withdrew her arm, prize in hand, weaving around the other things in the closet.

Much like everything else in the apartment, the longsword and accompanying sheath wore a thick dust coat. Lidria pulled the sword close, unsheathing the blade several inches. Metal caught sunlight, but the faint glimmer revealed little, save for "Lidria" written in script.

Lidria grabbed an old tunic and shook it until most of the dust came off. She padded over to the chair and plopped down. Tunic in hand, she used the article as a rag, dusting the hilt and sheath. The steel and black leather wrapping began to shine.

Dust flew. Lidria's face, hair, clothes; none were spared, but she didn't care. One thing mattered to her: cleaning her father's last gift to her. Tears blurred her vision. She shook and tossed the filthy rag of a tunic to the floor and clutched her sword to her chest.

Lidria wept. Memories of her parents drifted through her mind. She remembered the times her father taught her how to fish and fight and the pride on his face when she joined Odwyn's army. Her mother always comforted and nurtured her as well as showed her a thing or two about fighting behind father's back.

There was a time—Lidria couldn't have been more than thirteen—when she got into a fight with some local kids. She came out on top. When her father came home, he asked what happened. She cherished his priceless expression when she told him about the trick her mother had shown her.

A smile slid onto Lidria's face. They might not be with her anymore, but the things they instilled in her, her memories, they would be with her for life. Loneliness no longer consumed her. She met several people she could turn to now, and they didn't seem to be going anywhere.

Lidria stood and unfastened the latch on her sword's scabbard. She reached over her head, swinging the sword around behind. The strap lowered against her neck, resting on her right shoulder and across her chest. She secured the buckle fast and headed for the door.

Willard Square appeared minutes later. Two soldiers eyed Lidria, but, when she saluted them, they relaxed, throwing a salute back. She passed with a toothless smile. The square, until the attack, stood as Odwyn's commercial hub. Now, naught but ruins remained.

A skirmish had taken place. Human and Quelan bodies dotted the area, but most of the human ones lay near a crude pyre. Soldiers and civilians hauled the last few bodies as Lidria spotted Ren. He stood near the pyre, watching on in silence.

As she strode toward Ren, a woman to Lidria's left struggled with the body of a man. She stopped and helped. Soldiers soon took over for them. The woman closed her eyes, bowing her head. Lidria smiled before she took her leave.

Ren perked up as Lidria approached. "Ah, you're back." The rigidness of his posture eased, and he took a step forward.

"I told you I would come back," Lidria reminded Ren.

"You did." Ren's eyes flicked over Lidria's shoulder. "Is that what you wanted to get?"

Lidria's breath caught, and her eyes darted from side-to-side. "Yeah. I, uh, didn't want to lose it forever."

"Did someone give it to you?" Ren stared straight ahead, but Lidria couldn't meet his gaze.

"I," Lidria clamped her mouth shut, a lump forming in her throat.

"Lidria." Her eyes met Ren's. "If you don't want to talk about it, you don't have to."

"No, no, that's not it. I want to tell you; I just need a minute." Lidria took a deep breath to steady her irregular breathing.

"Take however long you need." Ren smiled. "I'm not going anywhere."

Lidria stared into Ren's compassionate eyes. How could she be reluctant to tell him anything? "This sword," she drew the weapon from her back, "was a gift from my late father." She held the blade out to him.

"It looks like a fine blade," Ren remarked, taking his time to examine the details. "It also looks like it needs some love. When was the last time you did anything to it?"

"At least six years." Embarrassment gripped Lidria. She withdrew her sword and sheathed it. A bit of dust floated down from her hair, sticking to the tip of her nose. She blew the dirt away.

Ren smirked. "Where did you have it tucked away? In a mountain of dust?"

"Close." Lidria's eyes drifted downward, but she brought them back up. "I haven't been there for years, and now I never need to go back."

"Was that your folks' place or something?" Ren asked.

"Uh, no. It was my place. I didn't feel like I belonged there since," Lidria paused, her heart hammering in her chest, "my marriage fell apart."

Ren appeared unfazed. "I can see why you wouldn't want to go back." She tried to say something, but he stopped her. "You don't have to give me any more details if you don't want to. I don't want you to feel forced."

"Ren, I don't; I want to be more open with the few people I have in my life." Lidria blinked back a tear.

"All right."

"I was married for three years before I became a breaker. The whole experience left me…depressed, withdrawn, and self-destructive. I drove away my husband, Ian, and he took our daughter, Evelyn, with him.

"I haven't seen either of them in six years. Sometimes I," Lidria took another deep breath, tears welling up, "sometimes I wish I could see her, but she deserves much better."

Ren didn't say anything. He closed the gap between them and placed his arm around Lidria. He pulled her close, holding her tight. She accepted his embrace and wrapped her arms around him. Her body trembled. She would do anything for another chance.

"I," Ren stammered, "I can't say I can imagine what that's like, but I can do my best to try to be understanding. I hope you've learned this already, but you don't have to fear any judgment on my part."

"I know, Ren," Lidria managed, choking back silent sobs. "Thank you."

"You're welcome, Lidria." Ren's head shifted to the right, and he loosened his tight embrace. "It looks like they're starting."

Lidria withdrew from around Ren and pulled away. She turned as several people approached the pyre with lit torches. They put them to the kindling, and fire crackled to life. The flames spread. Soon, an inferno raged.

Lidria stood silent. She bowed her head out of respect, and a chill ran down her spine. So many had died, an entire city rendered uninhabitable, and for what? The Quela came for something, yet no one—except perhaps Flinn—knew what they sought.

The woman Lidria helped strode forward, shaking her from her thoughts. Turning to the gathered crowd of thirty people, the woman began to sing. She started soft and delicate. As she went on, she got louder until her voice filled the square.

A minute in, several men stepped up and joined in. Lidria didn't recognize the bittersweet song—the words foreign to her. She closed her eyes and let the people's singing infect her. The song fit with a service for the dead, and her mood overall.

Chapter Eight

Selis poured over the ruminations of a madman. Flinn's notebook proved more of a crazed mess than she expected. One sentence he spoke of his work, his experiments, her, the next his breakfast. The disjointed nature grew jarring, breaking mid-thought.

Words repeated at random and in alarming frequency. They were not anything Selis thought held any deeper meaning: material, green, brand, and the phrase "it is fifty." She frowned when she read the twentieth "green."

Shaking her head, Selis grabbed a piece of charcoal and tallied every instance of the repeated words. She counted their place in the sentences they appeared and the space between each. Nothing correlated with anything she understood about cryptography or Flinn himself.

A nugget of imperative information existed amid the rambling. There had to be. Even paranoid, Flinn remained one of the three masters of the Enclave, and that carried incredible weight. He taught her what had turned into her way of life.

Selis flipped to the day before the attack. "I found it. It is fifty." More incoherent nonsense. She turned the page, but blank parchment stared back at her. Determination drove her to flip through several more.

Another tangent about his morning bacon and tea triggered Selis. She shoved the notebook across the floor. A breathy sigh escaped her, and she leaned back on her hands. Filth marred the canvas above. The dirt did not bother her, per se, but she had grown accustomed to more exemplary accommodations.

Selis' stomach grumbled. How long had she trudged through Flinn's useless notes? She rose, fighting past her tight, achy muscles. Curious, she poked her head out of the tent. The sun hung close to the horizon, and she let out a surprised little noise.

Selis slipped back inside and threw her cloak on over her plain, loose-fitting clothes. Food became her top priority. Lidria ate with Selis in the morning, and the camp cook did not take long to reach. He offered her a warm nod as she approached.

"Greetings," Selis said, her stomach rumbling again.

The man smiled. "Selis, was it?" She nodded. "The name's Max. It's pretty hard to forget meeting a mage, even more so when they have your hair and eyes."

Selis forced a smile as her heart twisted. "I suppose you are right. They are usually what people remember about me."

"I'm sorry." Remorse darkened Max's cheery expression. "I didn't mean to be rude. If it means anything, I think they suit you well."

"Thank you." Selis' smile turned genuine. "Most people stare or call me a freak."

"Bah, what do they know? You seem like a perfectly lovely young lady." Max's blue eyes sparkled.

Selis glanced away, and her cheeks flared. "I am glad there are some people like you that see me as a person and not some *thing*."

"That friend of yours from earlier—Lidria, I think her name is—she seems to be another one." Recognition flashed across Max's face. "Although, I supposed she would be in a similar situation as you, being a breaker and all."

"Yes," Selis managed. She lowered her head, her voice following suit. "People can be so cruel."

"Well, I don't think you came for my conversation skills. Here." Selis peeked up, and Max shoved a bowl of porridge at her. "Eat your fill and take solace in the fact that not everyone is that way."

“Thank you again, Max. I will keep that in mind.” Selis bowed her head.

Max smiled and leaned back on his bench. “I’m always here to cure empty bellies.”

Selis took the bowl and headed back to the tent. Once inside, she set the porridge down on the small crate and removed her cloak. She picked up her meal, sitting down in front of her collection of tomes, cross-legged.

The warm scent of honey and oats filled Selis’ nostrils. A growl emanated from her gut, and her mouth watered. She would need to remember to eat more frequent, but she knew she wouldn’t without someone else’s ministrations. Not while mysteries remained unsolved.

Selis snatched up one of the tomes, setting it on the floor. Her fingertips played on the edges of the cover, but she stopped. Though she still held the lukewarm bowl, she forgot her body’s desire for food. She took a quick bite.

Selis frowned. The porridge did not taste as pleasant as the aroma implied. She sighed but continued. Her stomach cared not about the food’s flavor, only seeking sustenance. She took a couple more spoonfuls before her curiosity, her drive, got the best of her.

Placing the half-eaten food down, Selis returned to the tome. She hooked the edge and flipped the pages open. The musty odor of old parchment overpowered her senses. She breathed deep, and her mind focused.

Selis ran her finger down the page, scanning the index. All manner of spells were listed but displayed no organization. Simple invocations to create water mingled with complex barrier projection. She shook her head. Whoever compiled this tome had done a poor job.

An invocation jumped out from the jumbled list: Helgathin—the ritual used to enhance a person's connection to the Flow. Selis underwent the process six times, several more than the masters of the Enclave themselves. Flinn wanted to prove something, yet he never succeeded.

Selis turned to the indicated section. Nothing. She cocked her head to the side and slid the previous page between her fingers, checking for stuck pages. Her eyes narrowed in confusion—no evidence of removal.

With a wave of her hand, Selis cast a spell. A pale light glowed over the parchment before dimming. Nothing changed. They remained missing, no hidden markings or text, and a sinking sensation settled in her gut.

Selis flipped through several adjacent pages to reaffirm she had not missed anything. Countless questions set her mind abuzz. However, none would be answered staring at nonexistent parchment. She sighed, flipping back to the index to continue her search.

No other invocations stood out as odd or pertinent. Selis picked the tome up and snapped the cover shut with a dull *clack*. She pushed the useless volume aside, returning her attention to her food. Two more spoonfuls and she continued.

Selis pulled a well-worn, green-covered tome out of her bag. A loose sheet of parchment drifted to the floor. She reached for the page. Blank. She frowned. Under normal circumstances, she would not reconsider, but…

Light shimmered with Selis' gesture, sparkling bright. Sharp, slanted handwriting materialized. A small diagram surrounded by crossed-out calculations followed. She flipped the article over and inspected the writing on the back.

The curious parchment outlined the Helgathin ritual. Why would Flinn remove the page and hide it in another tome? He had become unstable of late, but she did not understand. Many underwent the ritual—why stash the information away?

Selis examined the back. The fundamentals of the invocation had been changed, and multiple iterations of odd calculations ran in the margins. She blinked, overwhelmed. Her name sat cramped in the upper right corner.

Selis set the sheet down and pulled her braid over her shoulder. Her silver hair glinted in the flickering candlelight. She choked back a silent sob, her vision blurring. Before being consumed, she let her building anguish out in a long, sharp breath.

Anger burned inside Selis. She had called him master, she had trusted him, but he never thought of her as more than a lab rat. The urge to storm out, march over, and confront him welled within her. The venture would yield nothing, yet rage clouded her judgment.

Selis stood, but a sudden chill cooled her temper. Black smoke drifted into the tent, expanding. The gas shifted and coalesced into a somewhat solid form before radiating magic. She uttered an incantation of dispelling. The words died on her lips.

The smoke projection glided past Selis, flitting about. Amethyst light glowed as the cloud enveloped the pile of tomes. Her heart leaped into her throat, and she decided on her course of action. She could not let whoever controlled the invocation do as they pleased.

Selis closed her eyes, losing herself in the Flow. The magic did not bend to her will as expected. She butted up against an invisible barrier, but she did not stop. More, she pushed. Something gripped her and tore her from her body.

Distance contracted. The blurry image of the world rushed by Selis, sending her head spinning. Her stomach lurched, and nausea flooded her being. As abrupt as the sensation began, her surroundings stilled. Cool, crushing dark enveloped her.

Moisture permeated everything. Dim-lit features grew clear. Stone, worn from countless years of runoff, surrounded Selis. Stalactites hung from the ceiling, water dripping into little pools on the floor. The musty air suffocated her.

Tiny pinpoints of light appeared in the distance, and Selis headed toward them. Quiet, bestial growls reverberated off the claustrophobic stone. Quela. The noises became more distinct the closer she drifted, sounding an awful lot like speech. Fascination drove her forward.

Flickering orange fire blossomed around Selis, and she found herself amid a herd. They went about their assorted activities unaware or unfazed by her presence. No one ever had the opportunity to see them down in their tunnels and caves like this.

Selis studied the creatures. Groups communicated with one another, some fought over indiscernible things, while others slept. Most people wrote them off as mindless beasts. However, seeing them like this proved the opposite.

A group of several small—yet taller than Selis—Quela sat huddled in a corner. They appeared sick, or at least weak, and none of the other Quela paid them any attention. She stepped forward but stopped when a larger beast with a crude sword approached.

The sword-wielding Quelan tossed the weapon on the ground before the scrawny group. They lifted their heads in unison. All five leaped, scrambling for the blade. One of them stole the blade away and drove its prize through one of the other's chest.

Several sleeping animals stirred. The ones fighting stopped, and their attention shifted to Selis' right. Something tugged at her ethereal form.

An unusual Quelan emerged, the tiny bells interlaced among its horns rang hollow. It bore a gnarled stone staff.

The shaman's unnatural crimson eyes scanned the cavern. Selis flinched when its gaze met hers. It bared its stained teeth in what she took for a smile, stepping toward her. As the creature advanced, two giant bestial heads slithered out of the dark.

Selis stared in horror as the rest of the massive winged monstrosity emerged from the shadows. She could not deny the creature's Quelan origins, but she had never seen one. The beast bobbed, and blue-white ooze dripped from its maws, crackling.

The shaman reached out toward Selis, and she flinched. Its plump paw passed through her. She shivered. The Quelan blinked several times in confusion. It uttered something in its guttural language, staring her down. She opened her mouth—

Venomous words echoed in Selis' mind.

"Found…you…trick…ster…" The beast snarled and gored her with its horns.

Selis gasped. Dizziness swarmed her head. Her heart pounded, and she swayed. Steadying herself against a crate, she stared down. The front of her clothes torn where the shaman would have impaled her.

Breaths came quick and shallow. A crushing sense of urgency rushed through Selis. She spun, staggering to her travel pack. One after another, she stuffed the tomes in and drew the strings closed. She shot upright, threw on her robes, and hurried outside.

Glancing left and right, Selis chose a direction. She ran, the sack slung over her shoulder. Several people gave her curious or appalled stares, but she ignored them. She would not be responsible for killing these people.

A small cluster of children barred Selis' path. She altered her course without slowing. One of them glanced her way: Hector. She pulled her cloak tight, trying to hide her features. Her attempt proved useless as he ran up to her.

"Selis," Hector called out. "Where are you going?"

Selis fought the urge to ignore him and run away. She took a deep breath and faced him. "I…I have to go. When Lidria gets back, tell her I am sorry. I do not want to put the camp in danger."

Hector frowned. "You're not dangerous. People say bad things about mages, but you're so cool and a friend of Lidi's."

"Hector, please." Panic set in, and Selis' limbs trembled. "Promise me you will tell Lidria."

"I will," Hector said. "Be careful and come back soon. I want to see more magic."

Selis swallowed down her fear. "I do not know if I will be able to come back."

"Oh…" Hector stared down, dejected.

"If I do," Selis said, placing a hand on Hector's shoulder. "I will gladly show you more, Hector."

Hector's face brightened. "Okay. I hope I see you soon."

"Me, too." Selis turned from Hector and resumed her flight.

Selis took little more than a few moments to exit the camp. The soldiers on duty at the perimeter tried to question her, but she brushed past them. They appeared confused but did not follow. She did not care. Distance from others mattered more than anything.

The sun vanished by the time Selis slowed her pace. She breathed heavy, and her shoulder ached. Tossing her pack on the ground, she sat on a fallen tree trunk. Her body thanked her for the rest. Bursts of physical exertion were not her forte.

Selis sighed and allowed herself to think. If the creatures found her, she did not hold high hopes of fending them off. Burying the tomes or throwing them in the river would eliminate them, but the thought repulsed her. So much information would be lost. However, the shaman would not take them.

Fear retreated to the back of Selis' mind. She leaned forward, retrieving the sack. With a deep breath, she stood. She would deal with the Quela if they appeared.

No sounds but Selis' breaths permeated the dark. She inched forward and broke through a small row of trees. Paranoia welled within her. The shaman's haunting words repeated in her mind, and a bolt of amethyst lightning shrieked down from the sky.

Chapter Nine

Lidria entered the camp, Ren at her side. He threw crisp salutes to soldiers who greeted them. Everyone appeared in improved spirits despite their dire situation. A smile spread across her face. Weight lifted off her shoulders, and she took a step forward with her life.

A familiar red-headed soldier outside the command tent saluted Ren as they approached. "Welcome back, sir." He nodded at Lidria. "Breaker."

"Thanks for holding down the fort, Deeter," Ren said, returning the soldier's salute.

"No problem, sir. Oh, that Hector kid was by earlier looking for either of you. When I told him you weren't back yet, he said he would wait for you at," Deeter's gaze shifted to Lidria, and a grin slipped on his face, "Lidi's tent."

Lidria uttered a curse under her breath and shook her head. Deeter's grin broadened. "He probably wants me to tell him a story or something. I'd better go rescue Selis. I'm sure she won't be too pleased to be interrupted."

"I'll go with you," Ren offered. "I'd like to ask her if she found anything yet."

"Okay." Lidria turned and headed through the camp to her tent.

Lidria flipped the flap open and went inside, Ren following. Hector sat on the cot swinging his legs. He snapped up and flew toward her. His arms wrapped around her legs and squeezed. She patted him on the head, and he gazed up at her.

"Lidi," Hector stammered. "Selis ran away. I tried to make her stay, but she wouldn't listen."

Lidria pushed Hector off her and knelt in front of him. “Hector, do you know where she went?”

Hector shook his head. “She didn’t say, but she went,” he pointed west, “that way.”

“Did she say anything else to you?”

“All she said was she had to go, and she didn’t want to get anyone hurt.” Worry danced with confusion in Hector’s eyes.

“Okay. Thank you, Hector.” Lidria ruffled his hair and stood. She turned to Ren. “She must have found something in those books. She took them with her.”

Ren nodded. “Let’s go find her.”

Lidria and Ren cut their way through the camp to the western perimeter. The stationed soldiers saluted him. “Something the matter, sir?”

“Did you see a woman, a mage, come through here?” Ren asked. “She would have been carrying a sack of books.”

“Yeah, we saw her,” one of the soldiers said, stroking his chin. “We thought it was weird. She just ran past on her own without a word.”

Lidria ran. The sun became little more than a glimmer on the horizon, yet she pressed on, heedless. She needed to find Selis. If Selis thought the danger was enough to flee from camp, she wouldn’t be safe on her own. Lidria would protect her no matter what.

The ground shook, and a flash of amethyst sparked in the distance. Lidria cut through a small line of trees, increasing her pace. A second tremor threw her against a tree. She stared out from the tree line. The field beyond lay empty save for two figures.

“Selis,” Lidria shouted as she drew her longsword and took off.

Lidria severed a link and closed the gap between her and the Quelan. The beast uttered a guttural snarl and leaped away. She whipped around in a sweeping arc, aiming for the neck. Her blade collided with the creature's stone staff, emitting a sharp clang.

Lidria hopped back, rocking on her feet. She withdrew her weapon before thrusting at the Quelan's gut. Tiny bells tinkled as her opponent dodged right. She tried to follow, but she wavered. A burst of emerald flames collided into the shaman.

A shriek pierced Lidria's ears, and she froze in her tracks. Heavy wings buffeted the air. The abomination from Odwyn's fall crashed in front of Ren. He stumbled backward, managing to remain upright.

Lidria's heart leaped into her throat. She didn't think she could face the monster again, but she needed to act. She tore her eyes off Ren and the monstrosity, glancing over her shoulder at Selis. Although appearing haggard, Selis gave Lidria a resolute nod.

Lidria flew past Ren. Her sword flashed, biting into one of the monster's heads. It reeled back in agony as the other head lunged at her. She dropped into a crouch, and jaws snapped shut above her. She ran before jabbing upward.

Murky brown blood oozed out of the beast's cheek. Lidria only scored a glancing blow, but her strike enraged her prey. The aberration beat its wings and lifted off the ground. Lidria cursed. She severed another link and, straining her muscles, bounded into the sky.

Thrusting, Lidria caught the leathery flesh of one wing. Her blade tore through from top to bottom. The beast crashed down with a terrible screech. It lashed out and thrashed around. She hopped back, dancing on the balls of her feet.

Ren rushed in. He drew his sword arm back and thrust into leg muscle. It let out a deafening howl, loping away from him. He wrenched his blade free as the monstrosity's head swung around and batted him away.

Lidria capitalized on the opportunity Ren created. She leaped on the creature's back, plunging her sword down, but the abomination rolled forward and flung her off. She crashed into Ren, shoulder blades against his chest, and slid to the side. His arm shot out and caught her.

Lidria stood, pushing off Ren. He helped with a hand on the small of her back. Her head twitched to glance back his way, but a crackling sound drew her attention. The monstrosity opened both maws, and webbed lightning bolted through the air.

Pink light sparked in front of Lidria and Ren. The sheet of lightning screeched and crackled against an invisible barrier in a dreadful cacophony. The excess energy fanned out, enveloping the surrounding air. Her gaze snapped to the right.

Selis lay on her side in the grass; her right arm extended. The Quelan shaman ignored her action and instead focused on the discarded tomes behind her. It snatched up the sack and slung the parcel over its shoulder, staff tamping the ground.

A primal instinct drove Lidria toward Selis, but a guttural growl stopped her. She turned to the winged monstrosity. A pair of slit, russet eyes stared at her. She stepped forward, and the creature drew back. When she moved right, intent eyes followed.

Ren tapped Lidria on the shoulder and gestured to the other side. She nodded and slunk to the side, the aberration watching her. Ren mirrored her movements to the left. The monster's heads tracked them before jerking back to the center and focusing on her.

The heads swayed toward Lidria as she continued. She glimpsed Ren out of the corner of her eye. He rushed forward, but their adversary's tail flicked out. The blow struck his side and sent him tumbling. She slid further around, her sword level.

Lunging, the beast batted Lidria away with one head and snapped at her with the other. She danced backward. The monstrosity growled, lightning oozing from its twin maws. Ren charged from behind, and she threw herself at the threat.

Lidria thrust at the right head. It snaked left, but she struck true. Her blade cut into the creature's neck, blood spurting from the gouge. Its head flashed at her extended arm. She pulled back, but her enhanced speed faded.

The abomination's jaws stopped short and let out an ear-splitting shriek. Lidria fell back, ears ringing. The monster's severed tail flopped on the grass. The appendage wriggled, spewing murky blood. Ren rebounded off the bulky body.

Limbs and wings thrashed around. A gout of emerald fire surged through the air. Ren called out, but his words faded. Lidria pitched forward and pressed herself flat. Flames rushed overhead before crashing into the aberration in a shower of liquid flame.

Lidria popped her head up. Selis stood bent over, clutching her leg. The shaman's arms held up against something solid. Selis flinched backward, and she collapsed with a loud gasp. The Quelan took a shaky, ponderous step forward.

Ren glanced Lidria's way. She pushed herself off the ground as Selis' fire dissipated. The thrashing stopped. Lidria locked eyes with Ren, and she gestured toward Selis with her head. He nodded and rushed off toward the mage and shaman.

Lidria, not wanting the beast to follow Ren, asserted her existence. She lunged at the creature's chest. It reared backward, heads parting. She swung to the right, but her adversary swayed away from the blade. Her sword weighed heavy.

A bubble of panic rose in Lidria's gut. She hoped to deal with her shame from not killing the creature before swift enough that she wouldn't need to break another link. Enough links remained. She could sense them, but she didn't desire to burn through more. She could dispatch the wounded beast without.

Lidria slid to the left as the aberration lunged. It stumbled forward, missing her, and yelped. Magic sparked, but she ignored the sound. She trusted Selis and Ren, focusing on her opponent. Despite its wounds and faltering, one misstep would spell disaster.

Lidria steeled herself and charged. Jaws snapped, but she dropped down and slid underneath. She thrust up with all her strength. A shriek rang out as steel sank into its stomach. She twisted before yanking free at an angle.

The creature shuddered, and Lidria realized her mistake. If the massive bulk collapsed, she would be crushed. She tossed her armament aside and tucked into a roll. Her world spun as she cleared the hulking mass, collapsing behind her.

Lidria exited her roll, snatched up her sword, and sprang to her feet. The beast growled and beat its wings. She could not fail—not this time. Pain shot up her arm as she severed a link. Her left hand waved over her blade, and azure flames flared to life.

Spinning, Lidria swung back around front. The creature balanced itself with the added effort of massive wings. However, the wounds she inflicted kept the monster grounded. She breathed a sigh of relief, raised her weapon, and brought her might down.

Lidria caught her target behind the ears. Her blazing blade sliced through hide, flesh, and bone. The right head screeched as the left plummeted. Blue-white lightning erupted from the severed neck, and a sharp tingle danced across her skin.

The monstrosity thrashed around, necks flailing. Lightning arced across the sky and crashed into the ground. Grass and dirt flew as the blast carved out a huge gouge along the undisturbed field. More continued to spill forth in a crackling cacophony.

Lidria fell back, lest the unending lightning fry her. Ooze dripped from above onto her. Her muscles convulsed, and her hair stood. She fought through the pain and the spasms to finish the job.

The aberration let out a blood-curdling shriek. It reared back, but Lidria kept pace. With an upward flash, she severed the other neck two feet from the body. She drew her sword close and plunged the blade into the beast's chest.

Lidria yanked her weapon free, backpedaling. The headless creature swayed before collapsing with a thud. Her blade's fire spread out from the wound until the entire mass became a blazing azure bonfire.

Lidria stood tall as the fire raged. She redeemed herself from her previous cowardice. The flames around her blade dwindled and sputtered out, and she heaved a relieved sigh. She nodded to herself, pleased, and snapped her gaze to Selis.

"Lidria," Ren's familiar voice called. Her eyes jumped to the tree line, and he waved at her.

Lidria rushed over. She couldn't see much, but his slouched posture betrayed his injuries. "Are you all right?"

"Yeah, I'm fine." Ren turned, favoring his right leg, to reveal Selis. She sat propped against the tree with her leg extended. "Selis has a nasty wound. We should—"

Lidria blew past Ren and knelt at Selis' side, grabbing her by the shoulders and locking eyes. "Selis, what were you thinking?"

"I am sorry," Selis managed in a soft, shaky voice. Her eyes, to Lidria's surprise, stayed focused. "I did not have time to wait for you. All those people were in danger."

"Selis, you could have…" Lidria sighed, calming the butterflies in her stomach. "I suppose you do have a point. If the shaman and that thing attacked the camp, things would have ended badly."

"Yes, they would have." Selis grimaced and clutched at her wounded leg.

"We should head back so that Silvon can fix you up," Ren said as he stepped up to Selis. He offered her his hand.

Selis shook her head. "It is fine. I should be able to fix this. I just need a moment."

"I don't—"

Light radiated from Selis' right hand, and Lidria fumbled to shield her eyes. When the illumination dimmed, Selis' labored and pained expression relaxed. Tension drained from Lidria's tight muscles. A frown worked onto her face, but she buried her emotions.

Selis glanced between Lidria and Ren, a glossy shine to her eyes. "Do either of you have any wounds?"

"Nothing that won't heal on its own," Lidria said, rising.

"I'm all right." Ren scratched at the back of his ankle with the top his foot. "Thank you for removing that binding."

Selis smiled. "You are welcome."

Lidria raised an eyebrow, but they both dismissed her silent question. "So, what did you find that made the Quela come after you?"

"I do not know," Selis admitted. "I was digging through the tomes I salvaged, but I had not discovered much. Then, a magic projection materialized in our tent, searching for something.

"I tried to dispel it, but I was dragged through instead. I saw them in their caves and tunnels, and that is when I saw the shaman. It said it found me and pushed me out of the spell.

"Not sure what else to do, I packed them up and ran."

"A what?"

Selis stared up into Lidria's eyes. "There is an invocation that allows the caster to project a portion of their consciousness across great distances. They can see their surroundings, but other interactions are quite limited. Or so I thought."

Ren stepped forward. "How much did you see? Do you have any idea where they are now?"

Selis shook her head. "No, I do not. It must not be far from here if it was able to find me so quickly."

"How did it track you?" Lidria asked.

"Everyone leaves their own unique mark on the Flow." Selis patted down her robes. "Some are adept at tracking those marks."

Lidria glanced around, realizing Selis' pack vanished. "I'm guessing the shaman got away with the books?"

"Yeah," Ren said, shifting back. "I had to choose between stopping it and protecting Selis."

Selis met Ren's eyes. "You should have gone after it instead of helping me."

"I," Ren faltered, staring back at Selis, "I couldn't do that to you. If the lightning hit you…"

"I am aware, but my life is not worth much in the larger scheme of things." Selis tugged her disheveled braid across her chest.

"Selis," Lidria said, placing a hand on her slender shoulder. "Your life matters."

Selis raised her hand and touched Lidria's arm. Lidria smiled, which coaxed a weak smile out of Selis. "Do not get me wrong," she glanced at Ren, "I am thankful you did protect me. I only hope the knowledge the Quela seek is not as destructive as Flinn thinks or it is simply not among those tomes."

"We'll deal with that if and when it becomes a problem" Ren surveyed the area. "Can you walk?"

"I believe so." Selis turned to Lidria. "Help me up?" Lidria slipped her arm underneath the smaller woman.

Selis' arm wrapped around Lidria's waist and squeezed. Despite her exertion, Lidria lifted Selis' weight with ease. She moved to let Selis stand on her own, but she didn't let go. A nervous smile spread across Selis' face, and Lidria sighed, smiling back.

Chapter Ten

Selis awoke, groaning. Her right leg throbbed. The invocation she had used to heal her wound proved weak and slap-dash. She did not want to worry Lidria and Ren, but she had come close to bleeding out. The shameful trek back only exacerbated the embarrassment of her failures.

Ignoring the shooting pain, Selis sat up and rubbed the sleep from her eyes. Cool air rushed to greet her. Pale morning light shone through several tears and gaps in the tent canvas. Her gaze drifted to the space where she kept the sack of tomes. She sighed and cursed herself.

Lidria stirred on the cot. She shifted around but remained asleep. Hector lay motionless, curled up against her. The kid had awaited her return, and Lidria did not want to send him away so late. Selis admired Lidria's compassion.

Selis' cheeks flared. Her heart beat fast. She sat at attention, hoping to hide her weakness if Lidria awoke. Strength radiated from Lidria. Any hope such a woman would—she needed to leave.

Selis rose, resting little weight on her injured leg. The venture proved awkward and slow and, in the end, hurt. She frowned and shuffled forward, her muscles stiff. She tried to stretch, but the confines of the tent barred her progress.

Grabbing her cloak, Selis slipped outside. The chill morning air struck her. A shiver ran down her spine, but she savored the brisk breeze. It reminded her of her childhood mountain home. Wistful, she left her robe unbuttoned to drink in the cold.

Selis wandered around camp, working the tightness out of her leg. Soldiers and civilians milled about their morning routines. She did not resent the noise nor their presence, and some greeted her. She smiled and offered greetings of her own. Perhaps she had found a place she belonged.

McCrear's command tent appeared before Selis. Flinn popped into her mind, and she clenched her jaw. Without the tomes, she had no leads on what the Quela sought. Flinn held the answers. Her attempt would be futile, but what other option did she have?

Filled with determination, Selis strode forward. The two guards stationed outside waved. One, a man with a coppery-red beard that shone in the sunlight. The other, a dark-skinned woman whose eyes never left Selis.

"Mornin', miss mage," the man said, suppressing a yawn.

"Good morning. My name is Selis." She bowed and presented a warm smile.

"Name's Deeter." He gestured toward the woman beside him. "And that's Joan."

"Good morning, Selis," Joan said. Selis stared into her almond-colored eyes, and Joan smiled.

Deeter slid up next to Joan. "See something you like, Joan?"

"Deeter," Joan warned. He backed away, but a grin split his face. She turned her attention back to Selis. "You've got some gorgeous eyes, Selis."

Selis' cheeks burned. "I, uh, thank you. Not many people positively comment on them."

"They don't know what they're talking about, then. Trust me," Joan gazed into Selis' eyes, "a girl could get lost in them."

Selis shied her eyes away from Joan. "I need to speak with McCrear."

"No problem." Joan ushered Selis forward with a hand on the small of her back. "He's inside."

Selis entered the tent and found McCrear leaned back in a chair with his eyes closed. She stepped up, and his eyes shot open. "Selis," he muttered, shaking his head and blinking. "What are you doing up so early?"

"My leg was stiff, so I decided to walk around and stretch." Selis made an exaggerated effort of rolling her weight to her left.

McCrear frowned. "I thought you healed it with magic."

"I did, but I was so drained I could not heal it fully." Selis lowered her head. "I made a mess of things."

"Selis," McCrear stood, "you did what you thought you had to. If you hadn't, that shaman would have leveled the camp. You saved lives."

"I am glad no one else got hurt," Selis said. "Although, I would have liked to hold on to those tomes. Now, I have nothing to go on."

"Don't worry." McCrear strode forward and placed a comforting hand on Selis' shoulder. "I'm sure we'll have more opportunities to figure out what's going on."

Selis swallowed hard and stared McCrear in the eye. "We do. I decided that I will speak with Flinn."

McCrear clenched his jaw, and his eyes wandered. "His guards say he's grown rather incoherent since you and Lidria brought him here." He removed his hand from Selis, a thoughtful expression on his face. "I'll have Joan escort you. In case things get out of hand."

"All right." Selis tried not to let her anxiety show, but she tugged at her sleeve. "I appreciate that, lieutenant."

"No problem, Selis. You can call me Ren, though." He smiled before he slipped out of the tent. Selis followed.

"Joan," Ren said, "please accompany Selis to Master Flinn. I want someone dependable nearby if something happens."

"Gladly, sir." Joan threw a crisp salute.

Ren nodded and left, prompting Deeter to smirk at Joan. “Well, it looks like you got what you wanted.”

Joan glared at Deeter.

“What?” Deeter grinned. “Tell me I’m wrong.”

“Come on, Selis. Let’s go before the resident idiot here gets any more ideas.” Joan spun and walked away, and Selis trailed behind her.

“I apologize if Deeter and I made you uncomfortable,” Joan said after several minutes of traveling in silence.

Selis frowned. “No, it is all right. You did nothing wrong.”

“Good.” Joan nodded to herself. “I’ve been told sometimes I can come on a little strong.”

“After all the years of deceit,” Selis took a deep breath, “I find your straightforward nature pleasant.”

“Flinn was your master in the Enclave, right?” Joan asked, more reserved.

Selis choked down her resentment. “Yes, for many years. He taught me everything I know about the Flow.”

“I’ve only heard bits and pieces before you and Lidria brought him the other day. What happened?”

“He was paranoid,” Selis explained, “obsessed, with keeping something from the Quela. He did not think it wise to join the rest of you here after the attack. He did not trust anyone, not even me or Cent.

“I hoped to find out what he was trying to keep secret, but I lost the tomes I was searching through last night. And so, here we are today. If I have no other options, I must ask him. Although, I do not expect much.”

Joan furrowed her brow. “Cent? Was he another pupil of Flinn’s?”

“He was, in a sense.” Selis wiped a tear from her eye. “His family was contracted to serve the Enclave. I knew him nearly as long as Flinn.

When Lidria came, and I wanted to go back with her, Flinn and Cent tried to stop us. I," she stared at her feet, "killed Cent."

"Oh," Joan breathed. After a quiet moment, she placed a hand on Selis' arm. "I'm sorry."

"It is fine," Selis affirmed, staring straight ahead. "It had to happen."

They continued in silence until they arrived at Flinn's tent. Joan spoke with the guards out front, and they left. Doubts filled Selis' head. Rage at what he had done to her sparked back to life. She suppressed her emotions, knowing that going in hot-headed would yield nothing.

"If," Joan croaked. Selis turned her head toward the other woman, waiting. "If you ever need anyone to talk to, I'll be there for you."

Selis gazed up into Joan's compassionate eyes. "Thank you, Joan."

"Anytime, Selis." Joan flashed her a coy smile. "You going to be okay in there?"

"Yes," Selis said, though she did not believe herself. "I will be fine. I must do this on my own."

Hesitation came over Joan's face, but she nodded. "I'll be here if you need me—just holler."

Selis took her leave and headed inside. The pungent, heady stench of dauein filled the tent and wrinkled her nose. Flinn, disheveled and pathetic, sat on the ground, hands and feet bound in manacles lashed to a stake.

Flinn raised his head when Selis closed the flap, leaving them alone. His dark brown eyes locked on hers, and she noted anger in them. From his perspective, she had betrayed him. A voice in the back of her mind told her the same. She—at least a part of herself—believed that as well.

Selis opened her mouth to say something, only to realize she did not know what to say. Too many things, conflicting emotions, warred for supremacy. She stood, silent. Her heart rate escalated, and her breaths came short and rough.

"Well, spit it out, girl," Flinn snapped.

Flinn's voice cut through the unending spiral of thoughts in Selis' head and anchored her. She took a deep breath. "I wish to know what you have been keeping a secret. If it is, in fact, as important as you claim, someone else should know and do something."

"Like you?" Flinn asked, eyes wild.

Despite the shame the admittance brought, Selis chose to be honest. "I am not sure."

Flinn let out a bark of laughter. "You might be strong with the Flow, but you have a lot to learn. You also need to work on your meek temperament if you want to make anything of yourself."

Selis choked down her rising anger. "I may not be able to do anything, but I would be willing to find someone who could and share it with them, unlike you."

Flinn shook his head. "Cannot tell you, cannot tell you." His head swiveled to the right, and he stared off into space.

"Why do you not trust me? Was I not a diligent enough student? I followed everything you ever said."

"No-no one else must know." Flinn's attention darted everywhere but in Selis' direction. "Only I can keep it safe."

"Please," Selis pleaded, "Please, tell me. I want to help keep people safe." She drew in a shaky breath. "M-master, please."

Clear eyes snapped up. "Selis." He blinked, cocking his head to the side. "I am sor—no. No. No. No."

Selis strode over to Flinn. "You keep making excuses and hiding the truth from me." She knelt beside him, giving in to her darker emotions. "I do not care how fragile your mental state is; I will have my answers."

Selis placed her hands on Flinn's temples. His eyes flicked back and forth but never at her face. Resentment fueled her aggression. She closed her eyes and sighed. Magic flowed through her, down her arms, and into Flinn's mind.

A sharp shock jolted Selis. She gasped but kept her eyes shut tight. Burning pain swept through her as she forced herself past the barrier. The resistance blinked out of existence with a tangible snap. Every sensation left her until nothing but information remained.

Selis drifted. The texts detailing the invocation had done little to prepare her. Knowledge pressed in from every angle, threatening to overwhelm her, but she only wanted one thing. She inhaled deep and reached out, searching.

Something bumped against Selis, and she retreated. Caution tempered her movement, probing the barricade. Twinges shot through her. Another barrier, stronger than the last, blocked her. She had not expected this. As paranoid as Flinn acted, this took on a whole other level.

Each time Selis prodded, magic seared her core. She enveloped the wall, spreading herself thin. She would overtake the obstacle in one move. If not, she would cause herself untold pain or worse. However, she needed to understand what had driven Flinn insane.

Selis collapsed on the obstruction, squeezing with all her might. Anguish, frustration, and anger compelled her to push harder until…pop! The barrier gave way, shattered into a thousand fragments, and vanished. Her magic ran thin and wispy, yet she did not relent.

Selis pressed on deeper inside Flinn's mind. Nothing leaped out at her. No more barriers, no traces of the Flow, no feelings, no memories. Nothing. A void greeted her at every turn, no matter how deep she reached. The revelation broke her.

Severing her connection, Selis returned to her body. Tears streaked down her face, and her hands slipped from Flinn's head. She opened her eyes. He stared back at her, empty. She swallowed hard, stood, and took a step back as a tear fell from her chin.

"Why?" Selis sobbed. "Why would you do something like that?"

Flinn's cold, vacuous eyes offered no response.

Selis turned away, unable to meet the gaze of the shell Flinn had become. "I-I did not want this. I merely wanted to understand why you acted the way you did."

Silence.

"You," Selis swallowed down the lump in her throat, "you were so paranoid, so deluded, that you would destroy your mind to keep your secrets?"

Silence.

"I do not—I…I will never know why you tampered with the invocation that gave me these eyes and this hair. I will never…" Selis collapsed to her knees.

Silence.

"What have I done?" Selis buried her face in her hands and stopped holding back the tears. "I only wanted to help, to figure out what the Quela want, but you would not tell me. Your only apprentice." She sucked in shaky breaths between sobs. "Why? Why did you make me do that?"

Silence.

"I hate you," Selis shouted. The words echoed in her ears. "I hate you, I hate you, I hate you, I hate you." She gasped for breath, and her whole body shook. "You always wanted others to do your dirty work. Well, I guess you got your wish in the end." She lifted her face.

Flinn's vacant eyes held hers.

“How many have to die?” Selis demanded. “How many more have to die for the sake of your paranoia? If only you cooperated. Maybe…”

Silence.

Selis burned with rage. She shot to her feet, tears blurring her vision. She shoved her right hand toward the husk. Emerald flames danced to life in her palm and between her fingers. She urged more power to gather, forcing the fire brighter and larger. Her hand trembled as she reached her breaking point and…

All tension rushed out of Selis’ body and the magic with it. The flames winked out of existence. Her arm dropped to her side as a ragged breath escaped her. Flinn deserved her ire, her hatred, but that…thing was not be Flinn. He had disappeared, taking all his secrets with him.

Selis staggered outside. A gasp preceded Joan rushing over to her, but she ignored the other woman. The thought of Joan seeing her eyes twisted her gut. She did not want her to see the hatred, the shame, the sorrow, the emptiness she carried.

“Selis,” Joan pressed. “Are-are you okay?”

“I am not,” Selis whispered.

Joan placed a hand on Selis’ shoulder. Selis wished to remove the other woman’s hand, but strength failed her. “Selis, what happened? I heard you shouting, but I didn’t want to interrupt.”

“Flinn is gone.” Joan’s hand slipped off Selis. “I appreciate your concern, but I need some time to myself. I do not—”

“It’s all right,” Joan said in an awkward upbeat voice. “I understand. Just…if you happen to find yourself wanting some company later, keep me in mind.”

Selis allowed herself a glance at Joan. “I will. Thank you.”

“You’re welcome.” Joan offered Selis a bright smile. “I hope you feel better.”

Selis forced a smile. Although thankful for Joan's compassion, she could not bear to be around anyone. She turned without another word and headed east. The solitude of the forest would prove sufficient. Tears streaked her face.

Chapter Eleven

Something shoved Lidria, and her eyes shot open. Beside her, Hector fidgeted. She frowned and opened her mouth to scold him for waking her with his—Sobs filled her ears. A sigh escaped her, and she wrapped her arms around him. He flinched and melted against her.

"It's all right," Lidria murmured.

Hector nuzzled against Lidria's chest. "I miss my mom."

"I know, I know." Lidria squeezed Hector. "I'm worried about her, too."

"Do you think she'll ever come back?" Hector asked between sobs.

Lidria paused. Things didn't look good, but she couldn't tell Hector. "I don't know."

Hector squirmed in Lidria's arms until she loosened her embrace. His head raised, and he stared into her eyes. "You-you'll keep me safe, right?"

"Of course."

Hector broke eye contact and buried his face in her chest. "I don't want you to ever go."

"Don't worry; I'm not going anywhere." Lidria withdrew her hands and ruffled Hector's hair.

"Promise?"

"I promise," Lidria whispered. "I'll be here whenever you need me."

Hector wrapped his little arms around Lidria and squeezed her. "I love you, Lidi."

Lidria froze. Her heart skipped a beat, her breath caught in her throat, and her eyes widened. Glimpses of Evelyn's blonde hair and green eyes flashed in her mind. Evelyn's face and voice burrowed deep in her memory. She trembled, fighting back anguish.

Steady breathing brought Lidria out of her panic attack. She focused on the empty tent canvas. Evelyn vanished from her mind's eye, but she would return. Lidria never forgot her daughter, no matter how dreadful a mother she had been.

"Lidi," Hector said as sense returned to her. "Are you okay?"

Lidria swallowed down her lingering remorse. "Yeah, I'll be fine. Thank you, Hector."

"I'm glad." Splotches of red marked Hector's eyes, but he beamed up at Lidria.

"Let's get up." Lidria pulled away from Hector. "I need to meet with Ren; we're taking another group into the city."

Hector bounced out of the cot while Lidria groaned at her aching back. "Can I come?"

Lidria shook her head. "I think it would be best if you stayed here."

Hector lowered his head and turned away. "Lidi, can you look for my mom?"

"I can try," Lidria offered. "Go play with the other kids and try to forget about it for now. I'll be back before sundown."

"Okay." Hector trudged over to the tent flap and pawed at the canvas until he passed through.

Lidria strode over to the water basin and realized something missing: Selis. Her heart skipped a beat, and she spun toward the exit. She sighed. Selis wouldn't run away. She could be out for breakfast or a walk. Lidria cursed herself and breathed deep. Selis would be fine.

Ridding her mind of misplaced worries, Lidria stripped out of her dirty clothes. She used a washcloth and the basin of water to clean herself. She wiped down her left arm, but the pleasant sensation stopped at the shoulder joint.

Lidria sighed. Six years, yet she found herself lingering on mistakes. Her eyes wandered her tattoo as the cloth left her arm. So many links broken, and recent events had pushed her to use them faster. At this pace, the rest would be severed soon.

Lidria tore her eyes off her shame, her fleeting strength. Many scars marked her skin from all the conflict she had endured over the years. Most of them small, faint reminders of battles lost to memory, but several stood out. A long, curved scar ran up her abdomen, stopping short of her chest.

Lidria closed her eyes, inhaled, and carried on. She slipped into clean clothes and threw a chainmail hauberk over her head. The fasteners tightened for a snug fit. Her worn boots popped on with ease. She slung her sword over her shoulder and patted the strap.

Outside, the sun cleared the trees to the east. Lidria yawned and worked a kink out of her neck. She proceeded toward Ren's tent, meandering about the camp. The brisk morning air made her regret getting out of bed.

"Mornin', Lidria," Deeter said as she approached. The lack of his other half brought a frown to her face. "Don't worry; nothing's wrong. Joan's escorting your friend Selis."

"Escorting her where?" Panic flared up inside Lidria again, filling her gut.

"She went to go see if she could pry any information out of that master of hers." Lidria turned and stepped away, but Deeter grabbed her by the wrist. "I think we would have heard if something went wrong by now. Joan won't let anything happen to her."

Lidria stared Deeter down. "Flinn treated Selis like she was his property. I don't think the encounter will be good for her."

"I guess that's where you'd come in."

Lidria scowled, which caused Deeter's grin to broaden.

The flap to Ren's tent rustled and flipped open. "I thought I heard you out here."

"Yeah, Deeter just told me Selis went to confront Flinn." Lidria glared at Ren.

"I wasn't going to deny her," Ren asserted, brow furrowed. "I think yesterday hit her hard."

Lidria shook her head. "It did. I just…"

"I know."

"If anything happens," Deeter interjected, "I'll send a runner. Otherwise, you two should go get ready."

"Thank you, Deeter," Lidria said, the knot in her stomach untangling.

Deeter grinned. "You're welcome. I'm here to help."

"I promise you'll get to go into the city tomorrow," Ren said, placing his hand on Deeter's shoulder.

"No worries, sir. You wouldn't be that heartless." Deeter's voice rang calm, but uneasiness stiffened his posture.

Ren smiled before he turned toward Lidria. "I guess we should gather everyone up and head out."

Lidria traced the wreckage of the citadel, brushing a hand along the smooth silver-gray stone. Her fingers bumped into the cool bronze ornamentation, and she withdrew her hand. She followed the tip to where she had blacked out in the attack.

A massive fissure of crumbling stone opened before Lidria. The spire collapsed in the street, shattering the cobblestone and drilling into the earth. Halfway down, the stone snapped. The north road nestled the other half between rows of deformed buildings.

Lidria frowned. The ground beneath must be hollow for this kind of damage, but she didn't know of any subterranean tunnels. She gazed into the cavity; however, nothing but shifting dirt, broken stone, and darkness greeted her.

Lidria spun from the crater. More important things demanded her time. Hector had asked her to find his mother, and, despite the odds, she meant to. Even if she found Nell dead, knowing would at least be better than not having a clue.

As Lidria moved to leave, a faint voice followed. She stopped and listened. Nothing. She spun back to the crumbling hole. Sifting dirt echoed off stone slabs and cobblestone fragments. Fifteen feet down, an opening large enough to fit a person appeared.

Voices drifted up from the crevice. Lidria strained, but no further sounds came. She glanced around, chewing her lip. Her ears played a trick on her—no one else was around. Ren and the rest of the day's group operated a quarter of the city away.

Lidria inched her way to the edge of the hollow and crouched. With little effort, she could reach the bottom. Getting back out would prove more difficult, but nothing drastic. She checked if her sword drew clean, sighed, and climbed down the precarious debris.

Loose stone and dirt shifted under each step, but Lidria finished the climb without incident. She brushed the debris off herself before inspecting the opening. To her surprise, a glimmer of light danced within. Curiosity consumed her.

Lidria squeezed inside. Her weapon and armor scraped against the irregular stone walls, announcing her clumsy approach. She feared nothing. If attacked, she could handle herself.

Lidria emerged from the crack. The twenty-by-twenty chamber carved out a simple but clean space. Nothing but an oversized lamp across from her dotted the room. She expected the rough-cut stone of the passageway to encapsulate the entire subterranean complex.

A woman's cry ripped Lidria from her confusion. She drew her sword and crept toward the single doorway in the room. The hallway stretched on for thirty feet. Shadows obscured the mid-point before more dancing light illuminated the way.

Lidria strode forward, and voices drifted down the hall. "…want to do with her?"

"I don't know," a second male voice said, agitated. "She looks pretty roughed-up. We'll have to ask Bal."

"I'm sure he heard her." Lidria pressed against the right side of the door. "He'll be back."

Lidria shifted to take the corner and the men inside. A sharp blade pricked her skin between her ribs, and she froze. She expected the person holding the weapon to push it into her lung, but they didn't. Taking a deep breath, she turned her head.

"Hello, breaker," a man said, hovering near Lidria's ear. Cold blue eyes and black stubble peeked out from under his dark hood.

"And who do I have the pleasure of threatening me?" Lidria stared at the man over her shoulder.

He cracked a smile. "Just a lowly agent of Master Janus, but you can call me Bal for our little discussion."

"I'll cooperate." Lidria lowered her sword. "So, how about you ease up?"

"Don't try anything funny, or I will put you down." Bal slid a long, needle-thin knife out of Lidria's chainmail, and she released her breath.

Bal shifted and gripped Lidria's sword. She relinquished the blade. Once disarmed, he nudged her forward. She stepped inside, and the two men went rigid. They reached for their waists and drew hand crossbows in one synchronized motion.

"Easy, lads," Bal said, sliding out from behind Lidria. "She won't cause any trouble, right, breaker?" She nodded, and Bal's men lowered their weapons.

"Sir," the shorter man on the left urged, "what do you want us to do about her, though?" He gestured to the motionless form of a woman at his feet.

Lidria's eyes widened: Nell. Before her mind parsed the information, she rushed across the chamber and interposed herself between the men and Hector's mother. "Don't you touch her."

The short man raised his hand crossbow, aiming at Lidria's chest. "You're not in any position to tell us what to do."

"What did you do to her?" Lidria snarled.

"Calm down," the taller man said, placing his hand on his comrade's arm and lowering his crossbow. "She's just unconscious. We found her down here. Looks like one of her legs is broken."

Lidria spun and crouched beside Nell. Her clothes were torn and dirty, her hair a knotted mess, and her face covered in filth. Not surprising if she had been down here since the attack. Lidria's gaze drifted down to Nell's legs. The unnatural angle told her Nell's leg broke at the shin.

"I have to get her to a doctor," Lidria muttered. She glanced over her shoulder and stared at Bal. "Whatever you wanted to discuss will have to wait. She needs medical attention."

The shorter man stepped forward. "What makes you think you—"

Bal flashed a dismissive wave of his hand at his subordinate. "Very well. But first," he strode toward Lidria, sword in hand, "I must ask you: do you work for Master Flinn?"

“No,” Lidria snapped. Her outburst came as a surprise. However, the thought of being aligned with the man who abused Selis drove her anger.

Bal studied Lidria for a long moment, expression stoic. Without a word, he spun the blade around and offered it back to her. “An enemy of Master Flinn is a friend to Master Janus.”

Lidria snatched the hilt and pulled her sword to her. She sighed, relishing the creak of leather as her fingers sank in. Her blade slipped into the sheath upon her back. She needed a plan.

“Is there another way out of here besides that crack down the hall?” Lidria asked, anxious.

Bal smirked. “Yes. This whole complex is attached to the citadel.”

“This is connected to the citadel?” Bal nodded. “What’s it here for? All I’ve seen are empty rooms.”

“Let me show you.” Bal waved to his two subordinates. They retrieved the lamps on the ground, and the shorter one headed for the door.

Lidria shifted her scabbard to the center of her back and bent down. She hoisted Nell up. The taller man offered to help carry the other woman, but Lidria refused. She had promised Hector she would find his mom, and no one would compromise that.

Bal followed his comrade, and Lidria trailed behind. They meandered to the door in the hallway, entering the chamber beyond.

Lidria glanced around the furnished room. Monolithic bookshelves lined the walls, packed tight with countless volumes. A lone table sat askew to the side. Books, loose sheets of paper, writing utensils, and candles lay strewn atop the table. Faded chalk markings dotted the floor.

“What is this?” Lidria asked, balancing Nell on her shoulder.

Bal turned and spread his arms. “It appears to be Master Flinn’s hidden research area.”

"I guess his paranoia isn't a new trait. Is this what you were looking for down here?"

"Only partially." Bal frowned, shaking his head. "Unfortunately for us, the information we seek has either been taken or destroyed."

Lidria's face scrunched up. "After Nell's safe, I can ask Lieutenant McCrear to let you speak with Flinn. Maybe you can get your answers that way."

A sly grin slid onto Bal's face. "That would be splendid. You're quite cooperative, miss…"

"Lidria." She shied her eyes away from Bal's. "And I'm no friend of Flinn's, so I don't see a problem with helping you out."

"If things work out," Bal started, "Master Janus can help whatever survivors you've gathered up. Kal'Den is closer than anywhere else you could go."

Excitement fluttered in Lidria's stomach. "He has the means to facilitate two hundred people out-of-the-blue?"

"He is a master of the Enclave. His resources are quite vast, and you require aid." Bal locked eyes with Lidria.

"Of course, he wants something first." Lidria shook her head and reined in her emotions. "Aren't we all on the same side?"

Bal waved a dismissive hand at Lidria. "Now, now. It's not much. Besides, we didn't know how much influence Master Flinn had here."

"All right. Let's go." Lidria secured Nell and took a step toward the far door.

"As you wish," Bal said, taking the lead.

Chapter Twelve

Lidria walked in silence between Bal and his two men. Nell weighed heavy on her right shoulder, but her determination spurred her on. Besides the broken leg and some bruises, Nell appeared in decent shape. Soon, she would be safe and Hector happy.

Lidria imagined the joy on Hector's face when she returned with his mother, and she couldn't help but smile. The kid's been through enough. She wanted everything to work out.

A group of civilians approached around a corner. Shocked expressions greeted Lidria before they spotted her escort. If they feared her appearance, the sight of the unfamiliar armed men pushed them to panic. Several backed away from her and her entourage.

"It's clear," a solider addressed the civilians as he emerged from the building to Lidria's right. None acknowledged him; their eyes fixed dead-ahead. He frowned and turned Lidria's way. "B-breaker," he stammered. "What's going on here?"

"Everything's fine," Lidria said. "I need to get this woman to a doctor and find McCrear."

The soldier regarded Bal and his men. "The lieutenant is two blocks to the south, but who are these men?"

"They work for Master Janus of the Enclave. They have a matter to discuss with McCrear." Lidria understood why the man held reservations, but she didn't waste time easing them.

He scratched the back of his head. "I don't know much about mages aside from that they're dangerous. But," he caught Lidria's eye, "if you vouch for them, all right. You saved my fellow soldiers and me from that…thing the night of the attack."

Lidria smiled, and pride filled her. "I'm glad I was there to help. What's your name?"

"Sam," he said, surprised.

"Lidria." She nodded, and Sam reciprocated. "Have a good day, Sam. And thanks."

"No, thank you." Sam threw Lidria a crisp salute. She saluted back, heading off to find Ren.

Bal craned his neck toward Lidria. "Seems like you have a knack for protecting people."

"Just doing my job," Lidria said. She regretted her feeble denial the second the words left her lips. "She's personal. I promised her son I would find her and bring her back."

"Isn't it serendipitous that we all met here today, then?" Bal asked with an impish grin.

Every time Lidria thought Bal might be plain with her, he did something to stoke her suspicions. "That remains to be seen."

"Don't be like that." Bal peeked over his shoulder at his subordinates. "You didn't hurt the poor woman, did you, Theas?"

Theas shook his head. "No, sir. Merely knocked her unconscious. She was in enough pain."

Bal turned back to Lidria; his grin gone. "See? No harm done. I'm sure the boy will be thrilled you found her."

"You're right," Lidria admitted despite herself. "But I still don't like how your men treated her. I heard her screaming."

"Well," Bal stuffed his hand in his pocket, "that doesn't matter now, does it?"

"I suppose not."

Lidria spotted Ren a block later. He sat on a pile of rubble outside a section of homes. None of the civilians or soldiers he led were around. He shot to his feet, and she offered a nervous smile. Frowning, he rushed over.

"Lidria, are you all right?" Ren asked.

"Yeah, I'm fine." Lidria shifted Nell around, the woman's weight catching up with her. "More importantly, where's the medic?"

Ren's gaze drifted over Lidria and Nell to Bal. "He's helping out in that building over there." He gestured over his shoulder with a hooked thumb. "Who is she?"

"Nell." Confusion played in Ren's eyes. "Hector's mother."

"Oh," Ren breathed. "Hector will be ecstatic. I'll be right back." He spun and headed off.

Lidria staggered over to the knee-high rubble, managing to hold Nell aloft. Muscles trembling, she placed the unconscious woman on the ground. Her legs gave out, and she wavered. She grimaced. Carrying Nell this far had been nothing short of a miracle.

Lidria plopped down before she collapsed and closed her eyes. A weary sigh escaped her as her body sagged. She needed far more sleep, and she had planned nothing else for the evening…after getting Nell back and making sure nothing had happened to Selis.

Selis. Worry wormed up from deep in Lidria's gut. She wished Selis had stayed away from Flinn. The depth of her concern surprised her, yet she didn't want anything bad to happen to her. Pain didn't suit Selis' captivating eyes.

Movement shook Lidria from her brooding. Bal stood before her, a broad grin on his face. "What?"

"Nothing," Bal said with a shake of his head. "I'm just admiring your tenacity. Master Janus could use someone with your skills and temperament."

“After this is over,” Lidria leaned back and shook her head, “I think I’m going to find something else to do with my life.”

“That’s a shame. It would be nice to have another breaker among us.” Lidria bolted upright, but Bal turned from her.

“Are you—”

Ren emerged from the building, a soldier with a backpack and red and white armband in tow. Lidria hesitated, but she eased back. Bal winked over his shoulder before he strode to his men. Shaking her head, she turned her attention to where it belonged.

“What happened here?” The medic asked, eyes examining Nell.

Lidria grimaced. “I found her in another part of the city. It seems like her leg is broken, and,” she flicked her gaze to Bal, “they knocked her unconscious before I arrived.”

The man gestured at the three dark-clothed men. “Who are they?”

“They claim to work for Master Janus,” Lidria said, eyeing Ren. “I don’t believe they’re lying, but I don’t understand their exact motives.”

“Master Janus, huh,” Ren mused. “I’m not too familiar with him. Master Flinn was the Enclave’s representative here.”

“Speaking of Flinn,” Lidria chewed her lip, “their leader, Bal, wants to speak with him. Apparently, he and Master Janus are at odds, and he sent these men to find something.”

Ren didn’t hide his suspicion. “I suppose I should ask him some questions, then.”

Lidria, weary muscles groaning in protest, stood to follow Ren. She glanced at the medic, and he shifted his attention back to Nell. He wouldn’t be able to do much, not here, but having an expert looking after her eased her concerns.

“Ah, lieutenant,” Bal said with a grin. “Just the man I wanted to see.”

“Lidria tells me you’re agents of Master Janus.”

Bal's grin broadened. "And she told me you're keeping Master Flinn in confinement."

"And what exactly do you want to speak to him about?" Ren folded his arms as Lidria came up beside him.

"About his research," Bal glanced around, "and why the Quela destroyed this city."

Lidria had been so focused on herself, Hector, and Selis that she hadn't questioned why the attack happened. "What do you mean?"

"They might be destructive and deadly, but this was an outlier," Bal explained. "We've seen them be quite territorial and attack settlements unprovoked, yet those instances were not of this scale.

"They joined for a single purpose. We believe he is either responsible, or he simply knows why."

"I'm assuming this has something to do with Flinn's secret research area," Lidria said, running different possibilities through her head.

"It does." Bal stood stone-faced, but rage burned in his ice-blue eyes. "That is why Master Janus sent us here. That is why I must press him for answers since he saw fit to destroy or remove any evidence."

Ren shifted to the side and rubbed his chin. "I don't know how much information you're expecting to get out of him. From what I understand, he's not very talkative, even to the people closest to him. I can't imagine he'd spill to someone directly opposed to him."

"I'm willing to try. With your permission, of course," Bal added. "He is your prisoner."

"You may have your attempt, but it'll have to wait until we're done here. I have promises to keep to the citizens of Odwyn."

Bal grinned. "Splendid. We have time; take yours, lieutenant."

"Sir, breaker," the medic interjected. "This woman appears stable, but we're going to need to treat her leg, and I can't do that here."

“I’ll help take her back,” Lidria blurted out. “If that’s all right.”

Ren smiled. “I know how much it means to you. Go.”

Lidria nodded and spun. The medic doffed his backpack and produced a makeshift stretcher. He unfolded the device, placing it on the ground beside Nell. Lidria gripped Nell’s ankles and, with the medic’s help, moved her onto the stretcher. They lifted her and headed back to camp.

Lidria gazed at the pink-orange sky and breathed a relieved sigh. Hector caught them the near-second she and the medic—Arnval—entered. He thanked Lidria, embraced her, and cried. She told him to stay with his mother. Content, he let Lidria leave to check on Selis.

Their empty tent worried Lidria. She couldn’t imagine Selis, being her timid self, would want to do anything after another encounter with Flinn. Deeter mentioned earlier that Joan escorted Selis. Perhaps she kept her company. Lidria exited and made for Deeter’s post.

“Welcome back,” Deeter said as Lidria approached. “Things go well?”

“It went great, actually.” Despite her concern, Lidria smiled. “I found Hector’s mother, and it sounds like she’ll recover well.”

“That’s wonderful. I’m sure the little guy is ecstatic. You’ve treated him very well.” Deeter clapped Lidria on the shoulder, and she jumped at his touch. “You’d make a pretty good mother yourself.”

Lidria’s heart leaped into her throat, and she swallowed hard. She had been a terrible mother—nothing changed that. She shied away from Deeter, unable to meet his gaze or his ill-suited praise.

Deeter shifted around. “Uh, I take it you came here to find out where Selis is?”

“Yeah.”

"Joan took her in after she spent a while by herself." Lidria raised an eyebrow. "She looked…distraught."

Lidria sighed. "That's what I feared would happen." She cursed herself for not being there for Selis, but she had made a promise to Hector.

"Joan's tent is over by the supply stock," Deeter said, appearing less awkward. "It's a little blackened due to her carelessness."

"Thank you," Lidria whispered.

"No problem, Lidria. I hope everything is well." Deeter flashed a smile, but Lidria couldn't find it in her to reciprocate.

Lidria spun from Deeter and hurried through camp. Selis would be all right with Joan, yet Lidria still worried about her. She couldn't help but worry. Lidria understood enough about what Flinn had done and what had happened the day she found Selis to imagine the encounter turning out poorly.

Within moments, Lidria spotted a tent with a charred black section. She hurried forward, ignoring the odd gawks from onlookers. Laughter drifted from inside the tent—something she hadn't expected. She pressed on and flipped the flap open.

"You're so tiny," Joan exclaimed, squeezing Selis with her arms around her stomach. The pair sat on the floor, Selis in Joan's lap.

"I am not," Selis protested. She turned to face Joan but caught sight of Lidria in the entryway. "Lidria." Selis sprang up out of Joan's grasp.

Lidria remained still; the interior of the tent reeked of wine. "Hi, Selis. Joan. I see you two are getting along well."

Selis lurched forward, placing a hand on Lidria's lower back. "Join us, Lidria." Selis' hand slipped down to Lidria's backside.

"I don't know if I should," Lidria said. She tried to shift away, but Selis stuck to her.

"Awww, come on," Selis whined. "We are all friends here, right?" Selis squeezed.

"Okay, okay." Lidria brushed Selis' frisky hand away.

A huge smile came over Selis' face. "I will get you plenty of this wonderful wine." She spun and headed for a crate of bottles, several of which lay empty on the ground.

Lidria sighed and removed her sword. She placed her weapon aside, rolling her aching shoulder. She plopped down. Joan wore a distant smile on her face, but she didn't appear as drunk. Her eyes focused on the mage.

Selis knelt beside Lidria, folded her legs underneath herself, and wrapped her arm around Lidria's waist. "Here, you need to catch up."

Lidria took a tentative sip, humoring Selis. The fragrant, sweet wine tasted almost as pleasant as Selis insisted. She downed a few more gulps.

Selis pressed up against Lidria, jingling the mail between them, and let out a dissatisfied noise. "Let us get this off." Her clumsy fingers pawed at the fasteners of Lidria's armor.

"Selis," Lidria admonished. She set the bottle down to stop her, but her chainmail jerked up over her head, dragging her tunic up in the process.

Selis tossed the armor aside. She slipped back around Lidria, catching the hem on her forearm. Three of Selis' fever-hot fingers played on Lidria's bare skin. "Much better."

"Are you trying to make me jealous?" Joan huffed. "Because it's working."

Selis drew herself up next to Lidria. Lidria turned her head toward Selis, but, as she turned, the small woman pressed her lips against her cheek. Lidria's eyes shot open, and her breath caught in her throat. If she had moved a little faster, Selis would've kissed her on the lips. She froze.

Selis pulled back from Lidria, adoration shining in her half-lidded golden eyes. Lidria had never experienced another woman expressing interest in her. Her heart fluttered at the thought of being close to someone again.

Before she stopped herself, Lidria wrapped her arm around Selis' waist. Selis' eyes flicked down, and a lazy smile slid onto her face. Selis rested her head in the crook of Lidria's neck. She muttered something unintelligible and went still.

"I think I gave her a little too much," Joan said, snapping Lidria out of her warm daze.

Lidria wanted to be angry, but she couldn't bring herself to scold Joan. "Thank you for looking after her."

"I couldn't abandon her." Joan locked eyes with Lidria, alert. "She was upset earlier. I figured this might help. If just for the evening."

"What happened?" Lidria took a sip of her wine, its warmth traveling down her throat.

Joan broke eye contact. "I'm not sure. She went to confront her former master, I heard her shout a lot, and she came out in tears. He never raised his voice. She said she needed some time alone and left.

"When she came back, I kept her company. She still didn't want to talk, so we started drinking. You can see where that led."

"I'll talk to her about it when she's sobered up," Lidria said, surprised by the edge to her voice.

"I'm sure she'll open up to you." Joan shook her head, an amused smile on her face. "After she had some to drink, she kept saying how much she hoped you would show up."

"Oh." Lidria eyed the top of Selis' head, and a faint smile curled her lips. "I don't want to disturb her, but I'm exhausted myself."

“You two can stay here,” Joan offered. “No point in breaking you up.”

Lidria’s heart raced. “Are you sure?”

“Of course. She’ll be glad you’re here when she wakes up in the morning.” Joan cracked a grin. “She might not remember you came otherwise.”

“I suppose you’re right.” Lidria nodded with a hint of a smile.

Joan rose to her feet much steadier than Lidria expected. “I’ll go grab you two some bedrolls.”

Lidria’s eyes closed the second Joan exited the tent. Exhaustion weighed heavy, and she slumped to the side. She jolted upright when her head bumped Selis’. Something tugged at the back of her mind—she didn’t deserve anyone’s affections, even drunken ones.

Lidria wanted to fight, but she didn’t have the energy. Giving in, she leaned her head against Selis’ and inhaled deep. Selis stirred but didn’t wake. Contentment wrapped Lidria in warmth, and she drifted off to join Selis in unconsciousness.

Chapter Thirteen

Selis' right leg ached, her head pounded, and a cavernous emptiness bloomed inside her. Guilt and loneliness crushed her, threatening to ruin her. She tried to resist, to focus on something, anything else, but the gnawing would not go away.

Selis stared out from the edge of the forest at the distant camp and sighed. Her body shuddered as she exhaled, and tears welled in her eyes. Things had spiraled out of control around her. She had done terrible things, and for what? Childish selfishness, spite, and hatred.

Lidria popped into Selis' mind, and the sobs stopped. She had taken her in and accepted her at her lowest, saving her from Flinn's abuse. Her company reassured her. She adored when Lidria's lovely green eyes glanced her way. She even…

Selis curled her knees up and buried her face in them. How could she think about getting close to someone after what she had done? She could have found another way, done something different. A killer like her did not deserve anyone's affection.

Self-loathing oozed up from inside Selis, dragging her down into the deep dark. Her chest tightened, and her breathing became thin and raspy. Her heart pounded as panic set in. She drowned in her disgust. Failure. Murderer. Abomination. Her last thread of self-worth snapped, and she—

"Selis?" a soft voice called, catching her before she slipped into the darkness.

Selis wanted nothing more than to slip away, but she also craved interaction. She drifted in her thoughts. The voice hauled her up out of the drowning sea her dark emotions had become. Air filled her lungs, and she opened her eyes.

Lidria stood before Selis, staring down at her with a distraught expression on her face. Selis gazed into her eyes, and a spark of hope ignited. She said nothing; fearful her words might come out garbled, wrong. She tore her eyes away from Lidria's.

"May I sit with you?" Lidria asked, her voice competing with the rustling brush.

Selis did not wish to venture to speak, so she nodded. Lidria crunched across grass and leaves before she sat. Two inches separated them, and Selis twitched her head to the left. Lidria wore her silver and blue military uniform without armor or a weapon. Selis scooted closer.

Lidria draped her arm over Selis' shoulders, which made her jump. She hid, and Lidria let out a confused, disappointed noise. A moment later, Lidria withdraw. Selis' right hand shot up and gripped Lidria's above her shoulder.

"I," Selis squeaked. "I am having a difficult time. I did not mean to make you feel like your gesture was not appreciated."

"It's all right," Lidria said, her posture relaxing.

Selis pulled Lidria's arm tight around her shoulders, melting against the larger woman. "I thought you were heading into the city again with Ren."

"I wanted to check on you." Selis' heart leaped into her throat. She turned her head, but Lidria shied away from her gaze, a rosy hue to her cheeks.

"Thank you," Selis whispered, wrapping her left arm around Lidria's waist.

Lidria hugged Selis tighter. "You're welcome. I was worried about you after last night."

Selis' head pounded to remind her of her foolishness. She remembered flashes of her drunken antics and cozying up to Lidria came through the clearest. Waking up beside Lidria had surprised and scared her so much she ran before anyone else woke up.

Selis shifted away from Lidria, but her halfhearted attempt failed. "I am sorry."

"You have nothing to apologize for, Selis." Lidria embraced Selis' shoulders.

"What about…" Embarrassment burned Selis' cheeks.

Lidria shook her head. "No."

"Oh," Selis breathed, dumbfounded. Her heart raced.

Awkward, oppressive silence settled upon them. Selis wanted to say something, anything, but words escaped her. Lidria's presence provided comfort, yet her terrible actions haunted her. She betrayed all the goodwill and concern Lidria showed her. How could Lidria accept her if she told her what she had done?

"Selis, what happened with Flinn yesterday?"

Anguish twisted Selis' heart. "I-I am not a good person. I killed people." She curled into a small ball.

Lidria jerked upright. "What are you talking about?"

"Cent," Selis said in a stronger voice than she had thought possible. "We shared a connection—we were both chasing after our master's approval. That, along with our frequent proximity, made me feel close to him despite his hatred.

"I told myself there was no other way, I had to kill him, but that was a lie. I was always stronger than him. Maybe that was why he hated me so: he could never outdo me, some nobody."

Lidria gave Selis a tight, one-armed hug. "I didn't realize how personal it was, but you weren't very talkative on the matter."

"I lied to myself and thought it was not, but it was." Tears welled up, and Selis trembled. "I cannot believe I killed him."

"He wanted you dead," Lidria reminded Selis.

"Yes." Selis squeezed Lidria, her warmth soothing. "Although, it was more because of his hatred and less to stop me from leaving Flinn."

"It doesn't matter why," Lidria started. "You did what you had to, and you saved me."

A spark of frustration burned in Selis' gut. "You do not understand. I could have suppressed his magic, knocked him unconscious, restrained him."

"You can't second-guess yourself like that, Selis. You didn't take any pleasure in it, so own it and try to move on." Lidria moved her hand and caressed Selis' hair.

"Maybe you are right," Selis admitted with a sigh. "However, even if I can accept what I did to Cent, Flinn"—she flinched when she recalled the emptiness in his eyes—"was completely defenseless, a prisoner."

Lidria stopped. "I thought Flinn was still alive."

"He is alive…technically." Selis shuddered.

"Selis, what happened yesterday when you spoke with Flinn?" Lidria resumed her stroking, much to Selis' comfort.

"I wanted to know what was so important to keep hidden that he would abandon his countrymen as well as more personal things. Flinn did not want to speak with me, even in his moments of clarity. So, I," Selis swallowed and blinked away her tears, "used an invocation to force myself into his mind.

"I encountered the typical barriers put up to safeguard secrets and knowledge, but I blew past them with ease until I came upon the last one. It took some doing, but I broke it, too. In my haste and rage, I did not realize it was different than the others.

"When I destroyed the barrier, it, uh, erased all his thoughts and memories, everything that made Flinn the man he was. The…thing being held as a prisoner is no longer Flinn but an empty, mindless shell."

Lidria grew tense as Selis spoke. She stopped her comforting gesture, and her body went rigid, wooden. No doubt revealing herself to be a monster would chase Lidria away, but she did not wish to hide anything from her. Selis let her arm drop from around Lidria' waist.

"I," Lidria stuttered. "That's—I don't know what to say."

"Go ahead and say it," Selis challenged. "You are afraid of me. You think I am a monster."

Lidria jerked away from Selis, causing her to glance up. "No." Lidria held Selis' gaze, but horror twisted her vibrant eyes. "Not of you—just what you're capable of when pushed to an extreme."

"It is all right. You do not have to lie or twist words. People should fear me. I am some…*thing* to be feared." Selis' voice dripped with venom.

"You slept in my arms last night," Lidria said, and Selis flinched as her heart stopped. "You are not a monster."

Tears streamed down Selis' face. "Lidria, please. You are making this worse. I do not deserve your, anyone's, concern or friendliness. Leave me be."

Without hesitation, Lidria wrapped her other arm around Selis and pulled her close. Selis froze, unable to put up a fight. Lidria leaned back in the grass. She guided Selis' head to her chest, hugging her tight. Lidria's rhythmic heartbeat echoed in Selis' ear.

"I'm sorry, Selis." Lidria's voice reverberated. "But I can't abandon you when you need someone the most."

"I," Selis gasped between sobs. She tried to continue but found her despair too much to overcome.

Lidria squeezed Selis tighter. “It’s all right. I got you.”

Selis gave in and curled up against Lidria, burying her head in the other woman’s chest. She did not understand why Lidria accepted her—she admitted to being a monster. How could Lidria hold her like this?

Lidria patted Selis’ back and brushed hair from her face. A ray of warm sunlight hit her face, and she stopped gasping and weeping. She wanted to gaze upon Lidria, to drink in her beautiful, compassionate eyes, but her body would not listen.

“I do not deserve this,” Selis managed, muffled against Lidria.

A little giggle bubbled up through Lidria’s chest. “Of course you do, and I’m glad to be here for you.”

Selis lifted her head so her voice would come out clearer. “T-thank you.”

“You’re welcome, Selis.”

“Lidria,” Selis murmured. The other woman tilted her head down, expectant, and she curled to hide her flushed cheeks. “Please, do not…do not leave.”

“Hey. Hey—look at me,” Lidria coaxed. Selis uncurled herself enough to meet Lidria’s sincere eyes. “I’m not going anywhere. I’m all yours as long as you need me.”

Selis inched her way up until her head rested on Lidria’s shoulder. She wiggled around, her head finding its way into the crook of Lidria’s neck. Her lips brushed against warm, smooth skin. She stifled her desires and settled for curling up at Lidria’s side.

Selis cleared her throat after a long spell of blissful silence. “How did things go in the city yesterday? I did not get to ask you.”

“Oh,” Lidria croaked, shaking her head. Selis smiled—Lidria enjoyed the opportunity to rest as well. “Things went well. I found Hector’s mother alive. She’s a little beat up, but she’ll make it just fine.”

“That is great,” Selis squeezed, and Lidria reciprocated. “I am sure he was happy to see his mother again.”

“He was.” Lidria’s voice dropped, and she shifted around. “I hope that I can—never mind.”

“Lidria?”

Lidria turned her head, and conflict darkened her eyes. “It’s nothing. Don’t worry about it.”

Selis frowned. “You can speak to me. I made a complete fool of myself, and you were here for me.” She held Lidria’s gaze and hugged her. “I can be here for you, too.”

“I know, Selis,” Lidria whimpered. “It’s just hard for me to talk about my past.” She sighed and tore her eyes away from Selis. “I hope you don’t take it personally.”

“No, not at all. I…” Selis trailed off. The fact Lidria would not open up to her did hurt.

“You’re the first person I’ve been close to in years.” Lidria’s voice struggled to be more than a whisper. “Trust me, I’ll tell you. I,” shame flashed across her face, “need some time, though.”

The disappointment within Selis vanished. “I will be here for you when the time comes. Do not forget it.”

Lidria smiled, and Selis’ heart melted. “I have a feeling you won’t let me forget.”

Selis settled back against Lidria’s shoulder, content. She wished to sleep more, and no better place existed. Her heavy eyes closed, forgetting all her worries. The gentle, warm breeze washed over her, almost as calming as Lidria’s presence.

Lidria’s arm snaked around until her hand reached Selis’ hip. Selis placed her left hand on Lidria’s stomach, which made her jump. Selis wanted to say something to still her, but no words came to her.

Lidria cursed under her breath and tried to sit up, seeming to forget Selis' presence.

"What is the matter?"

Lidria's fingers drummed on Selis' hipbone. "I was so worried about you that I forgot the other thing that happened in the city yesterday." Lidria attempted to rise again, and Selis untangled herself.

Anxiety tightened Selis' chest. "I thought things went well."

"I didn't think anything of it," Lidria said, tearing her eyes away from Selis'. "But now that you told me about Flinn, we might have a problem.

"I met a man named Bal in an underground section of the city—the same place I found Nell. He claimed it was Flinn's secret research area and that he was an agent of Master Janus' sent here to find out what Flinn was researching.

"Bal said he and his men couldn't find anything worthwhile down there, that Flinn removed or destroyed anything potentially useful to them. I…told him he could speak with Flinn himself."

Selis' stomach dropped. "Oh."

"Did you know Flinn had a library underground?" Anxious eyes met Selis'.

Selis frowned. "I did not. I only knew of his workspace inside the citadel itself. It makes sense, though, especially with how he acted."

"I suppose it doesn't matter anymore. Whatever they were looking for is gone, and so is Flinn." Lidria lowered her head, staring into her lap.

"Is there something else going on that I am not aware of?" Selis asked, drawing Lidria's gaze. "I did not think you would worry about something like this."

Lidria chewed her lip. "What do you know of Master Janus? I don't have much to go on myself."

“I have not seen him in many years,” Selis explained, trying to draw from her memory. “So, I cannot speak for why he would want Flinn’s research, but he did not strike me as a bad or petty man.

“He took care of the people in his home of Kal’Den, and I remember him treating me well. There is not much else. He and Flinn did not see eye-to-eye, so Flinn cut off all interactions with him seven years ago.”

“Would you trust him?”

“If you asked me last week, I would have said yes. Now,” Selis shook her head, “I am done with the Enclave. I do not know if I would trust them.”

A guilty expression swept over Lidria’s face. “I should go tell Bal what happened. I’m sorry.”

“It is fine.” Selis stretched her legs, no longer yearning to curl into a tiny ball. She smiled at Lidria. “I will go with you.”

“Are you sure?” Lidria asked, frowning. “I don’t want you to push yourself.”

Selis nodded. “I am fine. Thanks to you.”

“I’m glad,” Lidria said with a smile as she stood. She turned around and offered her hand to Selis. “Let’s go speak with Bal and see if we can figure anything out.”

Selis took Lidria’s hand, and Lidria hauled her off the ground. She adjusted her robes and straightened her hair. “All right. Let us go.”

Chapter Fourteen

Selis strode through the camp, following Lidria. Despite the brave face she put on, her mind and body were drained. However, she did not wish to send Lidria alone. No doubt Bal would want to ask her a few questions after he learned what happened to Flinn.

The sun rose high in the sky, and Selis' stomach growled. She had left in such a hurry that morning, she had forgotten to eat. Looking back, running away from Lidria had proved foolish. Selis did not need to worry around Lidria.

"Are you sure you're up for this?" Lidria asked, concern evident on her face. "I can speak with him on my own."

Selis stepped close to Lidria and stared up at her, resolute. "Yes, I am sure."

"All right."

Halfway through camp, a soldier jogged up to them. He gave Lidria a quick salute, which she returned. "Lidria," he took several shallow breaths, "I've been trying to find you."

"What is it, Sam?" Selis raised an eyebrow.

"That man you were with yesterday," Sam started, alarmed, "Bal, I think his name was, demanded to see Master Flinn. The lieutenant told him he'd have to wait until either you or he was present, but Bal forced his way in."

Lidria glanced at Selis with an apologetic expression. "I'll take care of it. Thank you for informing me."

"No problem, ma'am." Sam threw a less panicked salute. "I'm glad I found you. Good luck."

Lidria took off. Selis followed her, if more hesitant. Panic set in at the mere thought of seeing Flinn's empty husk, and her steps wavered. Her heart pulsed in her throat, her mind swam, and dizziness swept through her. She tried to take deep breaths, but they would not come.

A hand clasped her shoulder, and Selis jumped. Lidria stood in front of her, sympathetic. Selis' breathing returned to her in short, shallow bursts. Prying eyes stared at her, and she realized she had stopped in the path. She shook her head.

"I am all right," Selis managed despite her emotional turmoil. "I just do not want to see…what I did again."

A lopsided smile appeared on Lidria's face. "You don't have to. I'll deal with anything that comes up."

"Okay." Selis nodded several times to herself. "Thank you."

"Of course," Lidria said, her delicate smile transforming into a stronger one. She removed her hand, pivoted, and continued on their way.

Selis' chest grew tighter the closer she got to Flinn. The dread of what she had done crushed her enough without worrying how Bal might react. She did not consider Master Janus' intentions nefarious, but recent events stoked her skepticism.

Three men in black clothes and armor stood in front of the holding tent, the lead man pacing. His disheveled short black hair accentuated his dissatisfaction. He stopped midstride and shot his gaze toward Selis. His ice-blue eyes unnerved her, and she perceived magic.

"Ah, Lidria," Bal said, an unsettling grin sliding onto his face. "I'm glad you're here"—he spoke through his teeth—"maybe you can tell me what happened."

"Calm down." Lidria's purposeful stride exuded confidence while Selis' limbs trembled. "How about we take this somewhere else?"

Rage burned in Bal's cold eyes. "Tell me why you lied to me, and I'll deem whether or not to kill you."

Selis wanted to say something, to absolve Lidria, yet she did nothing but stand still like a fool.

"I didn't know Flinn was like this; I only found out about it this morning myself." Lidria stepped closer to Bal and held his wrathful gaze. "If you're insistent on killing me, I'll show you I'm not so easily put down."

Bal's men reached for their weapons, but neither Bal nor Lidria made a move for theirs. The two stared at each other for a long, tense moment before Bal eased back. Lidria followed suit, unclenching her fist. The knot in Selis stomach loosened.

"You'd better have a good explanation," Bal growled.

Lidria took a deep breath, and the magic around her arm uncoiled. "Let's discuss this over lunch. I'll explain everything the best I can."

Bal's eyes flicked to Selis for the first time, and a shiver ran down her spine. "Very well. I'm sure Master Flinn's apprentice can fill in any details."

"Don't worry about her," Lidria said, drawing Bal's gaze. "You're speaking with me."

"Then, why did you bring her?"

Lidria opened her mouth, but Selis placed a hand on her shoulder. "Lidria, it is all right. I will be fine."

"Okay."

"I will do my best to answer any questions you have," Selis said as she tried to ignore her growling stomach.

"Let's get lunch." Bal gestured to his men, and they relinquished their weapons.

Lidria cut through the camp toward Max's kitchen. She pulled Selis close. Selis did not mind being beside Lidria—she relished her presence—but Lidria's motive vexed her. Maybe she should not have bawled her eyes out earlier.

Selis sighed, shook her head, and shifted her thoughts elsewhere. Bal wanted to speak with Flinn and pry his secrets out of him. If he could not acquire Flinn or his research, he might try the next best thing.

A shiver ran down Selis' spine, and she inched closer to Lidria. Bal seemed aware of Lidria's strength. If he wished to take Selis to his master, he would invite rather than take. However, could she deal with another master of the Enclave?

Selis desired to curl up into a ball and disappear. She did not wish to undergo the venture and not alone. Whatever questions Bal presented her today, she would answer; nothing more. No matter how small or insignificant, she had a place here.

"Over here," Lidria said as she walked away from Max, waving to Selis and Bal.

Lidria lead them to a makeshift wooden table with a bench on either side. She sat down before she directed Bal to the other side. As Bal and his men complied, Selis took a seat beside Lidria. Selis glanced to her left, and Lidria flashed her a reassuring smile.

"So," Bal said, folding his hands on the table and leaning forward. "What happened to Master Flinn?"

"I, uh," Selis swallowed hard, "triggered something in his mind. I pressed him for information, and he would not answer me. So, I tried to procure my answers with magic.

"He had barriers set up, and I broke through them. The last one felt different, but I continued anyway. After I shattered it, he became an empty husk, devoid of memory and personality. I…did not intend to do what I did."

Bal eased back in his seat, his eyes never leaving Selis'. "A paranoid man to the end. Master Janus was always surprised by the lengths he would go to keep things from others."

"He was not always like that," Selis murmured. She shook her head, ridding her mind of pointless thoughts. "He kept so many things, even from me, but he had been more secretive recently. And for what?"

"I hoped you could tell me," Bal swept his hand toward Selis, "seeing you were the closest to him."

Selis' breath thinned, but she carried on. "Cent was closer to him than I, but he is gone, too."

"Sounds like things spiraled out of control pretty fast here." Lidria glared at Bal, which caused him to sneer. "Tell me they didn't."

"That's—" Lidria stopped herself, shaking her head. "Never mind."

"I did not have the time to figure anything else out," Selis said. "They both forced my hand even if I made the mistake of letting them."

Bal raised his eyebrow. "I didn't know anything of Cent, but I have to say: you don't look like much."

Others often remarked on their underestimation of Selis' abilities. That did not, however, improve her spirits. "I am not proud of it, but my appearance is somewhat deceiving. If nothing else, I am a dedicated learner."

"You are an interesting one." Bal curled his pointer finger against his mouth. "Master Janus could find some use for you."

"I am done with the Enclave," Selis asserted.

Bal let out a bark of laughter and shook his head. "Look at the two of you. Your way of life has been destroyed, yet you don't want to consider an offer of aid, some direction."

“I’m sorry,” Lidria interjected, leaning forward. “But after what’s happened here, I would much rather help the people here than rush off to be a lapdog for some aloof master.”

“I am with Lidria.” Selis’ gaze fell from Bal. “There is nothing for me at the side of another master.”

Bal opened his arms in a wide, sweeping gesture. “He can provide shelter for all these people.”

“What—”

Selis stopped as Max approached with their meals. He offered her and Lidria a smile as he set the bowls in front of them. If he held reservations about Bal and his comrades, he did not show them. Max withdrew without a word, and Selis stared down at her meal. Bits of indiscernible meat floated amongst carrots and potatoes.

Growling emanated from Selis’ stomach. She craved sustenance, but Bal’s statement drew her focus. Her gaze lifted from her stew to Bal. He, seeming quite content, finished blowing on a spoonful and ate. He grinned.

“That cook seems to know how to work miracles with what he’s got.” Bal took another bite. “I’ll have to give him my compliments.”

Lidria leaned forward. “Are you going to try to recruit him as well?”

A thoughtful look came over Bal’s face. “I hadn’t thought of it, but, now that you mention it, I might.”

“You—”

Selis squeezed Lidria’s leg under the table. “What did you mean when you said Janus could provide shelter for the people here?”

“Exactly what it sounded like.”

Lidria’s face scrunched up with conflicting emotions. “Ignoring how—why would he do that?”

"Because," Bal waved toward Selis, "Selis here is the only connection to Master Flinn left alive, and Master Janus would be interested in speaking with her. Interested enough to open his home if that's what it takes."

Selis took a deep, laborious breath. If complying meant helping all these people, how could she refuse? Flinn seemed responsible for what happened to Odwyn; her interactions with the Quelan shaman teased at the notion. Since he could no longer answer for his deeds, responsibility fell to her.

"For the survivors of Odwyn"—Selis trembled—"I will do whatever I can."

"Selis." Distress covered Lidria's face. "You don't have to do this."

Selis swallowed her rising doubts. "I…I do. Flinn might have caused all this; I feel responsible."

"That's ridiculous." Lidria neared shouting, but she managed to keep herself reigned in.

"I am going to do it. I want to help." Selis tore her eyes away from Lidria and focused her attention on Bal. "You can inform Master Janus I am coming."

Bal grinned. "You can tell him yourself. We'll leave tomorrow, and the rest can follow at their own pace. I'm sure it will take this group a while to make it to Kal'Den."

"I'm coming with you," Lidria blurted out.

"You do not need to, Lidria. I can handle it myself." Selis allowed herself to glance back at Lidria.

"I know. I just," Lidria lowered her voice to little more than a whisper, "don't want you to go by yourself."

Selis stared into Lidria's eyes, and she spotted fear—she did not want to be alone herself. "There is no one else I would rather have by my side."

Lidria nodded, relief replacing the worry in her eyes. Her rigid posture relaxed, and she eased back. "I'm glad."

"That's settled, then?" Bal asked with a hint of impatience.

"Yes," Selis affirmed, shooting Lidria a smile before she turned to Bal. "We will be ready to go to Kal'Den tomorrow."

"Splendid." Bal clasped his hands together in front of him. "I will leave you to your own devices until then."

Bal and his men finished their meal and left. An overwhelming weight settled down on Selis. She looked down at her bowl of stew, but her appetite had vanished. She wished to be done, yet she kept pulling herself in deeper.

Lidria sighed, shoulders slumping. "So much for being done with all this."

"Lidria, I—"

Lidria placed her hand on Selis' thigh and gazed into her eyes. "I know, and I support your decision. I just hoped to be past all this sometime soon."

"I am sorry." Selis scooted close to Lidria, leaning her head against the other woman's shoulder.

"You don't need to apologize to me," Lidria whispered as she squeezed Selis' leg. "How about we finish here, and then you can get some rest? I'll inform Ren of the plan."

Selis lifted her head. "All right."

They finished their food before they got up and left. Selis yawned, and Lidria tried to suppress a yawn of her own. A lopsided smile crept onto

Selis' face. Guilt tugged at her heart, but she could not help but be glad for Lidria's company.

Chapter Fifteen

"Lidi! Lidi!" An overenthusiastic voice pierced her ear. Tiny hands shook her by the shoulder.

Lidria groaned. She couldn't deal with Hector's absurd energy levels this early in the morning. "Hector, quiet. People are trying to sleep."

"Oh," Hector's voice dropped to little more than a whisper, "sorry."

"It's all right," Lidria said before she opened her eyes.

Dim light clouded Lidria's vision for a moment. When her sight cleared, she found Hector knelt at her side, beaming. Her eyes drifted past him to the cot on the other side of the tent. Selis lay motionless, and Lidria smiled. Hector didn't wake her when he barged in.

Lidria sat up, adjusting her loose tunic. "What do you need, Hector?"

"Mom's awake," Hector cried. Lidria grimaced and glanced over at Selis. She stirred but remained asleep.

Lidria couldn't hold back a smile. "Hector, that's great." She couldn't believe the luck.

Hector beamed. "Wanna go see her? I know she'll be glad to see you."

"I would like to," Lidria frowned, "but shouldn't she be resting?"

"That's what the doctor said, but"—Hector let out a bubble of laughter—"mom told him she'd do what she wants."

Somehow, Lidria didn't think things were quite so simple. "If she's up for it, I would love to go see her."

Hector's face lit up with excitement. "I'll go tell her you're coming." Before Lidria said anything further, he shot up and bolted outside.

Lidria shook her head. She wouldn't be able to keep up with him if she had to raise him herself. Her mind went to Evelyn. Before she stopped herself, she slipped down into despair. The past proved she couldn't support a child.

It surprised Lidria that, after six years, she still cared. That gnawing might never go away. After meeting Hector, she wished she could go back, change things. However, the possibility of seeing Evelyn again never once struck her.

Lidria wandered around, trying to work herself back up to leave. She wanted nothing more than to stay and hide, but she didn't want to disappoint Hector. He also knew where to find and harass her. Taking a deep breath, she straightened her clothes and headed to exit the tent.

"Lidria?" Selis murmured from behind her.

Lidria glanced over her shoulder at the scrunched-up form of Selis. "I'm going to visit Nell. Get some rest."

"She is awake?" Selis fidgeting on the cot. "That is good. Say hello to Hector for me."

"I will." Selis grumbled in affirmation and stopped moving. Lidria exited without reservation.

The bright morning sun burned Lidria's eyes, causing her to raise her arm to shield them. She staggered to the left before she managed to steady herself. Shaking her head, she squinted to focus on her surroundings. Few people noticed her floundering.

Lidria entered the medical section of the camp. Tents were torn down, moved around, and set to the side. Patients sat or lay around, but none appeared too bad off. Soldiers and civilians milled about the place, carrying more items than usual.

Hector bounced up from among a sea of random supplies and waved. "Lidi!" He stumbled his way through the mess. "This way." Grabbing her hand, he yanked her forward.

Several crates and wayward tent poles bashed into Lidria's shins as Hector dragged her. "H-Hector, slow down. We have plenty of time."

"Sorry, Lidi." Hector slowed down, but he didn't relinquish his firm grip "I'm just so happy, and I know mom will be happy to see you."

"It's all right." Lidria squeezed Hector's small hand. "I'm sure—"

"Hector," a stern feminine voice called. "Leave that poor woman alone."

Hector withdrew his hand from Lidria's and pouted. "But, Mom," he whined. "Lidi came to see you."

Nell sat on a bedroll. She gazed up at Lidria for a long moment before a smile curled her lips. Nell's frizzy brown hair outlined her cut, bruised, and exhausted face. Her eyes traveled from Lidria to Hector as he scurried over to her side, grinning.

"Hello, Nell."

Nell grabbed Hector by the waist and dragged him down beside her. He fussed, but she held him down. "Hello, Lidria. It's good to see you again. I'm glad you made it out of the city fine."

"I almost didn't, but I guess you saw." Lidria took a few more steps, glancing at the cleared space in front of her. "More importantly: what happened to you?"

"Take a seat," Nell offered as she gestured between them with her free hand. After hesitating a moment, Lidria sat and folded her legs. "The ground around where the citadel crashed gave way, and I fell.

"I don't know how long I was out, but when I came to, I was in an underground passage. My leg was broken, so I couldn't get far." Nell shook her head. "I'm surprised I'm still alive."

Hector's face scrunched up. "Don't say that, Mom."

"It's all right, Hector." Nell patted him on the head, and that pacified him.

Lidria chewed her lip. “Frankly, so am I. I’m glad you’re okay. Hector was very worried about you.” She grinned at him, and he buried his face in Nell’s hair.

Nell locked eyes with Lidria. “Thank you.”

“It-it was nothing,” Lidria stammered. She tore her eyes away from Nell’s as a lump grew in her throat.

A somber smile slid onto Nell’s face. “It was a lot to me. Hector…is all I have left. And if I had,” she swallowed, “not made it back, I would have at least known he was safe.”

“You’re giving me far too much credit.” Lidria wanted Nell to understand how little praise she deserved, but she couldn’t bring herself to explain. “I’m not someone that anyone would want to care for their child.”

“Nonsense,” Nell chided. “Hector told me what you’ve done for him, what’s happened while I was gone. He had nothing but praise for you. He even gave you a nickname. You did a wonderful job, and I’m thankful.”

Lidria glanced up from her lap, yet she still couldn’t meet Nell eye-to-eye. “I just did what I could and thought would be best. It wasn’t anything special.” Frustration burned in Lidria’s chest.

Nell frowned. “Please, Lidria, I mean it. Take the compliment and know you did right by us.”

“Okay,” Lidria whispered, nodding to herself. “I’m sorry. I—never mind.”

“It’s all right; you don’t have to explain. All I wanted was to make sure you knew how much I appreciate everything you did.” Nell hugged Hector, and he squirmed in her arm.

“I do. I just wasn’t ready for it.” Lidria shook her head and locked eyes with Nell. “You’re welcome.”

“That’s much better.” Nell smiled.

Awkwardness settled down on Lidria's shoulders. She didn't belong. "So, uh, I'm leaving today to go to Kal'Den."

"What?" Hector yelped, pulling out of Nell's arm. He rushed over to Lidria, and she leaned back to avoid him tackling her. "Lidi, you can't leave!"

"Selis is going to see Master Janus," Lidria explained, "and I can't let her go by herself. She needs someone to keep her company."

Lidria's words didn't calm Hector. If anything, they drove him into a feverish panic. "But why do you have to go? Who is Janus?"

"He's a master of the Enclave." Hector gave Lidria a blank, wide-eyed stare. "He's one of the best mages in the realm. He wants to speak with Selis, and she agreed."

"I still don't want you to go." Hector plopped down in Lidria's lap. She grunted as he landed on her.

"Hector—"

"Was that the deal?" Nell asked, scanning the surrounding camp. Lidria clenched her jaw but said nothing. "I heard we're marching to Kal'Den tomorrow."

"Yeah. Bal, Master Janus' man, said his master would open his home to everyone here if Selis talked to him about her former master."

Nell rubbed the back of her head and grimaced. "I wouldn't trust them if I were you."

"I don't," Lidria blurted out. "Not really, but Selis is determined to do this. That's why I'm going with her: to make sure nothing happens to her."

"Did you know Selis before the attack?"

Lidria shook her head. "No, I met her several days ago. Flinn, the member of the Enclave stationed in Odwyn and Selis' master, went AWOL. I went to retrieve him and met Selis.

"Flinn was crazed and paranoid. Selis wanted to come back to camp with me to help people, but he wasn't having it. We fought him and won, taking him prisoner. She's been with me ever since. She…has no one else."

"I like Selis," Hector chimed in, a sad expression on his face. "She has pretty hair and shows me magic and is nice to me."

Lidria smiled, her heart fluttering. "I like Selis, too, Hector. That's why I have to go."

"But—"

"We'll be right behind her," Nell assured Hector. "It'll only be for a few days. You'll survive."

Hector's face brightened. "Okay. Don't let anything bad happen to Selis, Lidi."

"I won't, and I'll be sure to tell her that you're worried about her." Hector glanced away from Lidria, embarrassed.

"Lidria," Nell said, interrupting her and Hector's exchange. Lidria stared at the other woman and fear ruled her eyes. "Be careful. I overheard Janus' men talking about what, I assume, Flinn had been up to before the attack.

"Not much made sense to me, and it was difficult to hear, but it sounded like the Quela were attracted to the city because of something he did. They were trying to find details, but it didn't sound like they found what they were looking for."

Finding out Flinn partook in something shady didn't surprise Lidria. "If that's the case, he got off far too easy."

Nell cocked her head to the side. "What happened to him?"

"It's a long story." Lidria hesitated. "But, to put it simply, he's gone now."

"I see." Nell nodded. "I guess that explains why Janus wants to speak with Selis instead of demanding you hand over Flinn."

"Yeah." Lidria urged Hector out of her lap until he got the idea. "Well, I should go wake Selis up and prepare to leave. I'm sure Bal won't want to wait."

"Take care, Lidria. We'll see you when we reach Kal'Den."

Lidria stood, trying her best not to knock Hector over. "You, too, Nell." Lidria tilted her head down. "See you soon, Hector."

Hector spun. He threw his arms around Lidria's legs and squeezed them tight. "Bye, Lidi."

Lidria ruffled Hector's hair, and he let go. "Goodbye, Hector."

A lump swelled in Lidria's throat as she approached Ren's command tent. She hadn't realized, but she had grown accustomed to her surroundings and the people. The camp had become more like home than the city in the past six years. She told herself what Nell told Hector: one week.

Lidria shook her head. She couldn't believe her foolishness. So little time had passed, yet she had developed attachments to the people around her. Perhaps after being on her own for so long and after so much death, she had jumped to form any relationship.

Joan and Deeter stood outside Ren's tent. They smiled and waved as Lidria got close. She returned their greeting, a smile of her own cracking her brooding façade. Part of her told her to reel in her emotions, she shouldn't feel anything for these people, but she didn't listen.

"Mornin', Lidria," Deeter said, chipper.

"Morning, Deeter." Lidria nodded and turned toward Joan. "Hello, Joan."

“So, you got us a place to move to?” Joan asked, eyeing Lidria. “Ren told everyone we’re marching to Kal’Den tomorrow.”

“It was Selis, actually.” Lidria shifted under Joan’s dubious gaze. “She came to an agreement with one of Master Janus’ agents. We’re leaving today ahead of the camp.”

Joan locked eyes with Lidria. “You’d better not let anything happen to her, Lidria.”

Indignation flared. “I don’t plan on it.”

“Good,” Joan said.

“It’s going to be a lot quieter without you two around,” Deeter quipped. Joan slapped him in the arm. “What? You know I’m only messing around. Things seemed to be getting heavy there.”

“Don’t worry,” Lidria forced a smirk on her face, “we’ll be out of your hair as soon as I talk to Ren.”

Deeter smiled. “Take care, Lidria.”

Lidria nodded to Deeter and Joan as she flipped the tent flap back and entered. Ren sat in his chair, and, the moment she stepped in, he straightened. He stood and walked around the table, locking eyes with her. Concern played across his face and in his eyes.

“So, you and Selis are leaving today?” Ren’s voice didn’t betray his visible unease.

“Yeah, Bal wanted to get moving.”

Ren shook his head. “I’m losing my two most capable fighters.”

“You have plenty of reliable soldiers here,” Lidria reminded Ren.

“They’re fine soldiers,” Ren turned away, “but none of them can fight magic or Quela effectively.”

“Expecting trouble?” Worry didn’t suit Ren. “It’s not too far to Kal’Den.”

Ren peeked over his shoulder at Lidria. “You never know.”

"I'm sure you'll manage," Lidria said. "Honestly, I'm more worried about what Master Janus wants with Selis. That's likely to prove more dangerous than your trip."

"I can't imagine his intentions are nefarious, but I understand your concern." Ren's words came wooden, but Lidria attempted not to let his distance affect her.

"Selis and I fought one Master already." Lidria shuddered at the thought. "I'd rather not do that again."

"See what I mean about capable?" Ren asked, cracking a smile.

Lidria stared Ren down with disapproval. "Flinn was unhinged. I don't think he was fighting at peak performance."

"Maybe not." Ren faced Lidria. "How'd Hector take the news that you're leaving?"

Lidria smiled. "He wasn't too happy, but Nell assured him he'd see me again soon."

"Oh, his mother's awake? That's great news." Ren's face brightened, and life returned to his eyes.

"Yeah." A weight lifted off Lidria's shoulders. "I was starting to worry."

"I thought her a lost cause until you found her the other day." Ren tore his eyes away from Lidria's and stared at the ground. "I'm glad we didn't lose her, too."

Lidria stepped forward and put her hand on Ren's shoulder. He met her eyes. "You did a fantastic job of rescuing people and keeping everyone together, Ren. I don't know how you did it, but you should be very proud of yourself."

"Thank you, Lidria. I," Ren paused, shaking his head, "don't know what else to say."

"Just take care of everyone." A lopsided smile slid onto Lidria's face, and guilt gnawed at her stomach.

"You make it sound like you'll never be back," Ren said, challenging her to say what she meant.

"You know what I mean." Lidria couldn't bring herself to say she intended on quitting this business.

Ren saluted Lidria. "I will make sure everyone is safe."

"See you in a week." Lidria tossed a salute of her own.

Chapter Sixteen

Selis tossed and turned. She whimpered, curling into a tight little ball. Terror gripped her, and her heart froze. Something weighed heavy upon her chest. Her breath caught in her throat. She attempted to break free, but she no longer controlled her body.

Flinn loomed over Selis, puppeteering her. She tried to wrestle control from him, but he did not care. He carried on, making her do whatever he wished. Anger erupted within her, and emerald fire bloomed around her. She need only will them forward.

Cent stepped between Selis and Flinn. She called for him to move, but he would not listen. The flames consumed him, all her rage draining from her. Nothing remained of Cent, yet Flinn stood unharmed, oblivious. She collapsed, hopeless, and closed her eyes. Cent stared back at her.

Selis bolted upright, gasping for air with a pitiful squeak. Colorful trees, wild grass, and lush shrubberies replaced the black nothingness of her nightmare. Flinn and Cent were nowhere to be seen. She sighed and cupped her hand in her lap. Emerald flames danced on her palm.

With a wave of her hand, Selis extinguished the fire. In the past, she found comfort in it. This time, disgust. She shut her eyes tight and held back the coming tears. Magic stitched together every fiber of her being. How could she reconcile what she had done?

"Oi," a gruff voice called, making Selis jump. "You all right, little miss mage?"

Selis frowned at Bal's flippant appellation. "I am fine. Do not worry."

"It's hard not to worry when you nearly burn the forest down around us." An impish grin spread across Bal's face.

"I am sorry."

Bal shook his head. "Maybe before you go to sleep next time, we'll dose you with some dauein."

Selis' eyes widened in horror, and her body went rigid. The thought of being cut off from the Flow terrified her more than what she had done to Cent and Flinn. "I—"

"Calm down," Bal said with a bark of laughter. "I was merely joking. I know how sensitive you mages can be about losing your magic."

Selis took a deep, calming breath, yet, no matter how hard she tried, she could not shake the dread Bal drudged up. "Where is Lidria?"

"Your…companion is in the woods over that way." Bal gestured with a dismissive wave of his hand to the east. "She hasn't been gone too long."

The rest of the bedroll slipped off Selis before she stood. Debilitating pain shot up her right leg, causing her to stumble. Her wound had not healed yet, and the past day of solid travel did little to accelerate the process.

Selis flexed her tight muscles, ignoring the deep ache accompanying the effort. Her cloak caught the strap of her bag. She yanked the robe free and slung the article around her shoulders with a practiced motion. Familiar calm enveloped her and drove her worries away.

Selis' eyes drifted over to Bal. He flashed an amused grin and shook his head but said nothing. She supposed she acted a fool. Picturing herself in reversed positions brought a halfhearted smile to her face.

Leaves and twigs crunched underfoot as Selis wandered through the sparse wood. Her muscles remained tight as anything, but the pain receded. Progress. She breathed a sigh of relief and took in the sun that broke through the canopy.

Lidria sat on a log fifty yards from their campsite. Her sword lay across her lap, several inches of steel peeking out the scabbard. Selis smiled. Something about Lidria twisted her heart the right way, and she did not wish the phenomenon to stop.

As Selis stepped closer, Lidria's head snapped up. "Oh, Selis." The rigidness in her posture melted, and a pleasant smile curled her lips. "Good morning."

"Good morning, Lidria," Selis said, her smile broadening. "May I join you?"

"Of course you can." Lidria scooted over to make more room.

Selis closed the gap between her and Lidria and sat down beside her. "What are you doing out here? If you do not mind me asking."

"Just thinking about some things," Lidria replied, distant. She slid the blade back into its sheath and set the armament aside.

"Where did you get that sword from?" Selis folded her hands in her lap. "It appears to be important to you."

Lidria regarded Selis, a bittersweet smile on her face. "My father gave it to me ten years ago as a," Lidria clenched her jaw, "wedding gift."

Selis' eyes widened in panic, and her heartbeat surged out of control. "You are married?"

"I was." Lidria's voice came out rough, and her eyes darted around.

"What happened?" Selis fiddled with the excess fabric of her robe.

"Becoming a breaker happened," Lidria spat. She shook her head and sighed. "It would have happened eventually, but my injury sped up the process.

"I was bold and stupid. I thought I could do things I had no right doing. In one of our battles against Crien, I disobeyed orders. The outcome seemed all but determined, and we were told to hold. We knew where the enemy commander was, and I, thinking to further my station, thought we could kill or capture them.

"With the Crien army in retreat, they collapsed on us as soon as we pressed the attack. My squad did the right thing and pulled back, leaving me behind. I sustained a lot of wounds…and lost my arm. I almost died.

"We were going to win the battle anyway. My ego got in the way, and I paid for it. You'd think I would've learned my lesson, but it only made me bitter and withdrawn.

"I was never what you could consider a good wife or mother. I was too preoccupied with my career to give Ian, and especially Evelyn, the time and attention they deserved. After my injuries, I was broken, and my mistreatment of them only got worse.

"Ian finally had enough and left me, taking Evelyn with him. I haven't seen either since, and I know he wouldn't want to see me. Evelyn probably doesn't even remember me." Lidria choked up. "It's for the best."

Selis could not believe Lidria's words. Wrapping her head around them proved difficult enough without trying to imagine their reality. She did not see those qualities. The Lidria beside her, while short with people at times, displayed compassion and bravery.

A thought occurred to Selis: perhaps Lidria put on an elaborate act. Perhaps she treated people with kindness as a form of atonement for her past. Selis shook her head. No. The support and openness Lidria offered her would not exist if she did not care.

Without hesitation, Selis placed her right hand on Lidria's left. Lidria did not react. An idea overtook Selis. She slipped her fingers between Lidria's, drawing her attention. Magic flowed through Selis and trickled out into a weak form around her hand.

Under normal circumstances, the barrier would singe and repel anyone who came into contact. However, because of Lidria's artificial arm and the fact Selis poured so little energy into the incantation, little more than Selis' touch would reach her.

Lidria's expression shifted from wonder to confusion. "Wh-what did you do?"

"Just some magic to let you know I am here." Selis stared up into Lidria's vibrant green eyes.

"Selis, I don't know what to say." Lidria blushed, but her eyes remained locked on Selis'.

Selis' cheeks flared, and her heartbeat quickened. "Tell me about Evelyn."

"It's strange." Lidria's face twisted with conflict. "I wasn't around very much after she was a year old, but I distinctly remember everything about her: her cry, her laugh, the way she called, "Daddy."

"Ian always remarked about how she looked just like me." Lidria let out a little nervous chuckle. "But I never saw it," she let her eyes drop from Selis' and shook her head, "I was so blind."

"I am sorry things transpired the way they did for you, but you seem to have learned from your past mistakes." Selis held Lidria's hand tight.

Lidria hmphed. "I don't feel like I've changed at all."

"Lidria," Selis coaxed, "look at me." Hesitant, Lidria lifted her head. "The Lidria you speak of would not have given Hector or me the time of day. None of us would have met if you were still that version of yourself. You have changed."

"But I didn't do anything special," Lidria argued, her eyes plagued with doubt. "I just happened to be in the right places at the right time."

Selis smiled, and confusion spread across Lidria's conflicted face. "You might not consider what you did exceptional, but I, for one, appreciate what you did; that you are here with me now."

“I-I.” Lidria shied her eyes away from Selis’. After a long moment, Lidria squeezed Selis’ hand. “I’m glad I’m here, too.”

Selis had never felt so drawn to anyone before, and the notion both excited and terrified her. She wanted to express her feelings without holding back, yet she hesitated. Part of her wished she could go back to her drunk self from the other night and kiss Lidria without worry.

Selis scooted closer to Lidria until their shoulders and hips touched. Much to Selis’ surprise and delight, Lidria did not jump or flinch away. Selis expected confusion or hesitation in Lidria’s eyes, but neither appeared. Instead, tranquility shone with a flicker of anticipation.

“Lidria,” Selis swallowed, preventing her beating heart from leaping into her throat, “I—”

Lidria shook her head. “I know. Let’s take things slow, okay?”

“O-okay.”

Lidria untangled her hand from Selis’, and Selis’ breath caught. Even if she understood and respected Lidria’s wishes, she did not want to part with her. No matter how hard she tried, she could not stop the fear of rejection from creeping ever—

Lidria slid her hand back under Selis’, only, this time, she took Selis’ tiny hand in hers, palm-to-palm. A placating smile grew on Lidria’s face. “I need some time.”

“That is understandable.” Selis turned her head to hide her burning cheeks. “I am sorry.”

“It’s all right. You don’t have to worry.” Lidria squeezed Selis’ hand.

The peacefulness Lidria inspired in Selis drove her negative thoughts away. She basked in bliss, thankful to have Lidria by her side. Lidria made Selis feel wanted, confident, safe, and like she belonged. None of her complications would impede her feelings.

Despite the pleasant silence, Selis wanted to know more about Lidria. Selis gazed at Lidria, giving her hand a little squeeze. Her beautiful green eyes drifted up to Selis'. She could not resist Lidria's infectious smile.

"You," Selis croaked, swallowing down her reservations. "You said your father gave you that sword. I take it your parents are not around anymore?"

Lidria frowned, shaking her head. "No. They died in the plague five years ago."

"I am sorry," Selis said, guilty. Being part of the Enclave kept her far from the strife and danger the common folk faced.

"It's okay." Lidria's eyes darted away from Selis. "These things happen, and no one is to blame."

"Were you close with them?"

A wistful smile lit up Lidria's face and curled her lips. "Yeah, I guess you could say that. They taught me a lot, and we always got along. My parents were the only ones who could get anything out of me after I withdrew from everyone else.

"I," Lidria trembled, and her hand clamped down on Selis', "I think my turn hurt them the most. I wish I had the chance to apologize to them. They deserved at least that much before…"

Selis squeezed Lidria's hand twice and let go. Ignoring her confusion, Selis lifted her hand and cradled Lidria's head. She coaxed Lidria down onto her shoulder and leaned their heads together. Lidria melted against Selis, wrapping her arm around her waist.

"I am sure they understood, Lidria," Selis whispered, placing her left hand on Lidria's thigh. "They were your parents."

"You might be right. I just wish I could have." Lidria sniffled and brought her right hand up to wipe away tears.

Selis held Lidria close. "I was born and raised in a small village in the Ars mountains. I left my parents when I was young to pursue magic under the tutelage of the Enclave. Neither of them wanted me to go, but the idea of controlling magic enthralled me.

"I got so caught up in my pursuit of magic that I lost touch with them. By the time I realized what I had done, too many years had passed. They did not recognize me.

"That detached, awkward, stressful encounter ruined any hopes of reconnecting with them, and I dove back into my studies." Selis blinked back tears and gripped Lidria's leg. "I…do not know if they are alive anymore. I hope they are well."

"Selis," Lidria said, lifting her head. Selis' hand slipped and brushed against her cheek. Lidria's eyes lit up. "I understand that feeling. You, however, can still try to fix things. If you're willing."

Selis' mouth worked to form words. The simple thought of meeting her parents again made her want to run and hide. "I do not think that is a wise idea."

"I know it'll be hard," Lidria admitted, hugging Selis tight. "But you don't want to make the same mistake I did and only realize it when it's too late."

"You are right, but things are a little too overwhelming for me. I can't." Selis' cheeks burned with embarrassment, and she tore her eyes off Lidria's.

"Think about it, okay?"

Selis nodded in affirmation. Even after everything Lidria confided in her, she could not continue thinking about trying to re-establish a working relationship with her mother and father. Foolish, yes, but she could not help herself. The idea triggered a fear she forgot, buried.

Shouting erupted from the direction of their camp.

Chapter Seventeen

Lidria skirted the empty campsite. For a moment, she thought to stop and throw her armor on. However, a guttural bellow dashed the thought and urged her on. She didn't care much for Bal or his subordinates, but she couldn't allow Quela to be so close.

Brush burst apart as Lidria ploughed through and into the woods. She shifted and swayed, avoiding any plant life which would slow her down. Another human cry rose above the rushing wind, and she corrected course. With confident, practiced motion, she drew her weapon and broke into a small clearing.

Three Quela, Bal, and his men faced off. One of the men lay behind his two comrades, clutching a bloody hand to his gut. Bal, his subordinate beside him, held their swords up. The beasts themselves bore no weapons nor wore a scrap of armor.

"Ah, Lidria," Bal said, hazarding a glance in her direction. "Help me deal with these beasts, will you?"

Lidria nodded and pressed the Quela from the flank. The Quelan closest to her turned, growling and brandishing gnarled antlers. She ignored the menacing display and slid to attack. She swung in an arc, and the creature recoiled in fear.

Lidria's sword clanged off lowered horns. She hopped backward as her foe advanced for a counterattack, emboldened. A roar deafened her ears. She danced to the side, avoiding the sharp points, and drove forward.

Black blood oozed as Lidria's blade sank into the Quelan's shoulder. It let out a howl of pain, whipping toward her. The motion yanked her along, and she lost her footing. She ripped her blade free and staggered, spinning with her momentum.

Lidria lashed out. Her adversary reeled backward but not far enough. A long line of blood appeared on the creature's stomach, splattering the grass. The beast whimpered and fell back out of range. Something slammed into her side.

The world spun as Lidria flew, tumbling. She landed hard, rolled, and slid to a stop. She grunted with the effort but shot back to her feet. One of the other Quela loomed before her. It stood taller than the other two, but she realized they were all small for Quela.

With a frown, Lidria cast her gaze toward Bal. He held his own against the remaining beast, but both his comrades were down. The uninjured man lay on his stomach. Pain flared up from her ribs, sympathetic. She grit her teeth and focused.

The wounded Quelan circled around to Lidria's right. A quick threatening wave of her sword forced her opponent back, waiting for an opening. She kept her eyes on the brute in front of her, but she never let the other vanish from sight. Magic coiled around her arm as she neared severing a link.

Selis broke through the tree line, skidding to a halt. Emerald flames sprang to life from her raised hands. Her eyes widened, the fire died, and she staggered backward. Confusion flashed through Lidria's mind. Why had Selis stopped?

Growling in frustration, Lidria flicked her weapon upward as the Quelan attacked. Her blade caught the beast's wrist. Dark blood splashed on her, the severed paw crashing into her chest. She flinched, stumbling, before she batted the appendage away.

Lidria pressed forward, taking advantage of her opponent's floundering. Before the beast reacted, she plunged her sword into its chest. The blade sank three inches into soft flesh, struck bone, and bounced to the side.

A jagged gash tore through the Quelan. Teeth gnashed at Lidria, and she pulled away, yanking her sword free. Blood sprayed, and she spun. Her victim dropped behind her with a dull thud. The other creature charged Selis.

"Selis!" Lidria shouted. Her heart leapt into her throat. She severed a link without hesitation and bolted toward Selis.

Selis shook her head and stumbled, falling backward. Lidria urged her legs to carry her faster, and they listened. The gap between them vanished. She would finish this before anything threatened Selis.

"Lidria, stop," Selis called, holding up her hand.

Lidria dug her foot into the ground. Her arms traveled forward, so she tipped backward. The tip of her blade whistled over her target. She came to a halt, the monster looming, motionless, above Selis. Lidria's heart hammered in her chest.

Selis inched back and stood. The creature scrutinized her motions but didn't move or attack her. Lidria remained ready to intervene if needed. She wouldn't let Selis die for…whatever she was doing.

Lidria lurched forward when Selis held her hand out. A curious expression came over Selis' face. She grimaced and clenched her jaw, straining. Lidria trusted Selis, yet she couldn't help but fear for her. Her hand hovered an inch shy of the beast's snout.

Selis' mouth moved, and the Quelan let out a huff of a growl. The beast shifted around, taking half a step back. Lidria advanced, prepared to spring into action should things go south. Another silent incantation crossed Selis' lips.

"If you're not going to kill that thing," Bal hollered, drawing Lidria's attention, "then I will, little mage."

Bal strode forward with purpose, holding his bloody sword out to the side. Lidria glanced back at Selis—she either hadn't heard him or chose to ignore him. Worry and confusion swayed Lidria, but she wouldn't let him ruin Selis' concentration.

Lidria stepped between Bal and Selis. "Give her some time. I don't know what she's doing, but I trust her."

"One of those things took out Dust and Theas." Bal scowled. "From that range, there won't be much left of your little girlfriend if it decides to attack."

"If it does, I'll put it down. Don't you worry. Until then," Lidria stared Bal down, "let Selis do her thing."

Bal lowered his sword and made a dismissive gesture with his off hand. "Don't come crying to me if she gets ripped apart." He spun from Lidria and stalked over toward his downed comrades.

Lidria eased back and turned. Despite knowing full-well what she would see, the sight of Selis so close to the Quelan sent a thrill of terror down her spine. Selis' brow furrowed in distress. Lidria couldn't let this go on any longer.

"Selis." Lidria stepped forward, but Selis didn't respond. "Selis, talk to me."

Selis' eyes snapped open, and her hand lowered. The creature let out a quiet snort and shifted back, shaking its head. She gazed at Lidria, a blank expression on her face. Lidria frowned, which prompted Selis to lower her head. Lidria took an impatient step toward Selis.

"It-it spoke to me." Selis brought her eyes back up to Lidria's. "It called me…kin, I think."

"What do you mean?" Lidria asked. The beast had made no noise she would consider speech.

Selis flinched at the edge in Lidria's voice, but she maintained eye contact. "I…do not know how else to say it. It is not the same as how you and I speak; it is broken, fragmented, foreign."

"I didn't hear anything, Selis." Lidria tried her best not to snap at Selis—her nerves shot. "Nothing I would even call a different language."

Selis stared for a moment, her eyebrow arched, until her eyes widened in recognition. "Oh. It was in my head. I am not sure how, but magic is involved. I can feel it coming off him, however faintly."

"Selis, that—that sounds crazy. Are you sure?"

"Remember when I told you about getting dragged through the shadow-projection and into the Quela's tunnels?" Selis fidgeted with her sleeves, and Lidria nodded. "When I was there, the shaman that took Flinn's tomes spoke to me as well."

"You didn't mention that. I always thought they couldn't communicate with us."

Selis winced. "I am sorry. I thought it only an oddity at the time, and I was shaken after the attack. I did not intend to keep any information from you."

"It's all right," Lidria took a deep breath, ashamed of herself. "I didn't mean to sound upset with you. I just—I'm shocked they can speak at all."

"I understand." Selis stepped closer to Lidria. "You do not need to apologize. I am as surprised as you are."

"So," Lidria began, shifting her eyes to the beast next to her. "Is it a threat?"

Selis shook her head, and her bright eyes gazed up into Lidria's. "I do not think so. I would let him go. He does not seem to belong anywhere. I…can relate."

"Okay." Lidria closed what little of a gap remained between her and Selis and placed a reassuring hand on her shoulder. "I'll trust your judgment, Selis."

"You two are adorable and all," Bal said as he strode toward them, "but I'm not going to let you release that thing. Especially not after it attacked my men."

"I am not going to kill him," Selis proclaimed, brushing past Lidria.

"I'll kill it. I have no issues doing so." Bal pointed his sword toward the Quelan, but Selis interposed herself between the two.

Lidria raised her blade, ready to defend Selis. "Hold on—"

"This is between me and the mage," Bal barked. "Stay out of this."

Selis took a defiant step forward, and Lidria's heart leaped up into her throat. Bal's blade hovered a mere foot from her chest. "I do not wish to fight you, but I do not believe this creature deserves death."

"Fine." Bal lowered his weapon, but his sharpness of tongue didn't diminish. "Bind it with magic so that I can bring it back to Master Janus. No doubt he'll be able to find some use for it."

"No, I will not imprison—" Selis stopped midsentence, lowering her head. "Okay, I will bind him."

Selis stepped back from Bal and turned. She exhaled, and her body trembled. Letting the creature live didn't sound like a wise idea, but Lidria didn't want to argue with Selis. With a sigh, Lidria let Selis do as she wished.

The Quelan stared at Selis, hooved feet scraping the grass. She raised her hand to the creature's chest, and it let out a surprised bellow. Her face twisted in agony as the beast writhed against invisible bonds. It lunged and gnashed its crooked teeth.

"Shhh," Selis cooed, taking a step closer. "It is all right. Please, understand."

Selis' hand touched the Quelan's snout, and it huffed an audible breath. The conflict vanished from her face, replaced with a visible curiosity. Her lips moved, but not a single word escaped. The whole situation made Lidria's skin crawl.

Bal made Flinn's intentions of researching Quela clear, yet even Selis didn't understand what the research entailed. Lidria held no doubts Selis told her the truth. However, no one ever communicated with the Quela before. Why Selis?

Lidria furrowed her brow. Selis explained the rituals she had undergone to enhance her magical capabilities and how one had gone wrong. The accident changed her. Perhaps more than her eyes and hair were affected. Flinn had done something different, something risky, to cause a failure.

Despite her limited knowledge of magic, Lidria knew the creatures had split from the Flow at some point. No mage had cracked the code and figured out how they cast. Perhaps that's what Flinn had researched, trying to figure out the riddle.

The thought that Flinn had used Selis as a test subject in pursuit of such perversions enraged Lidria. She tried to shake the anger from her head, but the emotion lingered. Though Selis had emerged alive, he hadn't the right to expose her to that. He'd gotten off far too easy.

Lidria attempted to focus on the present and the woman before her. Selis still stood close to the Quelan. Her lips no longer moved, but exertion took over her face. Her legs quivered, and Lidria realized how much the effort drained Selis.

"Selis," Lidria called, hoarse. "Selis, you're going to collapse if you keep that up."

A moment passed before Selis lowered her hand. She glanced at Lidria and gave her a frail smile. "I get a little carried away sometimes."

"I know." Lidria flashed a smile, and Selis' grew stronger. "It understands, I take it. As much as it can."

"Yes," Selis blurted out before she frowned. "I think. Communicating is still akin to trying to speak and comprehend a different language. He has settled down for now, at the very least."

Lidria sheathed her sword and stepped closer to Selis. Her eyes never left the pacified beast. "Good. I can't imagine it took too kindly to being bound."

"No," Selis gazed past Lidria, "he was angry. I did not mean to hurt him."

Lidria placed her hand on Selis' arm, which brought her eyes back into focus. "It was either that or have Bal kill it—him. You did the right thing." Lidria gave Selis an affectionate squeeze.

"Thank you, Lidria." Selis' hand twitched upward, and she bit her lip.

"You're welcome, Selis," Lidria said with a smile.

Selis glanced to the side, and she blushed. "I do not know what I would do without you."

"I think you're giving me far too much credit." Selis locked eyes with Lidria and opened her mouth, but Lidria shook her head. "You're more capable than you think."

"So are you."

Lidria's cheeks burned, but she couldn't tear her gaze away from Selis' beautiful eyes. "Selis, I—"

"Just kiss already, and come over here and help me," Bal mocked.

Lidria jumped, pulling away. Selis, however, continued to hold Lidria's eye and raised her hand. Their fingers entwined and squeezed. For a moment, Lidria contemplated giving in and doing as Bal said, but she didn't want to hurt Selis.

The moment passed before Lidria made a feeble attempt at reciprocating. She flashed Selis an apologetic expression, and Selis mouthed, "I understand." Nodding, Lidria turned and headed toward Bal and his downed comrades.

Bal knelt beside the man who had taken a hit to the gut. Deep crimson stained his clothing, and he clutched at his wound. To Lidria's left, Bal's other subordinate seemed to fare better. He sat in the grass, dazed and battered but intact.

"Take Dust's legs," Bal ordered as he inched around behind the other man, taking hold of him under his arms. "We'll get him back to camp and then go from there."

Lidria closed the gap, bent forward, and grabbed Dust. Together, they hoisted him off the ground. Dust groaned, and a twinge of remorse sparked in her. If she had arrived sooner, he might be better off. She shook her head; she would do what she could.

Chapter Eighteen

Selis lagged behind the group. Her lifestyle of studying had not prepared her for continued physical exertion, and healing Bal's comrade, Dust, a day prior did not help. Lidria offered to carry her pack, but Selis refused. No point putting unnecessary strain on Lidria for her weakness.

In front, the Quelan shuffled along. He had remained calm since Selis bound him. To her disappointment, he had not tried to communicate with her again. Her curiosity overwhelmed her, and she wished to connect with him. The possibilities swirled in her head.

Selis frowned, realizing she had drifted further behind. Lidria glanced over her shoulder, and Selis waved her concern away. As much as she appreciated Lidria's care for her, she did not want her to worry over nothing. She would not be a burden.

The sound of running water perked Selis' ears. Despite having only been a couple days since her last proper bath, she felt appalling. The overwhelming discomfort, blended with her overall fatigue, made her yearn to stop, rest, and wash.

"Bal," Lidria said, breaking the silence. A minute passed before the man turned his head. "I think it's a good time for a bit of a break."

Bal appeared to ignore Lidria's remark, but his men showed visible signs of exhaustion themselves. He sighed. "All right. We'll rest here for a while."

Lidria nodded and turned to face Selis. The gap between them closed, and a relieved smile slipped onto Selis' face. Lidria smiled back and straightened her shoulders. Selis' heart fluttered. Lidria stood tall, confident, and striking—Selis' absolute opposite.

“I figured now would be a good time to wash up,” Lidria offered, gesturing to the sounds of the river. “I don’t know how much longer we’ll be nearby, and you look like you could use some rest, too.”

Selis shifted around. “I do feel a bit drained, but I did not want to impede our progress.”

“Don’t worry about Bal. He’ll get over it.” Lidria grinned when Selis gazed up at her, grateful. “His men looked appreciative of my intervention as well.”

Selis pivoted to head toward the river. Before she took a single step, Lidria placed a hand on her shoulder. Selis jumped at the gentle touch, suppressing a yelp. She glanced, sheepish, over at Lidria to find an amused yet sweet grin curling her lips.

When Lidria removed her hand, emptiness did not fill Selis. Instead, warmth did. A smile lingered at the corners of her mouth. She pressed on through the slight brush, Lidria following close behind.

The brook drifted to the west, curving into the distance. Selis drew a long, relaxing breath, taking in the delightful scent of fresh water. She threw her pack aside and went about removing her robe. Only when the garment hit the ground did she remember Lidria beside her.

Lidria shied away from Selis’ eyes. “You can go first. I’ll wait.” She turned and strode toward a squat tree before Selis replied.

Once Lidria sat, Selis continued to undress. She stripped away her sweaty clothes at a steady pace, ignoring her desire to be rid of them. Her cheeks burned, though no one watched her. Maybe the simple fact Lidria need only peek…

Selis glanced over her shoulder, and Lidria’s leg stuck out from behind the tree. Selis’ heart beat faster as her mind wandered. She shook tantalizing thoughts from her head and instead focused on the shimmering water and getting clean.

Tossing the rest of her dirty clothes aside, Selis waded into the cool water. A shiver ran up her spine. The tranquil, wonderful water rose to her neck. She closed her eyes, took a deep breath and submerged herself.

The world around Selis dissolved. Her dampened senses and the gentle pressure in her ears soothed her. She drifted, surrounded by nothingness. The floating void calmed her, and, for a moment, she forgot everything else.

Selis obeyed her body's bothersome need for oxygen and popped out of the water. Water ran down her face, and long hair stuck to her skin. She parted her hair and opened her eyes. The sparkling water forced her to squint, but she did not mind. Optimism blossomed in her chest.

"I've been meaning to ask you," Lidria called from the shore, interrupting Selis' reverie. "Why didn't you attack those Quela?"

Selis froze. She had hoped Lidria had not witness her hesitation, but she knew better. For a second, Selis thought about going back under. However, she did not want to ignore Lidria; she deserved better.

"I was going to," Selis asserted. "But I could not bring myself to do it."

Lidria remained silent, and Selis turned in her direction. "It's because of what happened with Flinn and Cent, isn't it?"

Selis shrunk in the water, hugging herself, arms across her chest. "Yes."

"Selis."

"It is all right, Lidria." Selis did not think she would ever recover, but she needed to try to press on. "I will be fine."

Lidria shifted until her shoulder popped out around the tree. "Don't be afraid to talk to me if you need to. I'm here for you."

"I know you are," Selis said as she let the tension in her body drift away with the current and uncrossed her arms. "Thank you."

"You're welcome," Lidria murmured after a longer-than-average pause.

Selis finished the rest of her impromptu wash in silence. A yawn escaped despite her halfhearted attempt to suppress the outburst. She smiled, content, and drifted a moment longer. The shore called to her, and she left the calming caress of the river.

Quickening her pace, Selis padded over to her travel bag. She rooted around inside until she found the object of her search: a full-body towel. She dried her ample hair the best she could. A quick once-over and she deemed her job satisfactory.

Selis tossed the used item on top of her dirty outfit and rifled through her pack for a clean set. Her spare clothes were ill-fitted and worn, but she did not have a choice. She scooped up her emerald-colored robes, wrapping the comforting article tight about her shoulders.

"It is your turn," Selis announced. Lidria did not respond or move. "Lidria?"

Lidria sat fast asleep, head back against the tree trunk. Selis smiled. Lidria appeared so peaceful. Selis did not want to interrupt her—she required the rest. Tearing her eyes off Lidria, Selis decided to satisfy her curiosity in the meantime.

Selis left Lidria; she would return. She strolled back to the path and the Quelan. He lifted his head but made no further reactions. Bal turned his head her way, raising an eyebrow. His men neither said nor did anything as they sat and rested.

"Almost ready to leave?"

Selis shook her head, and wet hair tumbled into her face. She swept her hair to the side with the back of her hand. "No, not yet. Lidria is resting, so I wanted to look into something."

Bal gave her a long, hard stare "That wouldn't have anything to do with our beastly friend, now would it?"

"It does," Selis admitted, stepping closer. "I assure you I will not release him if you do not wish me to, but I want to look into something."

"Go ahead." Bal took a quick swig from his waterskin.

Selis approached the Quelan, trying her best not to startle him. He gawked at her with his beady amber eyes and grunted. She gestured for him to follow her. Nothing. This time, she attempted to bridge their divide with magic.

The creature cocked his head and stared back. She urged him on again, pouring her will into the Flow. He snorted and took a step forward. Breathing a sigh of relief, she thanked him and led him closer to Lidria.

A thought occurred to Selis: she did not know what she hoped to accomplish. Curiosity about the Quela—and this new development—drove her actions, but what did she expect to gain? Knowledge? Understanding? Control? Something more had to exist.

Selis did, however, make the right decision. She did not wish to cause any more destruction or take any more lives. She would defend herself if need be, but she would hold back. So much power flowed within her; she only thought it right she exercise restraint.

Shaking the bleak thoughts from her head, Selis focused on her surroundings. Lidria slept propped against the tree, and Selis smiled. Although she possessed the will to follow-through on her convictions, she took comfort in Lidria's encouragement.

Selis tore her eyes off Lidria and spun to face the Quelan. He stared through her, attentive to nothing. She did not need to do this. She could free him and spare him whatever fate Master Janus fancied, but an opportunity like this would never come back around.

Inquisitive, Selis lifted her hand. The Quelan's eyes met hers, and she flinched. No anger, hatred, or bestial aggression of any kind shone in his eyes. No emotion did. She scolded herself for her foolishness, composed herself, and resumed what she had started.

Selis opened herself up and reached out with the Flow. A shiver ran down her spine, and, for a moment, she thought to stop. Instead, she pressed on and attempted to communicate. Silence. She closed her eyes and proceeded to forge a mental link like on their first meeting.

What is your name? Selis posed to the void.

Nothing—not the tiniest flicker of activity or the quietest inkling of sound.

Selis concentrated harder and pushed out. *I mean you no harm. I just want to learn how this is possible.*

Remove... the Quelan whispered in his grating, guttural voice. *Magic*...

I wish I could, but I cannot. My companions will kill you if you are freed. Shame burned Selis, but she needed to maintain peace.

Fear sparked in Selis' gut. *Gor'an. No Kill.*

Gor'an, Selis enunciated, *you are safe with me. I will find a way to free you so that you can go back to your people.*

No back! Gor'an bellowed, and Selis reeled from his panic, straining their frail connection.

Selis took a deep breath and pushed the invading fear and unease out of her mind. *Why do you not want to go back?*

Small. Kill. Gor'an shrunk away until Selis sensed little but a fleeting fragment of his diminishing being.

Selis frowned. An image of the Quelan tunnels from the shadow-projection popped up. She remembered several runty Quela huddled together. Gor'an and his fellow Quela stood small in stature. She would be in a similar position had she been born Quelan.

I think I understand, Selis offered, an unexpected kinship formed between her and Gor'an. Kinship. *Why did you call me 'kin' last time?*

Silence.

Selis waited, patient; communication proved difficult. That did not mean; however, she would not wonder. Her mind raced with possibilities, but she always came back to Flinn's failed invocation. The process changed her and not the way he had intended.

Scent, Gor'an uttered, his being reaching out to Selis. *Same kin. Not kin.*

Scent? Selis repeated. *Is that why this is possible*? *I can somehow tap into your people's magic*?

A rush of affirmation filled Selis, and so many things made sense. The Quelan-based invocation, her changed appearance, Flinn's secret research, why she had been able to travel through their magic and Master Janus' interest in Flinn and, by proxy, her.

"Selis?" Lidria's distant voice reached deep in her thoughts. For a moment, Selis thought she imagined the sound until Lidria's call repeated, closer.

Selis opened her eyes. Lidria stood beside her, hand on her shoulder. Selis shook her head, trying, and failing, to shake the flood of exhaustion away. Gor'an let out a soft grunt and shifted back. Her legs gave out on her, and she collapsed against Lidria.

"Selis, are you all right?" Lidria held her tight.

Selis tried to support her weight, but her muscles refused to listen. "Yes. I am just tired. Communicating with Gor'an is much more taxing than I suspected."

"Gor'an?" The heat from Lidria's gaze burned the top of Selis' head. "Is that the Quelan's name?"

"It is," Selis affirmed and took a steadying breath. She tilted her head up to Lidria's anxious face. "I think I figured something out, too. I can access their magic."

Lidria blinked several times in quick succession and cocked her head to the side. "I didn't think anyone understood Quelan magic."

"I would not say I understand it, but I can use it to speak with him."

"How did you figure out how to do that?" Lidria asked, her eyes expressing the doubt and inevitable curiosity her steady voice did not betray.

Selis pushed off Lidria and stood on her own. To Selis' delight, Lidria did not remove her arm from around her. "I am not sure. It simply happened."

"Selis," Lidria turned to face her better, "do you think Flinn did something to you in his pursuit of researching the Quela? I remember when we met; you told me about a ritual that went wrong."

"That is what everything is pointing to, yes. I suppose one good thing came of his madness." Selis fished her hair over her shoulder and toyed with the damp strands.

Lidria withdrew, stepped in front of Selis, and touched her arms. Staring down into Selis' eyes, Lidria squeezed. "Selis, you didn't deserve what he did to you, but you can't let it get to you. You are so much more than what he thought of you."

"Lidria," Selis stammered, unable to run away despite her brain screaming at her to do so. "I know. I am trying not to let him control me even now, but I still have nightmares and sometimes cannot help it."

“I’ve had my fair share of nightmares,” Lidria whispered, glancing away. “I didn’t have anyone to talk to about them.” She brought her gaze back to Selis. “I want you to know you do.”

Selis stared up into Lidria’s vibrant eyes, determined. “I am thankful I have you to speak with, but I do not want to dwell on it too much. I should focus on what comes next.”

“Okay.” Lidria returned her hands to their place at her side. “I know you want Gor’an to be free. Here’s your chance.”

“Bal will no doubt hunt him down if I did,” Selis said, trying to prevent her inner turmoil from slipping into her words. “He made it clear he wants Gor’an dead or captive, and I do not want to start any trouble since we are going to be Master Janus’ guests soon.”

“Do you think Master Janus knows about Flinn, the Quela, and…you?” Lidria’s eyes flicked over to Gor’an.

“I do not know.” Selis furrowed her brow. “I also do not know how much I wish to tell him, but I will figure that out once we meet with him.”

“Sounds like a plan,” Lidria said with a smile. “I’ll be with you every step of the way, so don’t be afraid to lean on me if you have to.”

Selis threw her arms around Lidria and hugged her. “Thank you, Lidria.”

Lidria did not hesitate to pull Selis against her. “Anytime, Selis.”

Lidria sheltered Selis, and the vibrations of her voice soothed her further. Selis hugged Lidria tighter, not wishing to part with the woman who brought her so much joy. However, Selis would respect Lidria’s wishes and be patient. She eased back.

“We should get back to Bal before he comes to find us, huh?” Lidria asked, grinning.

“Probably.” Selis’ body did not want to move, but they must press on. “I hope your rest was enough.”

Nervous laughter escaped Lidria, and her cheeks turned a cute rose-color. “I didn’t realize how tired I was. It was nice, but it was missing some—never mind. Let’s go.”

Chapter Nineteen

Kal'Den appeared, and Lidria tensed up. She didn't need to worry, yet her conversation with Selis about her and Gor'an had fried her nerves. Lidria didn't think the connection bad, and neither did Selis, but complications had often arisen of late.

Lidria reasoned Master Janus knew more about Selis, Flinn, and the Quela than Bal let on, but she would trust him until he proved he didn't deserve it. He opposed Flinn—even if for petty reasons. The fact he now opened his home to the survivors of Odwyn swayed her regardless.

Lidria snapped out of her brooding as Selis came up beside her. Relief played in Selis' eyes, yet exhaustion crept in around the edges. Lidria wanted to take Selis' hand in hers; however, her arm remained pinned to her side. Her emotions should be kept in check.

Instead of listening to her heart, Lidria listened to her head. She couldn't fall for Selis; it wouldn't be fair to her. Lidria deserved no one's affections and would drive her away. Hurting Selis didn't top the list of things Lidria desired to do.

Selis beamed at Lidria, oblivious of her internal struggle. Despite herself, she smiled back. She needed to pull away but following through proved difficult. Selis twisted and melted Lidria's heart. She cursed under her breath and focused on Kal'Den.

The walls around the town were an odd sort. Stone made up the foundation, leveling off at chest height. Wooden stairs and platforms rose and connected to the rising palisade. Thick, angled beams every six feet reinforced the wood wall.

Lidria frowned. The defenses seemed more a half-finished, slapped together mess than a substantial fortification. They would keep out wild animals and roaming bandits, but an armed force would break through without issue. Then again, a master of the Enclave lived here.

"Ladies," Bal said as they approached the entrance, spinning around, walking backward and extending his arms, "welcome to Master Janus' home: Kal'Den."

Lidria raised a disparaging eyebrow at Bal's theatrics, but he grinned before he swung back around and continued beyond the wall. Selis touched Lidria's arm, drawing her gaze. The corners of Selis' lips twitched, and she gestured forward with her head.

Inside, the dirt road turned to cobblestone. The road cut through the center of town, splitting the mass of buildings into defined sections. To Lidria's left appeared to be the town's market. The denizens were shutting down for the evening, and several of them stopped to stare at the newcomers.

Beyond, squat, wooden homes lined the visible edge of the street. They varied from home to home, but they all shared something in common: their craftsmanship appeared leagues above the rough walls. Polished metal accents by the doors, windows, and roofs shone brilliant in the fading sunlight.

The extravagance baffled Lidria until her eyes traveled down the main thoroughfare. Master Janus' manor stood higher than one story—the sole building in Kal'Den to do so. The dark maroon-painted roof bore the same gold lining as the homes, breaking the shingles into square patterns.

A balcony extended out from the second floor of the side facing town—painted a lighter shade of maroon than the shingles above with a matching polished railing. Four large windows, two to a floor, broke up the otherwise flat face of the building. The double doors at the front stood tall and intimidating.

Lidria, realizing she had stopped to gawk at her surroundings, shook her head and picked up her pace. The gap between her and Bal shrank, and Selis stepped closer to her. Lidria ignored the disparaging voice in her head and took Selis' hand in hers.

Selis went rigid before the tension drained from her body. She squeezed Lidria's hand. Appreciation warmed Selis' face, and Lidria realized she was making the right decision. Standing by Selis proved the only decision in the past six years she held zero doubts about.

The entrance to Master Janus' manor came up quick. Two armed men stood on duty. To Lidria, they appeared no more than glorified doormen, but Bal greeted them by name. They welcomed him and his two subordinates home and opened the gate. Not a word about the Quelan came up.

An extravagant garden grew to the left between the fence and the building proper. Waist-high shrubs lined the perimeter and some of the flower plots. Lidria didn't recognize many of the different lush plants and colorful flowers, but she never did pay much attention to the flora.

Beside Lidria, Selis stared at the garden, a wistful smile on her face. Lidria hoped Selis would be able to find something to take her mind off things soon. Maybe after her meeting with Master Janus, she could find a place to relax and avoid further trauma.

Lidria fought back the impulse to frown. Hector and Selis had done a wonderful job breaking down her guard, and she didn't understand how to deal with such vulnerability. She felt her weakest but also relieved and accepted—an odd yet pleasant conundrum. She supposed she would acclimate in time.

Bal approached the manor, and Lidria let her hand drop from Selis'. Selis tilted her head and opened her mouth to say something but nodded instead. The corners of Lidria's lips twitched. Before either acted further, the knocker clacked.

One-half of the doors swung open. A lanky man, years older than Lidria, slid into the doorway and eyed them. "Welcome back, sir Bal," the steward said, clasping his hands behind his back. "I see you have brought guests."

Bal let out a *humph* before he glanced over at Selis. "I have, Thelin." Bal extended his hand. "This is Selis, former apprentice to the late Master Flinn. And," he motioned to Lidria, "her friend Lidria. I brought them here to speak with Master Janus."

Thelin's deep brown eyes shifted between them, his gaze lingering on Lidria's tattooed arm. "It is a pleasure to meet you, ladies." He performed a shallow bow.

"Greetings, Thelin," Selis expressed as she returned his polite gesture.

Lidria remained silent and offered a single nod in greeting. Awkwardness rested on her shoulders, but she figured Selis, a master's apprentice, dealt with situations like this often. Lidria reminded herself she had come for Selis' sake. She didn't need to open up to these people.

"Thelin, would you show them to the guest rooms? I have to deliver this"—Bal shot a glance at Selis—"creature to Lein and see the Master."

"Very well." Thelin bowed, unclasped his hands and gestured for Lidria and Selis to follow him. "Ladies, this way."

Lidria stepped inside the manor, her boot heel thudding on the polished cherry wood floor. The faint aroma of cinnamon filled her nose. Candles on waist-high golden stands flanked the entryway. The grand staircase diverged left and right at the top, the same candles continuing along in small alcoves.

Thelin paused at the base of the stairs, but Lidria ignored him. She continued to survey her surroundings. Several wooden doors—shut tight—lined the room on either side. The rest of Kal'Den seemed so open that all the closed doors teased out her anxieties.

Lidria came up behind Selis. The smaller woman glanced around, curiosity in her eye. When she turned her head toward Lidria, she jumped. Lidria smiled and pushed Selis forward. Thelin waited, patient, unperturbed by his guests' dawdling.

Selis blushed and turned from Lidria, approaching Thelin. He nodded, pivoted, and ascended the stairway. Lidria and Selis followed him up and to the left into a decorated hallway. Paintings in polished wood frames adorned the walls above more candles, small plants, and tables displaying statuettes.

Rows of doors lined the hall, most of which were closed. Several hung wide; Master Janus' means allowed him to host many guests in his manor alone. The fact surprised Lidria. Masters of the Enclave held incredible wealth, but this exceeded all expectations.

Lidria's curious thoughts came to an abrupt halt as Thelin stopped between two doors. "These will be your rooms, ladies. You arrived at the perfect time. The kitchen staff is about to serve dinner, and I'm sure you're starving from your travel."

Lidria's and Selis' stomachs growled in near-unison at the mention of food. "Make yourselves at home, and I'll have someone bring dinner up."

"Thank you, Thelin," Selis offered. "That sounds wonderful."

"You are welcome, miss Selis. I will inform Master Janus of your arrival. No doubt he will want to speak with you tomorrow. Have a good evening, ladies." Thelin bent forward with his arm across his chest, pivoted, and left.

What little energy remained drained from Lidria's body, and any reservations she held vanished. As much as her stomach grumbled, she didn't want to stay awake long enough to wait for dinner. The thought of sleeping in an actual bed again made her eager for sleep.

"I guess this is goodnight," Lidria said with much less conviction than she anticipated.

Selis' distressed expression betrayed her dismay. "Lidria, I do not want"—she shied away—"never mind. I am tired, too."

Guilt twisted a knot in Lidria's stomach. "Selis, everything will be okay. I'm right here if you need me."

"You are right," Selis whispered, shaky. "I do not mean to be so—"

"You're fine." Lidria rested her hand on Selis' arm and smiled. "I'll see you in the morning."

A weak smile brightened Selis' face, and she nodded. "Goodnight, Lidria."

Lidria pulled back, but her hand slid down to Selis'. A frail smile grew on Selis' face, and Lidria's cheeks flushed. She didn't comprehend why; embarrassment didn't suit her, yet she couldn't shake the sentiment. Time, she hoped, would set her straight.

Tearing away, Lidria turned to her room. Her hand fiddled with the doorknob. The thought to invite Selis inside flitted through her mind; she would enjoy the other woman's company. Regardless of her fondness for Selis, she needed sleep.

The door closed behind Lidria. A cherry-wood table with two seats sat to her right. Paintings, bookshelves, matching wood dressers, and lit candle fixtures lined the walls to either side. She ignored the excess and focused on one thing.

The tall, plush bed called to Lidria. Little more than a week had passed since she slept in an actual bed, but the luxury became a distant memory. She removed her sword, setting the armament aside. As soon as she reached the foot of the bed, she kicked off her boots.

Without spending more precious time on inconsequential things, Lidria closed her eyes and flopped down, face-first. She sighed as she sank into the bedding. Her entire body ached, and her spine decompressed. Blissful sleep couldn't come soon enough.

Lidria remained awake. She frowned and pulled herself closer to the center. Considering her exhaustion, she couldn't believe her body's resistance. Troublesome thoughts wormed their way into her mind, and she groaned. Why now? Why couldn't she—

A soft rap came at the door. For a moment, Lidria considered ignoring the disturbance. She didn't need food if she fell asleep. Her stomach growled, and she huffed. Perhaps her body would be more inclined to sleep after eating.

Lidria hauled herself up until she sat at the foot of the bed. "Come in," she called, trying to summon the will to stand.

The door creaked open, and Selis—dressed down in a loose tunic and trousers—entered the room, carrying two silver food trays. Lidria stared at Selis, surprised. She took half a step back toward the door. Lidria's surprise turned into reserved delight.

"W-would you like to eat together?" Selis asked from the doorway.

Lidria smiled—she couldn't say no to Selis—and stood. "That would be wonderful, Selis." She strode across the room as Selis closed the door and took the platters from her.

Selis gazed up into Lidria's eyes. "I did not want to interrupt your rest, but I thought food would do us both some good. And I…did not want to be alone."

"I know." The fear in Selis' eyes made Lidria elaborate. "Don't worry; I couldn't sleep. And you're right—food and company would be great."

Lidria padded over to the table and set the trays down, pushing two long-stemmed glasses aside. Selis followed. They both sat, and Lidria pulled the lid off her platter. A meal of sliced ham, roasted potatoes, and sautéed vegetables greeted her.

Before Lidria could say anything, Selis produced a bottle of wine. Lidria frowned, remembering the night Joan got Selis drunk. "I thought you weren't going to drink again."

Selis' cheeks turned a rosy hue. "I…need to relax a little." A lop-sided smile slid onto her face. "Besides, you are not Joan."

"No," Lidria agreed, unable to suppress a soft chuckle. "I guess you're safe."

Selis uncorked the bottle and poured two glasses. Lidria took hers, raising it. Selis lifted her glass, and they tapped them together with a sharp *ting*. They sipped their wine and smiled. Lidria relished being able to share a dinner like this with Selis.

Lidria dug into her food to quiet her rumbling stomach. The juicy, semisweet ham filled her with warmth. She grinned; she hadn't tasted anything so delicious in so long. The meal didn't disappoint, and she soon cleared half her plate.

Lidria slowed her pace, wishing to savor the food. She reached for her wineglass and caught Selis' eye. Selis smiled at Lidria as she finished a bite of ham.

"This is nice," Lidria murmured, settling back and taking a sip of wine.

"I am glad to have this opportunity with you." Selis blushed, but Lidria saw joy in her eyes. "It gives us a chance to speak about some lighter subjects."

Lidria took another quick sup of her wine and tried to still her hammering heart. "What would you like to talk about, then?"

"I know things have been rough for you for a while," Selis raised her glass to her lips and took a hasty sip, "but what do you enjoy doing in your spare time?"

"I," Lidria stammered, working out how to answer Selis, "I haven't really done much outside of military work these past few years—not that I ever did much else before, but"—she smiled—"I did play cards with some of my fellow soldiers."

"What did you play?" Selis asked. "I am not too familiar with card games."

Lidria sat forward. A rush of nostalgic excitement took her. "There were a few games that went around. Sometimes we'd stick with one for a night; sometimes, we would switch off. It was…a lot of fun and a good way to relieve some tension."

Lidria glanced around the room, and the smile drained from her face. "I wish there were a set here; I'd love to teach you a game or two."

When Lidria's eyes returned to Selis, an adoring gaze met her. "What?"

"This is the first time I have seen you excited about something." A broad, beautiful smile spread across Selis' face. "It is cute."

Lidria's breath caught in her throat, and she froze. "I…don't know what to say."

Selis placed her hand on top of Lidria's. "You do not have to say a word."

Lidria bit her bottom lip, trying to suppress the burning sensation in her cheeks. "I, uh, what do you enjoy doing?"

"I am quite boring," Selis admitted while squeezing Lidria's hand. "If I have a tome to read, I am happy. Even more so if I have some tea."

"I don't think you're boring."

Selis retracted her hand, and her eyes flicked down to her lap. "What do you think of me, then?"

"You're a lovely, captivating woman that I'm glad I met." Lidria stared at her plate of half-eaten food and hooked a loose strand of hair behind her ear. "F-forget I said that."

"I am afraid I cannot, Lidria." Lidria lifted her gaze and stared into Selis' mesmerizing eyes. "That is the sweetest thing anyone has ever said to me."

"I suppose I can live with that," Lidria relented, a lop-sided smile tugging at the corner of her mouth.

Selis giggled. "Good. Because I will not forget it."

Lidria and Selis continued to eat in silence. Selis took a long draught of her wine, her eyes half-lidded, as she glanced across the table. Lidria jumped as Selis' leg touched hers. Selis smiled and sank into her seat. Lidria finished the rest of her meal before acknowledging Selis.

"Selis?"

Selis didn't respond. Her eyes remained closed, and her chest rose and fell in slow, steady breaths. An amused smile spread across Lidria's face. She sat back and yawned. Her eyelids weighed heavy—no wonder Selis passed out.

Struggling, Lidria escaped her chair and rounded the small table. She reached down and slipped her arms beneath Selis' legs and behind her back. With a muffled grunt of exertion, Lidria hoisted Selis up. Selis made a soft groaning noise but remained asleep.

Lidria swayed as she carried Selis. The wine and her exhaustion rendered the short trip arduous, but she managed. As she approached the bed, she leaned forward and set Selis down. Lidria gave into her protesting body and laid down beside Selis.

Lidria closed her weary eyes, ready for sleep, but a gnawing grew inside her. She whined and struggled until she gave in, scooting backward and pressing up against Selis' back. The void vanished and warmth surrounded her.

Chapter Twenty

Selis tugged at the hem of her sleeves as she waited outside of Lidria's room. Her mind wandered, returning to earlier that morning. They were both surprised when she woke up in Lidria's arms. However, she could not think of a way the morning could have been improved.

Excitement and embarrassment accelerated Selis' heartbeat until it pounded in her chest. She shook her head, dismissing enticing thoughts. She attempted to focus on something, anything, else. The hall remained empty, save for herself and the lavish decorations.

A door thirty feet down the hall opened, and an older woman in a tailored dark brown coat stepped out. Selis flinched away from the cold glare of her hazel eyes, self-conscious. The woman flicked her long, graying hair over her shoulder and approached Selis.

The door beside Selis creaked open, and Lidria emerged. She wore a light gray tunic with the left sleeve pinned up. The woman's gaze snapped to Lidria's exposed arm, and she *hmphed.* She continued past them without a word and rounded the corner.

Thelin appeared, hands clasped behind his back. "Ah, good. You seem to be ready. I hope breakfast was to your liking."

Selis nodded. "Yes." She frowned and glanced to her right. "I do not mean to pry, but who was that woman?"

Thelin's stoic face cracked into what Selis presumed to be the closest thing to a frown the man would allow. "That is Lady Shanna. She's a prominent merchant from Theovan."

"No wonder he spared no expense on his home," Lidria spat, staring at Thelin. "He's hosting criminals."

"The master has always been pragmatic." Thelin unclasped his hands, but he showed no other form of agitation. "He does not let borders or unnecessary ideals prevent him from business."

Lidria made a confused face, and her left hand twitched. "I see. That makes his generous offer all the more baffling."

"You may see it that way," Thelin admitted, "but I assure you that he cares for his countrymen. He built Kal'Den into a living town instead of simply some isolated home for that reason. He provided for people who believed in him or those that were merely lost."

"Still, I—"

"Lidria," Selis interjected, placing her hand on her arm. "He opened his home to us—let us trust his intentions."

Lidria nodded. "Okay." She focused her attention back on Thelin. "I'm sorry, Thelin."

Shaking his head, Thelin let a small smile shine through. "No need to apologize, miss. I'm aware of how some things may appear to others, and I have no problem explaining Master Janus' side to clear up any issues."

"I suppose Master Janus is waiting for us," Lidria proposed. "Shall we?"

"Very good." Thelin folded his hands behind his back, pivoted and strode down the hallway.

Thelin led Selis and Lidria to the grand staircase. Selis hesitated when a young girl danced onto the landing. The girl's long, golden-blonde hair flared out as she twirled. She froze; her green eyes locked on Selis. The girl blinked once and retreated down the stairs.

A surprised noise came from beside Selis. She turned, finding Lidria mid-stride, right hand extended. Selis' eyes followed Lidria's outstretched arm; she reached after the little girl. Distress clouded her face, and she pulled back, turned away, and lowered her head.

Selis cocked her head to the side. "Is everything all right, Lidria?"

"Yeah, I just thought"—Lidria shook her head—"Never mind. It's not important."

"Please tell me later." Selis placed a hand on the small of Lidria's back and pushed.

Lidria stumbled forward a step before she met Selis' gaze. "Okay."

Selis followed Lidria and Thelin down to the landing and up the other side. A sheepish glance down the stairs and Lidria's posture changed. Her straight back and shoulders slumped. Selis frowned. She would make Lidria open up after their meeting.

Thelin stopped in front of a door halfway down the hall and, upon knocking, spoke: "Master Janus, Miss Selis and her companion are here to speak with you."

Footsteps creaked across the wooden floor, coming closer. The knob turned, and the door swung into the room. Master Janus appeared in the doorway. He stood a full head taller than Selis—although, not much of an achievement. She frowned as her memory returned.

Master Janus' black hair faded and covered his ears, streaks of gray running throughout. His cheeks plumped, and his gut strained against an embroidered blue vest. Despite his other changes, his ice-blue eyes remained crystal-clear, and Selis wilted under his discerning gaze.

"Welcome, ladies," Janus said. He stepped to the side and swept his arm in an arc. "Come in, come in."

Selis entered Janus' study. Tall bookshelves lined the walls. Crooked and worn spines stuck out in a miss-matched patchwork of organization, loose parchment poking out between volumes. The disregard toward so many tomes made Selis' head spin.

A massive mahogany desk encroached on the glass doors leading to a balcony. Upon the desktop sat countless unorganized tomes as well as sheets of paper, writing quills, and other indiscernible items. For how well Kal'Den seemed organized, Janus himself kept a mess.

Janus thanked Thelin before he closed the door. "Please, take a seat." He gestured to two chairs as he strolled toward the fireplace. "Would either of you like some tea?"

"Yes, please," Selis blurted out. Her cheeks flared as Janus gave her an amused smile, and she sat down.

Lidria stared at nothing as she took her seat. "No."

Janus hung a silver kettle over the fire. He stepped back and spun around. "I hope you have found Kal'Den accommodating."

"It's quite nice to have a roof over our heads again," Lidria said, crossing her legs. "It's a miracle there's enough room for all the refugees coming on such short notice."

Janus strolled over and rested his hip against his desk. "We're countrymen. It's a tragedy what happened to Odwyn, but I'm glad some survived and to be of service to you."

Lidria's harsh gaze softened. "I'm sorry for my hostility. I've been anxious after everything that's happened." She shifted in her chair. "On behalf of everyone from Odwyn, thank you."

"You don't need to thank me," Janus replied with a dismissive wave of his hand. "I have the resources, so it's no imposition to me."

"I—"

A sharp whistle pierced the room, reverberating in the bookshelves' deep recesses. Janus flashed a smile, turned, and headed to the fireplace. He lifted the kettle and set the vessel on a serving table with several porcelain teacups. After pouring two cups of boiling water, he produced a teabag for each.

"Would you like some honey?" Janus asked, his piercing eyes fixed on Selis.

Selis nodded. “Yes, that would be lovely. Just a bit, though.”

Janus spooned a small portion of honey into Selis’ teacup and a larger one into his own. He dipped the teabags, added a stirring spoon, and ushered Selis’ tea over to her. She took the cup, warmth sinking into her fingers and spreading up her arms.

“I hope it is to your liking.” Janus stirred his own beverage with a light touch.

Selis brought the teacup up and inhaled the tea’s fragrant aroma. She preferred tea strong, and the honey added a pleasant warm sweetness. “It smells wonderful. Thank you.”

Janus smiled, sitting behind his massive desk. “You’re welcome.”

“If only I had something to read,” Selis muttered as she stirred her tea. Her eyes widened when she realized she spoke aloud. “I am sorry. It just came out.” She took a long sip to hide her embarrassment. Strong, warm, and a hint sweet.

“Not a problem,” Janus said. “You may borrow any books in my library downstairs. Once we’re done here, I’ll have Thelin show it to you.”

The joyous thought of having an entire library at her disposal overshadowed Selis’ fleeting doubts. “That is generous of you. Thank you.”

“I cannot deny such enthusiasm for knowledge.” Janus blew over his tea before he brought the cup to his lips, taking a sip. “Now, onto business. What can you tell me of Flinn’s research?”

“Honestly,” Selis started, her voice shaky and hesitant, “I am not sure what you are expecting to hear. I know a lot about the man, but I am at a loss for exactly what you want.”

Janus took another sip. “I apologize for my vagueness. I would like to know about his research into the Quela.”

Selis remembered the secret ritual she found on the torn page, and her breath caught in her throat. “How much do you know?”

“Not much.” Janus’ icy eyes fixated on Selis’. “He was trying to do something. I don’t know what his goal was, but it sounds like you might bear some insight.”

“I…” Selis tore her eyes away from Janus’ and stared at the murky liquid in her cup. “I am fairly sure that he succeeded in what he wanted to accomplish. At least a part of it.”

Janus’ eyebrow arched before he composed himself. “Go on. Please.”

“I was young at the time,” Selis said, distant. “Flinn did something different in one of the Helgathin rituals. I found notes on the altered process. It used magic the way the Quela do.”

“I see.” Something played in Janus’ voice which brought Selis’ eyes back up. Jealousy. “So, you are a living, breathing example of his success. I have to say, and I mean no offense, but that is alarming.”

Indignation flashed through Selis. “You do not have to worry about him continuing his research; he is no longer able.”

Janus shifted in his chair. “What can you tell me of the spell he placed on his mind. Were you able to locate anything?”

“He had several barriers in place. I broke through them with ease. I did not notice anything outside my search. And when I broke the last one, everything vanished like it never existed.” Selis recalled the emptiness in Flinn’s eyes as she screamed at him, and those horrid emotions threatened to take her once more.

“I am sorry. Even though you parted ways with him before it happened, he was still your mentor for so many years. It must have been difficult for you, seeing him that way.”

"It is fine." Selis lifted her right hand and wiped a tear away with the back of a finger. "He had become a poor mentor of late. I wanted answers…answers that now I will never get."

"I understand how frustrating, how soul-crushing that can be. While they might not be as personal as the ones you seek, I want answers as well." Janus leaned his elbows on his desk. "Is there anything else you can remember or tell me about Flinn's recent work?"

Selis shook her head. "I am afraid not. I was looking into it myself. He saved several specific tomes, but I did not find anything of note before they were taken."

"Taken?" Janus asked, raising an eyebrow. "By who?"

"A Quelan shaman was searching for the tomes," Selis explained despite the quiver in her voice. "I went through the back door of a projection spell it cast. It discovered me and came after me. It managed to take the tomes and disappear."

Janus' eyes lit up, ignoring Selis' failure. "That's…fascinating. I didn't realize the Quela could understand or read our language. This changes things."

Selis thought to tell Janus of Gor'an, but she held back. "It appeared to be fixated on whatever knowledge I either overlooked or did not get to. Flinn was also paranoid about keeping everything a secret. That is why I tried to force answers out of him." She no longer reigned in her dark emotions, and her chest tightened.

"It's not your fault," Janus offered, sympathetic. "He never would have given the information up. Regardless of who pressed him or how he was pressed, the ending result would've been the same as it was for you."

"I suppose so. Besides," Selis grabbed her long braid of silver hair and fussed with the end, "the damage is done."

“One last thing before we’re done.” Janus eased back in his chair, curling a finger under his chin. “You said you used a Quelan projection—do you know where they, specifically that shaman, might be?”

“No, they were deep underground. The distance I traveled felt like it was at least a few miles from where our camp was.”

“Ah.” Janus frowned. “All right. Well,” he stood and rounded his desk, “it was a pleasure to meet you. The both of you. Thelin should be just outside; I’ll inform him to show you to the library.” He strode across the room.

Lidria cleared her throat as Janus reached the door. “Do you have any young children, Master Janus?”

“No, I do not.” Janus cocked his head. “Why do you ask?”

“We saw a young girl on the stairs when we were being led over,” Lidria said, her posture wooden.

A flash of recognition erased Janus’ fleeting frown. “Ah. That’s Evelyn. She’s still young, but I’ve been tutoring her in magic for several months now.”

“I see.” Selis expected Lidria to raise another question or Janus to press her on why she asked, but neither said another word. A distant look came over Lidria’s face, and she appeared to lose her surroundings.

Janus frowned but opened the door without further questioning, and Thelin swept in from the side. “Ah, Thelin. I would like you to show Selis the library. She is welcome to come and go as she pleases.”

“Very good.” Thelin bowed, shallow, before he focused on Selis and Lidria. “If you’ll follow me.”

“Good day, ladies,” Janus said with a placating smile.

Chapter Twenty-One

Lidria paced outside the library. Selis loved books, but Lidria had no interest—not now. Her mind focused on whether the girl Janus spoke of could be her Evelyn. The answer seemed obvious if a little farfetched. She would recognize her own daughter, even after all this time, right?

Lidria stopped. How could she approach Evelyn to find out the truth? She didn't know if she could broach the subject, let alone know how to communicate with her daughter. Her feelings didn't matter. She couldn't, shouldn't, reenter Evelyn's life.

A tear ran down Lidria's cheek. She sighed, no point wiping it away. The thought of being so close to Evelyn but knowing she shouldn't meet her crushed her spirit. Her body trembled as she began to sob. She leaned against the wall and slid to the floor, cursing herself.

Lidria tilted her head back, staring at the ceiling through blurry vision. She wanted to apologize for not being around, for how she had treated her even if Evelyn didn't understand. She wished she could atone for her neglect and shortcomings. Ian would never let her.

Ian. His name brought nothing but pain, regret, and anger. Lidria couldn't blame him for taking Evelyn away, but that didn't stop her self-pity. If she struggled with Evelyn, she couldn't fathom how to talk to Ian. Evelyn might not remember her, but Ian…he would remember everything.

"Lidria?" Selis stood in the hall beside her, clutching a selection of oversized books to her chest.

Lidria's hand shot up to wipe the drying tears from her face, but she stopped. Her hand dropped into her lap. "Hey."

Concern darkened Selis' face. "What is wrong?"

"I—that girl we saw before talking to Janus reminded me a lot of Evelyn, and I've been thinking about what I would do if I ever met her again."

Selis bent down, placed the books on the ground, and sat beside Lidria. "She did look a lot like you."

"She's the right age. She has my eyes and hair, and her name is Evelyn, but," Lidria wanted nothing more than to curl up in a ball and disappear, "it's been six years. I'm not sure I would recognize her."

"I can only imagine how you feel, but I believe you should find out the truth." Selis scooted closer to Lidria and put a comforting hand on her thigh.

A lump grew in Lidria's throat. "I wished for so long to see her again, but I never thought I might get the chance." She turned to Selis, tears running down her face. "What do I say?"

Selis chewed her lip. "I do not know. I wish I knew what to tell you, but I am not adept at these kinds of things. However, I do think you should be you and be truthful with her."

"I don't know who I am." Lidria's stomach churned as she spoke. "Who's to say I'm not the same selfish, neglectful person?"

"The way you treated Hector suggests you are not," Selis said without hesitation.

"Maybe," Lidria admitted, staring down at her lap. "I think I was overcompensating with him to absolve myself of my guilt. He reminded me of Evelyn and how much I wish I could've been there for her."

Selis squeezed Lidria's leg. "That proves, to me at least, you are not that person, that you care and are willing to try. You need not be so hard on yourself."

"Ian will be harder on me." Every bit of hope Selis' words gave her, Lidria's brain tore to shreds. "With Evelyn, I don't know what to say.

With Ian," Lidria sighed and slumped forward, "I don't think I can say anything. There's no chance he'll listen."

"You will have to convince him if that is the case." Selis stretched her legs, and her left foot rested against Lidria's shin. "Show him you have changed and that you want to make things right."

"I don't think any amount of proof, if I even had any, would prove that to him." Lidria gazed at Selis' foot on her leg.

Selis let out a sad little noise. She lifted her hand and draped her arm on Lidria's shoulders. "Whatever differences you have should be set aside for Evelyn's sake. You do not need to get along, per se, but she deserves to have both her parents."

"He thinks I'm a selfish person and a lousy parent." Lidria sucked in a deep breath before she met Selis' gaze. "I would like to prove him wrong."

"You must try," Selis encouraged. "That is all you can do, and I believe you should." An infectious grin spread across her face.

Lidria leaned back, taking comfort in Selis' arm around her. "I-I think I can do that."

"I am glad." The smile drained from Selis' face. "I do not want to see you miss this opportunity to reunite with your daughter."

Lidria cracked a wry smile. "I'll try not to disappoint you."

"Good," Selis said, beaming. "But I think I know someone that might be more disappointed than me if you do not make an effort."

Lidria nodded, the knot in her stomach twisting tighter. "You're right. I would never forgive myself."

Selis pulled herself closer to Lidria and gave her a one-armed squeeze. Lidria snaked her arm behind Selis' back and embraced her. Neither said a word. Lidria tried not to let her mind wander, focusing on something less traumatic. How could Evelyn be a mage?

“I can’t believe she can use magic. There were no signs when she was younger.”

Selis shifted. “There rarely are. I found out when I was a few years older than Evelyn. It manifests when you are ready for it.”

“But,” Lidria flicked her eyes up to Selis, “she’s only *ten*. How can she be ready?” Lidria held back her contempt—Selis didn’t deserve it.

“The Flow does not determine readiness by age,” Selis explained. “It determines if your body is capable of completing the circuit, if it can flow freely.”

“I didn’t know it worked like that. I still don’t understand a whole lot about magic. I only know”—Lidria lifted her left arm—“and that doesn’t make me feel great about Evelyn learning.”

Selis withdrew her arm, pulled her knees up to her chest, and hugged her legs. “I understand. I have been struggling with whether I find magic to be helpful or harmful. Though, I have to say it is not a bad thing. I would not worry.”

“I’m glad you haven’t given up. You’re always so passionate whenever you talk about it.” Lidria laughed and embraced Selis. “I’m a little jealous.”

“I guess I cannot help myself.” Selis stared down. “It has been such a massive part of my life for so long that it is not something I can separate from.”

Ignoring the disparaging voice in her head, Lidria leaned against Selis. “I understand that all too well. Even after everything that happened, I jumped right back into military work without hesitation.” Lidria managed a whisper: “It’s the only thing I’m good at.”

“I do not know.” Selis loosened her tight hold. “I am sure you can find something else if you try.”

“Maybe I should start looking,” Lidria muttered. “Our city’s in ruins, the surviving people will be cared for, and there’s nothing else for me. I’m,” she shuddered, “done with it all.”

Selis nudged Lidria with her shoulder, and she lifted her head. “I will be there to help you. If you want me to be.”

“Selis,” Lidria breathed as tears welled in her eyes. “Of course I want you to be. Thank you.”

“Lidria,” Selis removed her arms from around her legs, stretched back out, and placed her hand on Lidria’s leg, “if anything, I should be thanking you. You pulled me up and gave me a second chance.”

“Let’s work on making something more of our lives,” Lidria grabbed Selis’ small hand and squeezed, “together.”

Selis took Lidria’s hand in both of hers, raised it to her lips, and gave it a little kiss. “Together.”

Lidria’s heart raced. Her instincts told her to tear her hand away from Selis, but she resisted. Lidria sighed, content, and rested her head against Selis’. A happy noise escaped Selis, and she pulled their hands into her lap. The warmth of Selis’ lips lingered.

“So,” Lidria said, apprehensive of shattering the peaceful moment. “Did you find anything interesting in the library?”

“I was searching for anything about the Quela, but I could not find much. This one,” Selis fumbled with a book in the small pile beside her, “appears promising, though. The others are spell tomes I am not familiar with.”

Lidria frowned. “I never realized how much of a technical side there was to using magic.” She brought her left arm before her, eyes flicking down. “I always thought it was more feeling and instinct like how I can tap into it with my arm.”

"Basic invocations can be cast based on nothing but instinct alone," Selis clarified. "But anything that requires you to manipulate the Flow in odd or complex ways requires a lot of technical understanding and skill. It took me years to understand the process of infusing a single spell into a breaker."

"Is there a way to," Lidria raised her arm, glancing at all the severed links, "repair these or infuse it with more spells?"

Selis shook her head. "If there is, I do not know it."

A bubble of panic rose in Lidria's gut. "That's what I thought. I hope I don't have to use it again, but if I do, there's not much left."

"If it comes to that," Selis paused, causing Lidria to glance at her, "I will make certain nothing happens to you." Determination radiated from Selis.

"Selis," Lidria said, breaking eye contact. "I appreciate the sentiment, but I don't want you to do anything you'll regret."

Selis cupped Lidria's cheek, and Lidria allowed her gaze to be guided back up to Selis' enchanting eyes. They melted Lidria's heart. "There is no way I could ever regret protecting you, Lidria."

"I can accept that," Lidria conceded, her stomach fluttering as she smiled at Selis.

"Good." Selis smiled back, and her hand slipped from Lidria's face.

Lidria's cheeks burned, and she shied her eyes away from Selis. "I guess since you've got your books, I need to figure out something to do for the rest of the day."

"See?" Selis asked. "I told you I am quite boring." With a twist to her right, she scooped up the pile of books and held them in her lap.

Lidria shook her head. "You're fine." She stood, took a deep breath, and stretched her arms up over her head. "I'm going to take a walk. I'm not ready to—"

“Lidria,” Selis admonished as she scrambled to her feet, books against her abdomen.

“I know.” Lidria glanced away. She didn’t want to disappoint Selis or make her worry any more, but she needed time. “I-I just need time to think about what I’m going to say.”

Selis’ face screwed up in thought before her beautiful eyes met Lidria’s. “I can lose myself in my own little world while reading, but do not be afraid to interrupt if you need me.”

A rush of emotion flooded Lidria, threatening to bring her to tears. She threw herself around Selis and squeezed; she couldn’t believe someone would treat her so well. Selis yelped, and books dug into Lidria’s ribs. She didn’t care—she wanted to show Selis her appreciation.

“L-Lidria,” Selis stammered, panicked. “The tomes.”

Lidria loosened and pulled back. “Sorry.”

Selis sighed and fussed with her small stack of books. “It is all right.” She flashed a warm smile. “You are welcome.”

“I—” Lidria wished to express her feelings, but something in the recesses of her mind restrained her.

Fighting back, Lidria bit her lip, closed her eyes, and planted a quick kiss on Selis’ cheek. Lidria’s heart pounded in her chest as she opened her eyes. Selis stared back at her. Lidria moved to apologize, but she stopped when a slow smile curled Selis’ lips.

“You know where to find me,” Selis said, struggling to hold in her delight.

Lidria grinned. She no longer doubted the path her relationship with Selis led her down. “I’ll see you later, then. I hope you find something interesting in those books.”

“I am sure I will.” Selis’ carefree expression turned thoughtful. “Do not forget what I said.”

“I won’t,” Lidria affirmed, knowing full-well she couldn’t if she wanted to. “I promise.” She gave Selis a brief, one-armed hug—mindful of her books—and headed off toward the manor’s entrance.

Chapter Twenty-Two

Selis placed her fresh cup of tea down beside the borrowed tomes. She sat, breathing in the robust and semi-sweet aroma. Easy access to such things thrilled her, but her mind soon wandered. She worried about Lidria and hoped her time alone would help sort out her thoughts and feelings.

Raising her left hand, Selis touched her cheek. Her heart fluttered at the thought of Lidria's lips, and she sighed. Things between them were going splendid despite Selis' concerns that Lidria would not want to be with someone like her. She did not need to worry any longer.

Selis smiled and, removing her hand, scooped up her teacup. Master Janus had been quite accommodating, and the tea he offered, delicious. The blend reminded her of what her mother had drank. Selis did not like tea as a child, but her tastes had changed during her years spent in Odwyn.

The smile drained from Selis' face. She wondered if her parents missed her or remembered she existed. Sure, she had moved away and became distant, but she did not recall them fighting for her to come home or visit. Not that she would know what to do if they had. How could she slip back into their lives after so long?

Selis shook her head. A problem for another time. She focused on finding out more about the Quela and what Flinn had done to her that allowed her to communicate with Gor'an.

Selis sipped her hot tea. Warmth spread through her as the liquid traveled to her stomach, and her nerves leveled out. She took another sip, relishing the delicious concoction. Holding the teacup, she reached for the tome on the top of the stack.

Selis rested her hand on the thick leather cover. Something inside her told her not to unravel the mystery behind Flinn's experiments on her. Pain rose thinking about the man. She did not know what she would find, if anything, but she needed to investigate.

An old, musty odor greeted Selis as she opened the pages. After years of studying, the scent comforted her. She ran her finger down the loose sheet of scribbles that aimed to organize the volume's contents. Some bits shone clear while others baffled her.

Selis stopped on the word "wards" cramped in the corner. She did not find an associated page number, nor did she believe the surrounding notes belonged. She tapped the parchment. If the number did not exist, perhaps she could extrapolate the location based on the available information.

Tallying up the listed numbers in her head, Selis soon compiled a short list of spots to search. She flipped through the stiff pages. A small, incomprehensible doodle marked the top right corner on the first page, followed by blanks. She frowned and continued to the next selection.

An intricate, precise tear-shaped rune jumped out at Selis. She recognized the ward the Enclave used in Odwyn to prevent the Quela from tunneling under the city. In the chaos of the attack, she had forgotten to question why the wards did not work.

Selis cursed. If she had not given into anger, Flinn would be alive to answer her questions. He played a role in Odwyn's destruction, but she did not understand how in-depth. Without a doubt, he experimented with Quelan magic—her existence proved that much—but everything pointed to something more.

The shaman had communicated with Flinn; it had searched for the tomes. A shiver ran down Selis' spine. Her fears that he had interacted with them, leading to the destruction of Odwyn, were realized. They needed assistance to manage such a feat.

Selis' breath caught in her throat. She traced the rune with her index finger and closed her eyes. Reaching out with the Flow, she descended through the manor. Potent magic radiated from the earth. Pressure built around her, growing more severe the further she probed.

Pain flashed in Selis' head, but she pressed on, determined to see her curiosity through. The wards should not affect her; the ones under Odwyn never did. She lost focus. Flinn's empty eyes appeared before her, and her concentration slipped through her grasp.

Selis' hand shook as she retracted from the open tome. The nothingness she found made her alter course. Instead, she opened her eyes and gazed at the wall, her chest rising and falling with rapid breaths. She pulled her braid over her shoulder and stroked it.

Selis' eyes drifted down. Her head sunk as she struggled to keep her crushing guilt at bay. She stared at her lap. Out of the corner of her eye, an unfamiliar color popped. She turned her head, and her eyes widened. Hazel-brown hair rested in her hand.

Selis blinked, sure her eyes played a trick on her. A memory of her natural hair rushed back to her. Guilt and fear gave way to confusion and intrigue. She held her hair out in front of her. The moment she did, however, the color drained and became silver once more.

Despite years of practicing magic, Selis had never experienced such a transformation, permanent or temporary, except the one that changed her. She let the braid slip from her hands, falling aside. She did not understand. Perhaps the wards here differed more than she thought.

Selis frowned. The more she indulged in her curiosities, the more questions she found. She thought herself smart and skilled enough to figure things out on her own, but that proved time and time again to not be the case. Frustration burned in her gut.

Shaking her head, Selis returned her gaze to the page before her. She scrutinized every curve and line; she must have overlooked some small difference. Nothing. The drawing matched the rune in her head, which made no sense. Unless Flinn had tampered with the ones in Odwyn.

Flinn had kept everything from Selis—his final act of indisputable dominance over her. She cursed herself again for allowing the shaman to take the only knowledge left behind. She rubbed her leg. Her muscles ached, reminding her of her failure.

Selis squeezed her thigh and shot out of the chair. Nothing would be gained from sitting around, wallowing in self-pity. She wanted answers. Her current path lead to nothing. She had to be strong and press forward in a new direction. One not so self-destructive.

Selis brushed her hair back, tightened her robe, and headed for the door. She would try to pry more information out of Gor'an. Her previous conversation with him, while arduous, proved to be a bountiful source of knowledge.

Selis slipped into the hall and searched for Thelin. He stood in the lobby, addressing some of the other manor staff. She descended the polished stairs and hoped he would finish before she reached the bottom.

"Miss Selis," Thelin said as he spun to face her. "Do you need something?"

Selis realized how crazy her request would sound. "Can you tell me where Bal is? I wanted to follow up on something we spoke about on our travel here."

Thelin regarded Selis for a moment, judging each of her words. "I will gladly escort you to him if you would like."

"That would be great," Selis replied, less anxious.

“I hope Master Janus’ library met your expectations,” Thelin offered as he led Selis down a long hallway.

“Yes, it did.” The simple thought of all the tomes she missed or overlooked brought a smile to Selis’ face. “It is quite outstanding. I will thank Master Janus again when I see him.”

Thelin turned his head toward Selis and returned her smile, if more reserved. “He will be glad to hear you are so enthusiastic. He could lose everything he has, and he would be fine as long as those books survived.”

Selis let out a bubble of laughter. “I can relate—”

“Ah, Thelin,” Bal hollered as he emerged from a door on the right. “You giving little miss mage the grand tour?” He grinned.

Thelin came to a halt in front of Bal and folded his hands behind his back. “Actually, she was asking for you.”

Bal craned his neck around Thelin, staring long and hard at Selis. “Were you now?”

“Yes. I, uh,” Selis glanced at Thelin, and he nodded.

“Very well. I’ll leave you to it. Come find me if you need anything else.” Thelin pivoted on his heel and headed back down the hall, his boots thudding on the wood.

“So, what do you want?” Bal asked, suspicious.

“I want you to take me to Gor’an.” Bal raised a questioning eyebrow, and she sighed. “The Quelan. The one you took prisoner.”

“If I remember correctly, *you* were the one that bound him,” Bal sneered.

Selis straightened her back and stared down Bal, feigning confidence. “It does not matter. I would like you to take me to him.”

“Well, since you asked so nicely.” Bal smiled, turned, and motioned for Selis to follow.

Bal led Selis toward the east end of the manor. She followed close behind in shock. She had not expected him to be so accommodating. With everything else going on, she did not think she bore enough energy to convince him.

Bal opened a side door leading outside. "Didn't want to say anything in front of Thelin?"

"I…do not know how much he knows." Selis did not trust Bal either, but she did not want to add yet another layer of complication to the interaction.

"I don't understand why you care so much about that beast," Bal said, flippant. "Regardless of whether or not you think you can 'speak' with it."

Selis tugged on the ends of her sleeves. "I am more curious than I am empathetic, to be honest. If I did not stumble into communicating with him, I would share your mindset."

"At least you haven't gone too crazy." Bal turned his head and grinned over his shoulder. "Yet."

"I assure you," Selis lowered her head and sighed, "I am crazy."

Bal shrugged, turning his hands palm-up as he led Selis toward an ornate barn. "I suppose you would have to be to get involved with a breaker."

Selis' heart leaped into her throat. "I—"

Bal patted his right leg without breaking stride. "Trust me, I know. But," a genuine smile slipped onto his face, "you two do go well together."

"I am surprised." Selis fiddled with her sleeve. "I expected something much less…sincere coming from you."

Bal stopped in front of the steel-slatted door to the barn. "Sometimes, you have to keep people guessing." The metal creaked, and he gestured for Selis to enter.

Inside, a redheaded man shot to his feet, skidding his chair across the floor with a loud screech. He put his hand on the pommel of the sword and stared, wide-eyed. Selis opened her mouth to speak, but Bal came in behind her. The guard composed himself, and his hand fell from his weapon.

"Oh," the man croaked, glancing at the chair. "Bal, it's just you. I'm sorry; I didn't recognize your guest."

Bal shook his head. "Don't worry, Lein. I'm taking miss Selis here to see her prisoner." He flashed her a grin.

"She doesn't look like much," Lein remarked, eyeing Selis. She frowned—sick and tired of being treated like some oddity.

"I—"

"No, she doesn't," Bal interjected as he stepped forward. He placed his arm around Lein's shoulders. "But the Quelan has been bound by her magic for days now without her even thinking about it. I wouldn't get on her bad side."

Lein's eyes widened, and he did not meet Selis' gaze again. "I-I won't."

"You'd better not." Bal laughed at the worry on Lein's face. "I'm just kidding. She's too soft."

Bal released a confused Lein and gestured for Selis to follow him. As she passed Lein, he took a couple of steps back. She sighed, and her cheeks burned with embarrassment. Bal offered no apology—nor did she expect him to—when they entered the stairwell.

"Did you need to do that?" Selis glared at Bal.

Bal grinned and shrugged. "Maybe not, but he was unprepared. If you had been an enemy, he wouldn't have stood a chance."

"I would appreciate it if you left me out of any further disciplinary practices." Selis gave Bal a long, hard stare. "I am not some tool for you to use."

"Fine, fine." Bal waved a dismissive hand at Selis and continued down the stairs.

Selis stepped off the staircase, and the air around her shifted. Pressure filled her head, her chest tightened, nausea washed over her and vanished. She floundered, lightheaded, before finding her stride. Taking a deep breath, she tried to ignore the sensation and followed Bal.

The fact that she experienced magic-induced pain often enough that she shrugged it off disturbed Selis. She fought her darker thoughts, telling herself to focus. An uncomfortable presence lingered despite her best efforts, and she wanted to do anything but stay.

Steel bars and the scent of musky fur drew Selis out of her head. She blinked twice. Bal stood beside the cell, eyeing her. She shook her head and stepped up. Gor'an sat curled in the corner. He lifted his head, and a soft grunt echoed from within.

Wrapping her hand around the cold steel bar, Selis closed her eyes and reached out to Gor'an. *I am sorry for how they are treating you. I—* Pain rushed into her, stealing her breath.

Out, Gor'an uttered. His voice distant, weak.

Selis steeled herself and attempted to not allow Gor'an's pitiful cry sway her. *I cannot do that. I wish I could, but I cannot. I will try to make them treat you better.*

Pain... Magic... Gor'an shrunk into a smaller, more wretched form until he almost disappeared.

I felt it, too, when I came down here. Do you feel this constantly? Selis asked, knowing his answer.

Gor'an's spirit flared up and struck Selis. *Away. Die.*

I will not let them kill you, Selis said as she projected her strength and resolve. *I promise you.*

Weak. Foolish. Gor'an shrank away from Selis, and an obstacle formed in the void between them.

Panic surged through Selis. *Wait.*

Release, Gor'an pleaded. The barrier flickered, and the Quelan's fear seeped into Selis. *Kin. Die.*

Selis did not understand. *I thought your kin would kill you.*

Magic. Worse... The agony Selis pushed aside rushed back, and she realized she contributed to Gor'an's suffering.

Shame weighed Selis down. She had not considered that, by keeping Gor'an alive, she subjected him to pain worse than death. *I...That was not my intention. I only wanted to spare you. I do not know if it means anything to you, but I am sorry.*

Words. Nothing. Their connection snapped, leaving Selis alone in the vast nothingness.

Selis sucked in a harsh breath and opened her eyes. Gor'an no longer paid her any attention, his head down, and his body curled tight. Regret burned within her. She had done everything wrong, and someone else was suffering for her failures. She let her hand slip from the clammy steel bar and the spell from around Gor'an.

"Release him," Selis demanded, her voice thin. She brought her eyes up to Bal's, and he stared at her with a raised eyebrow. "I said. Release. Him."

"I can't do that. Master Janus would never allow a Quela to run free in his home." Bal stood unwavering, oblivious to the whirlwind of emotions consuming Selis.

"Then, move him out of this place," Selis spat, limbs trembling. "He does not deserve to be tortured on top of everything else."

Bal's face scrunched up. "I'll see what I can do."

Selis let out a shaky sigh. Her body weighed heavy, and her head pounded. Bal's word would have to do; she did not have the energy to argue. She turned from the cell and staggered up the stairs, exhausted. She wanted to lock herself in her room and forget any of this had happened.

Chapter Twenty-Three

Sweat dripped from Lidria's chin. She lifted herself off the ground again, muscles straining. Her breaths came steady and controlled despite the effort required to lift her form. With a practiced motion, she kicked up into a handstand. A moment to balance, and she opened her eyes.

The world around Lidria tilted and swayed as her brain tried to right the image. Shrubs at the edge of the garden stretched downward. Blue nothingness and light clouds waved around her and dizziness crept up. She breathed in through her nose, holding her pose tight.

Lidria bent her arms, dipping into the sky. Her body wavered before discipline tightened her muscles. She inhaled as she lowered herself and exhaled when she pushed back—the strength burning through her the only thing on her mind.

Lidria fell into a slow, deliberate rhythm. She focused on nothing but the regulated flow of breathing and the contraction of muscles. Everything else faded away: Odwyn, the Quela, magic, Janus, Bal, Hector, Selis, Ian. None of them shook her.

Evelyn.

Fear spiked through Lidria's gut, and she lost control. Her vision swam as her breathing stopped and arms gave out. She pitched backward, crashing down on her spine. Trimmed grass pricked the small of her back, her limbs ached, and she wanted to hit herself for being so foolish.

Morning sunlight blinded Lidria as she laid back and stared. The only way to clear her thoughts, to relax, and she had ruined the moment. She closed her eyes, mumbling a curse. She couldn't change her cowardice, but she fought regardless.

Lidria sat up. She had to speak with Ian about Evelyn; nothing else would alleviate the nagging desire. Purpose filled her, yet the sensation felt hollow like she didn't believe herself. Her legs wobbled as she stood. Doubt ran rampant through her.

Sweat trickled down Lidria's face, and she wiped her brow with the back of her hand. She shimmied her tunic down to her waist. The confidence and focus from a moment ago vanished. Her eyes drifted down. How could she let something so simple break her?

Lidria's hands tightened into fists. No. She needed to see this through. Even if nothing came of it, she couldn't avoid talking to Ian. Selis' encouragement echoed in her head. Lidria took a deep breath, unclenched her hands, and headed to clean herself up.

Lidria strolled down the cobblestone streets. Pleasant faces greeted her at every turn, buoying her spirits. She returned several of the warm greetings people offered. There were reasons for her not to be receptive, but, for now, they didn't seem so oppressive.

Janus had made a happy home here for these people. Though she had started cautious, Lidria began to believe he deserved more credit than she afforded him. His reasoning for building Kal'Den appeared altruistic. He had done what he could for his fellow countrymen, including her and Evelyn.

The smile drained from Lidria's face. An armed guard strode past with a nod. She frowned and glanced at her exposed arm. Of course Janus' people knew what she was. She didn't intend to hide anymore, yet the vulnerability her decision put on her would take getting used to.

Lidria moved to the side of the road and, after sighing, inspected the shops around her. Tailors, street stalls, and various vendors lined the thoroughfare. One sign stood out. A memory of a mock-up badge with the words "Delvin's Bakery" carved into light-colored wood flashed before her.

Staring at the marker, pride filled Lidria. Ian always wanted his own bakery, but she hadn't expected him to own one here of all places. She took a step and faltered. Her dry mouth refused to work, and her breath thinned. What little confidence she had built up vanished, leaving her with nothing but anxiety.

A customer exited Ian's business and traveled down the way. Lidria inhaled, long and steady, steeling herself. She blocked out the nagging voice in the back of her head telling her to stop, to run away, and cut across to the shop.

Lidria opened the door and stepped through the threshold. The inside of the bakery smelled of fresh bread and stood empty, save for one man. He turned to greet her, but his warm smile soured. His blue eyes narrowed, and she breathed deep.

"Hi, Ian," Lidria managed. She thudded across the hardwood floor, trying to calm herself.

"Lidria? What are you—" Ian shook his head, and his eyes turned dark. "It doesn't matter. Get out of my shop."

Lidria's heart beat loud in her ears. "Wait, please. I just want to talk."

"What could you possibly want that you came here to find me?" Ian demanded, placing his hands on the counter.

"You know the answer." Lidria didn't meet Ian's harsh gaze.

"I don't think I do." Ian settled back and folded his arms across his chest. "I know you don't want to talk to me, so why are you here?"

The lump in Lidria's throat made her croak: "Evelyn."

Ian's eyes widened before a scowl took over his face. "Why?" He shifted his weight around. "Starting to regret how you treated her?"

"I…I've always regretted it, Ian. Even if you don't believe me." Lidria blew out a long breath. "I didn't think I would ever see her again. I just want a chance to—"

"No," Ian barked, and Lidria jumped. "If you want what's best for her, you'll leave her alone. I don't know why you're here but stay away from Evelyn."

Tears welled, blurring Lidria's vision. "Ian, I—please."

"What, you think you can just come back into her life now? Even if I thought you could change, she doesn't need you." Ian's chest heaved, his nostrils flared, and she feared he would leap over the counter at any second.

"I know she doesn't," Lidria admitted despite how deep the words cut her. "I was a terrible mother. I just want to see her, so I can have some closure. I will respect your wishes and stay out of her life after that."

Ian glanced away and chewed his lip. "I have a difficult time believing that, after going through the trouble of coming to talk to me, you would simply leave after seeing her."

"It's the truth. Everything you've said or thought of me is true. I'm not trying to prove you wrong." Lidria stared into Ian's impassive eyes. "I just want a chance to see my daughter one last time.

"And I promise you, once my business here is done, you'll never see me again." Tears rolled down Lidria's cheeks.

"I can throw you out of my shop," contempt dripped from Ian's voice, "and I'd never have to see you again."

Lidria choked back a sob. "You have every right. I wouldn't blame you if you did."

"I still don't understand. Why do you care now?" Ian's eyes flicked down to the counter and back up. "You never did when you had the right to see her."

"A horde of Quela destroyed Odwyn," Lidria said, taking Ian's slight in stride. She focused instead on her interactions with Hector and Selis and how they had changed her. "I've since met a few people and realized how poorly I treated her; how much I miss her."

"I see." Ian tried to hide his surprise, yet his rigid posture and forced words ruined the performance. "How many survivors?"

"That I know of? Around two hundred." Lidria hoped more had managed to survive without McCrear and his men and escaped into the countryside, but she didn't think their numbers would be noteworthy.

Ian cursed under his breath and shook his head. "I suppose I should be thankful for making me take Evelyn away from that dreadful place."

"Ian."

"What? You knew how much that place took from me. The only reason I ever stayed was because of"—Ian gestured to Lidria—"you."

Lidria's heart leaped up into her throat. "I know. Thank you for trying."

"You're thanking me?" Ian erupted into laughter. "It's been a long, long time since I heard you say those words."

"I'm sure it doesn't mean anything to you," Lidria reined in her emotions, "but I'm…sorry for what I did, what I must have put you through."

"You're right; it doesn't," Ian snapped. He ran a shaky hand through his hair and sighed. "I've been mad at you for far too long. I think I can at least try to accept your apology."

Lidria's lips curled, threatening to form a smile. "I'm glad. I never wanted to hurt you."

Ian's expression remained joyless. "I still don't think it's fine for you to see Evelyn. You only…complicate things."

"Okay. I'll respect your wishes." Lidria couldn't bear to meet Ian's gaze anymore. She fought back tears and surveyed all the fresh-baked bread. "I would like to make a purchase since I took your time."

"All right." Ian spun and wrapped a thin loaf with practiced movement. "Here, this was always your favorite, wasn't it?"

Sunflower seeds were baked into the crust, and Lidria's stomach rumbled. "Yeah," she said as she stepped up and took the bread in her hands—still warm. "I'm surprised you remembered."

Ian drew himself up. "It has to do with baking, of course I remembered."

Lidria shook her head. She fished out some coins, more than the loaf's worth, and placed the money on the counter. Ian didn't move. A frown didn't take her attention away from the food in her hand. She ripped off a bite. Her frown turned into a somber smile.

"You always were good at this." Lidria swept around the bakery with her chewed loaf until her eyes met Ian's. "I'm glad you have a chance to pursue it your own way."

Ian steadied himself. His eyes took a moment to focus on Lidria. "Thank you, Lidria."

"You're welcome, Ian," Lidria said with a smile. She took another bite of the bread to punctuate her point and turned to leave.

Ian muttered a curse as Lidria gripped the doorknob. "Fine." She turned around and gawked, stunned. "You can see her, but I'm going to be there. And when I say enough, you go. No hesitation."

"I promise."

"Meet me at the garden outside Janus' manor tomorrow." Ian's mouth worked before words came out. "Evelyn has a lesson, so I'll take her there afterward."

Lidria tried to keep her giddiness in check but failed. "Thank you."

"Yeah." A flicker of a smile broke his cold, stoic expression.

Hope and excitement rose inside Lidria as she exited the shop. The midafternoon sun shone bright, and she accepted the warmth. She took another bite of bread, savoring the sweet taste and airy consistency. Selis had to try it. Lidria's heart fluttered—she had Selis to thank for making this possible.

Lidria quickened her pace. The sooner she got back, the sooner she could thank Selis for giving her the push she needed. A smile slid onto Lidria's face. She envisioned Selis' gorgeous eyes and let out a little sigh. Whatever happened, at least Selis stood by her.

Chapter Twenty-Four

Selis stared at the tome. She did not want to open the pages, to read further. Things were not going to change from investigating some irrelevant writing. However, what other option did she have? The thought of speaking with Janus overwhelmed her. She did not wish to cause trouble.

Sighing, Selis pushed her empty teacup to the side and slid the volume toward her. Her fingers lingered, curled, on the cover. She had no drive, no desire, to delve any deeper. A sense of futility enveloped her. Each time she opened one for answers, she found herself with more questions.

The doorknob jiggled and turned. Selis jumped. The door swung open, and Lidria slipped into the room, a bright smile on her face. Unable to contain her joy at Lidria delivering the perfect distraction, Selis smiled.

"Lidria." Selis shot out of her chair. "How did it go?"

Lidria said nothing. Instead, she set down the loaf of bread in her hand, rushed across the room, and threw her arms around Selis. Selis squeaked and would have been bowled over if not for Lidria's strength clutching her to her breast. Laughter bubbled out of Selis at the sudden outburst.

Selis wrapped around Lidria and squeezed back, savoring the warmth between them. "It went well, then?"

"Thank you," Lidria whispered. Wetness dripped on top of Selis' head. "He said I was allowed to see her."

"That is great." Selis eased back, but not away, from Lidria, gazing up into her eyes. "You are welcome."

Lidria smiled and blinked a tear from her eye. "I can't believe it. Never in my wildest dreams did I ever think I would see her again."

"When are you meeting?" Selis asked as she pulled herself close to Lidria.

"Tomorrow." Lidria's hand stroked Selis' back in a slow, rhythmic manner. "She has a lesson with Master Janus, and Ian said I could talk to her after."

"I am glad. You deserve the second chance."

"I never would have had the chance if it weren't for you, Selis." Lidria beamed down at her, and Selis' heart beat faster.

A lump worked into Selis' throat; she fought to speak. "Lidria, I do not know what to say."

"I," Lidria started before she turned away, her cheeks flush.

"You are here," Selis held Lidria's hip against her, "and that is all that matters to me."

Lidria turned her head, timid. "Where else would I go?"

"There have to be plenty of people more suited for you than me." Despite her own words, Selis smiled as she spoke.

"No, you're perfect." A horrified expression popped onto Lidria's face, and she pulled away from Selis.

The floor creaked. Lidria snatched her bread off the table, tore a chunk off, and extended her hand to Selis. "Try this. It's my favorite."

Selis took the seed-encrusted bread, gazing into Lidria's eyes. The nervousness turned to expectancy. Butterflies whirled in Selis' stomach; she could not deny Lidria even if she wanted to. She took a small bite, and the light, sweet taste danced around her mouth.

"I can see why," Selis said, taking another bite. "Where did you get it?"

"Ian has a bakery here. I got it when I went to talk to him." A faint smile persisted on Lidria's face.

"How did a baker end up with a soldier?"

"He was a civilian cook at one of the barracks in Odwyn." Lidria's gaze left Selis'. "The rest…"

Selis shifted around, and her heart pounded. "I am sorry. I should not have asked."

"No, it's all right. I don't want to keep anything from you." Lidria hooked a loose strand of hair behind one ear and glanced at the table. "So, have you found anything in those books?"

Selis inhaled a deep breath to calm herself. "Not a whole lot. I spoke with Gor'an yesterday after realizing something was off about the wards here."

"You visited…him?" Lidria asked, taking a step forward. "Why didn't you tell me?"

"It was not pleasant, and I did not wish to burden you further. You had enough on your mind." Selis stared at the floor.

"Well," Lidria's feet appeared, and Selis tilted her head up to find a welcoming smile, "I'm here now."

"The Enclave placed wards under major population points to prevent things like what happened to Odwyn," Selis explained. "I found a ward pattern in one of the tomes I borrowed, but it was different.

"I tried to examine it like I had the ones in Odwyn. It…repelled me as if I were Quelan."

Lidria frowned, a thoughtful expression on her face. "Maybe whatever Flinn did to you effects how they treat you."

"That is the conclusion I came to. I had Bal take me to Gor'an, so I could try to figure things out. But, when I entered where they are keeping him, I felt the power of the wards pressing against me." Selis' chest tightened. "Gor'an was in so much pain."

Concern twisted Lidria's face. "Are you okay?"

“Yes, I was fine after I left and rested a bit. Gor’an, though…he does not deserve what they are doing to him.” Regret ran through Selis. She should have forced Bal to let him go; she had the strength to.

“If it means that much to you,” Lidria stood straight and rolled her shoulders, “let’s go free him. I have no problem standing up to Bal.”

“No.” Selis shook the dark thoughts from her head. “We cannot do it that way. He’d be killed before he could leave the town.”

“Not if we—”

“We are not going to hurt anyone,” Selis insisted. “They are just doing their jobs, protecting their home. I will speak with Master Janus about it since Bal will not budge.”

Shame clouded Lidria’s eyes, and she pivoted to the right. “I’ll come with you. No reason for you to do it alone.”

“I—okay. I planned on doing it by myself, but,” Selis smiled at Lidria, “I would be glad to have your company.”

“Good.” A smile played at the corners of Lidria’s mouth. “We can go whenever you’re ready.”

Selis took a deep breath and snatched her robe off the bed. Slipping the article on, she stepped toward Lidria. The door creaked before swinging open. Anxiety churned Selis’ stomach. She had backed herself into a corner, one she did not want to fight her way out of even with Lidria at her side.

“Now,” Lidria said as they strode down the halls, “what I don’t get is: if there were wards to keep the Quela out of Odwyn, how did they attack the city?”

“That is something I would like to know myself. I can only guess that Flinn had tampered with them while researching the Quela. For what reason, I do not know.” Wild possibilities spun around Selis’ head—none pleasant.

Lidria crossed her arms over her chest, a puzzled expression on her face. "Do you think those books the shaman took had anything to do with it?"

"They had to; it knew what it was looking for." Selis sighed. "I was too weak to stop it."

"Hey," Lidria took Selis' hand in hers and squeezed, "you did what you had to. You kept people safe."

Dread froze Selis in place, but her eyes met Lidria's. "What if losing the tomes causes more death than if I had stayed?"

"I…don't know. It's not your fault, though."

"It is." Selis pressed close to Lidria. "If I had gone along with Flinn, I never would have lost them."

Lidria dropped her hand from Selis'. "I'm sorry."

"No, no, no." Selis shook her head in time with her words. Her eyes never left Lidria's. "Lidria, you were only doing your duty. I am glad you showed up that day."

A somber expression played on Lidria's face, but she slipped her hand back into Selis'. "I am, too. I just wish it had been under better circumstances."

"Me, too, but," Selis gripped Lidria's hand tight, "we are here now."

"We are. Let's not forget that, okay?" Lidria's eyes sparkled with resolve and affection, quieting the guilty voices in Selis' head.

Selis inhaled the confidence Lidria exuded and took a step forward. She clung to Lidria, the connection providing a trustworthy physical anchor, but she pulled herself up straight. Even if no one else understood or cared, her beliefs were worth fighting for.

The door to Janus' office swung open as Selis and Lidria approached. Janus glanced up from the floor and, after a moment of surprise, greeted them. "Ladies, welcome. I was just on my way to make sure everything is in place for your friends. You're welcome to join me."

"That would be wonderful," Selis said. Lidria grunted in pain beside her, and Selis released her hand. The heights of her stress-fueled strength amazed her.

"So," Janus strode toward the manor's entrance, "what do you need to speak with me about?"

Selis hesitated. "I wanted to know: did you place the wards here yourself?"

"Yes, I did." Janus' movements became wooden. "Why?"

"I noticed they are different than the ones in Odwyn." Selis denied the urge to tug at the ends of her sleeves and focused. "I did not know any variations existed."

"No others do." An air of superiority surrounded Janus. Worthy master of the Enclave or not, Selis found his arrogance off-putting. "These are unique. I made some adjustments to make them last longer and be more efficient."

"I see." Selis tried her best not to reveal her displeasure. "Have you had any Quela activity around Kal'Den?"

Janus glanced over his shoulder at Selis with a raised eyebrow. "Other than the one Bal informed me of, no. I can't say I have seen a single one in years."

"What are your plans with the Quelan you have captive?" The closer Selis got to expressing herself, the more daunting speaking her mind became.

"I have not decided yet." The suspicion on Janus' face gave way to intrigue. "It's rare to find one so docile. It might prove a useful research tool."

"That sounds a lot like what Flinn was trying to do," Lidria interjected, a bite to her tone.

Contempt darkened Janus' eyes. "I understand that they recently destroyed your home and that the late Master Flinn's defection struck a nerve, but, if I have a chance to learn more about the creatures, I'm going to take it to better ensure that incidents like the one in Odwyn don't happen in the future."

Lidria's posture relaxed, but she continued to press Janus. "What do you hope to discover exactly?"

"Hopefully, what they're like when they're not attacking humans." Janus turned down a side road on the east side of Kal'den, and sunlight flooded their path. "We've had so few non-violent encounters that it's been impossible to work towards that goal.

"I would be lying if I said I also wasn't interested in figuring out what makes their magic work. They don't seem to be connected to the Flow like we are."

"From the little I have experienced," Selis fussed with the ends of her sleeves, "it seems like they function nearly identically. However, little things are different, almost as if it runs parallel with our own abilities." Patterns and sensations flashed in her mind as she visualized her connection with Gor'an.

"That's a good observation," Janus said in a tone befitting a parent encouraging a small child. "I have to say, I'm impressed."

Selis' head sank. "If Flinn did anything right, it was exposing me to vast amounts of knowledge and teaching me the technical, so I could realize those differences."

They continued in silence. The buildings, while not as lavish as the ones closer to the manor, were expansive and well-constructed. Selis did not focus on the homes; instead, she reflected on Flinn's teachings. Everything she knew, she owed to him. He had blessed her with this gift.

"What prompted you to examine the wards here?" Janus asked. His quiet voice echoed down the empty street.

"I saw a detailed sketch in one of the tomes I borrowed from your library." Selis slipped her hands in her sleeves to prevent further nervous ticks. "After I noticed it was different, I probed them."

Surprise widened Janus' cool eyes before he regained his composure. "And?"

"Nothing," Selis blurted out. "That is why I brought it up. I did not understand."

"Fair enough."

Lidria nudged Selis and pointed her chin toward Janus. Selis caught Lidria's eyes, and, for a moment, she thought to protest. Confidence remained something fleeting, alien. Flinn had given her the means to be something more, but he had always put her in her place—in a cage she could not break free from.

Selis followed her heart. "The Quelan. I would like him to be released."

Janus stopped and swung around to face Selis. "You what?"

"I do not believe your men are treating him right," Selis reasoned, afraid to catch Janus' eye.

"Bal told me you captured it." Venom dripped from Janus' voice.

"I did but," Selis swallowed hard, "only because Bal would have killed it otherwise."

Quick steps brought Janus close, and Selis flinched. "Why would you want to let the beast go?"

Selis met Janus' burning, resentful eyes. "He was separated from his people, an outcast, not a threat to anyone. I…sympathized."

"The Quela destroy Odwyn, kill thousands of people, and you want to spare one?" Janus boomed. "I have to say; I don't follow your logic."

"I do not think it is logical," Selis admitted, nervous laughter bubbling up. "But that is how I feel. Please"—tears blurred her vision—"he does not deserve to live his life in those conditions."

Myriad emotions flickered across Janus' face, and he let out a huff of air. "I will think about it." Hope blossomed inside Selis. "I'm not sure I want to give up this opportunity, but I see and respect your conviction."

"Very well." Selis nodded, holding back a sober smile. "This is your home. I merely wanted to voice my concern and ask you to act on it."

"I think Master Flinn had more of an influence on you than you realize," Janus said, his eyes lingering on Selis.

"I think you might be right." Drained, Selis retreated within herself, shut down. She did not want to think about Flinn, Gor'an, or anything.

Lidria swept up beside Selis, drawing her attention. "When do you expect McCrear and the other survivors?"

"Sometime tomorrow afternoon." Janus eased back on his heel and turned to Lidria. "I spoke with a scout earlier today, and he said they were on schedule."

"That's great," Lidria remarked in a pleasant voice. "I can't believe how generous you're being."

Janus waved a dismissive hand. "I do have somewhat of a reputation; your shock does not surprise me."

"I just wanted to say thank you again for everything. We'd still be lost without your aid." Hesitation slowed Lidria's movement, yet she bowed.

"You're welcome." Janus glanced up at the setting sun. "Now, if you'll excuse me, I have other matters to attend to."

Selis let Janus go, unable to feel anything. Her legs wobbled, and she collapsed against Lidria—not a scrap of strength in her body. Lidria wrapped her arm around Selis' shoulder and held her tight. She did not say anything, but she did not need to.

"I think I made a mistake," Selis muttered.

Lidria shifted, prompting Selis to gawk up at her. "What do you mean? It seemed to go pretty well."

"He knows I am withholding something from him." Part of Selis told her she was foolish not to tell Janus, but she could not imagine trying to explain her connection with Gor'an.

"You could've told him."

"I," a sharp breath escaped Selis, "yes. I do not know." She rested her head against Lidria's shoulder. "You are the only one I am comfortable talking about it with. Bal knows, but I believe he thinks I am crazy."

"Don't worry about him." Selis lifted her head, but Lidria continued before she said a word. "Either of them. If Janus presses you for more of an explanation, then you can tell him."

Lidria's words and presence were so gentle, so encouraging. "This is exhausting."

"I know." Lidria hugged Selis, pulled away, gazed down into her eyes and smiled. "It'll be all right. Let's go see if we can get some dinner."

"All right," Selis agreed with a shallow nod.

Chapter Twenty-Five

Lidria fought down the urge to tear off her sleeve. The tight clasp at her throat escalated her anxiety. She breathed quick and shallow, heartbeat rising in time. Her mind raced. Everything seemed wrong: her clothes, her body, her beliefs. She closed her eyes, lost to the chaos.

Fragmented memories, given shape by her resentment, flitted through Lidria's thoughts. She couldn't sift through the fabrications to determine what was real. They dragged her down until more fears and insecurities piled on, and she no longer thought anything. She couldn't do this.

"This is the first time I have seen you cover your arm," Selis said, confusion palpable.

Lidria's vision opened to Selis, and her inner conflict vanished. "I don't like to hide it; it's part of who I am."

"Then, why are you covering it now?" The simple question pierced Lidria's heart and stole her breath.

"I don't know." Lidria let her chin fall to her chest. "All I want is to make sure my meeting with Evelyn goes well. I'm afraid it might…complicate things."

"Lidria," Selis placed a hand on her arm, "I do not think it will."

"I just—"

"You do not have to bare it if you do not want," Selis agreed, squeezing Lidria's arm. "I only want you to know that you are fine the way you are."

Lidria pulled the excess cloth around her forearm into a clenched fist and trembled. Her eyes came up to Selis'. "I'm scared."

The smile drained from Selis' face. She wrapped her arms around Lidria and squeezed, but the gestured didn't comfort her. "I can come with you if you need me."

"No."

"I understand." Selis let her arms fall.

Lidria cursed her foolish outburst and snatched Selis tight to her chest. "I'm sorry. I appreciate you being here for me, but this is something I need to do alone. I hope you understand."

Selis hugged Lidria back, nodding against her. "I do. You will do great."

"Thanks, Selis. I'm glad you're here." Butterflies fluttered in Lidria's stomach.

"You are most welcome." Selis tilted her head upward and stood on her tiptoes.

A twinge of excitement shot through Lidria as she stared down into Selis' wonderful eyes. The thought to close the gap between them crossed her mind, but she couldn't—no matter how enticing. Not now. Selis deserved her at her best, not trembling in fear of a child.

Selis eased down on her heels, her eyes never leaving Lidria's. "You should get going. You do not want to be late."

"Yeah," Lidria breathed as their arms fell from around one another. "I…"

"I will be right here; you do not have to worry about that." A toothless smile rested on Selis' face.

Lidria took comfort, however fleeting, in Selis' smile. "I can do this."

"Yes," Selis flashed her teeth, "you can. I am proud of you."

Confidence pumping in her veins, Lidria turned from Selis and left their room. She stepped out into the hall and straightened her back. Her bones popped from being hunched and compacted all morning, and her muscles stretched. She needed to do this.

People passed by, but Lidria paid them no mind. One thought captivated her; she couldn't allow herself to be distracted by inconsequential things. Ideas for connecting with Evelyn took all her effort. She didn't know how, but she would try.

Lidria rounded the bannister at the top of the staircase and took the stairs. Anxiety crept up to mix with and dilute her conviction. Her quick steps slowed, becoming little more than hesitant inches forward. She gripped the handrail. Movement didn't stop but came to a crawl.

Why? Lidia fought countless battles and managed to escape death, but a little girl terrified her. Her hands trembled. Tears welled in her eyes, blurring her vision. She shook her head. Not here, not now; she couldn't let herself fall apart. The railing creaked and shifted.

Lidria sucked in a sharp breath and released the strained rail. She picked up her pace, her footfalls echoing down the empty stairway. The cinnamon scent of the candles lining the hall hit her nose. However pleasant the aroma, she couldn't linger.

Lidria opened one of the massive entryway doors and strode out into the afternoon sunlight. The cheery blue sky and the warm air painted a stark contrast to her inner turmoil. She inhaled, hoping some of the optimism would seep into her. Nothing.

Sighing, Lidria cut to the right toward the garden. All around her, flowers she had never seen before bloomed. Plenty of time remained before Ian brought Evelyn, but she made sure to be early. She didn't want to arrive late to a meeting she had begged for.

Shame seared Lidria to her core. Begging, pleading, and crying proved to be the only way to see her daughter, and she blamed only herself. She wouldn't let the humiliation bring her down—she had the opportunity she desired.

Movement caught Lidria's attention, and she lifted her gaze from the purple flowers. Ian strolled into view, a flat expression on his face. Every muscle tensed. Her eyes snapped down from his face to Evelyn beside him. A smile brightened her face as she glanced around at the colorful vegetation.

Lidria's lips curled, threatening to lighten her mood. She had dreamt of this moment for so long, she didn't think it possible. Even now, she couldn't believe her eyes. Her stomach churned, but she reigned in her emotions. Tremors rippled through her and shook her hands.

Evelyn tilted her head, and her green eyes came to rest on Lidria. Shock and fear played across her face. She swept behind Ian, peeking out around his thigh. Lidria's heart skipped a beat, overwhelmed by despair. Her body ceased quivering, frozen by Evelyn's shy reaction.

"Hello," Lidria forced out through her tight throat.

Ian glanced down at Evelyn clutching at his leg and up at Lidria. "Evelyn, this is Lidria. Your mother."

"You said"—Evelyn's voice came wispy, reserved—"she went away."

"She did," Ian said, staring into Lidria's eyes. A solemn sadness caught her attention and surprised her. "But," he knelt beside Evelyn, "she wanted to meet you again."

"She's scary." Evelyn spoke in little more than a whisper, yet her words hit Lidria with staggering force.

Lidria tore her transfixed eyes off Evelyn and opened her mouth, but Ian cut her off. "She's rough around the edges, but she wants to talk to you. What do you say? Will you give her a chance?"

Hesitation showed in Evelyn's movements as she shifted her concentration from Lidria to Ian. "Okay, but you're going to stay, right?"

"Yes." Ian put his arm around Evelyn, giving her a quick, one-armed hug before he pushed her forward.

Lidria stepped up and took a knee. "Hi, Evelyn. It's nice to meet you."

Blonde hair fell in front of Evelyn's eyes, which she did not attempt to remove. "Hi."

"Your hair is very pretty," Lidria offered, lifting her hand to brush the hair away.

Evelyn flinched at Lidria's touch. Lidria cursed her ignorant behavior. Of course Evelyn would shun her; she displayed nothing but apprehension toward her. Frustration coursed through her, blending with her nerves into a potent concoction of self-defeating thoughts.

"It's okay. I won't hurt you." Lidria eased back to provide Evelyn breathing room. "I just want to see your face."

With an uncertain wave of her small hand, Evelyn cleared her face and hooked her hair behind an ear. Lidria stared at a smaller, younger reflection of herself. Her strong jaw and sharp brow made themselves prominent despite Evelyn's young age. So few of Ian's softer features surfaced.

Lidria flicked her eyes up to Ian, and he showed no emotion. "So," she started, turning back to Evelyn, "Master Janus is teaching you?"

"Yes." Evelyn bobbed her head several times. "He said that if I try hard, I'll be able to use magic like him one day."

"I'm surprised. I didn't know you—" Ian scoffed, and Lidria winced, trying to hold herself together.

Evelyn glanced over at Ian, but he said nothing. "Dad was surprised, too, but he wants me to learn."

"I figured he wouldn't want you to have anything to do with magic." Lidria's left arm twitched, and she clenched her fist.

"Why?" Evelyn asked, cocking her head to the side.

Against her better judgment and the screaming voice in her head, Lidria gripped the hem of her sleeve. She blew out a quick breath and tugged on the loose fabric. Grim tattoos and jagged scars crisscrossed her skin from her wrist to her shoulder. She had grown used to the sight, but Evelyn reacted like so many others.

Evelyn staggered back, eyes wild. Regret slammed Lidria's gut. She shouldn't have done that without any context, explanation or tact—not with how skittish Evelyn was behaving. Pain lanced through Lidria's heart, but no other course of action would prevent this from happening.

Ian swept up beside Evelyn, and she hugged his leg. Lidria ignored him and stared at her daughter. "Learn as much as you can, so you don't make mistakes like I did."

"I want to go home," Evelyn whined, and Lidria's chest ached.

"I didn't listen; I didn't think my actions through." Tears escaped as Lidria ripped her sleeve back down her arm. "Most times when you screw up, you're not offered such an easy second chance. Remember that."

Ian placed a hand on Evelyn's head. "All right. We're leaving."

"Will I—"

"No," Ian snapped. "You scared her."

Lidria's eyes darted away; shame flushed her cheeks. "Okay." She struggled against her disgrace to gaze upon Evelyn one last time. "Goodbye, Evelyn. Ian, thank you."

"I hope you can find something to do with your life, I really do." The sharp countenance in Ian's eyes softened. "Goodbye, Lidria." He turned from her, leading an eager Evelyn where she wanted to go—far away.

Lidria's legs wobbled, and she staggered. Grief overwhelmed her as Ian and Evelyn left without so much as giving her a second glance. "Me, too."

All emotion drained from Lidria, leaving her close to oblivion. She stood alone in the garden unable to make her body move. No thought, no matter how positive or negative, inspired action. Ian's words were the one thing that filled her with something.

That one concept drove Lidria forward. She strode back into the manor with a twisted, fragile purpose. Thelin nodded as she entered, but she ignored him. None of these people mattered; they would forget her as soon as she left. She wished to forget, too.

Lidria froze as she touched the doorknob to her and Selis' room. The drive burning in her mind urged her to proceed, but her heart stopped her. How could she tell Selis? She would be heartbroken. Lidria blocked out the fear blossoming in her chest and opened the door.

Selis jumped as Lidria entered. A long braid of hair slipped out of Selis' hands and fell over her shoulder. "Lidria, I did not think you would be back so soon."

Lidria struggled not to smile upon seeing Selis. "I'm leaving."

"What do you mean?" Selis asked, panicked, and stood from her chair.

"I said: I'm leaving." Quick strides carried Lidria across the room before she had a chance to catch Selis' eyes.

"Lidria, wait." The wood floor creaked behind Lidria. "Slow down. Talk to me, please."

"There's nothing to talk about," Lidria asserted, her eyes, and attention, focused on her sword resting against the armoire. "I can't be here anymore."

Selis grabbed Lidria's wrist as she reached for her weapon. "Whatever happened, you do not have to do this. Just sit down. I am here for you."

"I know you are, Selis, but I…need to find something." Lidria wrapped her fingers around the hard leather scabbard. Her heart beat in her ears.

"You do not have to do it alone." Selis adopted a stronger sense of confidence, and her voice no longer wavered.

"No. You have a place here." Lidria yanked her arm free of Selis' light grip and glowered at her. "I don't."

Selis wilted, glancing down and away. Her hand rose in protest before falling back to her side. "You have…me."

"Selis," Lidria turned and stared at her, her face twisting in anguish, "please don't make this any harder than it already is."

"Where will you go? What will you do?" Desperation deformed Selis' beautiful face.

"I don't know," Lidria admitted, her concentration and determination crumbling.

"Then," Selis reached out and took Lidria's hands in hers, "stay here. At least wait until tomorrow. I…"

"Selis, please." Tears streamed down Lidria's cheeks, the first emotion she had allowed herself since scaring away Evelyn.

"I know you are upset. I cannot imagine how you feel, but you will not, cannot, scare me away. I will stand by you," Selis heaved an exaggerated, sad sigh, "even if you do not want me to."

Lidria shook her head, unable to hold back the tide of ugly emotions. "It's not that I don't want you to. I…I just…I'm so lost." Despair claimed her last scrap of willpower, and she collapsed on the bed.

Selis dropped beside Lidria, wrapping her up in her arms. “It is okay. I got you.”

Welcomed comfort surrounded Lidria yet didn’t take the pain away. “I scared her,” she wept as she trembled in Selis’ embrace.

“I am sorry,” Selis said and held Lidria’s head to her bosom “I know that is not you. You are a gentle person.”

Lidria attempted to let Selis’ rhythmic heartbeat calm her tumultuous emotions despite drowning in an ocean of despair. “I was stupid to think that anything close to what I wanted would happen.”

“You are not stupid for wishing to reunite with your daughter.” Selis’ words reverberated, and Lidria melted against her.

“I feel like it.” Lidria tilted her head upward, seeking the reassurance of Selis’ warm eyes. “And I can’t bear it.”

A smile spread across Selis’ face as she brought her chin to her chest. “You do not have to alone.” Lidria’s vision blurred. “If you want to cry, let it all out. If you want to squeeze me until you wear yourself out, I can take it. Whatever you do, please do not leave without speaking to me.”

“I promise I won’t.” Lidria buried her face in Selis’ chest and squeezed her tight. “Don’t let me go.”

Selis strengthened her embrace and whispered, “I will not. I swear.”

Chapter Twenty-Six

Selis slipped out into the hall and closed the door behind her with a soft *click*. Apprehension wormed into her gut. Lidria deserved the rest, but Selis found sneaking out and leaving her alone dishonest. However, she did not need to hide—she wanted to help.

The first couple of steps were agonizing. Selis' two utmost desires warred with one another despite their end goals being identical. She shook her head, her timid nature piling on her hesitation. A growl resonated in her throat. Frustration gave her movement purpose.

Selis struggled forward, staring at the unblemished wood floor. Her hand reached up to grab the cuff of her sleeve, but she stopped herself. Anxiety could, should, be conquered. She need only believe in her actions.

Morning sunlight cascaded down the staircase. Selis turned from the window, squinting her eyes. A yawn forced its way out, and she scolded herself. She could not let anything distract her or derail her mission.

"Miss Selis," Thelin greeted her as she crossed the stairs. "What may I do for you this morning?"

Despite her efforts building herself up, Selis glanced away from Thelin. "I was on my way to speak with Master Janus."

"Ah." The simple word brought Selis' eyes up. "Well, you won't find him in his study. He's teaching young miss Evelyn on the other side of the building."

"Perfect," Selis blurted out. A curious expression formed on Thelin's face, but she rushed on. "Can you take me to him?"

"That wouldn't be an issue. I'm sure he'll be able to spare a moment." Thelin folded his arms behind his back, clasping his hands.

Selis tipped in a shallow bow. "Thank you."

"You are most welcome." A faint spark lit Thelin's eyes. "Follow me."

Servants rushed around Selis as Thelin led her past the kitchen and pantry. Heady, tantalizing aromas assaulted her nose whenever the door opened. Her stomach growled. In her haste to sneak away, she had forgotten about breakfast. Filling up on delicious food could wait.

"How are your accommodations?" Thelin asked, his level voice calling Selis' attention. "I don't believe I saw you at all yesterday."

A frown ran down Selis' face. Lidria's troubles were not hers to tell. "I was preoccupied. The tomes I borrowed from the library have kept me busy."

"I am glad to hear you have found the library's contents to your liking. Master Janus takes great pride in keeping it stocked."

"I can tell." A rush of excitement tickled Selis at the mere thought of the massive library. "If I ever get the chance, I would love to discuss it with him."

"He's a busy man, but I'm sure he shares the sentiment." Thelin nodded and smiled.

Selis' cheeks burned, and she glanced away. "Do you know anything about Evelyn?"

"Only that she's relatively new here, and Master Janus has taken a keen interest in her training." The smile fled from Thelin's face. "He hasn't taken on a new apprentice in many years."

"Now that you mention it," Selis remarked, cocking her head to the side. "I do not recall him having an apprentice the last time I saw him."

"He's had his attention focused on Kal'den for as long as I can remember." A wistful countenance came over Thelin. "This is somewhat of a pleasant rarity."

"I am glad." With an absent-minded motion, Selis drew her braid over her shoulder. "He has done a lot for the people here; he deserves to share his passion."

"Maybe you can help him," Thelin offered in an almost whisper of a voice.

"How so?" Selis' hands gripped her hair tight.

Thelin straightened after a noticeable pause. "Well, you are no longer tied to Master Flinn. You could join Master Janus and help train new mages or with other magic-related prospects."

Selis bit her lip. The thought captivated something within her, but she did not know what her future held. "I…do not know."

"Something to think about while you're here." Thelin locked eyes with Selis, and she swore she perceived a hint of pleading.

Before Selis could think of something to say, Thelin stopped and pulled a door open. The room beyond lay empty, save for a small desk, several tomes and sheets of paper, and two people. Janus turned from Evelyn. A smile wiped away the dissatisfaction on his face.

"Ah, Thelin. Selis. Is something the matter?" Janus stood from his crouched position.

Thelin bowed. "Miss Selis wished to speak with you."

"What is it?" Janus asked, palpable tension in his voice and posture.

Selis shook her head to dismiss Janus' concerns. "I just wanted to know how Evelyn's training is going."

"All right, considering her young age. I must admit, it's been tough." Janus glanced over his shoulder at Evelyn, and nervous laughter seeped out of him. "I haven't had to do any real teaching in quite some time."

"Maybe I can help." Selis proposed. Despite the simplicity of her statement, her heartbeat escalated.

Janus nodded. "Yes, I think that would work. Some fresh perspective might be just what's required."

Anxiousness filled Selis, but she did not allow her concerns to paralyze her. Her proficiency with magic ranked the sole thing she held any confidence in. Yet even that had been twisted and damaged by Flinn. She let out a flustered huff and took a deep breath. For Lidria.

Selis sat on her knees, getting down to Evelyn's level. "Hello, Evelyn. My name is Selis."

"Hi." Golden locks danced in front of Evelyn's familiar eyes as she tried not to make eye contact.

"How has Master Janus' teaching been going?"

Evelyn's head snapped in Janus' direction and back to Selis. "Okay, but he seems angry today."

"He is not angry at you." Images of Flinn's twisted, belligerent face flashed before Selis. She blocked them out. "You have done nothing wrong."

"I can't do what he wants," Evelyn whined, but Selis noted frustration and fear pervasive in her every movement.

Selis frowned. "And what is that?"

"He wants me to," Evelyn paused, scrunching her brow, "har-harness the magic within me. He said everyone has a different way of showing their connection."

Selis held out her hand, palm up, and Evelyn's eyes tipped down. A small flash of emerald flame flickered as Selis cupped her hand. Nothing more came. The action came as natural to her as breathing. Every time she called, the Flow answered and filled her with comfort. This time, confusion sank in.

Shocked by her inability to produce fire, Selis stared down at her hand. She let her eyes slip closed and breathed deep. Calm found her once more, and she opened herself up again. Magic surged through her and ignited as it always had. She held a piece of herself.

The idea magic could fail her terrified Selis. She would be nothing. Each flick of the flame brought fear of disappearing, of losing everything. Her breathing threatened to break free of her control, but she composed herself. Nerves would not best her.

"This is what happens when I do it," Selis explained, staring at the wild, flickering fire. "I open myself up and let the magic flow freely. This flame is me.

"My former master told me it did not suit my timid nature, but I think it reveals the true me: vulnerable, passionate, and unique. Whenever I look upon it, I feel whole. I feel content. The Flow shows the truth."

Fascinated, Evelyn's gaze held on Selis' cupped hands and the part of her within. The sight of the young mage enraptured with her magic brought a smile to Selis' face. No other actions or words made her feel like she offered something worthwhile. She belonged.

"But…how do you do it?" Curiosity overpowered the hesitation and dejection in Evelyn's voice.

"Here, hold out your hands." Selis dismissed her flame and propped Evelyn's hands in hers. "Close your eyes and relax. Breathe in and out. Focus on the point in the palms of your hands.

"Now, let the Flow in and do not fight it. It is a part of you like anything else. Pour yourself out into your hands. Do not be afraid. I am right here."

Crimson light erupted. Selis flinched at the unexpected intensity. The magic receded before coalescing into a tiny swirling orb. Formidable energy pulsed within despite its diminutive size. Selis' heart leaped into her throat, and exhilaration took her.

"I-I did it," Evelyn exclaimed, rattling Selis. "Look!"

Selis eased back before Evelyn's excitement knocked her over. "You are strong." Selis' lips twitched. "Like your mother."

"What?"

"Nothing." Selis shook her head to dismiss the slip of her tongue. "You have strength you are not aware of yet. You will understand more when you are older."

Unease shifted to wonder on Evelyn's face. "Can you teach me more?"

"If Master Janus does not mind, I would be glad to." Selis pivoted to engage Janus, hopeful.

"No, by all means." Janus gestured forward from his place by the door. "You seem to have a talent for it and can connect with her better than I."

Selis' stomach whirled. Her knowledge and magic would be put to good use for the first time in a long while. "What have you taught her so far?"

"She's still new, so I've been trying to get her to understand the concept of the Flow. Most of the material we've been going over is on the table." The door to the room creaked open, and Janus gave Selis a shallow bow. "I leave her in your capable hands." He slipped out, leaving her alone with Evelyn.

Tension drained from Selis' body as she turned back to her eager student. "Evelyn, give me a few minutes, and we can continue. Okay?"

"Okay," Evelyn chimed and took an impromptu seat on the wood floor.

Selis shuffled the loose papers around on the desk, taking note of what they entailed. Clean, precise handwriting gave way to shaky, imprecise letters cramped in the margins and corners. The way Janus presented the information would prove difficult for a beginner.

Shaking her head, Selis moved the papers into a stack and pushed them aside. The tomes scattered around complimented the notes. She clutched one with the title "Flow Manipulation" emblazoned on the cover in faded gold. Flinn owned a copy of the tome, which she had found insightful.

"I am ready," Selis said with a rush of confidence and self-satisfaction. Not only had she succeeded in establishing a connection with Evelyn, she would help another mage find their way.

Chapter Twenty-Seven

Dark emptiness surrounded Lidria. She curled up tight, desperate to shield and comfort herself. Her stomach twisted, and a little mewling sound squeaked out of her. "You scared her," echoed in her head. Lidria thought she had accepted her identity, but, in truth, she scared herself.

Light filtered into Lidria's vision, and her eyes cracked open. With a vague sense of her whereabouts, she reached out. Nothing but an empty bed welcomed her. Turmoil built inside her. Panic rose to wrestle with her fear and hopelessness for control. She longed for Selis' presence.

Lidria shot up and searched the room, hoping Selis would be close. Selis had left. Loneliness overwhelmed Lidria, and she collapsed on the bed. Tears welled in her eyes. Why would Selis leave her alone? Selis understood her vulnerability…how could she?

A loud sob escaped Lidria as she wallowed in her dark, depressing thoughts and emotions. She had no one to count on, no one to be there for her. They had all left her, every one of them. She couldn't blame them—she had offered nothing. Selis could, would, find much better.

No. Selis didn't betray or abandon her. Lidria sucked in a long breath. Her body rejected her attempts at relaxing and shuddered before hacking coughs took her. She let the unpleasant reflexes run their course, reminding herself she had someone who cared.

Her mind clearer, Lidria scooted to the side and swung her legs off. She paused for a moment as her head spun. A nervous laugh bubbled up inside her. How could she be so foolish? Selis had only gone for breakfast or to borrow some new books. She would be back.

Lidria shook her head, took a deep breath, and stood. She wobbled, but a firm hand against the wall steadied her. The urge to grab her sword from the dresser filled her. She didn't need a weapon; the secluded room provided enough of a safe space.

Books lay scattered about the table, one of them open. Selis' excitement over Janus' library brought a smile to Lidria's face. Lidria found Selis quite adorable when she buried her face in a book or spoke about reading or magic. Her heart fluttered.

Shame flushed Lidria's cheeks. How could she think Selis would leave her? Selis couldn't make a conscious decision to hurt her if she tried. A hint of self-disdain attempted to ruin the moment, but Lidria didn't give in. She deserved someone that cared about her and to care for.

The chair scratched across the floor before Lidria sat down. She sighed, content to await Selis' return. Curiosity piqued Lidria's interest, and she grabbed the book. Text about a specific ritual marked the paper. Try as she might, she couldn't wrap her head around the material.

Lidria placed her left hand on the page to keep her spot and flipped ahead. She didn't know many things about magic or how to control it, yet she became baffled by how much eluded her. She had to admit; she found Selis' intelligence attractive.

Flipping back to Selis' spot, Lidria gave up on understanding anything. Her stomach growled. She hoped Selis would bring back breakfast. If not, she would need to silence her hunger on her own. The thought made her shiver. She didn't want to be alone more than necessary.

Tremors shook Lidria's hand. She pulled it back to her chest and gripped tight. Her eyes drifted to the tattoos peeking out from under her scrunched-up sleeve. Nausea rolled through her, and she hid her arm behind her torso. Long-buried feelings of self-loathing resurfaced.

The doorknob jiggled, and Lidria bolted upright. She tried to appear presentable, like she hadn't gone down a dark trail of thought. No matter how hard she attempted, she couldn't eliminate those emotions. The hope that seeing Selis would ease her mind didn't seem probable.

Selis slipped into the room, platter of food in hand. She jumped when her eyes caught sight of Lidria, but a grin spread across her face. Lidria couldn't help but smile back. What could she do? The simple pleasure of Selis' presence overwhelmed her.

"I am sorry," Selis blurted out, closing the door. "I did not want to wake you."

Lidria hadn't the heart to say much of anything. "Don't worry; it's okay."

The awkwardness vanished from Selis' posture as she moved to the table. She set down the food. "Your hair is a mess."

Without skipping a beat, Selis bent forward and brushed Lidria's hair. Lidria froze. The gentle caress shocked but also soothed her. Selis' absent-minded gaze shifted to embarrassment. Her hand shot back, and Lidria frowned.

"You don't have to stop," Lidria whispered, afraid to speak louder.

A rosy color flushed Selis' cheeks. "I-I brought you some lunch. I had some already, but I figured you would be hungry."

"Thanks, Selis." The nervousness Selis exuded tickled Lidria. "For stopping me yesterday, for this, for being here."

"You are welcome, Lidria. There is nowhere else I would rather be." As if to drive her point home, Selis pulled the other chair next to Lidria and sat beside her.

Lidria, overcome by Selis' words, reached out and grabbed her hand. A reflexive flinch shot through Selis' body, but she soon spread her fingers. Lidria gazed into Selis' beautiful golden eyes. Despite everything that had gone wrong, this felt right.

The food Selis placed before Lidria registered, and her stomach grumbled. She fought to tear her eyes away from Selis' and focus her attention on lunch. A selection of sliced turkey sat atop a thick piece of bread—potatoes and gravy at its side. Her mouth watered.

"So," Lidria said after taking the first bite of delicious food. "Have you been up for a while?"

"A few hours." Selis' voice came out quiet, reserved.

Lidria's eyebrow raised as she ate more turkey. "Were you reading the whole time? I'm surprised you didn't wake me."

"No," Selis confessed, squeezing Lidria's hand tight. "I thought I might be able to help give you another chance with Evelyn."

Lidria stopped mid-movement, fork buried in her meal. Her eyes drifted to Selis. "What did you do?"

"I-I visited while Master Janus was teaching her. He was having issues getting her to learn, so I stepped in and helped." Selis trembled, but Lidria focused on the betrayal lancing her heart. "Things went well. I connected with her over magic. I believe I can convince her to talk to you again, given a little time."

"I had my chance, and I blew it." Frustration over her failures ruined any semblance of self-worth Lidria had built up earlier. "Ian was right to be reluctant to let me see her."

"But I saw how much it hurt you." Selis turned to face Lidria head-on, clutching her hand with both of hers. "If I can help at all, I will try. You deserve it."

"No, I don't," Lidria snapped and wrenched her hand away from Selis.

Selis stared Lidria in the eyes, and she couldn't break away. "You may not think you do, but I know you do. I will support you in any way I can."

“If you didn’t have feelings for me,” Lidria lowered her voice, afraid of the answer to her question, “would you still think that way? Would you think a terrible, neglectful mother deserves anything but disdain?”

“Yes.” The nod of Selis’ head broke Lidria’s heart.

“Don’t lie to me, Selis.”

“I would not lie to you.” Revulsion rolled through Lidria as Selis touched her thigh. Her brain screamed at her to remove Selis’ hand, yet she couldn’t bring herself to. “You are trying to be better, to set things right. You deserve that chance.”

Selis wouldn’t relent. Why? What did she see? “I’ll just ruin it again. You’re wasting your time.”

“If all else fails,” Selis puffed herself up, confident, “I at least helped another mage connect with the Flow.”

“I can’t take this.” Lidria turned away and shot upright. She grabbed her sword and hesitated.

Selis’ chair skidded. “Lidria, wait.” Before she reacted, Selis stood at her side. “Why do you want to run from everything?”

Lidria spun around, towering over Selis, and anger filled her entire being. “She’s my daughter; it’s my problem.” She stormed past Selis, so close yet so far.

“I,” Selis sobbed, “won’t see her again if that’s what you want. I only wanted to help. Please.”

Tears blurred Lidria’s vision as she reached the door. Her heart beat loud in her ears, and her limbs shook. Each second slowed to a crawl, agonizing yet numbing. Nothing would fix the damage she had caused. Selis’ pleading wrenched her soul, but she had made up her mind.

Lidria locked eyes with Selis for a fleeting moment and slammed the door closed. The floor on the other side creaked, but the knob never moved. Part of Lidria prayed Selis would throw the door open and chase after her. She believed; however, things were better this way.

Forcing her body to move, Lidria lurched away from Selis. Nothing could stop her this time. She would be on her own again. Is that what she wanted—to be alone? The thought tied her stomach in knots, but she couldn't go back now. She had blown up on Selis.

Shame weighed Lidria down. Her legs carried her out of the manor, but she remained in shock. Soon, all this pain would fade into memory. No one would remind her of what happened, and no one would remember her. Despite her best efforts to reassure herself, tears ran down her cheeks.

Lidria stopped. She could turn around, go back and apologize. Selis, of course, would accept, but she didn't understand how destructive Lidria would be in her life. Nothing positive ever happened to those who cared for her. Her selfishness trumped any affection she held.

The street through Kal'Den buzzed with people. Lidria frowned before she recognized soldiers in familiar blue and silver uniforms. Her heart pounded. She needed to leave. She couldn't risk Ren or anyone else stopping her. The army had been her only true home but no longer.

Residents milled around the road, and Lidria tried to blend in. The sword on her back broke any sense of inclusion. If she avoided Ren and Hector, she would be home free. A pang of guilt struck her. She had told them both she would see them again; she couldn't disregard them.

"Lidria," a familiar male voice called. She pressed on, ignoring Deeter, the gate leading out of town so close. Only Selis could stop her.

"Lidria, where are you going?" She cursed under her breath as Deeter slipped into view on her left.

Lidria slowed her hectic pace and glanced in Deeter's direction. "I'm leaving." Her voice quivered, and she grimaced.

The smile on Deeter's face vanished. "Have-have you been crying?"

"Leave me be," Lidria demanded.

"Hey, hey." Deeter jumped in front of Lidria, barring her path. She growled her discontent. "Hold on. Once we're settled here, Ren, Joan, and I are going to get together and relax. How about you come with? You'll be in good company and forget whatever's bothering you."

Lidria peeked around Deeter at the exit behind him, anxious. "I don't think—"

"Deeter," Ren called as he approached them. "You found Lidria."

Slipping his arm around Lidria's shoulders, Deeter restrained her. "I was just inviting her to join us this evening."

"We'd be happy to have you."

"Okay." The urge to run didn't go away, but Lidria suppressed it.

"Great." Ren beamed. Lidria wished she shared his relief and optimism. "Once we get everyone settled, we can meet up. Tell Selis she's welcome, too."

The mere mention of Selis' name brought Lidria to the verge of tears. She fought them back and managed a nod as Ren turned to leave. Pressure built in her chest until her breaths came shallow and ragged. Staying would cause more problems, but she didn't have the strength to refuse.

"Don't go anywhere." Deeter squeezed Lidria and withdrew. "I promise things will get better."

Lidria stood in a daze, watching Deeter disappear into the throng of refugees. Her body moved on its own, but she stopped. She would humor Deeter and Ren and say her goodbyes. Then, she could leave with a clear conscience.

Chapter Twenty-Eight

Selis stared at the door in disbelief. She had let Lidria leave after she had tried so hard to show her she had a place. Time remained. Opening the door and chasing after Lidria required little effort, but she froze. She had said all, had attempted to help, and she had made things worse.

Hopelessness crushed what little will Selis clutched to. Her legs gave way, and she collapsed in the chair beside her. She closed her eyes as she shuddered. Tears ran down her cheeks and spattered the back of her hands. Her head swam in a dizzying conflict of thoughts and emotions.

Selis cast her gaze to the tomes, seeking anything to take her mind off Lidria. The text grew distant, hazy. How could she search for solace on the pages? Magic had caused all her problems. None of this would have transpired if she could not command the Flow.

Magic made up Selis' entire life, her being. She could not abandon nor remove herself from the Flow, but it prevented her from having room for other things, other people. Cent, Flinn, Lidria; their relationships all destroyed by magic, yet none would have happened without.

Selis' heart ached, pulled in opposite directions. She did not know what to do. The self-inflicted pain and torture threatened to tear her apart. No matter how hard she tried, she did not loathe magic the way she wished—how much simpler things would be.

Cupping her hand, Selis reached out, but, again, nothing came. Frustration mounted within her. She could not do the simplest thing in the world, and she tipped over the edge. More power swelled, unable to be released. Her temper flared.

Selis wound her arm back. "Why will it not"—her fist crashed down—"work." Emerald flames erupted from the impact.

Heat rushed around Selis, stealing her breath. She flinched from the fire, and the chair tipped back. The room blurred and swirled as her shoulder slammed against the floor. Crisp paper crackled and burned. Wood smoke filled her nose and spurred her to action.

Selis smacked at the flames licking the edges of her robes. Her head pounded, but she scrambled to her feet. The table sat ablaze with emerald fire. She waved her hand, quelling the raging magic. Only ash, mixed with charred fragments, remained of the tomes.

A nervous laugh echoed in the empty room. Selis did not believe herself. An hour ago, she had been ecstatic. Her misguided feelings for the woman who had saved her from living under someone else's thumb clouded her mind. No longer. She would act the way she wished.

The ash scattered as Selis strode toward the door. She gripped the knob and yanked. A surprised servant stumbled in the hallway, but she did not pay them any attention. Focus blocked out unnecessary concerns. One thing ruled her.

Selis flew down the stairs and cut across the manor to where Janus held Gor'an. Guests, servants, and guards alike shot her wary glances. Rather than allow them to inhibit her, she used the cautious gazes to fuel her purpose. She would not be intimidated any longer.

Cool wind nipped Selis' ears as she stepped out into the yard. She took a deep breath, reveling in the brisk air. The edges of her eyes stiffened, and she wiped away the lingering tears with the back of her hand. Her mouth twitched up into a lop-sided smile; she must appear a mess.

"Oi." Selis jumped, jarring her out of her thoughts. "What are you doing out here, little miss mage?"

Anger swelled, and Selis spun on Bal. "Do not call me that." She stared up at him, fire crackling around her fists. "My name is Selis."

"Okay, okay," Bal said and pumped his hands. She backed off, but her determination remained. "What's gotten into you?"

"Nothing." Selis pivoted and strode away from Bal.

Bal's footsteps followed Selis. "Where do you think you're going?"

"To set Gor'an free." The hairs on the back of Selis' neck stood on end, and concern fluttered her stomach.

"I can't let you do that." Steel scraped behind Selis.

Selis whirled around, channeling the Flow into her right hand. Instinct took over, and her eyes locked on the sword in Bal's hand. The gap between them vanished. She threw her hand out and gripped the blade. Magic surged as she crushed the threat.

Fragments of Bal's weapon splintered to the ground. Selis glared up into his wide eyes. "Try to stop me again, and I will not hold back."

"Master Janus isn't going to be happy," Bal managed, regaining his composure.

"I do not care." Selis' chest rose and fell in rapid succession, and her heart pounded. "He is treating Gor'an like a test subject, like an animal. I cannot allow that to go on any longer."

A frown came over Bal's face. He took a half-step back, and his shoulders relaxed. "You've made your position very clear. I'm just trying to warn you."

"I appreciate your concern," Selis drew herself up, struggling to match her physical appearance to the strength of her will, "but I can handle myself."

The chill wind blew, tossing around loose strands of Selis' hair and causing her to shiver. Bal's mouth moved, but he did not speak. She held no more words for him, and he none for her. A small victory, yet her resolve bolstered.

Selis turned from Bal and headed toward the building where Gor'an languished. He did not follow her this time, nor did he make any sound. Excitement rushed through her. In a few moments, she could say she had followed her feelings through for once in her life.

Warmth settled around Selis as she entered the small structure. Lein's head snapped up from his seated position at the desk on the far side of the room. He appeared to have been sleeping before her intrusion—Bal's scolding did not make the man any more attentive.

"Oh, Selis," Lein said, trying, and failing, to act composed. "If you're looking to see the Quelan, now's not a good time. He's—"

Selis strode past Lein. He stammered something after her, but she did not slow her pace. The stairs flashed by in a blur. Pressure constricted around her the moment her foot touched the ground. She grit her teeth, forcing herself forward. So close.

A guttural groan and frantic scratching came from Gor'an's cell. Selis clutched one of the steel bars, and her heart sank. Gor'an pressed himself into the dingy corner. Fresh wounds dotted his flesh, stretching in long swathes or precise divots; his fur matted and torn to match.

Selis reached out to Gor'an, and her grip loosened. *Gor'an, what happened?*

Silence.

Please. Speak to me. Images of Flinn's lifeless eyes staring back at her flashed. Her breath caught in her throat.

Gor'an lifted his head enough for Selis to recognize movement. *Hate. Attack. Pain.*

I am so sorry. The knife twisted in Selis' gut, and she blinked tears from her eyes. *I will release you. I should have done this earlier, but—*

No. A wall of fear struck Selis, knocking the air from her lungs. *Will. Chase.*

What do you... Selis sensed an enchantment around Gor'an—one not there before. Taking a steadying breath, she poured her magic out and plucked at the edges. The spell began to unravel, and she soon freed him.

There. He will not be able to find you. Selis took stock of all Gor'an's injuries and grimaced. *This may hurt a bit, but I am going to heal what I can. Hold on.*

Serenity overcame Selis' distress, and she placed her hand on the lock. The Flow surged through her, obeying her call, and sparks flew. Clear-cut fragments of metal plinked on the stone below. She yanked open the door and slipped inside before kneeling next to Gor'an.

Selis touched Gor'an's bloodied arm and, sucking in a deep breath, went about her task. Pain erupted in her mind and body. She gasped. Not all his injuries would heal well—some were too severe—but she continued. Her conscience weighed heavy, and she would do her best.

The constant strain from the prison's ward and the effort of healing soon caught up with Selis. She squeezed out as much magic as she could before her body rejected her actions. Her eyes shot open, and her balance wavered—nausea her reward. She fell against the wall.

Selis' labored breathing echoed off the dirty, worn stone. A long moment passed before she regained her composure. She had been down here for only a few minutes; the anguish Gor'an must suffer. His eyes greeted hers, and their connection strengthened.

You should be able to leave now, Selis said as her eyes grew heavy. *I am sorry I put you through all this, but I could not let them kill you.*

Confusion ebbed and flowed, and Selis grit her teeth. *You. Strange. Different.*

Selis did not hold back a chuckle. *I suppose I am. I do not know what I am doing. I only wanted to help, but I made things worse.*

Better. Gor'an shifted and, grunting with the effort, stood. He used the wall for stability, but Selis' spirits lifted seeing him stand on his own.

I am glad you think so. Selis fought down the urge to shrink back from Gor'an's tall, imposing form. *I was worried you hated me for what I did.*

Out. Kin. A strong desire to flee, to find where she belonged, filled Selis.

Selis glanced away, ashamed. The feelings of utter desperation and pleading when last she saw Gor'an pervaded her mind. *You said your kin would kill you, but when I visited last, it sounded like you wanted to join them. What changed?*

Hate. Magic. Death. Gor'an turned toward the open door, but Selis grabbed his massive arm. Her heart leaped into her throat as his narrowed amber eyes swung toward her.

What was Master Janus trying to discover? Selis pressed, hoping their fragmented communication proved sufficient to convey a close enough understanding.

Silence stilled the air. Selis did not think Gor'an understood her, but he eked out a single word: *Home.*

He placed the spell on you, knowing I might free you. Selis shook her head. Once again, she had caused more problems instead of making situations simpler. *But,* a frown came over her face, *he must have known I would dispel it. I do not understand.*

All. Dead. Gor'an's heart beat in Selis' ears. Dread coursed through his veins, and he shuffled out of her grasp.

Selis' mind raced. Master Janus wanted to comprehend how Quelan magic worked, like Flinn; however, except for their connection, Gor'an did not appear to hold any. The shaman she encountered over a week ago had been strong. Maybe Master Janus hoped to find such a candidate if she released Gor'an.

A thought came to Selis: if Master Janus did not learn anything, he would want to kill the Quela. Her actions with the invocation intact would have also worked to that end. She was missing a piece, something to tie everything together. One bit of information to illuminate the way.

Gor'an, Selis called. He stopped but did not turn around to face her. *Do you know a shaman of your people searching for human tomes?*

Gre'cha. A shiver ran down Selis' spine. The visage of the one who humiliated her flashed before her.

Selis shook her head, clearing her mind. Her right hand drifted down to her leg. *Why did Gre'cha want them?*

Trickster. Bitterness flooded Selis and mixed with her own disgust. Flinn.

What did this trickster want with your people? Selis asked despite fearing she knew the answer.

Gor'an glanced back over his shoulder, sorrow, and fury in his eyes. *Kin. End.*

Everything Flinn had tried to accomplish clicked into place. His research on the Quela, his experiment on Selis, his paranoia, and the attack itself. He had wanted to solve the riddle of Quelan magic, and, upon failing, sought to destroy them. They had razed an entire city to stop him.

Guilt settled in Selis' gut. She could have stopped Flinn, prevented Odwyn's destruction, if she had been smarter. He had been so close, and she had had so many opportunities. One time, one question, one action would have saved everyone. She would not make the same mistake again.

Selis swept in front of Gor'an. *I will make sure you get out.*

Determined, Selis led Gor'an out of prison. The moment she stepped on the stairs, the unrelenting pressure dropped from around her. She sighed and straightened her back. Her attention focused on seeing her action through. Lein may try to prevent her from leaving when he saw Gor'an.

The guard room upstairs appeared empty. Selis cocked her head to the side, but she heard voices outside. She prepared herself for whatever she had to do and opened the door.

"Sir," Lein protested. "What do you mean?"

Bal stood stoic in the face of his subordinate's questioning. "I told you to let Selis do what she wants."

"But Master Janus—"

"Bal," Selis interjected as she exited the building. "Please escort Gor'an outside the walls."

Bal gave her a long, hard stare before he nodded. "Very well." He waved his hand at Gor'an with his usual dismissive flair. "Come on."

Lein stared at Selis, a baffled expression on his face. She expected him to say something, but he did not. A moment passed until Bal and Gor'an disappeared. She trusted Bal. Her mission a success, and her mind and body exhausted, she struggled back to her room.

The trip went by in a flash. Overwhelmed, Selis did not think of much of anything. All she knew, all she felt, crystallized into one feeling—pride. She had accomplished what she had set out to do, and no one could take that away from her—not even herself.

Selis stumbled into her room. The door closed behind her, and she managed not to topple over. She ignored the ash on the table, chairs, and floor and made straight for bed. Her face struck the bedding, and she curled up. Tears dampened the pillow. She had achieved her goal on her own. Why did she feel so empty?

Chapter Twenty-Nine

Lidria stared at the cup in front of her. The pungent scent of ale assaulted her nose, but Deeter showed no signs of letting up. Reluctant, she reached out and grabbed the offered drink. She downed a quick sip. Bitter and potent; her body revolted for partaking in such swill.

"C'mon," Deeter urged, downing the last bit in his mug. "You've got a lot of catching up to do. Might as well get a start on Joan while you're at it."

Lidria grimaced. "I don't drink often, and this is certainly not the kind of thing I would drink when I do."

"This is all we could get on such short notice." Ale sloshed as Deeter poured another glass. "It'll get better after you drink some more."

The thought of keeping up with Deeter's expectations nauseated Lidria. "I don't think I have the stomach for it."

"You'll feel better if you do." Deeter cracked a warm smile. "I promise."

"Feel better about what?" Joan asked. She balanced several bottles of wine in her arms as she fumbled with the door.

Deeter's chair squeaked as he struggled to face Joan. "Dunno. She's been tight-lipped about it."

"Well," Joan set her haul down, "that's not very helpful." Her curious eyes met Lidria's. "Can you at least give us a hint?"

Lidria gave in to the pressure, downing a gulp of the terrible ale. "I…I'm not speaking to Selis anymore."

"Is she okay?"

"I answered your question. Please," Lidria wiped a tear away with the back of her finger, "drop it."

Joan frowned and eased back, tense. "Okay."

"Lidria here was on her way out of town before I stopped her." Smug self-satisfaction graced Deeter's face.

"I still plan on leaving," Lidria remarked, building up her resolve.

"I'm going to talk with Selis." Joan pivoted on her heel but turned back around and gestured to the wine bottles she brought. "You can have those. You look like that ale is trying to kill you." Her footsteps echoed across the room, the door creaked, and she vanished.

Lidria leaned back and avoided eye contact with Deeter. The urge to come clean and explain the situation bubbled up, but she couldn't speak. Words failed her and would make her sound like a blithering idiot. She remained content to deal with the silence a little longer.

Ren nursed his mug, silent. His eyes caught Lidria's. Uncertainty flashed across his face before he glanced away. A flutter of uneasiness filled her with anxiety. He took a long draught of his ale and sat up in his chair.

"So," Ren drawled. "What have you learned about Master Janus?"

Lidria reached forward, pulling one of the bottles close. "Not a whole lot. I've only spoken with him a couple times since I got here. He seems like he has everyone's best interests in mind."

"I'm meeting with him tomorrow; we've been too busy with getting everyone settled today." Ren set his drink aside, and his shoulders relaxed.

"Sel—" Lidria's mouth snapped shut, and embarrassment flushed her cheeks. She cracked open the bottle and gulped some down before she let anymore slip.

"Something's clearly driving you crazy," Deeter slurred, leaning forward. "What happened?"

Ren gripped Deeter by the shoulder and shoved him back in his seat. "Don't mind Deeter. You don't have to talk if you don't want to."

The warmth of the wine mingled with Lidria's relief, eroding her fears. A small smile curled the corner of her lips. "Thank you for being so understanding."

"It's no problem," Ren said with a dismissive flick of his wrist.

"Yeah," Deeter leaned against the table and pointed at the booze in Lidria's hand, "once you get some more drink in you, you'll get to talking."

Tension caught Lidria's breath in her throat as Ren turned to glare at Deeter. "I could order you to leave."

"Sorry, sir." Deeter gulped down more ale before he grinned. "Off duty. Your orders mean nothing."

Ren shook his head and grabbed his cup. "Maybe this was a bad idea."

"No, it's all right." Ren and Deeter's attention shifted to Lidria, and she sighed. "You should be happy that everyone's safe. Don't let my issues bog you down."

"You're fine, Lidria. Deeter's just being his usual difficult self." With a practiced grace, Ren took a swig of his ale.

Deeter blew out a harsh puff of air. "I'm not difficult—Joan's the difficult one."

"I'm glad she went," Lidria whispered. Her heartbeat spiked when she realized how loud she spoke.

"What do you mean?" Ren asked. He appeared as curious as Deeter at this point.

The embarrassment Lidria expected never came. Words came slow, but she would be honest. "Someone should treat Selis well."

"As much as I am for letting you twist and turn," Deeter sank back in his chair, drink in hand, "not knowing what happened is really making it hard to talk about."

"It's complicated." Lidria lowered her head and took a deep breath. "And I'm a complete idiot."

"Welcome to the club," Deeter sang and tipped back, coming close to spilling onto the floor. "Now, find your courage and out with it."

Lidria downed too much wine to stall for time. Coughs wracked her body, trying to dispel the misplaced liquid. She cleared her throat as her episode ended and focused. Thoughts and emotions flitted about her head in a jumbled mess. What could she say to do any of them justice?

Hesitation plagued her, but Lidria raised her gaze and fought on. "I found out my daughter's here. She's being trained by Master Janus. I haven't seen her in six years since my husband left me and took her with him. I convinced him to let me meet with her.

"I," Lidria swallowed back her self-pity, "did something stupid and ruined my chance at becoming a part of her life again."

Ren waited for a long moment before he spoke. "And where does Selis come in?"

"She's the one that pushed me to have the meeting; told me I could do it," Lidria said, shaking her head in disbelief. "I believed her, too.

"When I failed, I was distraught. Selis tried to cheer me up, but I was difficult. She"—a nervous laugh echoed in the small room—"went to help teach my daughter to get close to her to give me another chance.

"I lost it, got angry with her and said some things I shouldn't have. I stormed off, saying I was leaving, and now I'm here." Lidria stared at Deeter, resentment seeping up inside her. "If you hadn't stopped me, I would be long gone by now."

Deeter waved his sloshing mug in an arc. "You're welcome."

"Yeah," Lidria wavered forward as she snorted in indignation, "now I get to be harassed instead of on my own."

"Hey," Deeter protested, setting his drink aside. "I can't pretend to know how any of that feels, but it sounds to me like things could be patched up if you went back and talked with Selis." He locked eyes with Lidria.

Panic surged in Lidria, and she tore her eyes away from Deeter's. "I can't. She wanted to help, she cares about me, and I threw it all back at her. Me leaving is best for her." She exhaled and trembled.

"Did you tell her that?" Ren interjected.

Lidria shook her head. "No, she would have just said she didn't believe that."

Ren's eyes met Lidria's, lacking the same edge as Deeter's. "Do you believe that?"

"Yes." Tears welled up in Lidria's eyes and holding them back took all her strength. "I'm a terrible, selfish person. She doesn't deserve that. I would have only caused her more trouble if I stayed."

"Since I've known you," Ren started and leaned forward, elbows on the tabletop, "you have strived to do what you could for people. You could have abandoned Hector, left his mother to die, left Selis with Flinn, and let countless other people—including me—die, but you didn't.

"I don't know what happened in the past, but you're not the person you think you are anymore. And I would say those people don't see you as that person either." Ren smiled and eased back in his chair. "Give yourself some credit."

"That's not the real me," Lidria blurted out. She couldn't accept that, after everything she had done, people might believe her to be anything better. "I've been pretending to be someone else to avoid acknowledging who I really am this whole time. It only took me seeing my daughter to realize that."

"How old is your daughter?"

Lidria swallowed hard, and a tear streaked down her chin. "Ten." So many wasted years. If only she could go back and do things right.

"She probably doesn't understand who you are." Ren's words of reason exasperated Lidria's inadequacy, her self-belittlement. "I'm sorry things didn't go well, but I'm sure she just needs to be older to understand."

Pain fueled Lidria's rising ire. "I'm not going to wait around in this hell to get rejected again."

"I'm not saying that," Ren said, frustration sneaking into his voice. "I'm saying this isn't the last chance unless you make it so."

"You make it sound like it's easy. I thought I had gotten over this a long time ago. Then," Lidria no longer held her tears, her emotions, at bay, "Hector reminded me of what I was missing. I let Selis get close, and I let my feelings cloud my judgment." Weak sobs escaped her. "I should have known better."

A sad, thoughtful expression came over Ren's face. "It's all right. Let it out."

"No judgment here," Deeter chimed in as Lidria's vision blurred. "I may tell a few people, though, if you ever get on my bad side."

"I'm so sorry." Lidria crumpled forward and buried her face in the crook of her arm, ashamed.

"We're not the ones you should be apologizing to." Ren's voice came soft and comforting despite his message.

Lidria sniffed back part of her mess and raised her head. "I know, but I don't think I can."

"If you value her, or her feelings, at all, you need to make things right." Ren's eyes softened. "It might not be easy, but she will appreciate it."

“I—you’re right.” Wet stains dotted Lidria’s sleeve as she wiped her face dry. She glanced side-to-side at herself and chuckled. “I’m not going to go see her like this, though.”

Deeter raised an eyebrow and smirked. “What, you’re fine looking like that for us but not for her? I guess Joan was right.”

“About what?” Lidria asked, her heart pumping faster.

“You and Selis.” Deeter’s finger waggled back and forth like Selis sat beside her. “Have you—”

“Enough, Deeter,” Ren ordered, slapping Deeter’s hand down. “Lidria’s been through enough of your hounding.” Lidria’s cheeks burned.

The smirk returned to Deeter’s face as he tilted his head toward Ren. “Jealous?”

“Of what? If they’ve found something in each other, I’m happy for them.” Something flickered on Ren’s face, but Lidria didn’t catch it before it vanished.

“Don’t worry, sir.” Leaning over and avoiding falling to the floor, Deeter put his arm around Ren’s shoulders. “I’m right there with you.”

Lidria’s head pounded, and she wanted nothing more than for the terrible day to end. She pushed aside her quarter bottle of wine. How she went through so much in such a short amount of time she didn’t understand. Fatigue and alcohol slowed her every thought and movement until her consciousness faltered.

“I think I’m going to go lie down,” Lidria said, drawing Ren and Deeter’s attention. “Today’s been exhausting.”

“Okay.” Ren forced Deeter away and sat up straight. “Goodnight, Lidria.”

“‘Night,” Deeter managed before presenting her with a sloppy salute.

Lidria kept her hand planted on the table for support as she stood. "Goodnight." Her wobbly legs carried her to the back room with minimal effort.

Overwhelmed, Lidria collapsed onto one of the beds. Cold invaded her as she sank into the fresh bedding. Selis occupied her drunken, weary thoughts, and Lidria longed for her presence. She had no clue what she would say to make things right, but she needed to say something, to try.

Lidria squirmed around, pulled the covers up over herself, and curled into a ball. The tears she expected never came. Instead, serenity enveloped her. She would apologize and thank Selis for everything she's done. A smile crept onto Lidria's face as she thought about Selis and drifted off.

Chapter Thirty

Selis sipped her tea. The warm herbal concoction soothed her body but did not fill the void. She sighed and stared into the cup, watching the steam rise and the small bubbles drift across the surface. She did not know what to do with herself, every option worse than the last.

Nothing piqued Selis' interest, and nothing would shake her from her stupor. The fact she managed to acquire tea spoke volumes of her desire for comfort, for some semblance of normality. It was hard to believe how quick she had sunk into hopelessness, yet she did nothing to stop.

Lidria popped into Selis' mind despite her best efforts. She did not understand. The thought of bridging the gap between Lidria and Evelyn thrilled Selis, but Lidria reacted harsher than she ever imagined to the prospect. Lidria was struggling with the entire situation, which is why Selis had wished to help.

A sad sigh escaped Selis. She had driven away the one person she had made a connection with in a long while. Had she acted too hasty? Lidria wanted to take things slow, Selis understood, and still, she kept pushing. She overwhelmed Lidria with her foolish pursuit.

Selis needed to face the truth: Lidria would not come back. Not that there would be anywhere to come back to. Once Master Janus found out about Gor'an, he would throw Selis out. On top of having nothing else, she would need to find a place to stay.

Another sip of her tea and Selis did not find any comfort. She could do nothing but face things as they came. Her mind and eyes wandered. Tiny heaps of ash rested against the wood trim running along the bottom of the wall. Magic would not solve her problems.

Curiosity gripped her, and a frown weighed heavy on her face. Her intermittent loss of command over the Flow did not merit top priority.

Now, what else did she have to worry about? If magic abandoned her, she would be nothing.

One thing caused such disruptions: dauein. However, the drug blocked the use of magic, or it did not—no in-between existed. She should not be able to call upon the Flow at all, not be limited in frustrating spurts.

Selis shifted her weight, and a chill ran down her spine. Before she realized, she cupped her hand and summoned emerald flames. They obeyed and came as naturally as they had for years. She closed her eyes, shaking her head. Shame usurped her fear, her paranoia.

A soft rap came at the door. Selis bolted upright, and her eyes snapped up. Her heart raced. She waited for someone to speak or to knock again, but nothing came. Master Janus would no doubt throw the door open and storm in. Hope rose in her tightening chest.

The door creaked, and a familiar dark-skinned woman poked her head inside. Her almond-colored eyes locked on Selis as a smile spread across her face. Selis stared, dumbfounded. In the whirlwind of activity surrounding her the past two days, she had forgotten about the refugees.

"Hi, Selis," Joan said, upbeat, slipping into the room and closing the door behind her.

Selis bit down her surprise and disappointment. "Joan. I did not think you had made it here yet."

"We just got in this afternoon." Joan's eyes darted around the room, and Selis frowned. "May I sit with you?"

"Oh, yes. Come." Selis collected herself and pushed the other chair out with her foot as she scooted hers over.

Joan strode across the room and took the seat Selis offered. She leaned her elbow on the table, her posture relaxing. "How have things been here?"

“I—” A lump formed in Selis’ throat. She swallowed hard, trying not to let Joan’s confused expression dissuade her. “It is complicated.”

“You can talk to me. I won’t tell anyone.” Selis’ breaths came short despite Joan’s comforting words.

“It is not that simple,” Selis asserted, afraid of what she might do if she spoke further.

Concern flashed across Joan’s face. She placed her left hand on top of Selis’, gentle. “I saw Lidria before I came here.”

Selis filched backward, but Joan’s strong hand held hers in place. Panic shortened Selis’ breath until she thought her chest might explode. “It is more than that. Nothing I do goes right. I end up hurting everyone around me or driving them to hate me. I, I”—tears flowed uninhibited, and she sobbed—“please tell me she did not leave.”

“She didn’t,” Joan whispered, squeezing Selis’ hand.

“Where is she?” Selis did not care about her tears, about what they said; she needed to see Lidria. “I need to go.”

“Easy.” Joan slid closer to her and moved her hand to Selis’ shoulder, forcing her to stay seated. “She’s not going anywhere. Ren and Deeter will see to that.”

Selis’ leg bounced up and down, and the urge to run burned in every muscle. “But I have to. What if she leaves anyway?”

“I have faith in them.” Joan cracked a small smile. “Even if Deeter is an idiot, he’s the one that stopped her.”

“So, I am supposed to sit here and wait?” Selis’ heart sank, her shoulder slumped, and all drive fled her.

“Yes.” Joan leaned back, removing her hand from Selis. Her hand over top of Selis’, however, remained. “Your emotions are clearly running high, so calm down, cool down, and approach this with a more level head. How about you talk to me for now and tell me what happened?"

"Okay," Selis managed as she attempted to relax and figure out what to say. She wanted to express many things, but she decided to start when she and Lidria had come to the manor. "When we arrived, we encountered Lidria's daughter, Evelyn. Lidria had a—"

"I know," Joan said. Selis stared at her. "She told me back in Odwyn the day after she brought you back."

"Oh." Considering how much prodding Selis had done to force Lidria to speak about anything, she found the fact that she had opened up to Joan surprising. She shook her head to clear her thoughts. "Evelyn has the capacity to command the Flow, given time and training. Master Janus took her in as his apprentice, so she and Ian are living here.

"Lidria was uncertain about trying to meet Evelyn. I urged her to try; she owed it to Evelyn and herself. She took my advice to heart and set up a meeting. It did not go well. She ended up scaring Evelyn.

"Lidria came back here a wreak and said she needed to leave. I stopped her. Seeing an opportunity, I went and tried to bond with Evelyn by helping her learn magic. Lidria did not find my attempt to be anything but a betrayal. She stormed out and left. I could not bring myself to follow her."

Selis lifted her hand and wiped away the tears running down her cheeks. The ease with which she spoke with Joan, while cathartic, did little to soothe her pain. She realized each time she pushed someone, they lashed out. Her cravings for things she should not have tainted her every action.

"I, I have feelings for Lidria, and she for me, but she wanted to take things slow." Selis turned her head away from Joan. "I understood, yet I kept pushing her. I think all my advances, added up, drove her away. I would have kept pushing and pushing if she stayed, and I do not wish to force her to do anything against her will."

"Selis." Joan closed the gap between them and wrapped her arms around Selis. Warmth surrounded Selis, but it only made her cry harder.

"I always make things worse. I cannot help myself." Selis' words came out jumbled between sobs and sniffles.

Joan squeezed Selis tight. "You did nothing wrong. You only wanted to help someone you care for. That's not something to condemn."

"Then," Selis gripped Joan, afraid to let go, "why do I always drive people away or worse?"

"It's not your fault. People are complicated and can act in ways you do not anticipate. Don't take these experiences to mean you need to stop being yourself, that you should stop caring." Cool air replaced Joan's body heat as she pulled back. Selis tilted her head up until Joan's eyes encompassed her view. "Please."

Selis recoiled. How could she continue being herself if that meant more disasters like Cent, Flinn and Lidria? The idea crushed her soul. Nothing would have any meaning at that juncture. She could not, would not, live her life that way. Joan could not expect her to.

"I killed two of the three people closest to me and ruined whatever could have been between Lidria and me." Strength left Selis, and her arms slipped down to Joan's waist. "How can you say I should always be myself?"

Joan cocked her head to the side. "You had to defend yourself. Flinn was a mistake; you couldn't have known. You still have a chance with Lidria. She was as distraught as you when I saw her."

"That is because I betrayed her trust." The utter betrayal in Lidria's eyes lanced Selis' heart.

"Do you really believe that?" Joan asked, remaining as close to Selis as ever.

"Well," Selis chewed her lip, "no. But it does not matter how I feel; Lidria feels it is."

Joan's eyes hardened for the first time, and Selis' breath halted. "It does matter, Selis. You shouldn't be so hard on yourself. If anyone's wrong, Lidria is. However, I can see she wasn't in the right mindset and just needs to clear her head."

"If I did not try anything, Lidria would not be mad at me." Defeat plagued Selis, dragging her down to nothing.

"Think about it this way"—Joan pulled back from Selis and propped her up straight until they met eye-to-eye—"if you hadn't tried, would you be okay with that?"

Selis shook her head. "I do not think so. The whole point was to help her."

"Then, you're fine. You have nothing to worry about or apologize for." A bright smile drove away the darkness encroaching on Joan's face, and Selis found herself reciprocating.

"Maybe." Selis sighed and stared at her cold tea. "I am so used to being talked down to and blamed that I struggle with the idea I did nothing wrong, so I must blame myself."

Joan's strong hands squeezed Selis' shoulders. "I'm sorry you had to deal with that so much in your life, but you're free of that now. I only ask that you try to realize that and not be afraid."

"I will try," Selis said, more confident. "Thank you, Joan."

"You're welcome, Selis." Joan gave Selis one more hug before separating.

Joan's warmth lingered around Selis. She appreciated the other woman's kindness, but one thing consumed her thoughts. Instead of stopping herself, she pulled her braid across her chest. Her hands tugged and teased in a nervous fit. She did not want to wait.

"How long do you think I should give Lidria before I talk to her?" Selis squeaked, worried over Joan's response.

"I don't know." Joan shrugged. "Give her a couple days to get her head on straight."

Selis' eyes lowered to her hair, gripped tight, in her lap. "I doubt he will provide me that much time."

"What do you mean?" Concern played in Joan's voice, but Selis did not raise her gaze.

"I went against Master Janus' wishes today." A knot formed in Selis' stomach; she feared his retribution. "I freed a Quelan he held captive after he told me not to."

"Why would you do something like that?" Joan demanded, and Selis' heart twisted.

Pushing her pain aside, Selis lifted her head and stared at Joan. "I share a connection with him. I do not understand it, but I am able to communicate with him. My desire to help got in the way again, but I could not let him suffer any more torture."

"You can speak with the Quela? That's—" Confusion flashed across Joan's face. "I've never heard anything like that before."

"Neither did I until last week. I was surprised, but I would be lying if I said I did not find it intriguing." Being the first one, the only one, to bridge the gap between humans and Quela brought both a sense of pride and trepidation. She sat up straighter.

"Yeah, I can understand that. That means they're not just vicious beasts." The uncertainty and revulsion vanished, and curiosity danced in Joan's eyes. "What's it like, talking to one?"

"Difficult," Selis expressed, strained. She attempted not to fall back into the hole of misery she found Gor'an in earlier. "Our communication is not as clear as the conversation you and I are having; it's more feeling-based. I understood his emotions more than heard his curt, broken words."

Joan nodded, and her posture relaxed. "I guess you feeling its pain explains why you freed it."

"His name is Gor'an." Selis took a deep breath and dispelled her irritation. "But, yes, I could…even when I was not connected to him."

"What does that mean?"

"The reason for our connection when no one else has ever spoken to a Quelan before is because I share something in common with them." The ward, crisp and agonizing, burned itself into Selis' mind's eye. "Something happened to me to give me a part of their magic."

"Does that have something to do with your eyes and hair? I mean, I think they're lovely, but gold and silver aren't natural colors." Joan's eyes lingered on Selis' for a moment longer than usual.

Selis' cheeks burned. "I believe so. I also believe Flinn did it to me. Both he and Master Janus were obsessed with figuring out how Quelan magic works."

"Maybe what happened," Joan mused in a soft and wispy voice, "was less of an accident and more him getting what he deserved for experimenting on you."

"I was angry when I figured it out, but I now think it is more a blessing than a curse." Peace filled Selis for the first time, and a weight lifted off her chest. "Because of what he did, I was able to save someone's life."

"See," Joan smirked, "you don't always do the wrong thing when trying to help."

Selis did not deny Joan's infectious grin. "In this one case, you are right."

"Better now?" Joan asked, throwing her arm over the back of her chair.

"Yes," Selis admitted despite herself. "I think so. I do not know how to repay you."

Joan locked eyes with Selis. "Don't give up on finding happiness."

"I will try not to." Selis nodded as she spoke, a faint smile tugging at her lips.

"Good." Joan let out a cheerful little laugh and placed a hand on her stomach. "Now, I'm starving."

Selis stood, her stomach rumbling. She had not eaten anything since morning. "Let us go down to the kitchen."

Joan shot up, needing no further prompting. Selis pulled the door open and led Joan through the manor. Her anxieties melted and were replaced by a gentle calm. She would be all right, Lidria would be all right, everything would be all right.

Chapter Thirty-One

"Lidi, Lidi," Hector shouted over the din of milling refugees, emerging from a nearby knot of people.

Lidria swayed as Hector latched onto her legs. A smirk dashed the frown on her face, and she patted him on the back. He beamed up at her and squeezed tighter. Seeing him, and his overzealous enthusiasm, dispelled the uncertain thoughts swirling around in her head.

Hector's hair parted as Lidria ruffled the matted mess. "Hi, Hector. It's nice to see you, too."

"I was worried you might not be here." Anxiousness darted across Hector's face, and he hid against Lidria's hip. She lowered her arm and pulled him close.

"So, he did see you." Lidria's gaze snapped from Hector to Nell. She approached the two, struggling with a pair of shoddy crutches.

Lidria greeted Nell with a warm smile. "Yeah. I'm guessing he's been looking ever since you got in."

"Oh, he wouldn't stop. He's been running me ragged trying to keep him from running off." Nell hobbled close.

Hector peeled his face away from Lidria and glared at his mother. "I would have been fine looking for Lidi on my own."

Nell sighed, frustrated. She opened her mouth, but Lidria cut her off. "Hector, I know you wanted to find me, but you should think about listening to your mother. She's just worried about you."

"I know," Hector huffed, "but I could find you faster without her. It's not like there's anywhere to go."

"That's not the point." Lidria's words caught in her throat, and her chest tightened. "You two almost lost each other once; you shouldn't try pushing it."

Hector cocked his head to the side, curiosity evident in his eyes. "I don't see what the big deal is."

"You will when you're older. Treat your mother well, all right?" Hector nodded without further protest and wrenched his arms from around Lidria.

Nell crept forward and tried to grab Hector by the arm, but he danced away. He disappeared into the crowd. "Sometimes that child is exhausting."

"I wish I knew what that was like," Lidria blurted out. Regret set in, and she prayed Nell didn't notice.

A surprised laugh bubbled out of Nell. "Trust me, you don't." Her laughter came to an abrupt halt when Lidria didn't so much as smile. "Oh. Well, don't worry; you have time. You're still young."

"I had a chance, but I blew it." Shame drove Lidria's gaze away from Nell. "I'm not fit to be a parent."

"That's hard to believe. Even if you're not well-suited for it, you did a wonderful job with Hector. I can't thank you enough." Frustration welled inside Lidria, threatening to overflow and lash out.

Lidria took a deep, centering, breath. "I've just been trying to atone for my past mistakes."

"If that's the case," Nell placed a soft hand on Lidria's shoulder and smiled, "I'd say you've learned from them."

Minding Nell's frail state, Lidria wrapped the other woman in a tight embrace as a tear ran down her cheek.

"Needed to hear that, huh?" Nell whispered. Lidria nodded, suppressing further tears, and Nell hugged her back. "You've earned it."

"Lidi." Lidria pulled away and made sure Nell's crutches supported her. Hector stood beside them with a knotted and slanted wooden sword in his hands. "I…I made this. Can you teach me how to swordfight?"

“I can show you the basics,” Lidria cast her gaze back to Nell, “if that’s okay with your mother.”

Nell chewed on her lip for a moment. “Why not. He’s already a handful. At least this way maybe he’ll learn some discipline and not hurt himself with it.”

“Yes,” Hector exclaimed, jumping up and down. Lidria couldn’t contain the grin spreading across her face.

“What do you say to Lidria?” Nell asked, staring down at Hector.

Hector turned his head up at Lidria, his teeth showing. “Thank you, Lidi.”

“You’re welcome, Hector.” Lidria patted his head and glanced around over the mass of people and between the buildings. “Let’s go find someplace where we can work.”

Nell rested her weight on her uninjured leg, exhaustion draining the life from her face. “I’m going to rest after this morning’s excitement. You two have fun.”

“Okay. I’ll see you later, Nell. I promise I won’t teach him anything too crazy.”

“I’m sure.” Nell shook her head. “Now go on before he gets bored and runs off.”

Lidria cracked a smile and took Hector by the shoulder. They wandered around, winding in and out of streets and masses of people. With the addition of all the survivors from Odwyn, Kal’den had grown boisterous. Finding an open, quiet place to practice proved difficult.

Thoughts of the grounds surrounding the manor sprung into Lidria’s mind, but she squashed them as soon as they popped up. The idea of seeing Selis distressed her enough that her guiding hand fell from Hector’s shoulder. He paid no attention to her change in behavior, pressing on ahead.

A clear space sat along the slipshod hybrid wall, nestled in the southwest corner of town. Hector ran around the mud-paved ground in circles, wooden sword flailing at his side. Lidria reached for her back, only to realize she hadn't brought her armament.

Lidria moved to follow Hector but stopped short; no idea where to start. The moves, techniques and thought processes had become instinctual years ago. Trying to break down the movements that came without a second of contemplation into simple words and actions left her dumbfounded.

"C'mon, Lidi," Hector called, running up to her. "Show me what to do."

Hector's cheerful voice shattered Lidria's paralysis, yet she didn't have a clue what to do. "Okay," she extended her hand, "let me see your sword."

Without skipping a beat, Hector thrust his makeshift weapon at Lidria. She leaned in and grabbed the handle, biting her tongue—he's a child and didn't know any better.

"When you present your weapon to someone, you don't point it at them. You spin it around like this"—Lidria placed the flat of the blade against her fingers and turned the sword around, pointing the end at herself—"and offer them the hilt. If this was real, you could have stabbed me."

Hector bowed his head and hid his eyes. "Sorry."

"It's okay," Lidria assured Hector. "This is why we used practice swords when training in the army. I started with a wooden sword as well."

"Yeah?" The shyness in Hector's voice remained, but he gazed up.

"Yeah. No one starts out a master. Now…" Lidria took a step back and pivoted to her right. She held her arms out straight, level with the center of her chest. "We'll start with a few motions you can practice on your own. These'll get your muscles warmed up and used to swinging the weapon."

Lidria breathed in through her nose, assumed the stance, and swung. "You want to plant your feet, right foot forward, and swing in a diagonal arc from above your shoulder and down to your left hip." She repeated the motion several times. "This is a basic swipe. Watch how I flick the tip up each time I finish."

The anxiety filling Lidria vanished, and she fell into a familiar rhythm. "Now, it's important to keep your arms elevated in line with your chest. It gives you the most power behind your swings and keeps your body straight."

"Can I try?" Hector asked, inching closer.

"Of course." Lidria took one last swipe and brought the sword down, spinning it around for Hector.

Hector snatched up the makeshift sword, mindful of which way the end pointed. "So," he lined his feet up and held out his arms, "like this?"

Lidria couldn't help but smile at Hector's excitement, but his form needed some work. "You're close." She knelt beside him and placed her hand between his shoulder blades. With her right hand, she lifted his arms to the proper angle, keeping his back straight with the left. "Put your foot a little more forward like you're taking a step, and you're set."

Hector obeyed, not dissuaded by Lidria's corrections. She eased back and gave him the go-ahead. The first couple of awkward swings brought a frown to her face. She reminded him to follow through, and each attempt got better, more natural. By his twentieth try, he understood.

"All right. You're going to do the same thing, only now you'll swing from left to right." Lidria stood and stepped back to let him transition on his own. "Lead with your left foot and remember to keep your movements nice and smooth."

Concentration furrowed Hector's brow as he did what Lidria instructed. His left foot slid forward, and his stance changed. He held the crude sword up. She tapped his forearm until he raised it another inch. His questioning eyes met hers, and she flashed him an encouraging grin.

Hector went about his second set of practices with gusto equal to the first. While his left-sided swings weren't as strong as his right, they came out faster. The bit of practice he managed gave him confidence and a feel for the motions. He surprised Lidria.

"I thought you were done with the military," Ren said as he strode up to Lidria, disrupting her thoughts.

Lidria turned to meet Ren and his smirk. "Hector wanted me to teach him how to use the sword he made. I couldn't say no."

"See," Ren held out his arm, "you're not the selfish person you kept claiming you were last night."

"I get it." Lidria kept her voice quiet, annoyed. "Let it go, okay?"

"Don't worry." Lidria's body swayed as Ren nudged her with his elbow. "Your secret is safe with me."

Despite her best efforts, Lidria couldn't help but play along. "I think you've been hanging around Deeter too much."

"Perhaps," Ren agreed, shrugging. A wistful expression came over his face. "But I'm happy to have somewhere to call home. Even if it ends up temporary."

Home. Lidria had abandoned her home to distance herself from painful memories, but what had she received instead? Isolation and loneliness. The only times she felt she had a place were with Hector and Selis. They treated her well, like she belonged with them.

Lidria folded her arms across her chest and glanced over at Ren. "What are you going to do now?"

"That's a good question. I might see if Master Janus has any need of a—" Ren's words trailed off, and he turned until his left side became obscured by the rest of his body.

"Ren," Lidria said, turning to face him.

Ren waved his hand. "I know, I know." His anguished eyes met Lidria's. "I can't imagine someone would have use for a one-armed soldier."

"You're still a very capable man." Lidria clasped Ren's shoulder, and he glanced at her hand. "You can still fight, but you're more than that. You kept everyone together when no one else could."

"That's kind of you, but the people don't need me to fill that role anymore. They're safe." Ren sighed, closing his eyes.

A smile teased Lidria's lips. "Anyone would be lucky to have you lead. The people of Odwyn are still your people, not Janus'. He may provide the resources, but they'll come to you."

"I suppose you're right." Ren managed a lop-sided smile. "It's still going to take some getting used to, you know?"

"I do." Memories Lidria would rather forget flashed in her mind. "You can always talk to me."

"Until you leave." Ren's harsh words sent a wave of panic through Lidria, and she shuddered.

"I," Lidria's gaze drifted over to Hector, who now swung his sword around in wild circles, "might stay. At least for a little while longer."

"So, you're going to apologize to Selis." Ren stared Lidria down, challenging her.

Lidria moved her mouth, wanting to say something thoughtful, yet one evasive word squeaked out: "Eventually."

"I know you're worried, but you should do it sooner rather than later." To Lidria's surprise, Ren's posture relaxed, and his eyes lost their edge. "Joan let her know you didn't leave, but I can't imagine letting this fester will do either of you any good."

"Yes, I know." Apprehension shortened Lidria's breath. "I was trying not to think about it to clear my head. I still don't know what to say."

Ren clasped Lidria's shoulder and squeezed. "You'll think of what to say. She's important to you."

"She is," Lidria mused. The simple admittance lifted a weight off her shoulders. "That's why I want to make sure I say the right things."

"Don't think too long, okay?" Ren held Lidria's gaze until she conceded with a shallow nod.

Hector ran toward them. "What are you talking about?"

"Selis," Lidria said.

"Oh." Excitement radiated from Hector's face. "Can we go see her? I want to see more magic."

"Not today." With so many opportunities to go right her wrong, Lidria backed down again. "How about you show Ren what I taught you and we'll continue?"

Hector bounced back and fell into position. His flourishes came quick, too quick, and Lidria gestured for him to slow down. He listened and followed the motions as best he could. When he came to the end of the first set, he shuffled and proceeded with the second.

Confidence flooded Lidria. She studied Hector with a sense of contentment that had eluded her for what seemed an eternity. Each slash of his toy sword cut away another layer of her self-doubt. She smiled. Perhaps some hope remained for her.

Chapter Thirty-Two

Selis tucked a worn tome under her arm and meandered around the library. The musty scent of so many old and well-used volumes in one place brought a smile to her face. She blocked out everything else and went about scouring the room for interesting tomes.

Selis' mind pulled her to and fro, dancing between the shelves. Too many things to read and not enough time. Even if she locked herself in and only read, she would never finish them all. The thought excited rather than depressed her, and she plucked another volume from its home.

Joy filled Selis as she stared down at the cracked leather cover—"Connection to the Flow" emblazoned in faint lettering. Her recent failures troubled her, and she sought to find answers the only way she knew how. Research would see her overcome her difficulties.

A sinking sensation crept up on Selis. No amount of investigation or reading would fix the rift between her and Lidria. She prayed Joan had spoken the truth, for she could not bear the alternative. She shook her head and reminded herself that, either way, she needed to wait.

Her enthusiasm drained, Selis flopped into a nearby chair. She tossed the tomes on the table and stared at nothing. The fact that one errant thought derailed her positive mood paralyzed her. Why did she have to feel this way?

Wind rushed around as the doors flung open. Janus burst into the library and, after spotting Selis, stormed forward. She knew this to be the inevitable outcome, but the sight terrified her. Her future discarded for some creature everyone else wanted dead.

"What have you done?" Janus shouted, closing the gap between him and Selis.

Selis, holding herself together, stood. “I could not let him stay in your prison anymore. He would have died.”

Janus’ nostrils flared, and he loomed over Selis. “I invite you into my home, and you disobey my wishes. You ruined everything.”

“What did I ruin? Your torture of an innocent being?” Despite her bold words, Selis trembled.

Janus raised his balled fist before it fell to his side. “I told you what I was doing with it. He was to be the key to discovering their use of magic, and I was so close.”

“I understand your curiosity, but I do not understand your obsession. You,” Selis swallowed hard and fought to hold Janus’ gaze, “sound a lot like Flinn.”

Janus’ hand flashed up and slapped Selis’ face, forcing her head to the side. Pain burned from the impact. The impulse to return the slight coursed through her, but she denied vengeance. Her lashing out would do no good. He had the right to be mad at her.

“How dare you,” Janus spat. “I can’t believe you would even—get out. Get out of my home.”

“If that is what you wish.” Selis sucked in a quick, deep breath to give her muscles life. “I hope you do not fall the same way he did. I believed you to be much better.”

“You don’t know what your master did.” Janus glared at Selis, but, instead of apprehension, tranquility overtook her.

A bubble of laughter escaped Selis. “I know more than you think I do.”

“Leave.” Janus pointed toward the door. “You’re not welcome back.”

“Thank you for allowing me here. I am sorry I had to do what I did.” Selis did not glance back as she strode out into the hall.

Tears blurred Selis' vision, and she wiped them away before heading toward her room. Janus raged within the library behind her. She hurried to grab the few belongings she still had. Thelin walked past her on the stairs, raising an eyebrow. She said not a word.

Selis entered her room and did not waste time closing the door. The faster she threw her things together, the sooner she could leave. No more tears came. Gathering her pack took all her attention, and she moved quick. A minute later, she stepped out of the manor for the last time.

Regret seized Selis' body as she took the first step into Kal'Den. She stopped and caught her breath. The evening sun hung low in the sky, casting a pink-orange glow on the town. Where should she go? She would not survive out in the wilderness on her own.

Joan would shelter Selis, at least for the night. She strode forward and headed in search of familiar faces. Refugees lined the streets, mixing with the residents. None of them appeared recognizable, but some wore the blue and silver of Odwyn. She approached them.

"Excuse me," Selis said, drawing herself up. "Can you point me in the direction of Lieutenant McCrear?"

The two soldiers regarded Selis with curious gazes. "Yeah. He's over in the third building in the row closest to the wall."

"Thank you." Selis hefted the pack on her shoulder and cut straight for her target.

Selis hoped to run into Joan before finding Ren. As nice as he treated her, she did not wish to embarrass herself further. News would reach him soon, but she feared him spreading word to Lidria. She wanted to spare Lidria the additional stress.

An unexpected sight caught Selis' eye, and her pace slowed to a crawl. Lidria sat atop one of the watchpoints along the defenses, facing out. Relief shot through Selis. She smiled, despite everything, and relished the moment before reality crashed down.

Happiness, pain, anger, excitement ebbed and flowed. Selis' legs shook, her ears rang, and her heart pounded. There were so many things she needed to say, yet none of them were sufficient. How could words be worthy of expressing how she felt?

Lidria turned her head, and Selis dove around the corner of the building next to her. She cursed herself. Lidria could never frighten her; her actions were foolish. One path opened before Selis, and she would see things through.

The steps between her and Lidria did not register in Selis' head—her thoughts filled with words, what to say. No matter what she came up with, nothing worked. She ascended the small staircase regardless. The situation would not change if she did not try.

Lidria's head snapped to the right as Selis crested the top of the stand. Lidria stared, wide-eyed and froze. "Selis." Her voice came out little more than a forced whisper.

Selis' breath caught in her throat at hearing her name from Lidria's lips. "May I sit with you?" Lidria glanced away before nodding.

Discarding her pack, Selis inched toward Lidria. A knot worked into Selis' gut. Lidria refrained from making eye contact, and Selis swallowed down a pathetic plea. She took a seat beside Lidria, inches away. The desire to reach out and touch Lidria almost overtook her reason.

"Joan told you, didn't she?" Lidria asked. She kept her head forward, not so much as peeking at Selis.

"Yes, but I was going to give you time." Selis sighed and lowered her head. "Until I saw you."

Lidria shifted around, turning away from Selis yet getting closer to her. "More time wouldn't have changed anything."

"Lidria," Selis reached for Lidria's hand, "I am sor—"

"No," Lidria snapped. A huff of air escaped her, and she turned toward Selis. Tears ran down her cheeks. "I'm sorry. You didn't deserve what I did or said. You were just trying to help."

Selis shook her head and took hold of Lidria's hand, squeezing. Lidria's eyes flicked down, but she said nothing. "It is all right. I should have asked first, but I wanted to surprise you."

"I'm an idiot." Lidria slumped forward. "You're," she gripped Selis' hand tight and met her eye-to-eye, "important to me, and I don't want anything to come between us."

"I do not wish for anything to come between us either." Selis scooted up against Lidria, leaning in and savoring her warmth. "May I?"

Lidria licked her lips and blushed. "I've never…"

Selis giggled, and her own cheeks burned. "This is new to me, too." The desire she held back threatened to overtake her.

"Then," Lidria bent down, cocked her head to the side and closed her eyes. A second later, her soft lips touched Selis'.

Selis' heartbeat erupted in wild fury. She kissed Lidria back, closing her eyes and losing herself in the moment. All the worries and fears building up over the past two days melted as she found herself wrapped in Lidria's strong arms.

Selis let her hands wander around Lidria's waist and up her back. The hem of the loose tunic Lidria wore rose, and fever-hot skin greeted her fingertips. She wanted to touch and caress, but she controlled herself. Instead, she pulled Lidria in tight, enjoying her softness and their kiss.

A little smacking sound marked the end as Lidria eased back. Selis followed Lidria's movement, trying to connect with her a moment longer. She opened her eyes, Lidria her entire vision. Selis' lips curled up in an uncontrollable grin, and she could not stop staring. She needed only Lidria.

Uncertainty darkened Lidria's exquisite features. "What?"

Selis shook her head, unable to shake the smile from her face. "It is nothing."

"Didn't it," Lidria's arms dropped from around Selis, "make you feel anything?"

Selis cupped Lidria's face and pulled, planting her lips on Lidria's. Lidria yelped, muffled, as she fell forward. The pent-up feelings inside Selis rose, and she poured them into her kiss. Lidria's hands roamed up Selis' ribs before slipping back between her shoulder blades.

Potent sensations drove Selis, and she pressed into Lidria, forcing her back. The force of the impact would have knocked Selis off if not for Lidria's firm embrace. Selis' breath ran short. As much as she wished to continue, she had to breathe.

Lidria stared up, eyes widening. Amusement and pride tickled Selis, and she planted her hands on either side of Lidria's head. "How is that for an answer?"

"I-I don't know what to say," Lidria managed. Her fingers played along Selis' back.

"You do not have to say anything." Excitement sent tremors throughout Selis' body. She lowered herself to Lidria's ear and whispered: "Show me."

Selis collapsed against Lidria's chest as she sat up, lifting her with ease. A smirk popped onto Selis' face. Lidria nudged Selis' head to the side and teased her neck with her lips. Shivers ran down Selis' spine, and goosebumps rose on her skin. She had dreamt of this moment ever since her drunken indiscretions.

Chapter Thirty-Three

Morning sunlight filtered in through the half-covered window, casting a silvery glow around Selis. Lidria stroked Selis' hair as she yawned. Her heart beat slow and steady. Contentment ruled her, and she basked in bliss. She wanted to remain in bed with Selis forever.

Selis stirred, and her leg brushed against Lidria's thigh. Warmth surrounded her, blocking out other invasive sensations. The softness of Selis' body shifted, and her hand slid onto Lidria's stomach. Lidria giggled at the faint touch; she couldn't help herself.

"Good morning," Lidria murmured, hugging Selis with her right arm.

Selis drew herself up and nuzzled the crook of Lidria's neck. "Morning. You have not been awake too long, have you?"

"No, I just woke up." Lidria placed a light kiss on Selis' forehead. "I slept well."

"Good." Selis' lips brushed Lidria's skin, and she sighed.

Lidria raised her left arm and caressed Selis' forearm. The other woman snaked her arm underneath, clutching Lidria's hip. They shared an affectionate hug, and Lidria smiled. Years had passed since she felt so accepted, so wanted.

Selis' hand glided over Lidria's abdominal muscles, her fingers tracing the long scar up over her ribs. "You have so many scars."

"Yeah," Lidria breathed. Her scars made her self-conscious, and she wished Selis would stop. "I've been through a lot. I hope you don't mind."

Selis shook her head and stared up into Lidria's eyes. "No, not at all. I," she smiled, "like them."

Nervous laughter bubbled up from Lidria's chest. She shied away from Selis. "I don't. They remind me of my failures, of my mistakes."

"They show me your vulnerable side, and I am glad to see it. I adore it." Selis cuddled up against Lidria's side, her skin so warm. "I get to see the real you, not the front you put on for other people."

"I," Lidria hesitated. Selis turned her head up, expectant. Lidria's heart melted. "Come here." She pulled Selis' face close and pressed their lips together.

Lidria broke their little kiss, and Selis gazed at her, adoration in her eyes. "Is that what we do now when we do not know how to answer each other?"

"You started it last night." Despite defending herself, Lidria couldn't keep from smiling.

"I did not hear you complain," Selis teased, resting her leg on top of Lidria's.

Lidria's cheeks burned. "No, but…" She lost herself in Selis' beautiful eyes.

"It is fine. Besides," an impish grin curled Selis' lips, "you are cute when you are embarrassed."

Lidria smirked, pride washing over her. "You're a lot more confident now."

"I realized I cannot always be worried about what others think. I should do what I believe is right. Also, I am comfortable around you. I can be myself, as can you."

"That wouldn't have anything to do with"—Lidria's fingers strayed across Selis' smooth skin—"would it?"

Selis smiled before she kissed Lidria's collar bone. "I would be lying if I said that did not help."

"I'm sorry I refused you." Selis' hair fell forward, and Lidria brushed it away to uncover her eyes. "I let my hang-ups get in the way."

"You are fine," Selis said, hugging Lidria. "It was better this way. I did not want to push you into something you did not wish to do."

Lidria cupped Selis' cheek and stroked it with her thumb. "Thank you, Selis."

"You are most welcome, Lidria." Heat flashed through Lidria as Selis held her hand to her face. "It was worth it."

"Yeah, it was." Lidria drew Selis on top of her and joined their lips, savoring the intimacy.

Selis pulled back. A trail of light kisses formed from Lidria's jaw down to her chest. Each tender peck escalated her heartbeat. Selis stopped and rested her head on Lidria's breast. Lidria's ears grew hot. She thought to tell Selis not to stop, but the temptation vanished.

Easing back, Lidria held Selis close. Selis nudged Lidria and murmured her contentment. Weariness weighed Lidria's eyelids down, and she let them slide closed. If they stayed longer, she might as well sleep.

A thought came to Lidria before she drifted off. "I never got to ask you. Why were you out this way last night?"

"Oh." Selis groaned and wiggled her foot around Lidria's ankle. "I forgot I could not tell you. I freed Gor'an after you left. Yesterday, Master Janus threw me out. I should not be in town at all."

As Selis curled into a ball, Lidria squeezed. "You did the right thing."

"Do you believe that?" Selis asked, raising her head.

Lidria smiled. "Yes, I do."

"Are you," Selis' mouth worked for a moment, "sure you are not saying so because it is an easy excuse to get away from Evelyn?"

Agony pierced Lidria's heart. Selis had every right to call her out, but her words still stung. "If you asked me yesterday, I would have agreed with that. Now…I want to support you regardless of my own baggage."

"I do not know if that will be the wisest decision." Shame darkened Selis' eyes, and she shied away from Lidria's gaze. "I am going to be hard-pressed to find somewhere I am allowed after wronging two masters."

"Don't worry," Lidria comforted Selis, stroking her back and squeezing her hand. "We'll find you a place to study even if we have to go all the way to the edge of the kingdom."

"Thank you." Selis interlaced her fingers with Lidria's, and a faint tingle crept up her arm. "Do you want to give up on your last chance with your daughter, though?"

"There's not much I can do. Besides, Ian is more than capable." Tears welled and blurred Lidria's vision. "Far more than me." Her acceptance of the truth did little to dull the pain.

Selis propped herself up on her elbow and kissed away the tears running down Lidria's cheeks. "It is okay. I am here for you."

"I'm glad I found you," Lidria sobbed, overwhelmed by the myriad emotions whirling inside her.

A sweet smile spread across Selis' face. "Me, too." She leaned in and caressed Lidria's forehead with her lips.

Lidria's tumultuous emotions leveled out. Peace of mind bled into her as Selis settled back down at her side. She flinched at Selis' fingers teasing her abs, going about their idle tracing of the scars there. This time, however, Lidria didn't pray for Selis to stop.

"Where should we go?" Selis wondered, her voice quiet and fragile.

"I don't know"—Lidria twitched as Selis' gentle touch tickled her—"but I think we should stay here a little longer."

A soft hum reverberated in Selis' throat as she nodded against Lidria's chest. "I agree. There is no other place I would rather be."

Lidria fussed with her disheveled hair, opting for a bun. Beside her, Selis threw her robes on and flipped her braid back over her shoulder. A grin quirked Selis' mouth, and she turned her head to catch Lidria's straying eyes. Lidria wrapped her arm around Selis and pulled her into a one-armed hug.

Giggling escaped Selis. She hugged Lidria back before she stepped away and stood tall. Butterflies swirled in Lidria's stomach. Each time she saw Selis, they returned. She cursed herself for being so emotional, yet she couldn't stop. Her feelings were normal.

Selis padded across the room and reached for the doorknob. Lidria swept up behind her, resting her hands on Selis' hips. Rumbling came from both their stomachs—breakfast couldn't come soon enough. Lidria leaned past Selis, grabbed the knob, and yanked the door open.

Deeter came to an abrupt stop outside, and his head snapped toward the two. His eyes drifted down to Lidria's hands. Laughter erupted. "And you were so dour yesterday."

"I," Lidria stammered, pulling away from Selis.

Selis strode forward without skipping a beat. "The problem is solved. You do not have to worry about her being dour anymore."

"I can see that." Deeter shook his head, an expression of disbelief on his face. "Good for you."

Lidria rushed to catch up to Selis, placed her hand on the small of her back, and pushed. "C'mon, Selis. Let's get breakfast."

"Max is still providing his services a few buildings over," Deeter said, dropping his snarky attitude. "You should go there."

"We will. Thank you." Selis whispered something to Deeter Lidria couldn't understand.

Genuine empathy softened Deeter's face. "No problem." He winked.

Selis exited the house, Lidria following suit. They made their way down the busy street, and Lidria clasped Selis' hand. Selis drifted closer. Any odd stares they received, Lidria greeted with a smile. Nothing could sour her mood or make her believe she had chosen wrong.

"Did you have to play along with him?" Lidria questioned as they strolled down the road.

Selis glanced over her shoulder. "Did I say something incorrect?"

"No." Lidria frowned. "I—never mind."

"It is okay. Just relax." Selis squeezed Lidria's hand and tugged her close.

Amusement brought a smirk to Lidria's face. "This is weird. You're usually the timid one."

"I do not think I have changed that much," Selis cast her gaze at the people milling around, "but I do have you to thank for any changes. Without you, I never would have done any of this."

"I wish I had helped a little better. It would have saved us some trouble." Lidria stopped to let a group of people exit the building Deeter had pointed out.

Selis eyed Lidria with resolve and a faint grin. "You did what you should. If you had not, you would not be you."

Lidria held the door open. "I guess you're right. I should be glad how things turned out."

"I am." Selis trailed her fingers down Lidria's arm as she entered.

The warm scent of fresh-cooked eggs and grease struck Lidria. Her stomach grumbled, and she quickened her steps. A small line formed to the right of the kitchen, which she hoped would move fast. Food became the sole thing on her mind.

"Good morning, ladies," Max beamed from behind a short bar. Sweat soaked the bandana tied around his forehead, but he didn't appear to care. "I haven't seen either of you in a while."

Selis straightened herself. "Good morning, Max. It is good to see you again. I have remembered what you said."

Lidria gave Selis a confused look, but the mage dismissed it with a wave.

"Don't forget." Max turned around before coming back with two full plates. "Here. Eat your fill and enjoy the peace."

"Thank you," Selis said and dipped into a shallow bow.

Hunger turned to impatience. Lidria scooped up their meals and gestured with her chin toward the door. Selis' brow furrowed, but she said nothing. The bright smile on Max's face didn't fade or cloud over. Lidria nodded her thanks before she hurried out the door and back to the house.

After Selis took her seat, Lidria placed breakfast in front of her. She sat with her own plate and stared at Selis. "What were you two talking about back there?"

"I spoke with him the day I ran from camp. He reminded me that not everyone is cruel." Selis' eyes dimmed. "It can be hard to remember that when you have been treated like you are nothing most of your life."

"You made it through all that, Selis. You're the strongest person I know." Lidria rested her hand on top of Selis'.

Selis spread her fingers. "It sometimes felt like I would break at the slightest sign of adversity. That is," a lopsided smile snuck onto her face, "until I met you."

“I know having someone who believes in you helps,” Lidria blurted out, heat rising in her cheeks, “but you’re giving yourself too little credit. Think of how long you survived without me.”

“I would rather not.” Selis lowered her eyes to her food.

Lidria opened her mouth to comfort Selis, but the door opened. “Lidria, Selis,” Ren remarked, his eyes widening. “I’m surprised to see you two here. I didn’t think you were ready.”

“Selis found me and talked some sense into me. You won’t have to suffer my nonsense anymore.” Lidria retracted her hand and took a quick bite of her meal to hide her embarrassment.

“Please.” Ren snorted, slid out one of the extra chairs, and sat beside Lidria. “You’re no problem compared to what I have to deal with daily. You just needed some time.”

Selis lifted her head and looked to Ren. “Thank you for helping keep her here.”

“Joan told you all about it, eh? It wasn’t a problem.” Easing back in his chair, Ren flashed his teeth. “You’re welcome.”

“Well, now that I’ve been thoroughly embarrassed,” Lidria pushed herself away, “I’m going to—”

“Do not be like that, Lidria.” Selis stroked Lidria’s ankle with her foot underneath the table. “What were we just talking about?”

Lidria stared at Selis for a long moment before she relented. “Okay, okay.”

“So,” Ren’s eyes flicked between Lidria and Selis, “do you two plan on staying here?”

“No. I am not welcome here.” Selis popped a chunk of egg into her mouth, her shoulders slumping.

Ren raised an eyebrow and cocked his head to the side. “What do you mean?”

"I should not be here." Lidria pressed her leg against Selis'. Her face twitched. "Master Janus threw me out of his home for releasing a Quelan prisoner."

"Why?"

"I have my reasons," Selis proclaimed. "I would rather not talk about it. You can ask Joan if you are still curious."

"All right. If you're not staying, where are you going to go?" Ren asked.

The simple question froze Lidria. She had no clue where they would, or even could, go. "We don't know yet. It's not like we have a lot to go on. I just found out this morning myself."

A thoughtful expression came over Ren, and he propped his chin against his fist. "It's been years since I was posted there, but out west is nice land. Yermon would probably suit you. We can spare you supplies for the journey, but I don't know if it'll be enough."

"Thank you." Lidria clasped Ren's shoulder. "Any help would be greatly appreciated."

"You've earned it." Ren's eyes darted to his stump.

Lidria frowned. "Ren—"

"Don't," Ren barked. The harshness bled from his face. "We've already gone over this. I owe you my life." Selis tilted her head from Lidria to Ren. "The night of the attack, she saved me from losing more than my arm."

Selis nudged Lidria with her foot. "See? You are not as bad as you think you are."

"I get it. You don't have to keep drilling it into my head." Lidria shot Selis a glare, but she presented a smile.

"Have you learned, then?" Selis asked, staring down her nose with an air of skepticism.

Lidria sighed. "I'm working on it."

"I will keep reminding you until you cannot forget." No matter how bad she wanted to be upset with Selis, Lidria couldn't bring herself to say anything.

"I'm glad to see you two happy." Ren stood, his hand lingering on the back of the chair. "Let me know when you plan to leave, and I'll get you whatever I can."

"We will." Lidria threw a crisp salute. "Again, thank you."

Ren returned Lidria's salute and nodded. "Enjoy yourselves." The door creaked open and clicked closed, leaving her and Selis to themselves.

Unable to deny her stomach any longer, Lidria dug into her breakfast. Selis did the same, lost in thought. Lidria knew they had a lot to work out, but she didn't know where to start. Taking things one day at a time became her top priority.

Selis cleared her throat. "I guess we will see about going west, huh?"

"Yeah." Lidria slowed down and focused on Selis. "Unless we figure something else out."

"I," Selis fumbled over her words, "maybe I should visit my parents. I cannot see a better time to try and rekindle our relationship." She coaxed her braid over her shoulder and toyed with her hair.

Lidria gazed at Selis until her eyes flicked up. "If that's what you want to do, we can do that first and go from there."

"I think so," Selis said, more confident.

"Okay." Lidria reached her hand out, and Selis met her halfway. Their fingers intertwined. "We'll stay here another day or two, say goodbye to everyone, and then go. How does that sound?"

Selis pulled their hands toward her, bent forward, and kissed the back of Lidria's hand. "Wonderful."

Chapter Thirty-Four

"Do it again," Hector pleaded, jumping up and down—his little body unable to contain his excitement.

Selis spun a thread of magic. The strand blazed a vibrant pink and curled back in on itself. A faint sizzling snapped every time sections touched, but she paid them no mind. She poured more of herself into the display and wove longer pieces.

The familiar motions relaxed Selis as the Flow took on the form of unfurled ribbon. She bent her creation to her will, twisting and shaping the fiber. Hardpoints formed a cross-section parallel to the bulk. The wispy edges solidified and began to resemble a blade.

Selis grunted. Despite her knowledge and power, she never mastered the art of conjuring. Something as simple as forming a common object strained her concentration and body. The captivation and awe in Hector's eyes made the effort worth enduring.

Focus teetering, Selis squeezed. The magic hissed as pressure built. She imagined the crisp, clear shape of Lidria's long sword in her head and stretched. The unstable weapon popped into reality, finding a home in her hand.

Hector leaned in close, and Selis pulled the blade away. He stared up at her, curious. "Can I touch it?"

"I am afraid I am not good enough to make it safe for someone who cannot use the Flow." Admitting her deficiency aloud shamed Selis, but she intended to improve.

"But it's so cool." Hector wilted in defeat.

Hector's dejected display tugged at Selis' heart, and she dismissed the weapon. She wanted to be better. "I am sorry, Hector."

“It’s okay.” The liveliness that accompanied Hector lurched back into view. “I still have my sword, and Lidi’s been teaching me how to use it.” He flourished his wooden blade a bit too close for comfort.

Selis reeled back from the absent-minded swings. “You taught him?”

“One lesson,” Lidria said, shifting in her seat. “I figured Nell would appreciate him learning some discipline if he’s keeping his sword.”

Hector stopped flailing and scurried over to Lidria. “You promised you would teach me more. Can you now?”

Lidria’s eyes searched Selis, and she nodded. She would not prevent something that may boost Lidria’s self-worth. “All right. How about we take it outside and continue where we left off?”

“Okay.” Without waiting, Hector tore off across the room and out the door.

“Are you coming with?” Lidria asked, her eyes hopeful.

Selis shook her head. “I do not think it is wise to expose my existence any more than I have.”

“If anyone has a problem with you being here,” Lidria stepped toward Selis, squaring her shoulders, “I’ll stop them.”

As much as she appreciated the sentiment, Selis did not condone more violence. “I do not want anyone else hurt on my behalf.”

“If you’re sure.” Doubt played across Lidria’s face before she hid her eyes. “I don’t want you to worry about it.”

“It is fine.” Selis placed her hand on Lidria’s arm, stood on her tiptoes, and kissed her. “Enjoy your time with Hector. You deserve it.”

Lidria gazed down at Selis as she lowered back on her heels. Her cheeks blushed. “Selis, I—”

“I will be here when you are done,” Selis patted Lidria on the arm and smiled, “I promise.”

Lidria nodded, stole a quick kiss, and turned to leave. Selis let her go, heart fluttering. The rough edges surrounding Lidria vanished in the glow of her affection. Selis wished to nurture her, to allow herself to be vulnerable around others like she was with her.

Selis' contented smile lingered. No idle thought or lack of effort stripped her of it. A sigh escaped her, and she closed her eyes. Things were looking up. Relief and happiness replaced the turmoil and heartache of days prior. Nothing could shake her.

The door creaked, and Selis' eyes drifted open. Joan slipped inside. "I see you two made up."

"Yes, we did." Selis grinned like an idiot.

"I thought you were going to wait." Joan strode across the room and plopped down in the chair across from Selis. "What changed?"

"Master Janus found out about me freeing the Quelan," Selis admitted, a twinge of shame lowering her voice.

Joan's eyes shot wide before they narrowed in thought. "After the way you were talking, I thought he would have banished you from Kal'Den entirely, not just his home."

"He did." A knot tightened in Selis' stomach. She should stand up to him. "That is why I am here and not outside with Lidria and Hector."

"That's—" The disgust vanished from Joan's face. "I'll keep you company, then."

Selis shook her head. "It is all right. You have duties to uphold. I do not want to hold you up."

"Nah," Joan said, swinging her left foot up on her right thigh and leaning back. "We've got nothing. Once everyone got settled in, there wasn't much for us to do." She shied away from Selis' gaze. "Master Janus has it all taken care of."

"I see." Selis rested her arms on top of the table and eased forward. "Well, since you helped me twice now, I think it is time I return the favor."

For a moment, Joan's eyes gazed everywhere but at Selis. Joan chewed her lip. "It's weird not having anything to do, like I don't have a purpose anymore."

"I know what you mean. I do not know what I am going to do once we leave." Worry wormed into Selis' gut, but, as long as Lidria stood by her, she would figure something out.

Joan's foot slipped off her leg, and her back straightened. "You're leaving?"

"Yes. Maybe tomorrow." Selis' right leg bounced up and down. "I should not be here."

"That's a shame," Joan said as she cast her gaze toward the door. "Hector looked so excited running around outside with Lidria." Her eyes met Selis'. "I have to say, I think I'll miss you."

Selis did not want to think about the fledgling friendships she was throwing away. "I will miss you as well. You have been so kind to me, and I will never repay your kindness."

"Don't worry about it." Joan's wooden posture relaxed, and a smile crept onto her face. "Consider it my last act of protecting the citizens of Odwyn."

"Joan," Selis said, her heart aching.

Joan stared at Selis. Any objections Selis held disappeared. "It's all right. We all lost our home."

Home. Selis never considered Odwyn a real home despite spending almost two decades there. Her accommodations were welcoming enough, yet she always felt like an outsider, an impostor. There had been a time when she believed. Flinn, however, took that away.

"You will find a purpose," Selis encouraged, trying to dispel the dark cloud from Joan's face. "I wish I could help you."

"You have enough to fret over. No sense piling on regret over me." No bitterness tainted Joan's words, but they hurt Selis, nonetheless.

If she could not help Joan after si wihe left, Selis would do what she could now. "What do you like to do?"

"Drink." Joan cracked an impish grin.

"I am being serious." Selis glared until Joan's flippant mask shattered. She took a deep breath. "I would like to at least help you brainstorm potential ideas."

"I've been in the army most of my life," Joan offered. "Nothing else has been that important for so long." She nodded to herself. "I'm sure Lidria's told you the same."

"She has." The uncertainty and fear Lidria expressed flashed in Selis' mind. "We have not come up with anything yet."

"Yeah." Joan slumped in her chair, a thoughtful expression scrunching her features.

Selis mulled over some thoughts in her head. Many of Joan's skills were military-based, and she took pride in helping and protecting others. If the remaining forces of Odwyn disbanded, she could find a new way to carry on. Kal'Den needed protection.

"Maybe," Selis started, uncertain, "you should join Master Janus' forces. I am sure they would take you."

Joan frowned. "I don't know. It would feel weird changing uniforms."

"Odwyn's citizens are here." Selis' conviction grew stronger as the idea clicked in her head. "You would still be protecting them, only with some others now, too."

Joan humphed. "Pretty and smart." She folded her arms across her chest and smiled. "No wonder Lidria fell for you."

Selis' cheeks flushed, and she tried to bury her face in her shoulder. "I do not know about that." She cleared her throat, shaking off her embarrassment. "If you decide to join, ask for a man named Bal in the guard. Tell him…little miss mage sent you."

"Really?" Joan asked with a raised brow.

"Yes. He's a good man…even if he can be rather aggravating to deal with."

"Sounds like another soldier we know." Joan stared at the wall.

Awkward silence settled around Selis. She opened her mouth to say something before rethinking and continuing. "I thanked him for stopping Lidria."

"I knew you would," Joan professed. Her eyes never moved.

"If you do not mind me asking," Selis struggled to find the right words, "is there something between you two? Or are you just comrades?"

"We," Joan scratched her arm, "blew off some steam together years ago. After a while, we called it off because we were getting too attached."

Selis coaxed her braid over her shoulder, and her fingers went about their anxious ritual. "Oh. I am sorry."

"Don't be. That's the past. We've both grown since then." Joan unfolded her arms and bent forward, hands in her lap.

Deeter and Joan got along, despite their bickering and mocking, with a level of familiarity that amazed Selis. Now, their relationship made sense. However, she did not understand why they believed getting attached was a bad thing. How else were you supposed to connect?

"So," Joan said, dragging Selis out of her own head. "Did you and Lidria," Joan locked eyes with Selis, "you know?"

The previous night began to replay in Selis' mind, but she pushed the images out. Her heart beat quickened. "Yes."

Joan let out a bark of laughter before giving Selis a knowing wink. "And you were worried you'd never see her again."

"I," Selis stuttered. She held no ideals of purity but divulging her and Lidria's intimacy to someone else made her anxious.

"You don't have to be embarrassed. It's only natural with your feelings for each other." Joan smirked. "It's fun to tease you, though."

Selis' lips twitched. "Maybe it is a good thing we are leaving."

"C'mon," Joan threw her arms wide, "you know I have your best interests in mind."

"Thank you for keeping me from losing my mind." Selis bowed her head, humility flooding her.

"You're welcome. You've got a good head on your shoulders." Joan smiled. "Keep it that way."

Chapter Thirty-Five

Lidria swept up behind Selis as soon as she hung her robe on the hook by their bed. Her arms wrapped around the smaller woman's torso, hugging her. "Are you ready to leave tomorrow?"

"I should be asking you that question." Selis crossed her arms across her body and held Lidria's to her stomach.

"What do you mean?" Lidria asked, craning her neck to catch Selis' reaction.

Selis turned her head and stared up over her shoulder. "You are happy when you are teaching Hector."

"Yeah," bitterness sapped Lidria's strength, and her hold on Selis loosened, "but there's nothing else for me to do here. I don't have much of anything." She buried her face in Selis' hair. "I want to get away from—"

"I know," Selis affirmed, bringing Lidria's attention back to her concerned face. "You have friends here, though."

Lidria squeezed Selis tight and kissed the top of her head. "You do, too. Besides, I can't let you go alone."

The tension drained from Selis' body, and her voice came out little more than a whisper: "I would understand if you did."

"What's gotten into you?" Lidria spun Selis around by her hips. "We moved on with our relationship, and you want to drop it?"

Selis shook her head. "No, no. I only want what is best for you. I believe being around everyone brings out the best in you."

Lidria stared into Selis' troubled eyes. "So do you. They won't be gone forever; everything will be fine."

"I guess you are right." Selis sighed and fell against Lidria. "Forgive my foolishness."

“There’s nothing to forgive.” Lidria pushed Selis a few inches back. An inquisitive expression came over Selis, but Lidria leaned down and planted her lips on Selis’.

The tenderness with which Selis kissed her back sent a flutter through Lidria. She pressed further before easing back. Golden eyes met hers, and the conflict in them had vanished. Only adoration remained. She smiled, teasing the hem of Selis’ sleeve with her fingertips.

A loud banging came at the door. “Lidria, Selis,” Deeter shouted. “Quela are attacking the town.” Boots scraped across the floor; his footsteps faded.

Evelyn.

“Selis,” Lidria dropped her hands and pivoted half a step, “I have to go.”

Selis grabbed Lidria’s wrist. “I will come with you.”

“Thank you.” Lidria slid Selis’ hand into hers, squeezed, and turned.

Lidria reached for a set of chainmail that didn’t exist. Her years of service had trained her to prepare herself in a specific order. A sigh escaped her; she would need to be careful. She tossed her scabbard’s strap over her shoulder and lashed the weapon to her back.

Shouts drifted in through cracks in the structure. Lidria rushed over and threw the door wide, heedless of Selis’ lack of haste. She popped out into the common room, and, as she did, something struck the outer wall with a thud. She drew her sword.

Sounds of steel clashing pierced Lidria’s ears. Another deep *thump*, and the door flung open. “In here!”

A crowd of seven civilians flooded into the building. Lidria shoved past them, fighting her way to the exit. Snarls and growls deafened the screams. She pressed through the threshold in time to witness a soldier skewered on the end of a jagged spear.

Lidria grabbed Deeter by the arm and heaved him out of the path of a Quelan's attack. She batted the beast's follow-up swing to the side. Confidence surged through her as she rushed the Quelan and plunged her blade into its chest.

Gurgling leaked out of the creature's bloody mouth. Lidria drove forward until her adversary dropped to the ground. With a tug, she yanked her weapon free and scanned her surroundings. Several civilian bodies lay in the road, padded out with Quela and soldiers.

Selis emerged, and her eyes widened. A thought occurred to Lidria: Selis had refused to fight last time. Would she do anything now? If she didn't, she would slow her down. Lidria cursed herself. Selis wouldn't hinder her; she couldn't.

More Quela skittered around the corner at the end of the street. Lidria tore her eyes off Selis, taking off toward the enemy. Boot falls fell in step behind her as Deeter rushed to keep up. The urge to sever links and leave Selis and Deeter behind tugged at her mind.

Clenching her jaw, Lidria expelled the notion of abandonment. She slid to the side and dodged the opening attack. A quick slash, and one Quelan swung its horns at her. She grabbed them and let the momentum carry her to safety before letting go.

Lidria side-stepped the recovering creature and brought her sword down. The blade bounced off the gnarled mass. She reeled backward, staggering. Deeter interposed himself between her and the beast. A flourish of his weapon loped off a matted limb.

Warmth flecked across Lidria's face, but she didn't allow the momentary victory to slow her. She danced around to Deeter's right and swung at the creature's neck. In shock, the Quelan didn't react. Her blade sliced through flesh and bone with ease.

Lidria's opponent crumpled in a headless heap. However, before she moved, something massive slammed into her. She flew to the ground, tumbling several times across the cobblestone. Pain flared in her hip, shoulder, and leg, but she leapt back to her feet.

Lidria stared down the remaining two Quela, ignoring the blood dripping down her right arm. They rushed her without a sound or a second of hesitation. Pale pink light flashed in front of her attackers, and they fell backward.

Wind gusted past Lidria and drew her attention. Selis stood to the side behind her, arms finishing a sweep to the left. The Quela skidded and lifted into the air. They sailed over the wall into the field outside.

Selis caught up and placed her hand on Lidria's back. "Come on."

"Wait," Lidria said, spinning to find Deeter. "Can you make sure Hector and Nell are safe?"

Confusion spread across Deeter's face as his chest heaved up and down. "Where are you going?"

"To protect my daughter." Lidria held herself in place despite the burning need to rush to Evelyn.

"All right." Deeter nodded. "I'll see what I can do."

Lidria bumped Deeter's arm with her fist. "Thank you."

"Be careful." Deeter copied Lidria's gesture and headed back to the house.

Lidria grabbed Selis by the hand and hauled her down the road. She started to say something, only to stop short. Blood and gore littered the main thoroughfare. Several civilians lay groaning and twitching, but Lidria moved on—she could do nothing for them now.

Screams came from the left, and Selis broke away. Lidria chased after her, keeping pace without effort. A man fell, impaled through the gut on a wicked blade. The beast raised its arm to slaughter a woman and her child next. Lidria ran, yet Selis acted faster.

Ropes of crimson materialized and wrapped around the Quelan. The creature snarled and struggled against its bonds, failing to break free. Selis lifted her hand, and her spell finished cocooning her target. A huff of exasperation escaped her as her shoulders sagged.

Lidria placed her hand on Selis' shoulder, and the mage jumped before turning her head. Tired eyes stared back at Lidria. Lidria frowned, but Selis waved away her concern. She had seen Selis do far more and not be winded in the past.

Flames rose around them as a row of buildings erupted. Splinters of wood whizzed through the air, but they plinked off a thin pink-colored veil inches from Lidria and Selis' bodies. Lidria glanced back at Selis, and determination returned life to her eyes.

Lidria rushed over to the downed woman and child. The mother stared up at her, tears streaming down her face. Lidria's heart wrenched. She held out her hand to help the woman up, but she refused to take her hand. Baffled, she stepped back to give the grieving woman space.

Water splashed over the ruined structure, and the heat died. Selis strolled up beside Lidria. "I am sorry for your loss. You are safe now. The soldiers near the gate will help you."

Neither the woman or child spoke or moved. Lidria touched Selis' arm, drawing her attention. She tilted her head toward the mansion, and Selis nodded. They left the two survivors to their own devices and hoped they would survive by themselves.

The gates were cracked open and several guards stood watch. Three Quela lay dead outside, and Lidria stepped over them. Selis skirted around them, drifting close to Lidria as they neared the men. With all the fighting elsewhere, the place appeared tranquil.

"Where is Master Janus?" Selis asked, never leaving Lidria's side.

The closest guard eyed Selis. "In the manor. He's busy with something serious."

"I would think saving his people would be serious." Selis stood tall. "I will drag him out here myself if I have to." She took a step forward, and the man brandished his halberd.

"I know who you are. The master will not allow—"

Lidria batted the guardsman's weapon away and pushed him aside. "Out of my way. I won't be so polite if I have to repeat myself." The man stood down despite his, and his comrades', grumbling.

The manor doors opened without a sound. Lidria strode inside, allowing Selis past her before sealing the entrance behind them. No soldiers or servants filled the chamber, and the candles lining the walls were, for the first time since they arrived, snuffed.

Selis staggered, and her right hand shot up to her forehead. A harsh breath escaped her as Lidria rushed to her side. "What's wrong?"

"He put up a ward to keep the Quela out." Selis grimaced, and Lidria's heart rate spiked. "I can feel the pressure building in my head."

"Selis," Lidria glanced back over her shoulder, "maybe you should go back."

"No," Selis said, firm. She shook her head and straightened her back. "I must do this. He is letting people die."

Lidria locked eyes with Selis. "I won't let you die."

"I will be fine, Lidria. We do not have time to waste." Before Lidria protested, Selis strode away from her.

Lidria and Selis ascended the staircase. She scanned the area, panic rising as they did. No signs of anyone. While the lack of hostiles proved reassuring, the absence of people brought a new set of concerns. She needed to find Evelyn.

Thelin popped around the corner at the top of the stairs, caught sight of them, and pivoted. "Thelin," Selis took off toward the butler. He didn't run, much to Lidria's surprise. "Where is Master Janus?"

"I cannot tell you, miss Selis." Thelin stared her down as he clasped his hands behind his back. "Leave this place at once."

Selis stormed closer to Thelin, raising her voice. "You can, and you will. I want to save however many people I can."

"So does he," Thelin replied.

"Tell me." Selis trembled, and her fist clenched.

Thelin broke eye contact with Selis. "He's in the sanctum in the basement."

"Is that where Evelyn is, too?" Lidria asked, cutting in.

"No." Thelin shook his head and shifted his weight. "She's in the library."

Lidria snapped to the left and took two steps. Her body swayed as she stopped herself and half-turned back to Selis. Something tugged Lidria, pulling her toward Evelyn. She, however, couldn't tear herself away from Selis.

Selis closed the gap between her and Lidria, grabbed her arm, and pulled her into a firm kiss. "Go."

Lidria's breath caught in her throat as she stared wide-eyed at Selis. A smile curled Selis' lips. She pushed Lidria's hip, snapping her back to reality. A tingle ran down Lidria's spine as she severed a link. With a nod, she spun and took off.

A thud echoed through the empty chamber as Lidria landed on the hardwood floor. She sprung from her crouched position and flew forward. Her breathing labored, not because of physical exertion but the apprehension of seeing Ian and Evelyn again.

Lidria's legs carried her from one hallway to another, darting toward her destination. Doors, tables, paintings and other decorations rushed by her in a nondescript blur. The floor creaked, and she skidded to a halt. Bal rounded the corner and planted himself in her way.

Streel rasped, and Bal brandished his sword. "I can't let you go any further. Master Janus' orders."

"Bal," Lidria severed another link, running her fingers along her blade and coating the length in azure flames, "I don't have time for this. I need to protect my daughter."

"Master Janus was very clear that no one should be traipsing around the manor." Bal stood his ground, and Lidria's muscles twitched.

Lidria blinked away several tears, her grip tightening on her sword. "Please. I don't want to hurt you. I just want to ensure my daughter's safety. I finally got to see her, and," she swallowed down the lump in her throat, "I don't want to see her die today."

Bal clenched his jaw before he let out a long sigh. "I can see you're determined to kill me if you have to. It would be a waste if either of us were to die here." He lowered his weapon. "Go. Get your daughter."

Lidria nodded her appreciation. "Thank you." She sped past Bal, heedless of deception or danger.

Lidria threw the library door open as the flames on her blade flickered out. A high-pitched yelp echoed along the rows of bookcases, and she cursed herself. However, no matter how much she hated herself for scaring Evelyn, she couldn't tiptoe around.

Books lay scattered around the assorted tables in sloppy piles, open and askew. Lidria ignored them and searched for where Evelyn hid. As she rounded a row of shelves, a bolt sailed past her face. She flinched backward and pointed the tip of her weapon down the aisle.

“Lidria?” Ian crouched ten feet down the aisle, clutching Evelyn and a hand crossbow.

“Come on,” Lidria said. She took several steps toward Ian and Evelyn before she stopped. “I came to get you out of here.”

A disgusted expression came over Ian’s face. “Don’t think I can care for my own daughter?” he snapped, indignation dripping from his voice. “I’ve been doing it for the past nine years.”

Ian’s words knocked the wind out of Lidria. She floundered and took a deep breath. “That’s not it at all. I know you can; you’ve proven that. But…if the Quela get inside, you won’t survive.”

“Master Janus will protect us if it comes to that. He won’t let his newest pupil die.” Under any other circumstance, Lidria would’ve found Ian’s hostility justified and expected. Here and now, she thought him a bigger fool than she.

“Janus is AWOL.” Lidria sheathed her sword and took a step forward. “He’s locked himself in the basement. Selis went after him, but—”

“Get out. Now.” Ian aimed his weapon at Lidria despite the lack of a loaded bolt.

Lidria shook her head. “No. I came to keep our daughter safe.” Her reflexes returned to normal. “I don’t care what’s happened; her safety is my top priority.”

“We’re perfectly safe here without you.” Evelyn’s green eyes peeked out around Ian’s arm. “Don’t make this any harder than it has to be.”

“You missed me,” Lidria placed a hand on her chest and slowed her racing heart, “an unaware target, with your only weapon. I know you want what’s best for her—we both do—but you’re just not trained to handle combat.”

Ian glared back, unmoving. “This won’t change anything.”

"I know," Lidria breathed, little more than a whisper. "I will leave you two alone as soon as this is all over. You have my word, but this is something I must do."

"We've had this conversation before." Ian brushed Evelyn behind him and stood. "Leave."

"I'm sorry, but I can't. Now," no more than a foot separated Lidria from Ian, "please listen to me."

Ian's hand moved from the top of Evelyn's head. "I can't take you on in a fight, never could, but, if you're going to be so stubborn, I guess I'll have to do something."

Lidria frowned. "What—"

Sharp, hot pain radiated from Lidria's gut. Her eyes dipped down. A thin sliver of metal pierced her flesh, and Ian held it steady. She brought her eyes up to his face, but his features twisted in a disorienting haze. Her head spun as waves of nausea assailed her.

"I told you to leave us alone." Ian yanked the blade free, and Lidria wavered.

Lidria clutched her stomach. "What did you do?" she demanded, trying to remain upright.

"It won't kill you, but it'll slow you down." The needle clattered to the floor as Ian turned.

"Get back here." Lidria reached out to grab Ian, but her hand passed right through him.

Balance floundered, and Lidria stumbled into a bookcase. Ian disappeared, the room swirling around. She sucked in a sharp breath and pushed herself upright. Darkness crept in on her vision. She managed to take another step before her muscles and mind failed her.

Chapter Thirty-Six

"Take me to Master Janus," Selis ordered, turning from where Lidria had run off.

Thelin shifted in place. "What do you plan to do?"

"His people need him. I will drag him out and make him help if I have to." Power coursed through Selis, and restraining her violent impulses took all her strength.

"Why waste your time here if you care so much about saving people?" Thelin pried, a hint of defensiveness evident in his voice.

Selis sighed. "I do not have the power to save everyone; I am only one person." Her limitations were not the notion she held in contention. "He should be thinking about his people, the ones he swore to protect."

"I don't think he'll listen, but I'll take you to him." Thelin turned and waved over his shoulder. "Follow me."

Anxiety bubbled up within Selis, churning her stomach. She did not bear the capacity to force Janus to do as she wished if he denied her. He outclassed her by a huge margin in magical ability, and hers had proven unreliable of late.

Unfamiliar hallways passed Selis by as Thelin led her toward the basement. She tried to keep herself focused, to keep her resolve high, yet she found herself slipping. Every step away from Lidria drained her. She did not want to admit it, but she relied on Lidria's support more than she wished.

"Why did you release the Quelan against Master Janus' wishes?" Thelin asked, keeping his gaze focused ahead.

Selis suppressed an agitated growl. Everyone asked her the same thing. "He deserved freedom like anyone else. Just because he is Quelan does not mean he deserved to suffer."

"Many would say the beast-men deserve far worse. Didn't they destroy your home a couple weeks ago?" Selis appreciated the way Thelin kept his voice level, but he made it clear which side he believed in.

"They did," Selis admitted. Visions of the ruins and the dead seeped into her mind's eye. "However, that does not prove this one had anything to do with it. Or that the torture was necessary."

Thelin thudded to a stop in front of a massive, ornate door. "You may be right on the latter," his head swiveled toward Selis', "but the master's will is not something to be dismissed lightly."

Selis discarded her doubts and stared back at Thelin. "Neither is mine."

Thunder rumbled, shaking the manor. Selis wavered and steadied herself against the nearby wall. Something cracked above before thudding to the floor. The crossbeam snapped, and the ceiling gave way. Splinters of wood rained down as three Quela dropped before her.

Selis grabbed the door handle, ripped the door open and pushed Thelin inside. He shouted at her, but the slamming door drowned him out. One of the Quela held a gnarled staff, and tiny bells tied to his horns chimed. Gre'cha, the shaman, found her once more.

The two escorts charged Selis. She backpedaled and threw her arms up. Wind gusted, carrying her two opponents upward. They crashed into the wood with a loud *thud* and rattled the weakening supports. More debris dropped, but her captives did not.

Bands of pink lashed around the two beasts. Selis could find a more permanent way to deal with them after she dealt with her impromptu nemesis. Her attention and gaze focused on the hostile spellcaster. The creature eyed her with beady amber eyes, snarling.

Electricity arced from Gre'cha's staff. Selis swirled her hands out in front of her, and a thin veil appeared. The amethyst lightning slammed into the barrier, sparking pink and dissipating around her. She pushed forward and launched an attack of her own, her restraint slipping.

A gout of emerald fire surged outward. With a flick of its staff, her adversary deflected her flames. Paintings, tables, shelves, and the walls themselves caught ablaze. Selis charged, reckless. This creature would not humiliate her a second time.

The Quelan lowered its sharp antlers as Selis closed the gap. She juked to the right, avoiding the swing of horns thrown at her. Flat steps formed in midair, and she took them. Her momentum did not slow.

Selis launched another attack and struck Gre'cha square in the back. He howled in pain, but, as the sound pierced her ears, she fired again. The shaman dropped to his knees. She now stood near-level with the ceiling. A little longer, and victory would be in her grasp.

Glass shattered, and the magic holding Selis aloft vanished. She plummeted. Her shoulder blades connected with the floor, sending an agonizing shockwave through her body. She grunted and tried to lift herself up. Her head spun.

Standing over Selis, her opponent hefted the pointed end of his staff. She crossed her arms in front of her face before her assailant drove their weapon home. A clang echoed down the hall. Her attacker pressed harder against her barrier, yet her magic did not budge.

Flames billowed out from beneath Selis' shield, wrapping around to reach her target. Gre'cha flinched away from the raging fire. She continued to pour more of herself into the blaze until she engulfed the entire hall.

Shrieks snapped Selis out of her rage. She dismissed the blaze with a wave of her hands and shot back to her feet. The beast lay, fur singed, three feet away. Her eyes flicked upward, and the other Quela fared little better. She sighed and took a moment to steady her breathing.

Selis padded over to the downed creature. He did not react to her presence. She knelt beside him and, swallowing her pride, placed her hand on Gre'cha. Magic flowed through her, down her arm and out her hand. Pain flared, but she ignored the nuisance.

The shaman's fur appeared no better off, but Selis believed he would survive. She stood, staggering, and moved her captives. Simple repetition saw the duo healed like their leader. They were her enemies, yet she could not betray her beliefs. No matter how much torment adhering to them brought her.

Thelin cracked the door open and peeked out. Courage found him, and he stepped into the hallway. Selis bound Gre'cha and staggered backward. Her chest rose and fell with her labored breathing as her body attempted to counteract the exertion and torture she inflicted.

"You didn't kill them," Thelin said, his voice oozing astonishment.

"No." Selis took a deep breath and adjusted her robe and hair. "I am done killing."

Thelin eyed Selis for a long moment. "Given the circumstances, I don't know if that's a good idea. However, I am not here to judge you. Right this way."

Selis passed through the opening, and the air around her changed. The pressure at the base of her skull increased. She groaned but pressed on, determination outweighing discomfort. Her eyes flicked about the bare passageway, spotting nothing out of the ordinary.

Light flickered and danced at the end of the hall. Selis advanced as the door behind her closed. A quick glance over her shoulder revealed that Thelin had not followed her, and a shiver ran down her spine. While she did not wish for interruptions, the thought of being alone with Janus threw her off.

Frantic scratching drifted toward Selis. She frowned, advancing at a tenuous pace. If Thelin had lied to her, she might be walking into something far worse than a confrontation with a mage of Janus' caliber. The troublesome thought clung to her mind for a moment.

A vast, torch-lit chamber spread out before Selis, and she sucked in a sharp breath. White-blue lines etched every surface. The pattern they formed appeared familiar, yet the purpose eluded her. She hovered at the edge, afraid to progress. One misstep, and she could end up dead.

Janus knelt on the ground to the far right. He scribbled on the floor, drawing out a jagged circle. Selis stepped past the threshold, and a wave of goosebumps rose on her arms and neck. A tingling sensation danced across her skin. Pain seared her eyes, and she covered them with her hand.

"Somehow I knew you'd be back," Janus snickered. "I guess I should thank you. I thought I'd have to wait much longer for a proper specimen."

Selis slid her hand down her face and stared at Janus, who now stood. "What is all this? And why are you not out there helping your people?"

"I will save them; don't you worry. I'll save everyone from those wretched beasts." Janus scanned the chamber, his attention more so on his carvings than Selis.

"Listen to yourself. You sound mad." A terrible sensation of déjà vu settled in Selis' chest. "What are you doing?"

Janus spread his arms and locked eyes with Selis. "All my research has led to this: a way to destroy all Quela everywhere. Thankfully, your little sabotage came late," he smirked, and her heart skipped a beat, "and you willingly delivered the final piece of the puzzle yourself."

"I do not—"

"I needed a connection to their magic to make it all work," Janus explained. "Without it, I had no way to spread the incantation." His steps echoed in the empty room as he approached Selis. "It seems that fool Flinn ended up helping me despite his stubbornness."

Selis steeled herself, banishing the self-doubt creeping in from the recesses of her mind. "I cannot allow you to wipe the Quela from existence. They have the right to live as much as we do."

"Tell that to all the families of the people they killed, to all those who lost their homes to their marauding ways." The anger drained from Janus, and he shied away from Selis' gaze. "Tell that to the apprentices I lost."

Tears ran down Selis' cheeks; she understood the pain and death they had caused. "Yes, they have fought us for as long as anyone can remember, but they are not mindless beasts." She blinked away the tears. "I have spoken with the one you had imprisoned. That is why I freed him."

Curiosity played across Janus' face. "You spoke to it? That is very interesting, and it confirms my theories about you."

"This," Selis hooked her long braid over her shoulder and held the tail up, "is because of Flinn's tampering. I did not know how to feel before, but I now think it was for the best."

"Your ability to tap into their magic explains why you didn't lose your connection to the Flow." Janus paced to Selis' left, and she spun to keep him in sight.

"What?" Selis asked, fearing the answer.

"I saw you struggle the other day with Evelyn." Janus brushed his fingers over a rough line, and a faint glow followed in their wake. "You shouldn't have been able to cast at all after you ingested all that dauein."

Everything snapped into place. Selis' heartbeat accelerated, and her breath caught short. "What did you do?"

"Your tea," Janus said, continuing to circle Selis. "I slipped a small amount of dauein in, and you never noticed. Each cup was meant to inhibit your magic more. However, you've proved quite the special case." She followed him, but her stomach churned.

"Why?" Selis managed little more than a whisper in revulsion.

"At first, I was wary you might still hold ties to Flinn. And then it became an experiment." The predatory nature in Janus' eyes softened. "I am sorry for deceiving you, but I had to be cautious."

Selis shook her head, remembering the things Flinn had done to her. Her body trembled. "I was right when I said you were as bad a Flinn."

"Maybe," Janus agreed, much to Selis' shock. "But, unlike him, I will not be undone by you. I will succeed where so many others have failed."

"I do not wish to harm you, but," Selis took a defiant step forward, "I will stop you if you force my hand."

Disappointment dragged down Janus' posture, but he did not relent. "You can try. You're an adept mage, Selis, but you're no match for a master of the Enclave."

"That may be the case. However, I do not have to defeat you. Just interrupt your invocation." Selis' eyes strayed, searching Janus' pattern for some lead or clue for how to unravel it.

"You're welcome to try," Janus said as he came to a stop in front of the sole exit to the chamber. "I won't hold back."

Fear bounded down Selis' spine. "I do not expect you to, but I will not back down."

"Well," Janus gestured forward with an open hand, "what are you waiting for? Stop me."

Selis closed her eyes, extended her arms to her sides and let the magic flow out of her. Tendrils of energy writhed and swirled, seeking out the target of her will. A terrible screech pierced her ears as her spell connected with Janus'. She recoiled but did not release her concentration.

The invocation before Selis wove an intricate and strong web. Each time she thought she found a frayed or weak end, the lines wrapped back in on themselves and shored up any weakness. Her head spun from the complicated nature, and nausea wracked her entire being.

Despite her tribulations, Selis remained steadfast in her resolve. She needed to stop the spell before Janus activated it. However, each probe proved fruitless. She lacked the skill to exploit any faults in his designs. Unraveling this ritual eluded her grasp.

"Having trouble?" Master Janus asked, threatening Selis' teetering concentration. "I see you don't know what you're dealing with. Give up now, and I'll let you leave unharmed."

Selis cracked open an eye, Janus little more than a blur. "No. I want the killing to end. On both sides."

"They'll never understand or listen to you or anyone. You are proving my point," hatred dripped from Master Janus' voice, "with your perverted existence."

Agony tore at Selis' heart. She would always be different, something for people to look down on. However, not everyone considered her as such. "My existence is as legitimate as yours. I will no longer be anyone's pawn."

Chapter Thirty-Seven

Lidria's eyes shot open. Her vision swam, and a pounding in her head forced them shut. Bile rose in her throat and dribbled into her mouth. She swallowed hard, attempting to ignore the burning sensation as the unpleasantness went all the way down. What happened?

Tremors wracked Lidria's body as she propped herself up. She fought through the pain and lifted her gaze. Vague shapes dotted her blurred sight. Ian stabbed her with something, but she could've succumbed hours ago. The fact she lived surprised her.

Muscles straining, Lidria rose. She fell to the right, but a table caught her, legs screeching against the wood floor. Dizziness swelled. Her eyesight cleared until the outlines of massive bookshelves materialized all around. Evelyn and Ian were nowhere to be found.

Lidria stumbled through the library, searching and battling with her hampered body. Her sword lay on the ground three feet from her. She braced herself and bent over to pick up her weapon. Blood rushed to her head, and she reeled upright, blade in hand.

Thunder rumbled outside the mansion. Lidria headed for the door, her head foggy, and grasped the knob. With a yank, she ripped the door open. The hall before her stretched out into an infinite void. She shook her head and blinked. Nothing changed.

Lidria stared out, and the world twisted and turned. However, despite the shifting, the decorations remained in place. She reached her hand out past the threshold, but her action provoked no reaction. The need to protect Evelyn overpowered her confusion. She strode into the hallway.

Lidria's surroundings snapped into place. The jarring movement sent her head spinning, and she collapsed against the wall. Pain lanced her shoulder. Her tenuous grip on the hilt slackened until it almost slipped from her hand. She closed her fingers and squeezed.

The smooth walls provided an excellent guide rail to keep Lidria upright. She shuffled along, bypassing tables and ornaments as her crippled body allowed. Light flashed, and she shielded her eyes from the radiance. When she lowered her arm, the scenery changed.

A stark recreation of Lidria and Ian's home surrounded her. The furniture stood spotless, and the aroma of fresh-baked bread drifted through the air. She stared, unable to believe her eyes. Agony and confusion warred for supremacy. Regardless of which won, she would suffer.

Evelyn ran past toward the dinner table, but she appeared her current age. She struggled up into a chair and tore into a pristine loaf of bread. Crumbs littered the tabletop as she ate, and Ian swept into the room. He put his hand on her head and told her to slow down. Neither paid Lidria any attention.

Lidria wavered forward, weak. The floor creaked as she walked, but they ignored her presence. Her mouth moved, wanting to speak, yet nothing came out. She continued toward them. Try as she might, she couldn't connect with them. Her heart ached.

A happy little giggle escaped Evelyn as she bopped Ian with a piece of half-eaten bread. He gave her a stern glare, but the corner of his mouth curled upward. Lidria stopped at the edge of the table and rested her hand on the surface for support. The giggling came to a stop.

Ian and Evelyn turned their heads in unison and stared at Lidria. Ian's eyes narrowed, and hatred radiated from them. Despite the hostility he showed, Evelyn's reaction drew Lidria's focus. Big green eyes filled with terror greeted her. She couldn't tear her gaze from them.

Lidria extended her hand and attempted to apologize. Once more, her voice eluded her. Her trembling hand reached Evelyn's shoulder but passed through. Lidria's breath caught in her throat as both faded. Loneliness enveloped her as it had for so many painful years.

The world dimmed. Details blinked out of existence one-by-one. Soon, she stood in a dark, blank nothingness. She collapsed to her knees, burying her face in her hands. The tears she had held back trailed down her cheeks. She could only blame herself.

A golden color crept into the fringes of Lidria's sight. Her sobs ended, and a warmth embraced her. She slid her hands away from her face, opening her eyes. The entrance hall of the manor appeared. She knelt where the hallway spilled out next to some knocked over candles.

Tears clung to Lidria's face, but she needed to press on. She drove her sword into the floor and used the sturdiness to pick herself up. Sounds of battle pricked her ears. She ignored them. Only one conflict caught her attention, and the fight didn't exist outside.

Lidria headed for the stairs. She didn't know where to begin searching, but her gut told her up. Loud crashes came from above. Anything that barred her path to Evelyn would be dealt with quick and without hesitation. She couldn't afford to be lenient.

The steps creaked under Lidria's boots as she ascended. Dizziness returned, so she gripped the handrail with all her strength. She continued, one step at a time, and controlled her erratic breathing. If she did find Evelyn again, how could she protect her in this condition?

Lidria lifted her foot, but the landing stretched beyond her reach. The walls and railings around her rushed past as her stomach rose into her chest. She glanced around, panic rising. The ceiling grew closer, and she closed her eyes before impact.

Pain jolted through Lidria as her shoulder blades and tailbone slammed into the hard surface. Weightlessness overtook her. She gasped, and her eyes shot open. Instead of seeing the floor below, the ceiling remained above. Her addled mind had played a trick on her.

Lidria rolled onto her side and coughed. Her body ached, but she took comfort in the fact that she had imagined the event. She took a moment to catch her breath. The staircase stretched up before her, far more daunting than she ever thought possible.

Someone stood at the top of the stairs. Lidria squinted, but she couldn't discern the person's identity. If they proved hostile, she wouldn't be able to fight in her current state. She groped around for her sword and tried to stand. Her muscles allowed her to get one knee under herself.

"It's too late," the figure said in Lidria's own voice. Her eyes focused, and a perfect replication of herself loomed over her. "The damage you've done cannot be undone. You're a failure."

Lidria attempted to shout, to defend herself, but words disobeyed her.

The doppelganger smirked. "You can't deny it. You're selfish by nature. You drive everyone away."

Unable to speak, Lidria acted. She grasped the hilt of her weapon with a vice-like grip and forced her body to obey. The steps proved more difficult than the first attempt, but her will surpassed the obstacle. She lurched upward until a few short feet remained.

"You have no future with anyone if you won't accept yourself." Lidria's clone spread her arms, awaiting her to rejoin.

Acceptance and refusal conflicted inside Lidria as she stared at herself. Her pace slowed but did not stop. Even if her mind warped reality and preyed on her weaknesses, she would prevail. She kept her blade at her side, but she readied herself.

Lidria stepped up and locked eyes with the hallucination. "I know who I am." She drove her sword through her twin's abdomen.

Sharp hot pain stabbed into Lidria's stomach. She dropped her armament, clattering to the floor, and doubled over. The terrified green eyes staring back at her were no longer her own. Evelyn materialized before her, a jagged thread of magic in her right hand.

Lidria's gaze lowered as agony overwhelmed her. The conjured blade impaled her gut. She lifted her head, and shock froze her horrified expression. Tears welled in Evelyn's eyes. The conjuration dissipated, and she staggered away from Lidria.

"Why?" Lidria asked before coughing up blood. Her legs gave out, and she collapsed, cradling her stomach.

Evelyn sobbed. Quick footsteps approached, but Lidria couldn't see who they belonged to. She curled up, defeated by the fact her daughter had stabbed her. After everything, she only wanted to protect her…and Evelyn rejected her in the most brutal way possible.

"I'm sorry, Lidria," Ian said, his boot shuffling into view. "But we'll defend ourselves, even from you."

Lidria's eyes rose enough to see Ian's face. "I just wanted her safe. She's my daughter; I love her."

"She is safe now." Ian sighed and turned from Lidria, his eyes lingering on her.

Mustering what little strength remained, Lidria crawled after Ian. He didn't stop or glance back at her. She called out, but a deafening explosion rocked the manor. The force sent her airborne. Her head slammed into something solid, and consciousness fled her.

Red-orange flames roared around Selis. She centered herself, raised her arms out on either side and absorbed the inferno. The ritual pattern hummed. She split her attention between Janus and finding a way to unravel his spell. If she failed, so many would die.

Janus charged Selis, summoning a blade of magic in his right hand. She backpedaled to give herself more time, but he kept pace. The air buzzed where his construct slashed. Instinct took over, and she teased the foundation of the invocation.

A hairline fracture snapped partway through one of the lines. Pressure squeezed Selis' head, but she did not let the inconvenience slow her down. She worked more magic into the tiny crack. Her feet tripped over themselves, and she tumbled to the ground, landing on her backside.

Selis lost track of the location where she had weakened the spell. Her eyes flicked up as Janus barreled down on her. She thrust out her hand, and a gout of emerald fire burst forth. He spun to the side, slicing through the attack with a swing of his crackling blade. A pale blue glow filled the room.

Hesitation froze Selis in place. Janus came within striking distance, yet she could not stand. Needles pricked her skin, running up and down her body in waves. The sensation built until pain seeped in. She closed her eyes and searched for the cause but found nothing.

Sparks flew. Selis held her barrier firm, but cracks webbed throughout. More pressure, and the whole thing would shatter. She channeled as much power as possible into protecting herself. However, in spite of the added energy, the shield popped into ethereal dust.

Selis rolled to the right, avoiding Janus' fury. The lines beneath flared a harsh white-blue, and he fumbled backward. Something splintered. She finished her roll, safe, and sought out the fracture point. The gap grew, and the time for her to give everything came.

Taking a deep breath, Selis opened herself up to the Flow. She ushered the magic to her target. The invocation pressed back despite the weakening structure. Her limbs trembled, and she dropped to one knee. Even with her advantages, succeeding required exceptional strength.

Searing pain lanced through Selis' left shoulder, and all her effort halted. She screamed, clutching at the source, and snapped the end off. The solid object embedded in her flesh dissolved. Her wound did not close, but the excruciating anguish faded to a sharp ache.

"I will give you one more chance to stand down," Janus said, remaining behind Selis. "In honor of my fallen apprentices. We shouldn't throw away this gift so carelessly."

"You do not understand." Selis pumped enough magic into her shoulder to dull the pain. "I am not afraid to give up my life if it means stopping you from exterminating an entire race."

"If that is the path you wish to travel, you will not be able to act fast enough." The air grew thin, and Selis shuddered as she breathed.

Selis gripped the spell around her and tore the bindings to shreds. Half of her dove back into dispelling the rune at her feet as the other pushed Janus back. Instead of lashing out, he placed his hand on the etched wall. Her essence shrank, and she fell back to the edge of the breach.

Energies swelled and mingled, diminished and clashed. Selis forced herself to keep going, to fight for what she believed. She could not let Janus succeed. The lives of a whole race outweighed her own, yet the notion of disappearing terrified her.

The wound in her shoulder, the pressure at the base of her skull, the potency of Janus' magic, and her fear of death overwhelmed Selis. Her concentration slipped, and Janus pressed his advantage. She held onto her spell by a fragile, thin thread—one more distraction, and her grip would fail.

Selis grit her teeth. Her body strained to stay in one piece. She tried not to, but her mind went to Lidria. They would never get to spend more time together if she let herself die here. The ache the thought inflicted strengthened her resolve rather than broke her.

Magic spilled out, wild and savage. Selis shunted the flow and held her and Janus' rising power in place. He kept pushing, oblivious to the fact that everything grew out of control. Vast currents twisted and swayed. One little slip-up, and their conflict would backfire on them both.

"Please," Selis gasped, holding back the tide. "Stop. I do not know what will happen if we keep this up."

"Go ahead and release your spell." Janus continued to put his entire being into stopping her.

Selis' left arm dropped to her side, numb, and she grimaced. "I cannot. If I let go…I do not know what will happen."

"You will not stop me." Heat rose around Selis. "I will see the end of those beasts."

Selis took a fraction of her attention away from the invocation to deflect Janus' flames. The ritual collapsed. She reached out to hold the stitches together, but she did not act quick enough. A thunderous crash resounded around her. She flew, and the world winked out of existence.

Chapter Thirty-Eight

Lidria groaned and shifted. She pressed her hands to the floor and pushed down, but she fell to her left. Her shoulder hit the ground, sending a spike of pain up into her skull. She clenched her teeth. The wound in her gut strained, yet her attention focused on why she collapsed.

Nothing remained where her arm should be.

Confusion turned to horror. A hysterical noise escaped Lidria, and she groped for her missing limb. For all the difficulties she had faced coming to terms with the fake, the idea of having nothing terrified her. Her life would never be the same.

Tears welled in Lidria's eyes, but a cry ripped her from her self-pity. She rolled onto her back and struggled to sit up. Scuffling drifted down the hallway until her eyes caught Evelyn. She lurched forward, using her remaining arm as leverage. Her abdomen ached.

Ian stumbled and fell on his back. A limping Quelan rounded the corner, no armament visible. Lidria pushed her body past its limits and scooped up her sword. She staggered toward him. Even if he had caused her harm, he didn't deserve to die.

Purpose allowed Lidria to ignore her physical and emotional trauma. She quickened her pace, hefting her weapon. Evelyn turned toward her and froze. Her expressive eyes cried out for help, yet she shied away from Lidria. The heart-rending display didn't deter her.

Lidria brushed past Evelyn, wishing to reach out and touch her, to reassure her. In a moment, Lidria would have everything under control, and they would go back to hating her. She blinked back more tears. The time for petty disputes had passed.

The beast turned as Lidria approached. Growls and snarls emanated from the creature, but weariness showed. Ian took the distraction to back himself away. She gripped the hilt tighter, making sure she held a sound grip to end this as quick as possible.

Drawing on what little strength remained, Lidria thrust her blade toward the Quelan's chest. The brute shifted and pitched to one side. She followed her deviating target. Flesh gave way to cold, sharp steel, and she pinned her opponent to the fine wood floor.

Dark blood pooled from the creature's back. Lidria yanked, but her weapon wouldn't budge. She moved her left shoulder to add her other hand and stopped. Frustration seeped into her. Her time as a capable fighter seemed to be at a pathetic end.

Lidria let go and took a step back. The Quelan made no conscious effort to move or attack her. She lifted her leg and kicked the pommel of her sword, driving the blade deeper. Life vanished in the blink of an eye, and the body went slack.

Strength fled Lidria's body—her task followed through. She fell back against the nearby wall, chest rising and falling with her shallow breaths. Her eyes closed, and she didn't care. Evelyn and Ian were safe.

The wet sound of steel being pulled from flesh filled the hallway. "Thank you, Lidria." Ian's voice perked her ears, but she didn't open her eyes.

"Don't worry about it." A lump grew in Lidria's throat no matter how hard she tried to prevent getting emotional. "Go hide; I won't bother you. You're free of me once more."

Ian remained silent for a long moment, no movement of any kind. "Your arm."

Lidria grimaced. "It's not important. Just," she opened her eyes, found Ian's, and held them, "treat our daughter well, all right?"

A halfhearted smiled slipped onto Ian's face. "I wouldn't dream of anything else." His smile faded. "I'm sorry. For what happened here today, what we did."

"It's okay." Lidria attempted to move, but the gesture proved too much effort in her deteriorated state. "I have more important things to concern myself with than a few scratches." Selis popped into Lidria's mind, and the prospect of her being hurt, or worse, by the explosion roused her anxiety.

"Take care of yourself." Ian's expression softened. "I mean it."

Lidria laughed despite the action causing her wound to pull and tear. "That's what I've been doing, what I've always done."

"When you walked into my bakery after so many years, I could only remember how you had been—that you didn't, couldn't have changed. I'm happy to say I was wrong." Ian handed Lidria her sword before he took hold of Evelyn's hand. "Goodbye, Lidria."

"Goodbye, Ian." Lidria tilted her head down, and a tear broke free from her cheek. "Evelyn."

No more words passed between them. Ian ushered Evelyn off, and Lidria held herself together. She expected more of a response out of her herself. Maybe, with all her injuries, she couldn't feel much else. She hadn't the energy.

A tightness and ache in her chest caught Lidria's breath. She forced her body to inhale, to breathe again. The act proved difficult for the first few breaths, but she worked herself into a somewhat steady rhythm. Her entire body shook as her vision blurred.

Lidria shook her head, shoved herself upright, and started forward. She needed to find Selis. Janus wouldn't take her disobeying him again and returning well. If anything happened to her…No. She couldn't think that way. Selis proved herself time and time again; she would be all right.

Selis' eyes snapped open, and her heart raced. Her hazy vision cast about the chamber. The rune work etched into every surface vanished, leaving behind a series of scorched lines in the wake. An inhibited sigh escaped her lungs. She had succeeded.

Effort strained Selis' arms as she lifted herself into a seated position. She inched backward and leaned against the wall for support. The pressure in her head no longer existed. Relief flooded her despite the aches and pains throughout her body.

Selis inhaled a slow, deep breath. She searched the room for Janus. He lay face down fifteen feet away. Her first instinct told her to eliminate him, but she suppressed the notion. Instead, she raised her hand and sought to bind him.

Fire ripped through Selis' veins. She collapsed on her side, curling into a ball. Her entire body quivered as she fought to find breath. Tears ran down her face. She writhed on the floor, and the agony swelled. All thought twisted into incomprehensible begging and screaming.

A hand touched Selis' shoulder, but the pain continued to occupy her existence. She floundered and kicked. Something tried to hold her still despite her desperate, primal desire for the torture to end. Her head rose and rested against something soft.

"Selis." Lidria's voice reached her ears. Her suffering did not cease, but her violent struggles ebbed. "Selis, I got you. You're safe."

Selis stretched and clutched at Lidria's arm and clothes. She pulled herself close, being cradled, and sobs wracked her body. If nothing else, Lidria had survived. The sensation wreaking havoc on her receded to a dull throbbing. Spent, she melted against Lidria.

"I stopped him," Selis breathed as oxygen filtered back into her lungs.

Lidria hugged Selis tight. "Are you all right?"

"Yes. Although, I am not sure why that happened." Selis took comfort in Lidria's presence and wrapped her arms around her.

"It's okay. You seem better now." Lidria kissed the top of Selis' head before she glanced about the room. "What happened here?"

Selis tilted her head up until she glimpsed Lidria's face. "Master Janus wanted to exterminate the Quela. He transformed this chamber into a ritual, but I stopped it." Lidria bit her lower lip as Selis spoke. "What?"

"Nothing." Lidria shook her head. "I know how important stopping more killing is to you."

"I know it might not be the wisest thing to do, but I cannot allow an entire race to be wiped from this earth." Selis held Lidria's gaze, knowing full-well she would not challenge her.

A lopsided smile curled Lidria's lips. "I'm not going to argue against that. What was that explosion, though?"

"He tried to prevent me from unraveling his invocation. Our combined magical energies grew out-of-control, and it resulted in some kind of—" Selis noted Lidria's stump, and her eyes widened. "Your arm is gone."

"Yeah." Lidria turned her head and swallowed. "I woke up after the explosion, and it was gone. Not cut or ripped off. Just gone."

"His magic seemed to feed my countermeasure. That means," Selis took a breath, her attention focused on the nothing at Lidria's side, "anything created with the Flow inside the radius must have been dissolved."

"Are you able to cast?" Lidria asked, giving Selis' waist a gentle squeeze.

"I-I do not believe so. I wanted to restrain him before you came in, but it felt like I was being torn in half." Selis rested her head on Lidria's chest. The mere mention of what happened caused a sliver of the agony to return.

"That explains why you were screaming." Lidria spoke in a soft tone, her voice no more than a whisper.

Selis clung to Lidria and attempted to shut the experience out of her mind. "I am sorry if I worried you."

"You're fine." Lidria jostled Selis until she flicked her eyes up. "That's all that matters."

Janus stirred, drawing their attention. He lifted his head and stared at them. Pain flickered across his face before he pulled himself up. Lidria moved, but Selis grabbed her sleeve. Confusion registered in Lidria's eyes. Selis shook her head and eased back on her own.

"L-look what you did!" Janus snapped. He staggered forward, dropping to his knees.

Selis turned to face Janus, but she could not stand. "I told you to stop. You did not listen."

"Why do all this to save those wretched beasts?" Janus placed his hand on his knee and tried to rise, only to slump back down. "The damage you caused here is irreparable."

"I am willing to live with my choices," Selis said. Lidria rested her hand on her shoulder, and resolve washed through her. "The Quela have been abused like me. If people like you and Flinn left them alone, maybe they would not have caused us any issues."

Rage flushed Master Janus' face, and he shook his head. "You don't understand anything. They stole from us! That magic they cast was never theirs."

Selis cocked her head to the side. "What do you mean?"

"The Flow used to be more potent, more common. Those creatures stole part of it, separating it off for their own people." Janus paused, and his shoulders slumped. “Flinn and I were trying to figure out how to merge it back, but you had to get in my way.”

“We…had enough power. Whatever your plans were for it, I am glad I could put a stop to them.” Selis rose, clamping a hand down on Lidria’s shoulder to steady her wobbling legs.

Tremors wracked Janus as he attempted, once more, to stand and face Selis. He failed. “Do you hate your own kind so much you would see us remain stagnant?”

“No.” A twinge of curiosity tugged at her thoughts, but Selis shook her head. “But your way forward was not something worth pursuing.”

“You little—”

Lidria extended her sword out toward Janus’ face, standing beside Selis. “Don’t you dare talk to her like that.” Her heart leaped into her throat. She trusted Lidria with her life yet fear she would kill him rose.

“You’re going to defend her after she caused you to lose your arm, your power?” Janus appeared undaunted by the sharp point of steel encroaching on his person.

“None of that matters.” Lidria wavered, and her arm slipped down to her side. “I only care that she’s safe and that she was able to accomplish what she sought out to do.”

Janus’ eyes narrowed. “I can’t believe this. You two would throw away everything? And for what?”

“We did not throw away anything,” Selis said as she wrapped around Lidria’s waist for support. “You did.”

“Get out.” The bare walls and floor reverberated with Janus’ bitter voice.

“Selis.” Lidria shifted her gaze between her and Janus. Her sword arm twitched upward.

Selis tugged on Lidria, pulling her back. "No. He cannot harm anyone now. That should be is his punishment."

Lidria nodded. Relief washed over Selis, and she clung tight. Her legs no longer carried her weight. She did not think she could walk, but the exhaustion and pain in Lidria's posture and mannerisms made her think twice. They both needed a long rest.

The scrape of steel on leather snapped Selis out of her stupor. She tilted her head up and caught Lidria's vivid eyes. Every trial and inflicted injury were worth the struggle just to drink in such adoration and beauty. She wished to kiss her.

"Can you stand on your own for a second?" Lidria asked, maintaining eye contact. "I'll switch sides and hold you up."

Selis nodded, afraid her voice might fail her. She pulled herself up and, straining, let go of Lidria. Unease bubbled up inside Selis. Her stomach revolted, but the warmth of Lidria's embrace calmed her nerves. They made their way toward the exit in short, slow increments.

Dark blood dribbled into the hallway. Lidria's steps slowed, and Selis lurched in her arm. Two Quela lay on the ground, only a sword stuck out of Gre'cha's skull. Selis grimaced. She knew the beast needed to be dealt with, but the sight still upset her.

Selis nudged Lidria. "Did you?"

"No," Lidria said, her posture rigid.

"I did." Selis' eyes followed the voice and found Bal hunched against the wall, his right leg nowhere to be seen. "I know you're against it, but it had to be done."

"You were just trying to protect people." Something drew Selis' gaze back to the corridor, but she kept her eyes fixed on Bal. "Unlike Janus. I do not condone it, but I understand."

Bal gestured to the hall behind Selis and Lidria with a flick of his wrist. "Is he still alive?"

"Yes. However, like me, he is no longer able to connect to the Flow." Anxiety flooded Selis' thoughts. Her life would never be the same.

"Whatever you did," Bal let out a huff of laughter, "you really did a number on everything."

"I did not intend for things to get so out of control, but he refused to listen." Selis could not help but glance down at Bal's missing limb. "I am sorry about your leg."

Bal shook his head. "He's more to blame than you are. I'll have to have a word with him after I take a little break."

"Do not kill him," Selis pleaded, her throat tightening.

"Don't worry; I won't." An impish grin spread across Bal's face. "I might smack him around a bit just to get my point across."

Selis smiled. "You are a good man, Bal. I hope you find your way."

"I would say the same to you, but," Bal gestured with his chin toward Lidria, "it looks like you already have, Selis."

Selis' ears burned. "Yes."

"Thank you again, Bal," Lidria said, tipping forward in an awkward bow. "It didn't go the way I had hoped, but she's safe."

"No problem. It would have been interesting to see which of us was more skilled, though." Bal drew himself up but remained seated.

Lidria nodded, a wistful glint in her eyes. "Under different circumstances, I would agree."

Selis opened her mouth to assert her disapproval, but Lidria hugged her. The words died on her lips. She accepted silence—there were far more important things to worry about.

Lidria adjusted Selis against her hip, tightened her arm snug around her waist and left Bal. Sounds of the lingering battle outside penetrated the building. Selis did not know where they should go, and she did not know if Lidria did either.

The entrance to the manor burst open. Several guards surged into the antechamber. They shouted and started to barricade the door with nearby loose furnishings, but splinters exploded from the hinges. The men retreated as the massive wood panels collapsed.

Two bulky, armored Quela stood in the battered doorway. One smaller creature shuffled behind them, brandishing no weapons or armor. Selis recognized Gor'an. Her heart fluttered at the sight of him alive. She could convince him to tell his people to stand down.

Selis summoned all her strength and pulled away from Lidria. Lidria's hand remained on Selis' hip until she turned and nodded. The lack of security made her queasy, but she managed to take several steps forward. One of the guards hollered something at her. She ignored him and focused on Gor'an.

Pain flooded Selis. She ground her teeth and fought on through. If she did not reach Gor'an, any chance of things ending in peace vanished. She needed to try, even if she almost killed herself. Her body rejected her actions, crumpling under her weight and the stress of opening herself up.

Gor'an, Selis said to the void, grasping at the tenuous connection. *Tell your people they are safe. They do not need to continue this attack. Please, I do not want any more bloodshed.*

Gor'an's ears twitched, and his gaze snapped to Selis. Surprise and confusion flowed into her. He shifted and uttered several guttural barks. The two other Quela halted and turned their heads toward him. More growls and rumbles came from the group.

Kin. Lies. Frustration poured into Selis.

I am not lying. I promise you. Selis swallowed her apprehension, desperate. *What do I have to do to prove that?*

Gor'an grunted with his fellow Quela before he bobbed his head. *Give. Monster.*

I—temptation flickered inside Selis, but she struck the dark thought down—*cannot. I know he has done terrible things and wanted to kill you, but he can no longer use the Flow to harm you. He will no longer be a threat to anyone.*

Shaman, Gor'an uttered without deliberation.

Dead. Selis awaited an outburst, yet none came. She pressed her position. *That is why this needs to stop. Both of our peoples keep losing because of this conflict. Please. I know how righteous vengeance can feel, but your people are the only ones who can stop this.*

Try. Reason.

Agonizing minutes passed as Gor'an and his comrades argued back and forth. A myriad of half-realized emotions bombarded Selis. She remained upright, waiting, despite the exhaustion wearing down her body. One of the armored Quela glanced at her and shuffled out the door.

The second Quela followed the first and disappeared outside. Gor'an focused on Selis. *You. Save. Kin. Leave.*

Relief and appreciation calmed Selis' nerves. *Thank you*. She smiled. *I am glad we met*. Gor'an turned and left.

Selis collapsed to her knees. Her head spun. She pitched forward, but Lidria rushed over and grabbed her by the shoulder. Despite Lidria's firm grip, Selis swayed and teetered, drifting close to unconsciousness. Too many deaths; however, she took solace in having prevented more.

"You can still speak with them?" Lidria asked as she knelt beside Selis to help steady her better.

Selis turned her head. "It seems my connection to their magic is still intact. I struggled to use it, but it worked."

"I'd say so." Amazement played in Lidria's voice, and her gaze followed Gor'an out of the manor. "How did you convince them to leave?"

"The only reason they attacked here and Odwyn was because of Janus and Flinn trying to harm them." Selis leaned back against Lidria, closing her weary eyes. "Gor'an listened when I told him Janus no longer posed a threat to them.

"His people did not wish for any more death either, but they protected themselves. Janus would have killed them all."

Lidria guided Selis' head to her chest, and her voice reverberated in her ear. "I still can't believe they were so reasonable. Then again, I've never spoken to one."

"I am glad I got the chance. Perhaps Flinn had my best interests in mind after all." Selis lost herself in the soothing rhythmic beat of Lidria's heart and drifted off.

Chapter Thirty-Nine

"Do you have to go, Lidi?" Hector asked, tugging on Lidria's loose sleeve.

A somberness settled in Lidria's gut. "I'm afraid so."

Selis stepped around Lidria and knelt beside Hector. "I am sorry, but I asked her to accompany me on my visit to my parents."

Sadness darkened Hector's eyes, and his grip loosened. "Will you come back?"

"After we're done with her parents, we'll come back and visit. I'm not sure where we'll go from there, but you'll see us again. I promise." Lidria broke free from Hector's grasp and ruffled his hair.

Hector dipped out from under Lidria's hand and started swinging around an invisible sword. "I'm going to practice every day, so I can beat you when you get back. Ren said he would help me."

"All right." Lidria grinned. "You'll have to show me how much you've improved when I come back." Selis stood and settled in beside her, taking her hand.

"Don't encourage him," Nell said from her seat.

"Too late, mom"—Hector continued to dance around—"you said it was okay."

"I could always change my mind. I am your mother." A stern mask slipped onto Nell's features, and she crossed her arms over her chest.

Hector ran over to Nell in a panic. "No, don't. Lidi will be disappointed when she comes back."

Nell shook her head, lifted her gaze, and locked eyes with Lidria. "He cares more about disappointing you than his own mother."

Guilt tugged at Lidria's heart, but not as strong as the bitterness of rejection. "At least he cares about you."

"I'm sorry things with your daughter didn't turn out, but don't forget you have people who care about you, too." Nell's eyes flicked to Selis before she adopted a warm smile.

"I know." Selis draped her arm around Lidria's waist and squeezed. "Thank you."

Selis glanced up at Lidria over her shoulder. "We should get going," she said before Lidria opened her mouth. "If we do not leave soon, we will not make it very far before dark."

"Yeah." Lidria turned her attention back to Hector and Nell. "I guess this is goodbye for now. We'll see you when—"

Hector shot over to Lidria and clamped his little arms around her legs. She frowned. With a gentle motion, she pried him off her and dropped down to his level. His wet eyes stared back at her. She spread her arms, and he took the invitation, latching onto her.

Lidria hugged Hector. "I'll miss you, too."

"You promise to come back?"

"Of course." Lidria patted Hector's back. "Have I ever let you down?"

Hector shook his head and buried his face in Lidria's chest. "No."

"Saying goodbye is hard, but it's not forever." Lidria placed her hand on Hector's arm and coaxed him out of the embrace. She made eye contact. "Look after your mom, okay?"

Hector nodded several times. "Okay."

"Goodbye, Hector," Selis said, patting him on the head.

"Make sure Lidi doesn't break her promise." Lidria suppressed a chuckle as she stood.

"I will." A huge grin slid onto Selis' face. "You have nothing to fear."

Nell cleared her throat, and Lidria turned to face her. "Thank you. Again. For everything." She nodded. "Take care of yourselves."

Lidria strode over to Nell, leaned down, and hugged her. "You're welcome, and we will."

Lidria waved goodbye, which Hector returned with gusto, as she and Selis left. They drifted through the town for several minutes. A lump grew in Lidria's throat, which she was unable to swallow. Leaving now became a far more devastating prospect than it had been a couple days prior.

A soft nudge brought Lidria back. Selis bumped into her again until she glanced down at her. Warmth and reassurance radiated from Selis, and Lidria's melancholy faded. She had spoken the truth to Hector: she would come back. Leaving didn't mean forever.

Lidria stepped up to the open door where Ren made his command center. He stood behind a squat oak desk, and his head snapped up at the sound of her boots on the wooden floor. "You two are about to head out, then?"

"Yeah," Lidria said, a twang of guilt tugging at her heart. Selis swept up beside her. "Just wanted to say goodbye to everyone before we left."

"You're both welcome back here anytime." Ren rounded the table and strolled across the room. "Bal and I are the acting people in charge now, so you don't have to worry about anything."

Lidria grinned. "I guess you're going to be busy."

"Thankfully," Ren extended his arm, "Janus had this place set up well. That, and Bal being known among the native residents makes things pretty smooth."

"This is where you belong. You're a great leader." Lidria threw a quick salute, standing at attention.

Ren shook his head and waved away her salute. "That's awfully kind of you. I was beginning to doubt myself, but it seems as long as I have something to do, I'll be fine."

"I'm glad." A thought came to Lidria, and she snickered. "I didn't want to have to tell Deeter and Joan to keep you in line. I'm sure they'll give you a hard enough time without me adding to it."

"You're right." Ren raised his hand, but something behind Lidria caught his attention.

"Leaving already?" Deeter asked, slipping in.

"We're both well enough to travel." Lidria pivoted to accommodate Deeter. "Selis wanted to go. I don't see why not."

Deeter eyed Selis. "You're an impatient one, huh?"

"I do not see what the issue is. I simply want to reconnect with my parents." Selis gave Deeter a harsh glare, and Lidria stifled her laughter.

"Oh, there's no problem. I wish you the best of luck." Deeter smirked, draping his arms around Lidria's and Ren's shoulders. "I just have too much fun giving people a hard time."

Lidria slipped away from Deeter. "We hadn't noticed."

"I'm sure Ren told you that you're welcome here anytime, so I'll see you then." Deeter fired off a sloppy, two-fingered salute and ducked back out the door.

Lidria clasped Ren's shoulder. "Goodbye, Ren."

"Goodbye, Lidria." Ren returned Lidria's gesture before he turned his gaze to Selis beside her. "Selis."

"Farewell," Selis said and bowed.

The sun rose high in the sky as Lidria and Selis exited the building. They made their way toward the gate, but Selis kept glancing around. She stopped and turned up the main thoroughfare. Lidria followed her and realized why she deviated.

“I’m glad I caught you,” Joan called over the crowd of people.

Selis rushed over and threw her arms around Joan. The other woman stood stiff before she hugged Selis back. “As am I. Thank you.”

“You’re welcome, Selis,” Joan said. “Glad to help.” Lidria couldn’t help but smile.

Selis pulled back and released Joan. “We will visit once we have met with my parents.”

“Good. I didn’t think you’d be gone forever.” Something dark played across Joan’s face.

“No.” Selis shook her head. “After everything, it would be impossible not to come back.”

“That’s good to hear.” Joan gazed skyward, and a frown marred her features for a moment. “Well, you two better get going before you lose even more daylight.”

“Goodbye, Joan.” Selis squeezed Joan’s arm.

Joan smiled. “Goodbye, Selis. Lidria.”

“See you around.” Lidria and Selis parted ways with Joan and headed out of town.

As the walls of Kal’den drifted further behind them, a sense of tranquility washed over Lidria. She no longer fought herself at every step, every thought. Things had not transpired the way she wished, but she did everything she could. She had nothing to be ashamed of.

In time, Evelyn might even come to see Lidria without fear. The thought instilled hope in her—more than she could bear. As much as she told herself she was alright with never seeing her daughter again, a small part of her wanted to try again. She hoped Ian didn’t take her away once more.

Lidria reached over and took Selis’ hand in hers. A gentle squeeze reinforced the fact that she had friends, people who cared about her and for her to care for. She was no longer alone nor did she have to fear being vulnerable. The future, for once in so many years, seemed promising and exciting.

Thank you for reading!

If you enjoyed this book, check out my website for free short stories and other books at: https://www.andrewjlandis.com

Credits and Legal

Cover art by: Maerel Hibadita

Gallery: https://www.artstation.com/innervalue

Copyright © 2020 Andrew J. Landis

ISBN: 978-1-7347911-0-5

This is a work of fiction. Names, characters, businesses, places, events, locales, and incidents are either the products of the author's imagination or used in a fictitious manner. Any resemblance to actual persons, living or dead, or actual events is purely coincidental.

www.ingramcontent.com/pod-product-compliance
Lightning Source LLC
LaVergne TN
LVHW041108080826
845145LV00007B/1730

* 9 7 8 1 7 3 4 7 9 1 1 0 5 *